Game On

The House that Gamine Built, Volume 1

Dawn Dalton

Published by Dawn Dalton, 2024.

GAME ON

First edition. March 26, 2024.

Copyright © 2024 Dawn Dalton.

ISBN: 979-8224804955

Written by Dawn Dalton.

Table of Contents

Dedication:

To the angels in my life, thank you for believing in me.

Chapter One

"Was I wrong to not tell them I'm a girl?" Sam blew the lock of chestnut brown hair out of her face only to have it fall back in place. She reached to tuck it behind her ear only to have her hand smacked by her friend, Olivia.

"Stop fidgeting! Your nails aren't dry and I'm not redoing them."

"You're the one that insisted I try something new with my hair, including letting them cut face framing pieces. This," she gestured to the piece that escaped the clip holding up her hair, "is technically your fault."

"You needed the change. Admit it, you like it." Her friend reached across the table to tuck the strands behind Sam's ear before resuming painting her nails light pink.

Sam had to admit to herself that the amount of hair she had just lost was shocking, but Olivia was right. Cutting her waist length hair into long layers that fell just past her shoulders was freeing. But not so freeing that she was willing to go as short as her friend's light blonde bob.

She sighed and returned to the problem at hand. "It's not like the guys are going to miss the fact that I'm female tomorrow."

"You've been talking to these guys online for months. You don't think they've figured it out already?"

"I have a fairly gender neutral handle and picture. No one there knows me in real life." She thought of the guys as friends already, but the real test was when they met in real life.

"It shouldn't matter what your gender is. You've already proven yourself a knowledgeable player."

"It shouldn't, but you know as well as I do that female gamers are treated differently by the guys. Either they'll be assholes because I'm encroaching on their territory or I'll be an object of curiosity."

"You never know, they might surprise you. Look at Luke and Andrew."

Sam smiled at the mention of two of their roommates. "That's because Luke claimed me as his little sister almost right away. Andrew didn't know what to make of me until we started dating."

"At least you'll have them there for support tomorrow." Olivia capped the nail polish.

Sam blew on her nails to dry them. Luke burst in the door and swept Olivia into a passionate kiss. His long dark blond hair escaped his customary ponytail and tangled with his girlfriend's shorter hair.

Longing swamped Sam, making her look away from her friends. She missed having a connection to another person. She made gagging noises. "For someone who calls himself my big brother, you are doing a great job at scarring me for life."

"Don't you live downstairs? Go home." He ruffled her hair, knocking more of it out of the clip.

"I'll leave you two lovebirds to do whatever it is you do." She opened the door, careful not to ruin her nails. "See you in the morning."

She trudged down the stairs into the lower apartment, her stomach tying back into knots. She perched on the arm of the green couch and watched her other roommate, Eric, shuffle around piles of papers. Colored post-its and highlighters littered the coffee table. His ginger hair stuck up in spikes where he obviously ran his hands through it.

"Homework or game notes?" She studied the piles for clues.

"Game notes. I'm trying to pull people's back stories into the game and balance how much time I spend on each one."

"Sounds complicated."

"But rewarding if I can pull it off." He glanced at the clock. "I thought you were upstairs letting Olivia girlify you."

"We went out shopping, got haircuts, and deep conditioned. I even let her paint my nails." She showed off her hands. "We were having a good time until Luke came home."

"Made out in front of you again?"

"Yup, turned my stomach."

"Try not to smile when you say that."

She stuck out her tongue at him. One of the things she loved about her roommates was their close-knit group. They could call each other out on their bullshit.

He stared up at her. "Are you ready for your tournament tomorrow?"

Sam's stomach flip-flopped. "As ready as I can be. I have an alternate army list in case Ubel forgets or changes his mind about loaning me the mini."

"Or wants payment in some sweet Sammy action?" Eric sat next to her on the couch, momentarily abandoning his project.

"That too." She stared at her feet.

"Is that why Luke and Andrew are going?"

"They swear it's because they like the game, but I'm certain they want to make sure I'm comfortable and don't get harassed."

"I don't envy you."

She put her head on his shoulder. "It does suck having to justify my nerd credit all the time. But the other option is to not play."

He put his arm around her shoulder. "If it makes you feel better, I think of you as one of the guys."

"Oddly, it does, but I smell better than they do."

"Sometimes."

She smacked his shoulder. "Be nice or I'll mess up your notes."

3

BRAD ROOTED THROUGH the jumble of paints, brushes, and general debris on his desk. He just saw the bottle of cyan blue, but now he needed it, it had disappeared. *After this tournament, I'm organizing all my paints.* He knocked over his rinse cup, spilling the dirty liquid across his notebook and soaking the leg of his jeans.

"Son of a bitch!" He snatched a towel off the desk, knocking over papers and paint bottles. He cursed again. *I do not have time for another setback*, he thought as he mopped up the mess.

"Are you okay down here?" Steve poked his head into the basement.

"I'd be doing better if I could find anything."

"It looks like a tornado hit your desk." His roommate took the other three cups of dirty water and dumped them in the sink in the tiny basement bathroom. "Are you still painting minis for tomorrow?"

Brad patted the water off of the notebook that held all his client notes. Luckily, the water only hit the cover. "My stuff, finally."

"Way to wait until the last minute."

"Paid work takes precedence over my own projects. I just need this one last machine to round out my army."

"I thought your army was finished."

"I'm loaning out the Wrecker and need a replacement."

"I can't believe you're loaning out your Wrecker. That thing's your Precious." Steve finished picking up the bottles of paint and set them back on the desk.

Brad went into the bathroom to refill his rinse cup. He caught a glimpse of himself in the mirror. Great, he had multiple streaks of paint in his dark brown hair. When did that happen? Did he paint anything orange today?

"We need more players, so I'm helping out. More players mean better game play and more clients for my business." He settled back into his chair and picked up his brush. "Plus, she's a gamer girl. We don't see many of those."

"Here we go again." Steve gracefully flopped onto the leather couch. Brad envied the effortless way Steve lived his life, from the expensive way his jet-black hair was cut to the fact that he owned the house they lived in with their other friend, Chuck.

"Here we go again, nothing. She's a girl."

"This is your favorite theory. How are you so sure she's not a dude?"

Brad resisted the urge to throw his paintbrush at his friend. "She writes like a girl and never refers to herself in anything but neutral terms. No guy would be so cautious."

"You've spent way too much time obsessing over this. You're going to be so pissed that you've wasted all this time deciphering a guy's posts."

Brad would never admit how much time he had actually spent, but he had nothing better to do when he painted units of the same mini over and over. "Sounds like you want to bet on this."

"Twenty bucks says Sam-cat is a guy who uses that handle because he likes messing with guys and making them think he's a girl." Steve reached out a hand.

"You're on." Brad shook it. "Now, can I have some peace and quiet to get this mini done? I would like to get some sleep tonight."

Steve tromped up the stairs, muttering something about easy money. Brad found the bottle of cyan blue sitting front and center on his desk. Cursing his lack of organization, he went back to work.

An hour later, he stretched, his back popping from hunching over his desk. Satisfied with the paint job, he sprayed sealant on it and set it aside to dry. He double-checked his cases to make sure all of his clients' pieces were ready as well as his army.

Finally, he placed his new machine and the Wrecker in the case. *Please be a girl,* he stared at the miniature. *I'll never live it down if you're a guy.*

Chapter Two

S am yanked the door open and yelled up the stairs. "Luke, come on! We're going to be late."

She barely slept the night before. Excitement warred with her nerves and her early morning coffee threatened to come back up. She was about to go upstairs and pull her brother down by his stupid blond ponytail when she heard the door open.

"I'm coming." Luke thundered down the stairs. "What's the rush?"

Andrew slung a tanned arm around Sam's shoulders. "It's her first tournament." He pinched her cheeks. "Our little Sammy is growing up so fast."

She elbowed him in the ribs. "I wish *you* would."

"She's blushing." Andrew led the way out of the house.

Her cheeks heated up to her dismay. "I am *not*."

"Are you wearing perfume?" Luke sniffed in her direction.

"No." Both guys turned to her and she squirmed under their scrutiny. "Yes. I just wanted to make sure I didn't have gamer funk."

Andrew studied her with a practiced eye. "Hair's neatly brushed, she's wearing nicer clothes. Hell, I think she even put in all of her earrings." He reached out and touched the cluster of earrings. She smacked his hand away. "If I didn't know any better, I'd say Sam's on the prowl for a man."

She shot him a glare. "Because the last two times ended so well." Andrew looked away and she immediately regretted her harsh words. She stood on her tiptoes to kiss his cheek and ruffled the back of his auburn curls. "Sorry. I'm nervous about meeting these guys and taking it out on you. I just want to have a group to play with, not just forcing you guys to play."

"We love gaming with you, but I understand the desire to game with other people." He held the car door for her. " And I should be one of the last people to give you shit about your love life."

She slid into the back seat and set her game case next to her. She gave it a nervous pat. "I'd give you hell for having crappy taste in women, but you dated me, so you *can* occasionally pick a decent one." She winked. "Too bad you don't know how to keep one."

"Sick burn." Luke leaned back and fist bumped her.

The tension broken, they kept up a steady stream of teasing for the rest of the drive. She was grateful that the guys kept her mind off her nerves. All too soon, Andrew pulled into the parking lot of the Game Hut. Her stomach hit her knees.

He glanced at her in the rear-view mirror. "Are you ready?"

Sam took a deep breath and checked her game case one last time. "As ready as I'll ever be."

Luke put his arm around her and propelled her into the store's dim interior. She gawked at the racks of miniatures, paints, and dice. Part of her wanted to drop out of the tournament so she could wander the store.

The clerk gave her a double take as she signed in and paid her tournament fee. She sighed, so it began. They were directed down a dimly lit staircase. Halfway down, a door was propped open to an area for smokers. The stairs ended in a short hallway with two doors. The right-hand door opened into a filthy bathroom. She wrinkled her nose. The left-hand door led into a cavernous room with tables, chairs, terrains, and over a dozen guys. Yup, she didn't stand out at all.

"How do I know who Ubel is?" She scanned the room for anyone who stood out as the guy she had been chatting with, not that anyone used their real picture as their handle.

Luke glanced down at her and raised his voice. "Anyone here go by the screen name Ubel?"

"Asshole." She shrank behind the boys.

"That would be me." A tall, brown-haired guy cut through the crowd and offered his hand to Luke. "Are you Sam-cat?"

Of course Ubel would be hot as sin. And just when she swore off guys for the foreseeable future. He had just enough muscles for her to stand up and take notice while being tall enough to make her feel dainty. His shirt stretched tight across his shoulders. His dark brown hair was just long enough for her fingers to tangle in. Her tongue tied itself in her mouth.

I'M NEVER LIVING THIS down. Brad eyed the guy. The long blond ponytail meant that Steve would have a field day. The guy looked back at a petite brunette and nudged her forward.

She reached out and shook his hand. "I'm Sam-cat."

His eyes widened. "No shit?"

She cocked her head to the side and rolled her eyes. "Last time I checked, that was me."

"Come with me." He grabbed her arm and ignored her squeak of surprise. Steve was going down. He pulled her through the crowd and tapped his friend on the shoulder. "This is Sam-cat. I told you she was a girl. Pay up."

Steve looked her up and down. "Is this asshole telling the truth or did he hire you to win our bet?"

She ripped her arm out of Brad's grip and leveled a glare at them. She pulled herself up to her full height, which put her head just under Brad's nose. Her eyes snapped with barely contained rage, making the blue sparkle. Multiple piercings winked in her ears under the store's lights.

"For fuck's sake. This is why I hate going outside my regular group." She took a deep breath. Her words came out in an angry rush. "Yes, I'm Sam-cat. Yes, I'm a girl. No, I'm not playing because my boyfriend plays nor am I looking for a man. Yes, I play this game because I like it. You can call me Sam. Does that cover all of your questions?"

"That was impressive. I'm Brad." He curbed his urge to applaud her speech. He turned to Steve, held out his hand, and waited for his friend to place a twenty in it.

"Did you really just bet on my gender?" They nodded and hurt flashed through her sky-blue eyes. She held out her hand to him. "Rude. My cut of the bet please."

"How do you figure you get a part of it?" He pocketed the cash.

She held his gaze. "I helped you win it by actually showing up and being female. It's incredibly insulting to have your gender bet upon." She walked away. "It was nice meeting you."

"Sam, wait." He caught up with her surrounded by her guy friends. "I'm sorry. I didn't think about how you'd feel about the bet."

"Water under the bridge. Good luck today." She dismissed him.

"Let me grab the Wrecker for you."

"You don't need to. I brought a second list that doesn't use it."

"You came prepared in case I acted like a jackass." The realization hit him like a punch to the gut. "And I proved you right. Let me lend you the mini, please."

"I think you should leave her alone." The blond stepped between them.

"Luke, it's alright. I got this." She placed a hand on the blond's arm before turning to Brad. "Thank you for the loan. It is much appreciated."

"It's the least I can do." He headed back to his stuff, listening to her friends ask if she wanted to leave. So much for bringing new players and clients to the store.

The tournament organizer called for everyone's attention. After going over the rules, they were paired off for their first match. He brought his mini over to Sam's table. He got a whiff of her perfume, light with a hint of flowers. It caught him off-guard and he wondered what other surprises she had under that tough cookie exterior.

SAM STARED AT THE MINI Brad loaned her. She thought she was a decent painter, but he put her work to shame. The Wrecker stood out like a beacon amongst her minis. She forced her attention from her thoughts and looked at her opponent.

"I'm Sam." She held out her hand, despite her gut telling her to run. She chalked it up to his unkempt greasy brown hair and smug look.

"Curtis." He held her hand in his damp one until she grew uncomfortable.

She swallowed back her revulsion and discreetly wiped her hand on her jeans. She scanned the room for Luke and Andrew just in case she needed them. There was just something about this guy that didn't feel right.

Shrugging, she focused on the game at hand. She maneuvered her minis around the board to catch her opponent by surprise and pick away at his army. Seeing an opening, she took out his leader and won her first game.

"Good game." She smiled.

"Whatever." He stormed off.

She frowned at his abrupt departure but understood being upset about getting knocked out of the tournament in the first round. Single elimination was tough. She picked up her minis and turned in her results slip.

A brief check-in showed the guys were still in the tournament before she found her second game. She set her bag down across from the guy Brad bet earlier. It was a study in opposites from her last opponent. This guy looked well put together and friendly. Even though he wore jeans and a tee shirt, they seemed too well made to not be designer.

He held out his hand. "We weren't properly introduced earlier. I'm Steve."

"Sam." She relaxed a bit when his handshake was firm but brief.

"I want to apologize for my involvement earlier. My assumption was that you were a guy and Brad was wasting his time obsessing over your gender, which led to our wager. I meant no harm in it."

"Apology accepted." Her smile slipped as she mulled over his words. "Obsessed?" Her stomach back flipped and she lowered her voice. "He's not hoping for anything to come from the loan of his mini, is he?"

Steve let out a rich laugh. "No, it's more that he saw a pattern to your posts and had to prove his assumptions correct." He rolled his dice. "Five points of damage to the Wrecker's left arm. I'm happy he was right."

"Why's that?" She took her turn and wiped out a full unit of his minis.

"You set me up." Steve shook his head. "One, it's nice to have fresh blood. I hope you stick around despite us being assholes. Two, you seem to know your shit. And three, you improve the view."

"Thanks, I think." Her cheeks heated up. It had been too long since a guy had given her a compliment.

"Anytime." He took a few more of her minis before shaking his head. "I'll admit, this isn't my forte. Put a controller in my hand and I'm a god, but don't ask me to think five moves ahead."

"Sorry, I come from a chess background. My dad and I would play when I was little."

"I concede to your superior strategy." He shook her hand. "Are you going to the after party?"

"I didn't know there was one. I'll have to check with the guys."

BRAD PACKED AWAY HIS minis and congratulated his opponent. He passed out a couple business cards and looked around. Sam was sitting alone on a table in the back corner watching the games. He hopped up next to her.

"How is the tournament going?"

"Got my butt handed to me in the third round. You?" She sounded bemused about her loss, not upset like he thought she would.

"Scrubbed out as well. Single elimination is not my favorite format."

She picked his mini off of her case and handed it back to him. "Thanks for the loan. It made the rest of my army look plain in comparison."

"How so?" She was one of the few players with a painted army. He leaned over her to check out the models in her army case.

"Woah, there is such a thing as personal space." She shoved at him.

"Sorry. I get excited about painted minis. Not many players actually paint theirs." He sat up, shamed by his blunder. He was not making a good impression for the store's community. "May I see your army?"

She handed him her case. "My paint job isn't up to your level." Embarrassment etched itself over her face. "Where'd you learn to paint like that?"

"Trial and error." He shrugged. "And a lot of questions of the people winning awards." He looked over her pieces. She wasn't bad for a self-taught painter. "Your stuff is pretty good. If you want to learn more, we meet up here every Thursday night to play and paint. You guys should join us." His gesture encompassed her friends.

"We'll see." She gave him a sideways look. "What were you handing out over there?"

"Business cards." He passed her one. "I paint miniatures for a living."

"'Battle Extreme Miniatures, Providing High Quality Miniature Painting. Brad Werner, Owner.'" She flipped the card over. "Hey, that looks like the mini you loaned me."

"It is. The Wrecker's my favorite paint job."

Her mouth dropped open. "Why would you loan out your favorite mini to a stranger? I could've ruined it."

"I'd rather see it used than let it collect dust." He shrugged, uncomfortable under her scrutiny. "Why do you play Factionless? It's an uncommonly hard army to play with."

"They have style and female leaders."

"You could play Justice."

She wrinkled her nose. "I'm not into righteous fire, that's Luke's bag when he plays."

"Druids?"

"Only if I want to play with beasts instead of machines. They're my second choice."

"Weren't you playing with a male leader today?"

"I was. I did the math on the cost of the minis I wanted and found it would be cheaper to get the starter set and fill in other parts afterward. I haven't gotten a chance to pick up much else."

"Who's your leader of choice?"

"Ashley. I already have an army list made up and tested for her." Her face lit up with pride.

"Are you planning on getting her today?"

"Yeah, before we head out, I need some more paint and stuff to get my army up to snuff."

"If you want recommendations, I'd be happy to give them."

"I'd love a professional opinion to make my army look amazing."

"If you come up on Thursdays, I'll teach you some of the techniques I use."

"Why would you teach something you can charge for?"

"You don't seem the type to pay someone to paint your army." He hopped off the table. "And I could use someone to talk to while I paint."

Chapter Three

Sam hugged her knees to her chest and mulled over his offer as Brad walked off. Andrew sat next to her and put his head on her shoulder to get sympathy for his crushing defeat. Shortly after, Luke did the same thing on her other side.

"You two are such big babies." She loved the big dog pile but refused to let them know.

"We've been invited to grab food and drinks after the tournament wraps up." Andrew waggled his eyebrows at her. "I'm guessing they invited us so you would go."

She shoved him. "That's because no one likes you."

"I can leave you here."

"Luke would kick your ass for it." She shrugged and Luke nodded.

Their conversation was cut short by the tournament wrapping up and awards given out. Brad won best painted army, not that she was surprised. When her name was called for best sportsman, she sat in shock until the guys pushed her forward. She collected her prize, her smile hurting her cheeks. She found herself surrounded by all the other players congratulating her.

"Are you ready for my painting expertise?" Brad clinked trophies with her.

"Yes, please." She held up her store credit. "I even have extra money to spend."

Sam trailed behind him up to the store. After grabbing the new models she needed, she joined him at the paint wall. He spent a ton of time explaining the differences in paint brands and brushes. It was enough to make her head spin.

"I think you know way too much." She held up her hands in surrender. "What's the best bang for my buck?"

"Strett will take a lot of punishment." He pulled a couple of brushes in various sizes and handed them to her. "They hold their shape fairly well. For paint, Marko is a good line, fine pigments that thin down well."

"That's the brand I've been using. I just need a few more colors."

They stood at the rack and debated which colors would be the most useful for her collection. She liked the easy way he talked to her without talking down to her. The rest of the group came to herd them to dinner.

She sat squished between Brad and Luke at the restaurant. She looked over at Luke. "Hey, big brother, did you invite your girl to join us? You know how much she loves nights out."

"Hell no, the last thing I need is the two of you drinking together. I'd have to be your DD because you'd get into mischief."

"That's okay, I invited her myself." She laughed at his pained expression.

"You're siblings?" Brad looked between them. The table fell silent.

She fidgeted under everyone's stares. "Not exactly. Theater frats are co-ed, so Luke picked me to be his little when I pledged. We had a long talk about TV shows and books during initiation and hit it off."

"You're a theater kid?" Brad raised an eyebrow at her.

"I hold a BA in theater management and promotions, thank you very much." She gave a nod. "I didn't act in any productions, except the one act plays because Andrew begged me."

"'Begged' is a bit of an overstatement." Andrew gave her a pointed look.

"Yeah, more like he asked nicely after going down on you." Luke snorted and she shot him a glare. "What? Tell me that's not how it happened."

Heat flooded her cheeks. How dare he be so casual about something like that in front of new people? She spoke through her teeth. "Not a proper discussion to have in front of people we barely know."

BRAD WATCHED SAM'S face turn bright red and she squirmed in her seat. When her boyfriend didn't come to her defense, Brad turned the conversation away from her love life and back to game theory. She flashed him a grateful smile.

He fell in step with her on the way to the bar. "Do you want me to beat your brother for you?"

"Nah, I'll tell his girlfriend what he did and let her eviscerate him."

"Vicious." He did not want to get on her bad side. "I'm surprised your boyfriend didn't speak up."

"Andrew's not my boyfriend anymore. We broke up a couple of years ago." She held the door for him. "We live together."

He nodded his thanks. "I couldn't imagine living with my ex."

"It's not that bad. Eric, Olivia, and Luke keep it from getting weird."

"How many people do you live with?"

"There are five of us living in the House that Gaming Built."

He stopped in his tracks. There was no way he could live with that many people. Some days, it was hard living with two roommates. "You named your house?"

"Yeah, don't you?" She shrugged like it was the natural thing to do. "You name the type of gaming, odds are it's played in the house."

They settled around a big table in the back room of the bar. A couple of guys started jostling over the jukebox. She shot off a text before pocketing her phone. It didn't escape his notice that she stuck close to her guy friends to fend off the advances of the other guys.

He leaned over so she could hear him over the music. "Can I buy you a drink to make up for being an ass earlier?"

"You don't have to." She waved a dismissive hand. "The use of your favorite mini more than makes up for our rude introduction."

"Are you sure? I have this twenty burning a hole in my pocket." She frowned at him. "What?"

"I'm trying to figure out your motives."

Her suspicions punched him in the gut. "Honestly, I want to share my ill-gotten gains with you. I feel bad that I confirmed your low expectations for the day."

"Nothing more?"

He chuckled. "Cute as you are, I'm not in the market for anything right now."

"Bad break up?" Sam visibly relaxed.

"The worst. She got knocked up by her side piece and dumped me." He wasn't sure why he felt the urge to confide in her.

She patted his arm. "Ouch, my condolences. At least she wasn't stolen by the same person who took your previous significant other."

"Touché. What would be your pleasure?" He nodded at the bar.

"Rum and coke's fine." Her tone made him not want to believe her.

"Fine, but not what you really want." He bumped her elbow with his. "What do you want to drink? Be honest."

"I like sweet, girly drinks like a Fuzzy Navel or amaretto and Coke."

"Do you want to come with me or do you want to be surprised?"

She popped off her stool. "I'll come with you, if for no other reason than to save your male ego from ordering a girly drink."

19

"You make it sound like a challenge."

"No, if I were in a challenging mood, I'd say you're too scared to try a fruity drink." She raised her eyebrow.

Laughing, he shook his head. He had to hand it to her, she knew how to roll with the punches and wasn't afraid to rib him. They ordered their drinks and waited by the bar. He caught her glancing around the room like she was looking for someone.

She let out an excited noise and shot across the room to pull a blonde girl into a giant hug. They bounced and squealed before returning to the bar to grab Sam's drink.

"How long has it been since you saw each other?" He grinned at their antics.

"We live together." They answered in unison and dissolved into a fit of giggles.

LUKE ROLLED HIS EYES and pulled Olivia into a hug. "If you think this is bad, try living with them."

"We're awesome and you love us." Sam grinned at Brad, who saluted her with his drink. "No toast?"

"What would you like to toast to?"

"To bets won and new friends made." She clinked her glass against his.

She followed the group back to the table and got drawn into an animated discussion with Brad and Steve. She was really happy the three of them salvaged the day. They made her feel right at home. Olivia snapped a couple of pictures before pulling her onto the dance floor.

"What's the story with the hottie?" Olivia leaned into Sam's ear.

"Nothing. He bet that I was a girl against his friend." Sam glanced at the table.

"Shut up, seriously?"

"Yeah, he bought me the drink to make up for it. He felt bad for upsetting me."

"Do you need me to do recon for you?" Olivia's baby blues lit up with mischief.

Sam groaned. "No, he just got out of a bad relationship. And I'm not in the market for more heartache."

"Aaron and Hannah did a number on you. Sometimes you have to fall hard and fast." Olivia spun her around.

"I'm sick of crashing and burning. Don't forget, she tricked Andrew first."

Their conversation stopped when a group of guys joined them. Sam declined requests to buy her drinks or teach her how to play War Tactics, even though she did better in the tournament than some of them. Andrew saved her from the crush and brought her back to the table while Luke did the same for his girlfriend. They called it a night shortly after and she said her good-byes to her new friends.

Alone in her room, she unpacked her trophy with a grin and set it on her bookcase. She turned on her computer to find Brad online.

Sam-cat: Thank you again for the loan today.

Ubel: Not a problem. Are you coming out on Thursday?

She checked her schedule and made a face.

S: I can't.

U: Even if I ask nicely and promise not to insult you?

S: I work late.

U: :(

S: I'll be out the following week.

U: Awesome! Bring your painting gear and we can paint together.

S: Sounds like a plan. I'll see you then.

She smiled and logged off. She puttered around getting ready for bed and thought about the day. She could easily see herself fitting in with the group at the Game Hut.

"A GIRL AT A TOURNAMENT. What will they invade next?"

Brad raised an eyebrow at Steve. They ran later than usual to the Game Hut due to traffic. Curtis held court and ranted about his loss on Saturday to Sam. They set down their bags and joined the rest of the group.

"Next they'll want to vote or something." Curtis let out a derisive laugh.

"They can vote already." Brad crossed his arms across his chest. He didn't like the tone of the conversation or the fact that the troll was allowed to hold the floor. "What do you have against gamer girls?"

"Fake gamer girls."

"Haven't seen any of those around here."

"Maybe your eyes weren't working. There was one at the tournament on Saturday. About this tall, brown hair, blue eyes."

"There was nothing fake about Sam." Steve spoke up, his ice blue eyes flashing a warning.

"She totally used her tits to win games." Curtis pressed his arms to his chest to give the illusion of breasts and tittered.

Brad struggled to keep from punching the troll. "Yeah, she totally used her breasts as ammunition. That's why her shirt covered up any hint of cleavage." He leaned against the table, needing something to steady himself. He now understood Sam's wariness in coming to the tournament. "She got knocked out in the third round. So much for your theory on why you lost to her."

"Of course you'd stick up for her. You were all over her like white on rice before the tournament. Just remember, bros before hoes."

"You are not my bro and Sam is definitely not a hoe." He rose to his full height so he could look down at Curtis. "Nor is she a fake gamer. She knows more than you do about this game."

"She only lost to me due to rotten dice luck." One of the other guys spoke up. Brad let out a sigh of relief that he and Steve weren't her only defenders. "Her set up was sound and she's got a head for tactics. But there's nothing you can do when you roll that many ones."

Curtis's eyes darted around the group as the tide had turned against him. "Are we going to talk all night or are we going to play?"

Brad threw down the gauntlet. "Just waiting on you to shut up long enough to challenge you."

He had the irrational urge to stomp the slime ball into the ground. He understood now why Sam never said she was a female online, if this was the crap she had to put up with. He played aggressive, never letting up on the other guy. When he finished beating Curtis, Steve stepped up and gave the guy a solid second beating.

SAM LET HERSELF INTO Julie's dorm room. She set down the bag of junk food on the floor and opened a can of soda. As much as she loved the guys, she enjoyed the hell out of Saturday girls' night. Even if it meant occasionally dealing with Julie's bitch of a backstabbing roommate, Hannah.

"Where's Olivia?" Julie's jet-black curls obscured her face as she snagged a bag of gummy worms.

Sam crawled onto the bed with her bag of chocolate and soda. "She'll be along in a minute. Last I saw her, she was in a lip lock with Luke."

"We can't start girls' night without her. She promised pedicures."

"At least someone's getting some around here." She directed a pointed look at Hannah's bed. "Hannah's not going to be here, is she?"

"She's in the library, studying or something. She shouldn't be back before midnight at the earliest."

"Good. I can't stand her smug face." She popped a piece of chocolate in her mouth. She savored the smooth texture as it melted slowly.

"You still haven't forgiven her for dating Aaron? She apologized for that."

"Hell no, I haven't forgiven her. Taking away one guy, forgivable—*maybe*. Taking a second? Not fucking happening." Sam took a big swig of soda. "Not only that, but she made herself out to be a submissive version of me to snag Aaron and then cried about him tying her up. She knew what he liked and made him feel like shit for it."

"Fair enough. I hadn't heard Aaron's side. Are you two still talking?"

"Yeah, he felt like shit after we broke up. We both knew it was coming, but not like that. He said she lost it over everything he suggested, even tame stuff, and would pull these long guilt trips over it."

"Damn, I feel bad for him."

"Apparently, his little sister read him the riot act for dumping me for Hannah."

"Sorry I'm late. Did I miss anything?" Olivia breezed in and dropped her purse next to the bed.

Sam eyed her friend. "The fact that Luke left a hickey the size of Texas on your neck?"

"That shit. I told him no marks." Grinning, Olivia checked out her neck in the mirror. "I guess that's what I get for telling him we were going to pick up guys."

Envy bubbled up in Sam's stomach. She squashed it back down. "I wouldn't blame you for getting rid of him and upgrading."

Julie plumped up a pillow on the floor. "I never heard about the tournament. How'd it go?"

"I won best sportsman."

"How'd they react when they found out you were a girl?"

"They bet on my gender and then felt bad about it. So, as well as could be expected." Sam got comfortable at the head of the bed.

Olivia pulled out a bottle of nail polish. "Our Sammy had them falling over themselves to buy her a drink."

"Any prospects on a new boy toy?"

"None." Sam cut off Olivia. "I'm not in the market."

Olivia didn't take the hint. "There was one really good prospect, Brad. Totally her type. He was the one that bought her a drink because he was one of the ones that bet."

"I'm sitting right here." Sam hugged a pillow to her chest, not ready to think about a relationship now, even if he had the prettiest chocolate brown eyes. "He's also not in the market. I thought we were going to watch a movie and paint our toenails, not talk about my non-existent love life."

"We can do both."

"Yeah, we're great multi-taskers." Julie laid her head on Sam's knee. "We just want you to be happy. And you haven't been happy since you broke up with Aaron."

"I don't need a man to be happy." Sam felt like a broken record when it came to her love life.

"But you want one." Olivia coated Julie's toes in sparkly blue polish.

"You look at Chris Hemsworth like you're a starving dog and he's a steak."

"That's because he's Thor and hot as hell."

"Why don't you want to date anyone?" Olivia studied Sam out of the corner of her eye.

Sam stared at the TV without seeing the movie. She wanted to date. Hell, she wanted what Olivia and Luke had with a need that clawed at her stomach and heart. She just couldn't handle another repeat of her last two relationships.

"My track record has been shit lately. I'm two for two on guys leaving me." She shrugged with a nonchalance she didn't feel. "I'll date eventually." *After Julie moves away from Hannah.*

Chapter Four

"Do you want us to come with you?" Luke poked his head into Sam's room, causing her to jump.

"You could knock."

"Your door was open." He shrugged.

"And no, I don't need a baby-sitter." Sam packed her paints in her case.

"That's not what I'm suggesting. You just look nervous."

"This isn't nerves, this is excitement." The half-lie left her lips easily. "If everything works out, I'll have a group to play with and can stop forcing you to play games with me."

"I like learning new games." He leaned against her door frame.

"Go spend some time with your girl." She shooed him out of her way.

Halfway to the store, she had second thoughts about going alone. Maybe she should have brought someone along as a buffer. She shook her head at her nerves. It wasn't like she hadn't met these guys before.

"You came!" Brad swooped in and pulled her into a big hug.

"I think we need to have another discussion about personal space." She tried to ignore how good he smelled, like soap and something distinctly male. Her body reacted to it and relaxed. Damn Olivia for putting thoughts of dating him in her head.

He relaxed his grip and searched her face. "Sorry, I'm just happy to have someone to paint with. You did come to paint, right?"

"You promised to help my painting techniques, how could I refuse?"

"You could just let him paint your army, like your last boyfriend did." A voice piped up from across the room. Curtis patted the seat next to him. "And then come over here and watch the big boys play."

She tightened her hand on the strap of her case and raised an eyebrow at him. "Are you suggesting that I only play because I either have a boyfriend or am looking for one?"

"I'll come right out and say it if it makes you feel better, sweetheart."

She suppressed a shudder at the way he leered at her. "Wow. Now we know why *you* play." The guys around him chuckled. He turned a mottled purple. "I'll have you know that I introduced War Tactics to my gaming group. I paint all of my own minis, which I can see you don't bother to do." She waved a dismissive hand at his unpainted army. "As for watching the big boys, I'm fairly certain I kicked your ass at the tournament."

She waited a beat to see if he had a retort before turning her back on him.

"That was harsh, but amazing," Brad whispered.

"Sometimes you need to be harsh to prove that you belong." She dug in her bag so he wouldn't see her face.

"You sound upset."

"If you had to prove to every group you meet that you actually belong, you'd be disappointed too."

"Every group?"

"Pretty much." She gave him a half smile. "At least you only bet on my gender."

"TOUCHÉ. WOULD IT HELP if I said I was sorry again?" Brad wondered how long Sam was going to hold this grudge.

"I'm kind of used to it. First time my gender was bet on that I know of though." She spun her empty cup with her finger.

Brad picked up his rinse cup, plucked hers out of her hand, and went to fill them with water. He spent so much time in the last few weeks wracking his brain for how he could make up for his epic faux pas and still didn't know if he could. He set the cups on the table and shifted uncomfortably next to her.

"Look, Sam... I..." Still nothing. Nothing he could say would fix his fuck up and they both knew it.

"How about we start over?" She turned to him and stuck out her hand. "I'm Sam-cat, but you can call me Sam."

He breathed a sigh of relief and shook her hand. "I'm Ubel, but I'd prefer if you called me Brad."

"Okay, Brad, I hear you're an amazing painter. Can you teach me some of your secrets?"

He shouldn't like the way she said his name as much as he did. He focused on going over the basics of painting. She had primed her minis and had a rudimentary knowledge of painting and shading. Definitely self-taught. He explained why she should thin her paint to do thin layers instead of one thick one. He kept going over different techniques and styles for her to try. Her initial efforts met with varying levels of success.

"My brain's going to explode. How many different ways are there to paint a mini?" She rinsed her paintbrush.

"Everyone paints differently. The trick is to try a bit of everything and see what you like." He contemplated the mini he was working on.

"You can bring it to life with just a couple brush strokes. I feel like I should break my brushes and have you paint my army." She brushed a lock of hair out of her face. "I'm not going to, but it's kind of disheartening to work so hard and not have it look like I imagined it."

"You'll get there. I've been painting for years and I still learn new things."

"I might have to invest in one of those." She gestured to his wet palette in front of him. "It seems like you can get a smoother blend of paints on it."

"Like everything else, it takes practice. But I will admit it keeps my paints liquid long enough for me to actually use them."

SAM OPENED THE DOOR to exit the disgusting bathroom and almost ran into Curtis, who stood in the doorway. "Oh! I hadn't realized anyone was waiting for the bathroom."

"I was waiting for you."

"Why?" She tried to keep her tone light, but her hand tightened on the doorknob.

"You insulted me in front of my buddies."

"You insulted me first." She shifted to step around him.

He blocked her exit. "Your smart little mouth can be put to a much better use and I'm just the man to show you."

"I doubt there is anything a little boy like you can show me."

He inched forward. "Sweetheart, you're about to find out just how much of a man I am."

"Let me pass or I'll scream." Her heart beat in her throat. Would anyone come if she yelled for help? Why didn't she bring one of her friends with her? Her mind raced through all the scenarios, none of them good.

"I don't think you will. I think you're using that big bravado to hide the fact that you want me."

She tried to slam the door shut, but he was too quick. He shoved the door open. The knob hit her in the hip and knocked her back a step. While she was off balance, he followed in after her and locked the door behind him. He stalked her across the tiny room.

"Even now, you're thinking about what it would be like if I covered that smart mouth with mine." He stroked her bottom lip with his thumb.

She recoiled and searched for a way around him. "Not a chance in hell."

He crowded her into the corner. "I like them feisty to a point." He ground against her. "Be a good girl and tell me you want me."

Bile rose in her throat. She could feel how much this power trip aroused him. "I wouldn't kiss you if you were the last man in the world."

"Lies." He slapped her across the cheek. Pain exploded in her head. "Now, tell me sweetly how you want me."

"No, let me go." Her voice came out tiny. She darted a look at the door, so close but impossibly far away.

He leaned in to breathe in her ear. "No one's going to save you. Struggle and I'll keep hurting you. Give in to your desire and it won't hurt."

She pushed against his chest, desperate to free herself. He grabbed her hands and pinned them over her head with one of his. She struggled to be free of his grip, but he slammed her head back against the brick wall a couple of times. Dizzy and trapped, she could do no more than plead for him not to hurt her.

BRAD LOOKED AT THE clock. Sam was taking an awfully long time in the bathroom. He looked around the game room and realized Curtis was also missing. A sick feeling propelled him into the hallway.

Scuffling noises came from the bathroom. Her voice sobbed and asked to not be hurt. He tried the knob to find the door locked. The fear in her voice propelled him to kick the door until it gave way.

Time froze as he took in the tableau before him. Curtis held her pinned against the far corner of the room. From the looks of it, Brad had come in just as the slimeball was about to undress her. Tears ran down her cheeks, one of which sported a handprint.

Brad saw red. He pulled Curtis off Sam, tossing him into the hall. "Get away from her!"

"Stay out of this." Curtis snarled.

"Not on your life." Brad swung at Curtis, his fist connected with a satisfying crunch.

"You'll regret that." Curtis spat at him before Brad's fist connected a second time.

"Not as much as you will." Steve stepped in and stopped Brad from pounding the creep into the ground. "Get Sam out of here." Steve grabbed Curtis.

Brad nodded his thanks to Steve and went over to where Sam had curled into a ball. He squatted down and gently brushed the hair from her face. She flinched at his touch until she looked up at him.

"Let's get you out of here."

He stood and pulled her to her feet. He shielded her with his body as he helped her leave the bathroom. Once they were clear of the scene, she threw her arms around him with a cry. He patted her back awkwardly, unsure of what injuries she had sustained. Her sobs tore him to pieces.

Slowly, her crying slowed. She shifted in his arms so he loosened his hold, but kept his arms around her if she needed it. She wiped the tears from her cheeks.

"Sorry about melting down on you."

"There's nothing to be sorry about." He offered his hand. "Come on, we'll go talk to Alex. He's the owner." He led her upstairs to the office. Steve followed with Curtis. "Alex, do you have a minute?"

"Sure thing. What's up?"

"I need to report another player for misconduct."

"Caught another cheater? This isn't a tournament." Alex frowned at Steve and Curtis.

"No, for physically assaulting another player in the bathroom." Brad gestured to Sam, who shrank against him. "Curtis tried to force himself on Sam."

"Curtis, is this true?"

"Of course not." The slimeball shrugged off Steve's grip and oozed up to the desk. "She wanted it until that asshole broke down the door."

"Bullshit." Brad stared down at Curtis. "Explain the handprint across her face."

"She likes it rough." Curtis shrugged.

"You're being awfully quiet." Alex turned his attention to Sam. "Is it because Curtis is right and you're embarrassed you got caught?"

"Brad got it right." She pulled herself upright. "Curtis cornered me and locked us in the bathroom with the intention of forcing himself on me." Her voice trembled.

"What did you do to provoke him?"

Her mouth opened in shock. Brad felt his mouth do the same. He couldn't believe the way she was being questioned. He had to bite his tongue to keep from launching his anger at Alex, but could tell by the look on her face that she needed to answer for herself. She had a spine of steel that he admired.

"Are you seriously asking me what I did to get assaulted?"

Alex held up his hands. "I've known Curtis for many years. He says it was consensual. You say it wasn't. I'm trying to get both sides of the story."

"I beat him at the last War Tactics tournament. Tonight he insinuated that I only play to get guys. I flipped it back on him, maybe that's the reason he plays. I spent the rest of the night painting my minis." Sam's calm voice was in stark contrast to her trembling hands. "I went to the bathroom and he was waiting for me when I got out. He slapped me and pushed me against the wall. He hit my head against the wall when I tried to fight my way out."

"Did you do anything to lead him to believe you wanted his advances?"

"Other than telling him to stop? No."

"Are you sure?"

Brad couldn't take it anymore. "For fuck's sake!" His outrage boiled over and he slammed his fist against the desk. Sam flinched away. "I was with her until she left to use the bathroom. She has done nothing wrong. Why are you treating her like she has?"

"BRAD, RELAX." SAM PLACED a hand on his shoulder and felt the anger vibrate through him. His outrage on her behalf went a long way to make her feel better. "You wanted to know why I rarely play outside my group? Tonight is an extreme example of what I put up with."

"It's not right."

"I know, but it's easier to blame the victim." She collected the ragged ends of her nerves to give Alex a cool once over. "Thank you for ensuring my safety while I'm in your establishment. Don't worry, I can see myself out."

She walked out of the office with her head held high, silently congratulating herself on how little she was shaking. Behind her, Brad and Steve continued to argue for her. She'd have to do something to thank them later.

Vaguely, she contemplated if the numbness she felt was a good or bad sign. She headed back into the game room, ignoring the stares of the guys around her. She made quick work of packing her things and mourned the loss of a potential new group. All she needed to do was make it to her car before the numbness wore off.

Two hands slammed on the table on either side of her. Sam jumped and let out a squeak. Her heart hammered in her ears. *Not again.*

Curtis's breath was hot on her neck. "Where's your great protector? Still arguing your innocence so hard that he didn't even notice me slip out after you?"

"Go away."

"No. We're going to finish our discussion about the uses for your mouth." His hands slowly crept up her arms.

Her brain froze before kicking into high gear. "The only use you will get is me telling you to leave me alone."

"You don't mean it. I can hear the desire in your voice."

"Get your hearing checked." He ignored her attempts to dislodge his hands. "Don't touch me!"

"Get your hands off of her!" Steve skidded into the doorway.

Curtis continued to rub her arms. "She likes this. She's feeding off the attention she's getting."

"She told you to stop. Either you will, or I will make it so you can never touch another person again. " Steve stalked toward them. His intensity should've frightened Sam, but his attention was on the slimeball behind her.

"She doesn't mean it."

She found her voice. "I never want you to come near me, let alone touch me."

Curtis's hands clenched painfully on her arms. And then, they were gone. She turned around to see the other guys in the room holding him back. He cussed about how much of a bitch she was. She blinked back tears as Steve gently pulled her into a loose hold.

"What the hell is going on in here?" Alex walked into the room with Brad hot on his heels.

"What do you think happened?" Steve turned his focus on the owner. "He followed her back down here, intent on finishing what he started earlier. Apparently with your blessing." The rest of the guys nodded.

"Alex, man, you know I wouldn't do that. The little tease gets off on the attention." Curtis's voice oozed across the room.

"Bring him to my office." Alex turned to her as the group filed out. "I'm very sorry for not believing you earlier. We've never had this type of problem before, but I take full responsibility for my part in it. If there is anything you need to make up for this, let me know."

BRAD WATCHED SAM STRUGGLE to keep her composure after the group left the room. He touched her arm, unsure if she'd welcome any physical comfort after what she'd just gone through. "Are you alright? Do you want me to take you to get checked out? Do you want to go to the cops and fill out a report?"

"It's just a bunch of bumps and bruises, no need to file a police report." She let out a small sob. He pulled her out of Steve's hands and into his arms. She clung to his shirt. "Would it sound bad if I said I don't know if I'm alright?"

"It would sound honest." He stroked her back until she calmed.

She blinked up at him with her big blue eyes. "Can I get the hell out of here?"

"Let me grab my stuff and I'll walk you to your car." He packed his stuff while she picked up her bag.

Steve placed a hand on his arm. "Are you going to let her drive home alone? She's awfully pale."

"I'll see if she'll let me drive her. Would you mind following so I can get home?"

"Not a problem."

Brad caught up with Sam at the stairs. She gripped the railing as she climbed. He stuck behind her, ready to catch her if she fell.

He walked her to her car. "Are you okay to drive home by yourself?"

"I'm not a weak little girl that needs to be coddled." She toyed with her bag strap.

"I'm not suggesting you are. You were just assaulted and said he hit your head against the wall. I don't know if you'll go into shock while driving and get hurt." His heart squeezed at the thought of her hurt on the side of the road with no one to help her.

"How would you get home?"

"Steve will follow us and drive me home."

"You don't mind?"

"Not at all. So long as you don't mind me moving your driver's seat." He held the passenger door for her

"Thank you for playing knight in shining armor. You and Steve both." She stared out the window.

He reached over and squeezed her hand. "I'm sorry it was necessary."

They both fell silent. He couldn't help but wonder if there had been anything he could've done different to save her from this pain. He pulled up in front of her house and looked over at her. Tears streamed down her face, breaking his heart.

She didn't respond or move when he said her name. She stumbled when he helped her out of the car, so he picked her up. She was so light in his arms, he didn't know how she managed to keep

Curtis off her as long as she did. Steve beat him to the front door and opened it so Brad could carry her inside.

Andrew took one look at her and called for Olivia. "What happened?"

"She was assaulted in the bathroom. We stopped it before she was..." Brad couldn't bring himself to say the word. He cradled her as carefully as he could, frightened by the fact that she had barely moved. "He beat her pretty good, but she didn't want to go to the ER or police. I think she's in shock."

Olivia barreled down the stairs with Luke on her heels. "Baby, let's get you cleaned up. Luke get me a pair of pajamas for her." Brad gently set Sam on the edge of the tub. "Thank you for getting her home safe."

Chapter Five

S am curled up on the couch and stared at the TV. "You don't need to hover."

Andrew handed her a cup of tea. That seemed to be everyone's solution lately. Can't sleep? Tea. Woke up from a nightmare? Tea. She was sick of the stuff.

"I didn't realize I was hovering."

"Everyone's been acting like I'll break for the last week or so." She struggled to remember what day it was. The days had all blended together in an exhausted haze.

"We're worried. You're not sleeping properly."

"Sorry for waking you again last night." She picked at the fuzz on her blanket. "I hadn't realized you could hear me pace."

"It's the perk of having rooms next to each other. Do you need anything else?"

"No, but I do have to say that walking on eggshells isn't helping."

"I'll let everyone know." He picked up his jacket. "If you need anything, you have my number."

"I need to get ready for work myself." She sipped her tea while she dressed. Most of her bruises had become a bad memory so she opted for short sleeves.

Busy shifts meant less time to dwell on the shit show that had become her life. She finished her shift exhausted and headed home. Andrew must have passed along the message because dinner was more lively than it had been. She was grateful for the slice of normality.

After helping with the dishes, she changed into her pajamas, intent on reading something that would allow her pleasant dreams.

She looked at her gaming bag with a shudder before tucking it further back in her closet. She logged into the gaming boards out of habit while checking her online comics.

Ubel: Hey you

Her stomach sank. She avoided logging on so she didn't have to deal with any of the guys from the store. She stared at the message. It wasn't fair to Brad to keep avoiding talking to him.

Sam-cat: Hey yourself.

U: I saw a new painting technique that I want to try out. Are you game for learning together this week?

Her heart gave a painful thump. She wasn't ready to face anyone yet. Luckily, she had a ready-made excuse.

S: I promised Olivia I'd help her with a project for school. Maybe afterward.

U: What kind of project?

S: I'm modeling for her. She's a photography student.

U: That's wicked cool.

S: Yeah, you never know what she's going to throw at you.

U: I'll see you Thursday.

S: Maybe, it depends on how long the shoot takes.

She logged off before he could ask anymore questions. She hated being a coward. She hated not sleeping and not wanting to touch her minis or practice painting. Reading forgotten, she sat on the couch next to Eric.

"What are we watching tonight?" She watched him flip through the channels.

"I hadn't settled on anything." He looked at her out of the corner of his eye. "What are you planning on doing this week?"

She knew he meant what was she planning on doing about the Game Hut. Her stomach twisted. "Olivia scheduled a photo shoot with one of the theater kids and needs me to help."

"That's convenient."

"It beats the alternative."

"SHE'S NOT COMING THIS week, is she?"

Brad glared at Steve and then the clock. "I guess not. I figured she would've told me that she's no longer coming instead of saying maybe."

"Or she needs more time." Steve studied him. "You're worried about her."

Brad made an inarticulate noise. "Yeah, that was some scary shit. She doesn't come online much and when she does, it's only for a minute or two. I can't get more than a couple of words out of her before she logs off again."

"I'm beginning to think you're developing feelings for Sam."

"No." He mulled it over. "I don't know. She's awesome, but let's be honest, she's not looking for anything and I don't need to have a Brittany repeat." He finished his turn. "And she's probably been scared off for good so it's a moot point."

"You'll never know if you can't get her to talk to you. Why don't you pack it in and see if she's online?"

"You don't mind?"

"You owe me a make up game."

Brad rushed through packing his minis and went home. *I'm an idiot.* He turned on his laptop and logged into the forums. Bingo, Sam was on.

Ubel: Hey you.

Sam-cat: You're home early.

U: You never showed up, again, and I can only play Steve so many times.

S: Sorry. Something came up.

U: That's it? 'Something came up?'

He winced. He had no right to question her. She didn't owe him an explanation. He was about to tell her he was sorry when she replied.

S: Yeah, we held a house meeting to talk about a few things.

U: I was hoping you weren't avoiding the store.

S: Was Curtis there tonight?

That one question told him she had been avoiding the store. His heart dropped.

U: No, he was permanently banned from the store. It might take Alex a bit to get the right idea, but he doesn't tolerate abuse in his store.

S: That's good to hear.

U: Are you coming next week?

He held his breath. He wasn't sure how he could tempt her into coming back. The longer she took, the less likely it was she'd ever show back up.

S: I should be there, barring an emergency.

He let out a huge sigh of relief. He told himself it was because he enjoyed having someone to paint and talk with, not because he had developed anything more than feelings of friendship for her.

U: Good, because I still have a lot to teach you about painting.

S: Good, because I still have a lot to learn about painting from you.

"WHO'S THAT?"

"Eric, the one roommate that you haven't met." Sam blew out her breath and set down her bag. Brad had already set up her spot next to him, bringing a smile to her face.

"Why's he here?"

"It was decided that, after what happened, I would bring one of the guys along with me until we're sure I won't be assaulted again."

"You don't sound thrilled about this."

"Tell me how you'd feel having a baby-sitter because some douchebag cornered you and the store owner wasn't going to do dick about it. They hovered over me for a week. I just want to forget it happened."

"What's he going to do all night?"

She pulled her minis out of her case. "Other than follow me to the bathroom? Work on his role-playing campaign for the most part." She heard the irritation in her voice, but refused to apologize for it.

She was grateful he didn't push any further about the subject of her baby-sitter. Olivia understood why she needed to push herself into confronting her fear. Eric offered to be the first of her keepers. Sam agreed because he was the one that did the least hovering after the attack.

She watched Brad work, glad to have a diversion. "How the hell do you paint so good so fast?"

"Practice." He grinned at her. "Also, I'm painting all of them the same so I do all the same color on each model before starting the next color."

"Those are for a client, aren't they? Color me impressed at your organization and skill."

"It doesn't feel impressive most of the time. Big armies of the same model make me feel like an automaton." He shook his head and gave her a crooked smile that did all sorts of crazy things to her emotions. "I don't mean to bitch. There are worse jobs to have. I just feel like I need to restructure my business."

"How much longer until you're done with this army?"

"No clue. It's stupid huge and the client wants to add more."

"Is it worth it?"

"Yes and no. It's a good chunk of change, but as an hourly rate, it sucks."

She debated helping him restructure his business. Her brain churned over ideas, but she kept quiet. She wasn't sure he'd appreciate her butting into his life. "At least you're living your dream, even if it isn't turning out exactly the way you want it to."

"Has anyone ever told you that you're too sweet for your own good?" Brad's eyes softened.

She grinned at him. "My roommates. But it's usually 'oh my god, knock it off.'"

"That would be me and Luke." Eric said as he walked over to them and set his book on the table. "You should see this girl when she's caffeinated and baking with Olivia. Are you going to be okay if I use the restroom?"

"I'm sure Brad will keep an eye out for me." She turned her attention back to her mini.

"YOU WEREN'T KIDDING when you said you had a baby-sitter." Brad felt bad for Sam's predicament, but he couldn't fault them for wanting to take care of her.

Her shoulders slumped. "Whether I want one or not, I'm stuck with one."

"Anything I can do to help?"

"Not really."

"I'm confused why Eric is still hanging around. Most of the room has your back." He gestured to the other guys. "Hell, they even scrubbed the bathroom to make it more female friendly."

He left out the part where he washed her blood off of the brick wall. Blood that was too high on the wall to be anything but her head. The memory still tortured him, partially because he hadn't noticed the head wound that night. Had he seen it, he would've insisted that she go to the ER.

"That's so sweet of them." She smiled at him. "Can we not talk about my shadows or the reason behind them? Can we just paint?"

He dropped the topic, making a mental note to see if her friends would shed some light on it. He made it his mission to keep a smile on her face for the rest of the evening. "Of course. Now that you've gotten blending down, do you want to try your hand at washes?"

He alternated his attention between the minis in front of him and watching her work. She took to painting like she was born for it. With a bit of practice, he could see her as a business partner. They worked side-by-side until they had to pack up, occasionally commenting on each other's work.

They continued to chat about painting techniques on the way to their cars. Brad watched her drive away and shook his head. *Business partner? Where did that come from?* He dropped his bag next to his desk and flipped open his laptop.

Sam-cat: Sorry for being in a sour mood.

Ubel: Nothing to be sorry for. It's completely understandable.

S: I think they're overreacting.

U: I'd be the same way if you were my friend.

S: You mean I'm not your friend? I must have been mistaken then.

U: Twisting my words already? I meant if I were as close to you as they are, I'd be overreacting too. Are you coming next week?

S: Let me check.

He watched the cursor blink. He was too impatient for her answer. Maybe Steve was right. Maybe he cared for her.

S: No. Can't get anyone to go with me.

U: That sucks. Would they make an exception if I came out and got you?

S: That's a resounding no from the house. You're still too new to the group for them to get a read on you, even though you saved me and made sure I got home in one piece.

U: I understand. Can you promise two weeks from now?

S: Yes, Olivia pinky-swore that she'll make Luke come with me.

U: Great, see you then.

SAM PACED AROUND THE empty house. The restrictions placed on her by her friends chaffed and made her feel weak. She was ready to go to the store on her own without a chaperon. At this rate, her army would be painted sometime next year and there were only so many tips Brad could give her over chat. Hell, she was running low on a couple of colors. A thought skittered across her brain that had her snatching her purse and heading out.

She pulled into the parking lot of the Game Hut and panicked at the thought of Luke catching her. *Screw it, I'm an adult*. She slammed her car door in defiance and marched into the store. She bought a couple bottles of paint before heading to the basement, hoping to catch Brad before he went home.

"I thought you weren't coming tonight." He did a double-take and looked behind her. "Where's your entourage?"

"Shh, if anyone asks, you didn't see me and I was never here." She placed her finger on his lips. They were as soft as they looked.

He tugged her hand away from his mouth. "Did you slip your handlers?"

"No one was available to come with me, so I decided to go shopping. It just so happened I needed more paint."

"If no one knows where you are, I could kidnap you and no one would ever find out." He rubbed his hands together.

"You wouldn't." Her stomach flipped. She looked into his brown eyes, focused on the mischievous smirk on his face, and smiled back as her mind flashed through a few scenarios she wouldn't mind.

"Don't tempt me." His voice held an edge of promise.

"So you would kidnap me and what? Lock me in your basement? Turn me into your harem girl?"

He rocked back in his chair and his eyes lit up. "It would be Steve's basement, but basically, that's exactly what I'll do. Thanks for the idea."

"You're so weird." Her phone rang. She stared at the number and cussed. "Hey Luke, what's up?"

"Where the hell are you? I came home and you were gone." Luke sounded pissed.

"Shopping." She winced at the sound of rolling dice.

"You slipped away to the Game Hut, didn't you?" He slammed a door. "Damn it, Samantha Marie! We're doing this for your protection."

"Calm down." She turned away from Brad and lowered her voice. "I don't think you understand that your protection, as thoughtful as it is, makes me feel weaker." She couldn't believe she admitted that. "It's been over a month since the incident, the guys here are my friends too, and the nightmares have stopped. I think I'll be fine on my own. Plus, I'm an adult."

"We will talk about this when you get home." Luke hung up on her.

"Can't wait." She spun and found Brad's eyes glued to her. "What?"

"You had nightmares? Why didn't you tell me?"

"I had it under control."

"Define under control." She shook her head. "Seriously, if we're friends, you can talk to me about this stuff."

She contemplated his serious expression. "Under control meant waking up in a sweat and screaming the first couple of nights. Sometimes it meant Olivia came and slept with me, sometimes I took a shower and stayed up for a couple of extra hours." She waved a dismissive hand and picked up the closest bottle of paint so she didn't have to see his reaction. "It hasn't happened in a while."

BRAD WATCHED SAM FIDDLE with the bottle, pieces falling into place. He covered her hands with his and she stilled. "I wish you'd said something. I understand not wanting to be saved, but you could've talked to me."

"We barely knew each other. I didn't want to burden you when you had already done so much for me."

He ran his thumb over her knuckles before he could stop himself. He let go of her hands before he did something stupid. "We're friends now, or at least, I hope we are."

"Of course we are." She set aside the paint. "If I had known I was going to be caught so fast, I would've brought my painting stuff with me."

"I have all my stuff here. You can borrow it to get some painting in." He missed having her next to him.

"I can't stay too long." She slid into her usual chair. "Stop making faces. The sooner I have it out with my roommates, the better."

"I could beg." He wanted to rip his traitor tongue out of his head.

"Next week, I'll be here the entire time."

"Promise?"

She held out her pinky to him. "Promise."

He wrapped his pinky around hers. She hung out for a while and watched him work on a commission piece. He had to stop himself from brushing the lock of hair off her face. He wondered if it felt like satin when threaded through his fingers. Sam tilted her head and stared at him.

"You're looking at me funny." She waved her hand in front of his face.

He racked his brain for anything to say besides the truth. He didn't know how she'd react to him telling her he was thinking about touching her. "Are you signing up for Tactics Weekend?"

"What's that?"

"It's a weekend long event for War Tactics. We only go for the big tournament on Saturday."

"When is it? I don't know if my army will be ready in time."

"You have two months. I'll help you get ready."

She pulled out her phone and checked her schedule. "That should be my weekend off. What time do we leave?"

"I'll get you the details." His insides lit up at the idea of spending more time with her.

Chapter Six

Luke met Sam at the door, frustration radiating off of him. "I can't believe you'd sneak out like that!"

She slipped around him. "Relax. I ran out of black paint and needed some to work on my army. How was I supposed to know you'd have a conniption fit over it?"

"You'd risk getting hurt just to see a guy?"

"Woah, back that shit up. I didn't go out because of a guy." She threw her purse in her room, his remark hitting a little too close to home. "And even if I did, it's my life and I get to dictate how I live it, not you."

"This is serious, Sam. We're doing this to keep you safe."

She stepped toe-to-toe with him. "Obviously, I feel safe enough to leave the house without you and, yes, go back to the place where I was attacked."

"There's a difference between feeling safe and being safe."

"You don't think I know that? You're smothering me and making me feel like I can't continue living my life because of something forced on me."

"That's the last thing I want, but I need to make sure you're okay."

"I'm fine."

He narrowed his eyes at her. "Yeah? When was your last nightmare?"

"I haven't had one since the second week." She crossed her arms. "I'm getting better, but you acting like I'm under house arrest isn't helping. I control my life, not you."

"What's going on down here?" Olivia stepped between them.

"Samantha Marie snuck out to go to the Game Hut."

Sam hated that he used her middle name like she was an errant child. "It's nothing. Luke's overreacting to me running out to get paint."

"Sometimes I swear you two really are siblings." Olivia rubbed her temples. "Sam, you should've let someone know you were going out. We were worried when we got home and you were gone." Olivia turned her attention to her boyfriend. "Luke, stop smothering and yelling at her. If she feels she's ready to go out without you, it's her choice. Who knows? It might actually help."

"Thank you." Sam hugged Olivia. Luke walked off in a huff.

"I could hear the two of you upstairs. I can't say I fully agree with you going to the store by yourself, but I do understand why you'd want to. Some of those guys are really cute."

"Oh, sweet baby Jesus. I'm not into any of the guys at the store. We're friends and that's it. We're getting our armies ready for a tournament."

"Just friends? Even the guy you spend most of your nights talking to?" Olivia raised an eyebrow.

"He's a great painter and teacher. I'm not ready for another relationship and neither is he. We're friends and that's all." She refused to admit he made her heart race anytime he was near. It was just that he was hot and she was in the middle of a long hiatus from guys.

"I SHOULD'VE KILLED that douche bag when I had the chance."

Steve looked up at the venom in Brad's voice. "Who?"

"Curtis. Did you know the whole reason her group's been overprotective is because she's been having nightmares?"

"I figured there had to be more to the story than she was telling us. Is that what her phone call was about?" Steve was always perceptive.

"Apparently, she decided to come here alone against the wishes of her group. Didn't tell a soul where she'd be."

"That's fucking risky. She barely knows us. If she were under my care, I'd give her such a spanking that she wouldn't be able to sit for a week."

"I don't think she'd appreciate that, she isn't one of your little submissives."

"Submissive or not, sometimes a spanking is called for."

Brad shook his head. "I think she has a good head on her shoulders and can make decisions for herself."

"You're just saying that because you're smitten with her."

"I'm not smitten. I just enjoy having someone to talk about painting with."

"Keep telling yourself that." Steve's tone let him know he wasn't fooling anyone.

"For real, if she keeps improving the way she has, she could rival my paint jobs in under a year. She could have her own painting business if she wants it."

"Or she could join your business."

"It crossed my mind, if business keeps picking up the way it has."

"Yeah, you have it bad for her."

Brad flipped off Steve and headed back to the house.

SAM GOT HOME FROM WORK and grabbed leftovers before going to her room. She knew it was childish to keep avoiding her roommates, but her fight with Luke still stung. She logged into her computer and found Brad online. A smile crept over her face.

Sam-cat: How goes the great world of painting?

Ubel: Long hours full of spilled paint. I swear I keep Alex in business solely on how much crap I knock over.

S: You don't seem to spill much on Thursdays.

U: My desk is a bit messier.

S: You should do something about that. It sounds like it's eating into your profits.

U: After Tactics Weekend, I'll put it on the top of my to do list.

S: Speaking of that, how big is the tournament?

U: Point wise or player wise?

S: Both. I need to start firming up my list so I know what I need to buy and paint.

U: 500 points, two lists.

S: How much overlap can the lists have?

U: They can be as identical or different as you like, but they have to be the same faction as each other. I would suggest bringing one that's good against machines and one list if you fight beasts.

She made a couple notes and pulled up a few pages on her faction. She was already at a disadvantage because her faction was meant to supplement other armies and wasn't really tooled to be played by itself. That meant her tactics needed to be spot on.

S: How many players?

U: Last year there were over a hundred players. Luckily, it's not single elimination. You get points by completing objectives. Those points added to your wins are what decide if you make it to the finals.

S: Sounds tough.

U: It's the biggest tournament for War Tactics. Most of us go with the hopes of winning the supplemental prizes. Prize payout is more than worth the drive and entry fee.

S: That gives me a lot to think about.

U: You know you can always pick my brain.

Chapter Seven

A lock of hair escaped Sam's clip. She blew at it to get it out of her eyes, but it fell back where it was. Brad thought it was adorable that it happened pretty much every week. He gave into the impulse and reached over to tuck the silky smooth strands behind her ear. She froze under his touch.

"Sorry, but it looked like you needed a hand." He looked over at her, suddenly embarrassed by his action.

She blinked a couple of times. "It's fine. My hands were full. Thanks for the assist." She nodded at the mini in her hand. "What do you think?"

He studied it. "Can I hold it?"

"Yeah, kinda hard to check it out if you can't look at it closely." She passed over the mini, her cheeks staining pink.

Brad turned the mini around, half of his attention on her reaction to him. He couldn't figure out if she liked him touching her or if he was just another guy pawing at her. He didn't want her to think of him like Curtis, but he did seek out small ways to brush against her. She was addicting. Her hands free, she undid her hair clip and ran her fingers through her hair before putting it back up.

Realizing he had been quietly watching her, he refocused on her mini. "For a machine on the battlefield, it's awfully clean and shiny."

"I hadn't thought about that." Her face fell.

"I'm not saying it's a bad thing." He berated himself for not offering a compliment on the paint job before giving his criticism. "It was just a thought. Otherwise, it's a really killer mini." He lingered over handing it back. Her hand was warm and soft against his.

Sam frowned. "How do I make it more battle worthy?"

He picked out a bottle of brown ink from his case. "A little of this at the joints to make them look oiled and greasy. Maybe some heat scoring at the pipes and guns. You could even go crazy and splatter mud at the legs."

He went back to teaching mode and her eyes were on him. She leaned in to watch him paint and it was all he could do to stop himself from sucking in lungfuls of her perfume. He hoped she wore it just for him, but figured the chance was slim. His gaze landed on her lips and he wondered if they tasted as sweet as she smelled.

"Thank you for teaching me." She settled back into her chair. "I know you have better things to do than answer my questions."

"I enjoy teaching you." Brad found himself a little surprised at how true those words were. "If everyone learned like you, I'd be out of a job."

Her cheeks flushed. "Then you could make a living teaching gamers how to paint. What do I owe you for the lessons?"

He debated asking for a kiss. "No charge."

"That's no way to run a business." Sam scowled at him and wagged her finger. "How about I get you a snack?"

"Sounds like a deal." She bounced off and he groaned.

Steve leaned over to inspect Sam's mini. "She's getting good."

"I know." His chest swelled with pride at her progress.

"Then why the pained look?"

"I just realized I could've probably bargained for dinner instead of a snack, but I don't know how she'd react to the suggestion." Brad buried his face in his hands.

"Just ask her out."

"After what Curtis did to her, I don't feel right. Especially if she doesn't want to, I don't want to make things awkward around here."

"Your funeral."

SAM PAUSED AT THE DOOR to the game room, her arms loaded with snacks. Her mouth went dry just peeking at Brad. If she was being honest with herself, the snack break was just an excuse to get her head back together. She had been reading too much into his actions lately. He just wanted to be friends. If only her heart would accept that.

She set a soda and bag of chips in front of him. "Payment for the teacher."

"No apple?" His lips quirked up.

"All out." She took a long drink of her soda to cool off and to stop herself from leaning down for a taste of him. "Maybe next week."

"Does that mean I should come up with a lesson plan for next week?"

"If you want to." She kept her tone as noncommittal as possible, but was dying to break out in a dance at him wanting to spend time with her.

"I want to." His voice rumbled. She struggled to not read more into his statement. "What do you want to learn?"

What it feels like to have your arms around me. She swallowed back the thought and wracked her brain for the least sexy thing he could teach her. "Rust. I think my machines need a bit of rust on them."

"Rust it is."

"I'M IN OVER MY HEAD." Sam flopped onto Julie's bed.

"She's been moping since she got home Thursday night." Olivia shoved Sam aside to sit down.

"What's her deal?" Julie passed out the snacks.

"I might have a thing for Brad, but he totally wants to keep things platonic." Sam groaned and buried her face in a pillow. Saying it out loud solidified the feelings she tried to suppress.

"Apparently, his last girlfriend did quite the number on him and now Sam's convinced he doesn't like her as more than a friend." Olivia supplied.

Julie snorted. "Fuck it, ask him out. Life's way too short to miss out, especially if he's hot. Is he hot?"

"Oh yeah. He has these chocolate brown eyes that make you melt. And his arms, just muscular enough to get your attention without looking like he spends too much time at the gym." Sam stopped, aware that Julie tricked her into waxing poetic.

"He's so her type and we know he can pick her up, which she loves." Olivia nudged Sam with her elbow.

"What have you got to lose if he says no?"

"I could ruin what has the possibility of being an amazing friendship and have my heart broken, again."

"Chicken."

Sam ignored her friends' taunts and focused on the movie. She needed a break from puzzling out what to do with her feelings for Brad. Soon enough the conversation turned to the other girls complaining about their course loads and homework. When the movie finished up, she and Olivia packed their things and headed home.

"Seriously, Sam, you owe it to yourself to see if there is anything between you and him."

"I think I'll wait until after the tournament." She unlocked the door and walked towards her room. "That way it's not awkward on the way there."

"Just promise me you'll do it soon, okay?"

"The tournament's in a few weeks. Good night."

"AN APPLE FOR THE TEACHER." Sam set a shiny red apple in front of Brad before taking her usual spot.

"I was joking about wanting one, but it's sweet of you to remember." His heart sped up as he caught the first whiff of her perfume. It was not the apple that he wanted to take a bite out of. "Are you ready to start?"

"Let me grab our water." She picked up their cups and dashed to the bathroom.

He hooked his foot around her chair and scooted it a little closer to him. If she noticed, she didn't say anything. Her leg brushed him when she leaned forward to watch him demonstrate a technique. Was it his imagination or did she let it linger an extra moment before shifting it away? He deliberately left the supplies between them so he had an excuse to brush against her arm or hand.

"What am I teaching you next week?"

Sam gave him an apologetic look. "Steve challenged me to a game and I feel bad for monopolizing all of your time with my questions."

"Don't feel bad." Brad kept his voice low, debating on strangling his best friend. "I like having someone to talk to about painting."

"If there's time next week, do you want to play a game against me? With the tournament being so close, I feel like I need practice."

"I'd love to play against you." *Or with you*, his brain added.

"Good." Her face lit up with a smile. "I'm going to dump this cup, there is way too much rust in my water." She slipped away.

He went over to where Steve was playing. "Bastard."

"What did I do?" Steve feigned innocence.

"Challenged Sam to a game next week."

"You act like it's a crime to spend time with her."

"Thursdays are my time with her." Brad growled, knowing he was being baited, but couldn't stop himself.

Steve gave him a satisfied look. "Then do something about it. Ask her out, but don't mark her as yours and not do anything about it."

"I haven't marked her."

"You've all but pissed on her."

"Just keep your hands off of her."

"I don't think she's my style, but I wouldn't mind being proven wrong." An unholy light lit up Steve's eyes.

Before Brad could punch his friend, Sam came back into the room and walked up to them. "Am I intruding? This looks like a serious conversation. I'm totally intruding."

"Not at all, are you ready to try your hand at basing your minis?" Brad herded her back to their table and away from Steve.

She helped him pack up at the end of the night. "Is everything okay with you? You seem extra tense tonight."

Was he that easy to read? Did she know he wanted to kiss her? He zipped his bag and gestured for her to go ahead of him up the stairs. "Just stressed with the workload and getting my army ready on the side."

"It must be hard to juggle painting everything. And I'm not helping by stopping you to ask questions."

"Oddly, helping you reminds me how much I like painting."

"I'll see you next week." She touched his arm briefly before climbing in her car.

He was so screwed, pining for a girl that didn't want to date anyone. He snorted, he was one to talk. He even told her that he wasn't looking for anything. He mulled over what to do while munching on the apple she brought him. He deliberately took small bites to make it last longer. Yup, screwed.

"BRAD'S GLARING AT ME. What did I do wrong?" Sam kept her voice quiet as she finished up her turn.

Steve gave her a smile and patted her hand. "He's not mad at you. Me, on the other hand, that's a different story."

"What did you do?" She hated that the two friends were fighting. She walked in on a serious conversation the previous week, but it didn't seem like they were fighting then.

"Nothing he won't forgive me for in a couple of days." He waved off her concern. "How did you manage to kill my leader?"

"Tactics and playing the long game." She placed her minis in her bag and glanced at the clock. She should have let him win, then she would have had time for a game with Brad. She dropped into her usual chair.

"Did you enjoy your game?" He sounded pissed and she noted that he hadn't worked on anything all night.

"I did. Sorry it took so long." She studied his face, trying to figure out how to get him out of his funk. "Are you planning on being grumpy all night?"

"Just doing some heavy thinking."

"Whatever Steve did, I'm not sure it's worth the frown lines." Sam couldn't stop herself from smoothing her hand across his forehead.

He caught her hand before she could pull away. He toyed with her fingers like they held the answers he was looking for. "Even if he's right?"

"I guess it depends on what he's right about. Anything I can help with?" She shifted a bit closer.

"Why would you want to help?"

"We're friends, remember? We should be able to talk about what's bothering us." She said it to remind herself and tried to ignore how amazing his hands felt on hers. "And it's only fair. You helped me with my army."

"Friends, right." He muttered and straightened his shoulders. "Thanks for the offer, but I think I figured it out." He released her hand, much to her dismay. "Do I get a raincheck for our game?"

She couldn't put her finger on what was eating him, but her statement hadn't helped his mood like she thought it would. "Absolutely. How's next week sound?"

Chapter Eight

"You said something about a theater degree. What do you do with it?" Brad set up his army across from Sam. He wanted to learn more about her and so far their conversations had been primarily about painting or game theory.

"Theater Management and Promotions. Right now, I'm doing nothing with it. I work at a big box retailer, Ali Carte, and turn down promotions."

"Why would you turn down promotions? Don't you have a shit ton of student loans to pay back?"

"Not a cent." She gave him a smug look.

He took the obvious bait, grateful that she kept the conversation going. "How'd you manage that?"

"Grants, scholarships, and a job. I think I applied for every scholarship I remotely met the requirements for. Plus, my parents are divorced so my dad set up a college fund for me." She shrugged. "Every time he got a raise, he'd put as much of it in the college fund as he could after my mother took him for whatever she could get."

He frowned at her bitter tone. It was rare to hear that kind of venom out of her. "Sounds like you aren't on good terms with your mom."

"I don't like talking about her." She shifted from foot-to-foot and stared at the table before meeting his eyes. "Did you really ask me what I did for a living? That's such a cheesy question."

He could drown in those blue eyes. "I just realized that I didn't know much about you outside this game." He took his turn. "Does it bother you?"

"Not really, but turnabout is fair play. What made you decide to own your own business?"

Leave it to her to turn this into a game. He thought about his answer while taking his next turn. "I hated working for other people. I didn't go to college. Instead, I got a job as a drone in an office."

"I can't see you doing that for long."

"Two hellish, suit-wearing years. I painted on the side, learned the trade, and picked up small jobs here and there."

"What caused you to go full-time?"

"I was downsized. It was the kick in the pants I needed." He pretended to study the table while sneaking glances at her. "Why do you work at a crappy retail job when you're so smart?"

She killed off one of his minis. "I like where I live. After everyone graduates, we'll scatter to get jobs and I want to wait a bit longer. Plus, it turns out that most businesses don't count my degree as a real business degree even though I logged a ton of hands-on experience."

"Why theater management?"

"That's two in a row." She wagged her finger at him. For a moment, he didn't think she was going to answer his question. "I didn't know what I wanted to do when I got to college, so I concentrated on taking my core requirements. I took a theater class that entailed a lot of hands-on work. I fell in love with the hectic pace and decided to do management and promotions."

"You love a challenge." He took out one of her minis. He barely concentrated on the game set up between them.

"Most of the time." Sam picked up the mini and toyed with it. "Tell me about your family."

Brad knew that question would come up sooner or later. He took a deep breath. Better to just get it out of the way. "Not much to tell. Parents are still together, even though they shouldn't be. Older sister, married with two kids."

"Do you get along with them?"

"Do you get along with your mother?" He countered.

"You can't answer my question with one of your own." She perched on the table, the game forgotten for the moment. "And for the record, no I don't. She uses me as a pawn to hurt my dad."

"I'm sorry." He reached over and patted her hand. "My father had me arrested for hitting him after he beat my mother."

She came around the table and hugged him. "That's terrible. I'm sure your mom appreciated it."

He loved how Sam felt in his arms. "Don't be so sure. She sided with my father when the cops came, even though she was sporting more than a couple bruises." He stepped out of her hold, unable to bear her pity. "Now, I'm a violent criminal that's not allowed to see his niece and nephew."

"That's absolute crap. Is that why Steve stopped you from giving Curtis the beating he so very much deserved?"

This was the first time she willingly brought up that night. He studied her to see if it still affected her. "I think he was more worried about you. He's... very protective of the women in his life."

"It sounds like there's a story there."

"It's not mine to tell."

"WHAT IF I ASK NICELY?" Sam teased as she turned back to the game. She wasn't interested in Steve's story so much as Brad's, but she needed to steer the conversation back to happy things. She hated that she inadvertently hurt him with her questions.

"No. Don't waste your question on it."

"I thought it was your turn."

"I asked about your mother."

"Right. What's your happiest childhood memory?" She crossed her fingers that Brad had one.

He took a long time thinking it over. "Remember Fire Prevention Week?" She nodded. "Third grade, we had a contest to make posters. Best poster won a gift certificate to get a free ice cream. I won." Pride dripped off of him.

She tried to picture him as a little kid. "Artistic even back then."

"What's yours?"

Hers was easy, but she didn't know if he'd understand it. "Shortly before the divorce, my dad took the day off of work. We went to the zoo and studied all the animals. He bought me a stuffed panther and all the junk food I wanted. I think we rode the carousel half a dozen times. He took me to a movie. Afterward, he told me they were getting a divorce."

"That seems more bittersweet than happy."

"But it's not. My parents had been fighting a lot and I was happy it was going to be over. I was also under the delusion that I would be moving with my father to Missouri, but the judge sided with my mother." She wracked her brain for appropriate questions. "What's your favorite color?"

"Green. Yours?"

"Purple. Favorite movie?"

"Kill Bill, both parts. Yours?"

"Lord of the Rings, all three movies."

"Cop out."

"You did two movies, why can't I do three?" She stuck her tongue out at him, enjoying the verbal sparring.

"I'm joking. It's your turn."

"You just parrot my questions. I'm doing all the hard work in this conversation." Not that she minded, he had a great idea to get to know each other.

"How do you want to remedy this?"

She acted like she was in deep thought so she could stare at him longer. The clock behind him caught her attention. "I guess it doesn't matter because we're going to have to pack up to go home soon."

"Seriously? Where did the night go? We didn't get to finish our game."

"Spent too much time talking and not enough gaming." She shrugged, not caring that they didn't play much.

He packed his minis. "Do we try for another game next week?"

"I'm still short a couple minis for the tournament. Do you mind if we paint instead?"

"Not a bit. I still have some work to get done."

She slung her bag on her shoulder and waved good-bye to the other guys. They walked to her car. "What's your favorite animal?"

"I'm a dog person. You?"

"Stop asking my questions back to me. Cats, big cats."

"Your favorite being?"

"Tigers." She fiddled with her bag strap, not wanting to go home yet.

"I'm not surprised, Sammy-cat." He winked at her. "We'll continue this conversation online."

"Give me your phone." She took it, plugged in her number, and sent a text to herself. "Just in case you need to get a hold of me and I'm not online." She congratulated herself on getting his number. "Good-night."

She floated on cloud nine on her drive home. It shouldn't make her so ridiculously happy to get his number, but it did. Too bad she didn't have the courage to ask him out. She pulled into her spot and skipped past her roommates. She barely logged in before a message appeared on her screen.

Ubel: What's your favorite possession?

Sam-cat: My stuffed panther.

U: Mine's my painting desk. It was my grandfather's woodworking bench before he died.

S: That explains all the dents I see on it when you post pictures of your work. Are you a night owl or an early bird?

U: Night owl.

S: I figured as much. I'd be more of a night owl if I didn't have to work early most days.

U: Favorite day of the week.

S: Thursday.

She hit send before she realized the implications of her answer. She sat and watched the cursor blink for forever. He took a long time to respond. She chewed on the side of her finger, waiting for his answer.

U: Mine too. Any reason in particular?

S: I like hanging out with you and I'm learning a lot. I didn't expect to be as relaxed with all of you as fast I am.

U: Yeah, it was quite the rough start. Sorry for my part in all of it.

She smiled at the screen. One of these days, he would stop apologizing.

S: I think your part in helping me more than negates the bet. Why do you like Thursday?

U: Stimulating conversation. And you smell better than everyone else.

Not what she expected out of him. She stared at his response. How did she respond to that? You smell amazing yourself?

U: Did I embarrass you?

S: No, I just wasn't expecting to hear that you like sitting by me because I don't stink. What's your favorite smell?

U: What perfume do you wear?

S: I thought we had a talk about answering a question with a question.

U: Seriously, I think it's my new favorite smell, but I don't know what it's called.

Her mind churned over the reasons that he could possibly like her perfume over any other smell in the world. Did he like her as more than a friend? Unsure on how to figure it out, she started pulling up other questions to ask while answering him.

S: It's called Love Potion.

U: Interesting name. It suits you. What's your favorite?

S: The smell of cookies in the oven. It reminds me of Christmases with my grandparents.

U: I haven't had fresh baked cookies in forever.

S: Olivia and I bake a ton for Christmas every year. You'll get some this year.

U: I didn't mean for that to be a request.

S: We give them out to all of our friends. We just have to bake more than normal this year.

"HE'S BEEN GRINNING like an idiot for the last few days." Chuck poured himself a cup of coffee.

"I think he's in love." Steve waggled his eyebrows.

"You two know I can hear you, right?" Brad didn't bother looking up from his phone. Sam transitioned to texting him questions during her breaks at work.

"He's got it bad for this girl. Poor guy."

Steve sipped his coffee. "Poor guy, nothing. I think she has it bad for him too. Why else would she talk to him all hours of the day?"

"We're just friends." Again, Brad didn't look up from his phone.

"Keep telling yourself that. You've got it bad for her." Chuck rinsed out his cup and left for work.

Brad looked up. "Seriously, we're just friends. She says so all the time."

Steve sat across the table. "I've seen the way she looks at you. I think she's trying to tell herself that to spare her the pain of you not liking her back."

"She doesn't look at me in any particular way." Brad frowned.

"Like hell she doesn't. Did you miss the way she gravitates to you? Or the fact that she worries that you're upset with her when you're mad at me? If you don't do anything about it, you're a dumbass." Steve rinsed out his coffee cup. "I'm going to be late for class."

Brad sat at the table and stared at his phone. Just friends. She brought it up all the time. Their messages didn't feel like they were only friends. His screen lit up.

Sam: Do you like roller coasters?

Brad: Yes, you?

S: Hell yeah.

B: What risks are worth taking?

S: Deep. Going after your dreams, definitely. I used to think love was worth risking everything for.

He frowned at his phone. Those two words stopped him cold.

B: Used to?

S: My last two relationships didn't end well. Same girl used the same technique to steal both guys.

B: Harsh.

S: Are you going to answer your question or do I need to ask it?

B: I mostly agree with you, except I think love is worth the risk. Especially if you find the right person.

S: Back to work. Talk to you later.

"CAN YOU PASS THE BROWN ink?" Panic mode had settled into the Thursday night group and Sam was not immune to it. The months had slid by and now she had two days to get the last details done on her army before the tournament. Although, it looked killer thanks to all the tips and tricks she had learned.

Brad looked up from his mini and plucked the bottle from the box. "Are you really going to waste your question on that?"

"No." She laughed. It seemed like they were both really enjoying their game of questions. "I just wanted to add some oil to the joints of this machine."

"Good, because that would be a lame question and I'm waiting for the next one." He handed over the bottle and they both paused a beat before either moved. She could never be sure if he was making sure she had a handle on the bottle before letting go or if he liked touching her as much as she liked touching him.

She distracted herself by asking a real question. "If you were the dictator of a small nation, what crazy dictator stuff would you do?"

"How do you come up with some of these questions?"

"Googled questions to ask to get to know someone better. I was running dry. Now answer."

"Easy, a harem of painting girls."

Jealousy flashed through her. He didn't need a harem when he had her. She gave herself a mental shake. He wanted to be just friends and she needed to accept that before her emotions ran away from her.

"That is such a guy's answer."

"Tell me you wouldn't want the girl equivalent of a harem."

"Hadn't thought about it. But I would hold parades in honor of my genius-ness and put my face on all the money." Sam dabbed ink on her mini.

"Way too obvious. I'd have my own personal amusement park and movie theater."

"And my own zoo, complete with tamed large cats so I can snuggle them."

"Now you're getting creative with it." He thought for a minute. "What are some small things that make your day better?"

"Ooh, the perfect cup of coffee with just enough sugar and cream in it to cut the bitterness. Comfortable pajamas. Freshly washed sheets." She smiled. "Texts from friends."

"Texts from new friends are some of the best things during the day." She peeked at him from the corner of her eye. What she wouldn't give to read his mind. "Finding the bottle of paint I'm looking for right away. Clean paint palettes. Paid invoices."

"So, for your business to run smoothly."

"If you want to generalize it, yes."

"What's your favorite alcoholic drink?"

"Long Island Iced Tea. I already know yours, Fuzzy Navel."

"You remember my drink order?" Her mouth dropped open.

Brad tapped under her chin with the handle of his paintbrush. "Don't look so surprised. You joked that my manly honor couldn't handle ordering one. What would be your spirit animal?"

"Too easy. Tiger." She tried to wrap her mind around how much he remembered about her. Maybe he didn't want to be just friends and she wouldn't ruin what they had by asking him out after the tournament. If she got the courage to say something.

"Wolf."

"Are you ready for Saturday?"

"Almost. I have one more mini that's half painted sitting on my desk. All of my orders are packed and waiting to go. You?"

She contemplated the mini before her. "I think I'm finally ready after I seal this one."

"Hot damn, I think it's your best one yet."

Her cheeks heated up under his praise. "Thank you. I have this amazing teacher." She glanced at the clock. "Who needs to rinse out his brushes so I can dump our water cups so we can get out of here on time."

Chapter Nine

"How are you doing?" Brad pulled up a chair to the corner table Sam had claimed for their group.

She looked up from her bag as she double-checked that her army hadn't suffered any damage during the tournament. "I'm in it to win it, you?"

"I'm out. Lost too many games."

"That sucks. It would've been fun to play you in the finals." She pouted.

"It gives me more time to offer up my painting services."

"Glass half full, I like it." Her name was called for the final game. "Guess it's time for the last round." She patted his arm for good luck and headed to the center table. The other tables had been cleared away for the main attraction. She swallowed back her nerves. She got this far on her skills, but bad dice luck could knock her out.

"Well, if it isn't the Whore of Babylon." An eerily familiar voice oozed across the table.

Her head snapped up and she took in her opponent. "Hello, Curtis. It's so wonderful to see you too." Sarcasm dripped from her voice. She forced herself to reach across the table so he could shake her hand.

"Can't wait to touch me again?" He held on to her hand and tugged a bit so she stumbled forward half a step.

She pulled her hand back and wiped it off on her jeans, not disguising her disgust with him. A few of the guys from the store gathered behind him and nodded at her. They had her back in case things went south. "Actually, I'd prefer to never see your face ever again, but tournament rules say I have to shake your hand."

Sam tried to ignore the rest of his comments during the game. He seemed to have a sixth sense for when the judges were nearby and toned down his commentary. The old fear rose up in the back of her throat and she concentrated twice as hard to not let him shake her. Brad stepped near her and touched her arm briefly to let her know he was there. She took a deep breath and calmed. None of the guys would let her get hurt today.

They neared the end of the game and were still fairly evenly matched in points. The other players crowded around the table to see how it played out. She was not about to let it go to a tie breaker and have Curtis win on any technicality. She narrowed her eyes at the table. She made a risky move, put her leader in the forefront of the group, and cast a spell. The crowd drew in a breath. She took her pot shots at his leader and ended her turn. He fell into the trap without realizing it.

"Before you take your shot, you have three coming your way." She pointed out the minis in range.

"How do you figure?" Curtis sneered.

"Overwatch. The two machines have it as an automatic trait when paired with Ashley. And, as you remember, she cast it on herself at the end of my last turn."

"You bitch!"

The room grew quiet at his unsportsmanlike conduct. She gave him a feral grin. "I'll be using one spell power for hit and one for damage on each machine. Ashley will be using her one remaining power on damage."

She picked up her dice and rolled. Each machine scored a solid hit and decent damage, not what she wanted, but she would take it. It made killing his leader on three dice quite a stretch, but it was the risk she took with this move. She caught Brad's eye and he winked at her. She could do this. She rolled Ashley's attack. Double sixes, an extra damage dice, just what she needed. She picked up her dice and threw again.

She didn't even get a chance to see what numbers came up before Brad had her swept into his arms. She wiggled out of his embrace and offered her hand to Curtis. "Good game."

"Go to hell." The douche bag packed his things and stomped off.

"Sammy-cat, you are amazing." Brad hugged her again and she relaxed against him.

Sam headed up to the judge to accept her prize for winning the tournament. She stood up there and grinned like an idiot when Brad's name was called for the best painted army. There were a couple of other consolation prizes split up in the group. They headed to the car and loaded their things into the trunk.

"We need to celebrate!" Steve picked her up. "Our Sammy's first big win."

"Put me down." She laughed.

"I second the motion." Brad put his arm around her for a side hug. She leaned into him and hoped it looked natural. "All in favor?" Everyone shot up a hand. "Done, let's get dinner and go to the bar."

BRAD CLAIMED THE SEAT next to Sam in the back of the car. He placed his arm across the back of the seat to allow her space if she needed it after her encounter with Curtis. She shifted closer to him to give Steve room in the backseat with them. Steve winked at him.

"Are you okay?" Brad whispered into her ear so the rest of the car wouldn't hear him. She nodded. "Are you lying?"

She twisted to face him, her blue eyes serious. "I'm fine. I had a moment or two during the game, but then I saw you and knew he couldn't hurt me. You wouldn't let him."

Her trust humbled him and made him feel ten feet tall. He let his hand slide until it rested on her shoulder. She made no move to dislodge it, so he left it where it was. She felt right in his arms.

Steve held a chair for her at dinner, but she scoffed and sat next to Brad instead. She snagged the last breadstick in the container before he could. When he made a disgruntled noise, she broke it in half and handed it to him. Steve gave him a significant look across the table. The conversation mostly involved reliving her winning moment and everyone's thoughts of the tournament. He loved how animated she got talking to the guys. He could watch her all night, especially when she smiled at him.

When they got to the bar, he offered to buy her a celebratory drink. He handed her a Fuzzy Navel and toasted to her win. He watched her sip her drink and decided to push his luck before they went back to the group.

"How is it?"

"Delicious."

"May I have a taste?" He was envious of the glass. She offered the drink to him. "Not like that."

He took the glass out of her hand and set it on the table next to them. He reached up slowly and touched her cheek. Her skin was warm and soft under his touch. He ran his thumb across her lips, causing her breath to catch. He inched nearer, giving her plenty of time to turn away if she didn't want this. He teased her mouth with little nips and licks, urging her to open to him. His tongue slipped into her mouth, exploring every inch. She tasted sweet and he wanted nothing more than to devour her. She melted against him.

"You were right." He whispered in her ear. "It does taste delicious."

Brad picked up their drinks and handed her the fruity one. Sam took a big swallow from the glass. He mirrored her movement and let the cold liquid cool him back down. He led her back to the group, but stayed by her side until they got back to the store.

"Are you sure you're good to drive?" He walked her back to her car.

"Totally fine. I didn't drink that much." She fiddled with her keys. "Thanks for the celebration."

He tipped her chin up and captured her lips in a quick kiss. "You earned it. Good-night, Sam."

He walked away from her by sheer force. That girl was intoxicating and if he stayed near her any longer, he wasn't sure she'd make it home tonight. He drove home on autopilot and dropped onto the couch next to Steve.

"Took you long enough to get home and you're grinning like an idiot. I'm guessing things went well with Sam tonight." Steve looked up from the video game he was playing. "What were you doing at the bar tonight that took so long?"

"Can't a guy buy a girl a drink to celebrate her winning a tournament?"

"They will still get questioned by their friends when they take forever getting the drink." Brad stayed quiet, only to get hit by the pillow Steve threw. "You horn dog, I hope like hell you didn't scare her away from the group."

"She seemed to like it." Brad's voice didn't come across as confident as his words. Damn Steve for putting doubt in his mind. "I'm going to bed."

He headed to his room and logged onto his computer. Steve's words echoed in his head. He stared at the screen, watching her icon turn to online. Did he screw up and scare her away? How the hell do you ask someone if they were okay with you kissing them? Giving up in frustration, he shut down his computer and flopped onto his bed.

BRAD HAD BEEN SILENT all week since the tournament. What if he regretted kissing her? Sam fretted the entire drive to the Game Hut. She replayed the kisses in her head a hundred times during the week. She didn't think there was anything wrong with it, but each time she logged on, he either wasn't on or logged off right away. Her heart lodged in her throat as she made her way into the basement.

She looked around the room. He wasn't at their usual table. He always beat her. *He's not coming tonight. He regrets kissing me and doesn't want to tell me.* She set her bag down and set up in her normal spot. She gave a half-hearted wave to everyone as they came in.

A bag thumped onto the table next to her, shaking her from her thoughts. "Shouldn't you be on top of the world after that epic win on Saturday?" Brad pulled out his painting supplies. "Why the long face?"

"I was debating on what to paint next." She tried to hide the grin that spread across her face.

He sat down and they fell into their regular pattern of painting and debating army composition. The tension slowly eased out of her. Even if he did regret the kiss, he wasn't treating her like he didn't want to be friends, although it felt like he wasn't saying something.

Intent on getting to the bottom of it, she waited for him to head to the bathroom and sat on the stairs to wait for him. She wasn't sure what she was going to say, but she had to know where things stood with him.

He walked up to her. "If I didn't know any better, I'd say you were following me."

"Maybe I was just waiting for my turn in the bathroom." She made a move to go around him, her courage failing her.

"Or maybe, you were hoping to catch me away from the crowd for some reason."

"Nope, I'm good."

"Are you? Then why are you staring at my lips?"

She dragged her eyes up to meet his warm stare. "I was just wondering... Never mind. It's not important."

He grabbed her arm as she made to escape. The second she stopped, he let go. "What were you wondering, Sammy-cat?"

"It doesn't matter."

He tugged her back against his chest. His warmth seeped into her skin. "Does it have to do with Saturday?" She nodded, leaning back against him. "With the kiss?"

She closed her eyes and nodded again. She could do this if she didn't have to meet his eyes. "How much of it had to do with the fact that we were celebrating?" She kicked herself for how small her voice sounded.

"The truth?"

"It would be nice."

Brad turned her around and cupped her face. "I've wanted to kiss you for weeks. I wasn't sure if you wanted me to."

"Really?" Sam could hardly believe her ears.

"Asking for a taste of your drink was just an excuse to see if you would let me kiss you." He chuckled.

She stared into his eyes, giddy with relief. "You could've asked."

"I didn't want it to be awkward if you didn't return my feelings. You were so adamant that we were just friends."

"I only said it to remind myself to keep my hands to myself. I didn't think you wanted anything more."

"I didn't at first, somehow you snuck through my barriers."

She thought her heart would burst out of her chest. "Wait, weeks? You mean we could've been dating before this?"

BRAD WATCHED THE EMOTIONS flit across Sam's face. "I'm guessing you've been thinking the same things I have, not wanting to ruin the friendship."

"Very much so." She nodded vigorously. "So instead of asking, you decided to ask for a taste of my drink. How was that not potentially friendship ruining?"

"It wasn't, but I couldn't take not knowing. And it was more fun my way."

She melted against him. Her hands ran up his chest and tugged his head down to hers. He expected her to devour him with that wicked look in her eyes. Instead, she placed soft kisses and licks on his mouth, taking her sweet time to explore. He shifted to take over the kiss, impatient to possess her.

"You're right." She murmured against his lips. "Your way is more fun."

"Are you going to actually kiss me at some point?" His breath came out in ragged bursts.

"I'm enjoying taking my time." She peppered his lips with another couple soft kisses.

He pushed her against the wall. "You are being an evil little kitten."

He cupped the nape of her neck and pinned her against the wall with his body. Every inch of her curves molded against him like she was made for him. He angled her head and returned her teasing kisses, loving the way she tried to pull him closer. She stood on her tiptoes and pushed herself against his lips. He chuckled and let her take over the kiss.

"I was wondering where you two went off to." Steve's voice shattered their moment.

Sam broke off the kiss and ducked her head against Brad's shoulder. He flipped Steve off. "Can't you see we're busy?"

Steve put his hands up and backed up into the game room. Brad lifted Sam's head so he could stare into those gorgeous blue eyes. Her cheeks were flushed and her lips swollen from his kisses. He liked that look on her. He brushed his lips against hers again, unable to resist another taste of her.

"Maybe we should go back in." Her voice was soft and breathless.

"Maybe Steve should mind his own business."

"I think he was just looking out for me." She snuggled against him.

"Doesn't make the interruption any less irritating. Maybe we could go somewhere else." He nibbled her ear and delighted in her shiver.

"Where?"

His heart soared that she was willing to take off with him. He could get lost in the soft feel of her pressed against him, the way she surrendered herself to him. He tugged the elastic out of her hair and buried his fingers in the satiny strands. He nibbled his way along her jaw and back to her lips.

"Someplace quiet, with no interruptions." He peered down at her. Her eyes were half closed and she looked like she was struggling to make a coherent thought. "Or we could go back in and paint before I take advantage of you."

She nodded and allowed him to lead her back to their chairs. Steve gave him a hard look. Brad pulled Sam's chair closer to his. She gave him one of her shy smiles and hooked her foot around his. She fiddled with her paintbrush.

"Someplace quiet with no interruptions? What were you planning on doing with me tonight?" She whispered.

He handed her back the tie for her hair. "Whatever you'd let me do."

"I'm not that easy." She shot him an offended look.

"I wasn't implying anything, kitten. I wouldn't have gone any further than you'd let me." He winked. "But once I got you back to my place, I'd lock you up as the beginning of my painting harem."

"Keep kissing me like that and you probably wouldn't even have to lock me up."

He used every excuse he could to touch her or whisper in her ear. Once she warmed up to the idea that the other guys weren't judging them, she stole little kisses. He walked her to her car at the end of the night even though everything screamed in him to take her home. She fitted her hand inside his and leaned against his shoulder. She stood next to her car and pulled his lips against hers. He had to put his hands on her car to keep his knees from giving way under her assault.

SAM GLANCED AT HER phone and smiled. She typed a response to Brad. A pillow sailed out of nowhere and hit her in the head.

"I swear you are just as bad as Olivia. It's girls' night and you have your nose buried in your phone." Julie groused.

"Olivia's worse. She lives with her boyfriend and still sends sappy texts while we're here."

"It keeps the romance alive." Olivia looked up from the box of polish bottles. "Remember, no girls' night next week. I want you both rested and fresh for the boyfriend shoot on Sunday. Do you both have your lingerie picked out?"

"I've got some, but not much of what I own is sexy."

"I've got your hook up. We're about to mark down a whole crap ton of stuff at work to make way for the new line of fall and Christmas lingerie. Stop by my work early Saturday morning and it should be priced. You'll get first pick after all of the clerks. I have a stash waiting for me."

"Good, I've picked up and laundered the stuff we are borrowing from the boys and theater department, but if there is an outfit you specifically want to wear, let me know so I can rearrange the group shots. I'm asking everyone to send me pictures of their lingerie no later than Saturday evening. Sam, you can just bring your stuff upstairs."

Julie stole her and Olivia's phones before they could touch them again. "You will get these back at the end of the night. Now, it's time to pick out the movie of the evening and for Olivia to paint our nails."

"Toenails too because we're going to be showing them off next Sunday." Sam grabbed the remover and started cleaning off her nails.

They ribbed her for her new love interest. She didn't mind until Hannah came back into the room. She tried to shush her friends, but they were in too good of a mood to recognize the danger they put her in. The other brunette ignored them except to complain about the smell of nail polish. Olivia offered to do her nails too which seemed to placate her.

On the walk back to the house, Sam brought up the subject of Hannah. "I wish you two wouldn't talk about me and Brad around her."

"Honestly, I think you need to give her another chance."

"I've given her two, and both times she's taken my boyfriend. I'm not letting that happen a third time."

"People change."

Sam loved Olivia's optimism, but didn't share it. "Some people don't. I don't know what her problem is with me, but I swear she starts scheming whenever she sees I'm happy."

Chapter Ten

"Excuse me, miss. I was hoping you could help me."

Sam straightened and pasted on a customer service smile. Just a few more minutes and she could clock out. She turned to come face-to-face with Brad. "What are you doing here?"

"Obviously, I'm shopping. Steve wanted me to pick up garbage bags." He mirrored her grin. "And I knew you'd be working."

"So you drove two cities away to shop here to see me at my job?" She pegged him with a questioning look.

"I need to drop off the fig Luke had me paint."

"My shift is almost over. If you want, I can help you get your shopping done." She glanced back at the fitting room, remembering her purchases. "I need to grab a few things on my way out."

"I'll start my shopping and wait for you here so you can grab your things."

"How about I meet you at the entrance?" She ducked her head to hide the blush racing up her cheeks. "You don't need to watch me shop."

"I'm curious to know what you're buying if it turns you so red."

"Please don't be."

He tipped up her chin. "I'll meet you by the doors if it makes you that uncomfortable."

She straightened the last couple of tables in her section and clocked out. She glanced around to make sure Brad wasn't around before grabbing the clothes she picked out earlier. She hustled through checking out and met him at the doors, bags in hand.

"Am I following you home?" He transferred his bags to one hand so he could wrap the other around her.

"Actually, if you don't mind giving me a ride, Eric needed to borrow my car. His truck is in the shop getting the heater fixed." She followed him to a beat-up old car. "Your car is kind of a pig sty." She shifted the trash on the floor so there was room for her feet.

He glanced back at the stuff covering the back seat. "'Kind of' doesn't even begin to cover it. I've been meaning to clean it out before letting you see the interior of my car."

She gave him directions to the house, belatedly remembering he had been there before. She clenched her hands in her lap, consciously resisting the urge to touch him while he was shifting gears. He parked in front of the house.

"Welcome once again to the House that Gaming Built."

"I like the reasons for being here this time."

"Come on, I'll give you a proper tour." She tossed her bags in her room and gave him a quick tour. Eric pulled him away to talk about painting a few minis for his role playing game and Olivia came into Sam's room to check out her purchases.

"Oh, these would be perfect for tomorrow." Olivia held up a dark pink lacy bra and matching panties. "I'm thinking this under just a button-up shirt or suit jacket." The oven timer went off. She ran out the door. "That's the bread!"

"That's what you didn't want me seeing you buy?" Brad lounged against the wall just inside Sam's room.

Sam jumped and stuffed the lingerie back into bags. "Yeah."

He came up behind her and covered her hands. "Are you embarrassed that I saw?"

"A bit." She chewed her lip.

"Why? My mind is whirling with images of you in all this."

"Not helping my embarrassment." She leaned back into the warm cocoon of his arms. "I didn't want you to see me buy it because I didn't want you thinking I was buying it for you. And it feels like getting caught with my hand in the cookie jar."

"You bought slinky lingerie for yourself?" He turned her in his arms.

She curled her fingers against his chest, nuzzling her cheek against his shoulder. "I like knowing I have pretty things on, even if I'm the only one who sees them."

"Well, I hope we can get to the point where you're not embarrassed to show me."

"At some point." She pulled him down for a kiss. She couldn't get enough of his lips on hers.

He peppered her neck with kisses, raising chill bumps on her skin. His breath huffed hot in her ear. "Are you really going to be at the photo shoot all day tomorrow?"

"Sounds like it. This is Olivia's big push to prep her professional portfolio." She untangled herself from his arms to shove the lingerie in her closet. "She wants to be a boudoir photographer after she graduates."

BRAD COULDN'T HAVE heard Sam right. There was no way she would be posing like that, not when she was embarrassed by him seeing her lingerie. His heart skipped several beats at the thought of her posing.

"You're posing for boudoir photos tomorrow?" He swallowed hard.

She nodded, eyes averted. "Yeah, we're doing one of those wearing the boyfriend's clothes shoots apparently."

"But you didn't ask your boyfriend for anything to wear." He tried to keep his tone light, but it hurt that she never asked him for anything.

"Are you my boyfriend?" She puttered around her room, cleaning up nonexistent clutter.

Her question stung. He wandered through her room and studied the constellations painted on her walls and ceiling to appear nonchalant. He couldn't keep the hurt out of his voice. "Well, I hope you don't go around kissing just any old guy."

"You're not 'just any old guy.'" She touched his back. "Are we dating?"

"You needing to ask means we're doing something wrong." He stared down at her, losing himself in the depths of her blue eyes.

"I don't think so. I just want to know if I can go around saying you're my boyfriend or if we're still so new in this relationship that it's weird if I called you that."

He adored how her eyes softened when she said boyfriend. "I like you calling me yours, so long as I get to do the same." He kissed her forehead. "Do I get to see any of the pictures you take?"

"Maybe. We'll see how they turn out."

"Do you pose for her often?"

"Yeah, it's not always sexy shoots. I have copies of all the pictures Olivia's taken of me over the years." She gestured at her computer.

"Can I see some?"

"Sure." She pulled in a second chair. He shut the door and sat down next to her. She chewed on her lip while she took her time selecting a folder. "This was a 1920's shoot."

He stared at his cute girl in a black beaded dress. "You make a sweet flapper." He kissed her hair, unable to stop touching her. "What were the other folders you skipped?"

"Production shots from a student zombie film, class projects for other friends, or technique practice for the make-up students."

"Why would you let people practice make-up on you?"

"Participation hours for my theater classes." She shrugged.

"Will you let me see one of the less tame shoots?" He was intrigued as hell by the idea even though he'd rather have her naked in front of him.

"Why would you want to?"

"Why wouldn't I? Pretty girl, risque art photos." He sank a hand into her silky hair and rubbed the base of her scalp. "Plus, your eyes lit up when you were talking to Olivia earlier."

"You're cheating." Her head lulled under his ministrations. "One folder of pics. I can veto it."

"Liquid latex?" The title intrigued him.

"Don't bother. One of the dance kids thought it would make a good costume choice, but it rips when you move and doesn't breathe. It was uncomfortable and took forever to scrub off."

"Jewels?"

"You'd have to pick the most risque shoot." She whimpered.

He studied her for a moment. Was it fear in her eyes? "You still have veto power."

"Go for it. Most of the shoots get pretty indecent at some point, so I'd find reasons to veto." She got up, curled on her bed, and covered her face. "Might as well rip the band-aid off."

Part of him needed to comfort her, but his curiosity was piqued. He clicked through pictures of girls in catsuits, playing with piles of jewels. The sight of her in skin-tight leather stole his breath. He had no idea she could be so overtly sexy.

"Wow, Sammy-cat, you look good in pearls." He couldn't tear his eyes away from her costume unzipped to her navel and necklaces draped around her upper body.

"We were having fun with the idea of being cat burglars after a major score. The one with the gemstones a couple of pictures later is one of my favorites."

He clicked through a few more pictures and stopped breathing. Sam stared at him from the screen without her catsuit, lounging on a pile of strategically placed jewels. He couldn't think of anything sexier, except maybe her naked in his arms quenching the need that barreled through him.

"I..." He cleared his throat. "I'm going to agree it's my favorite as well."

"Thanks." Her voice was muffled by her arms. "If you want to look at more, feel free."

THE BED DIPPED UNDER Brad's weight. He gently pulled Sam's hands off her face. "How is it that you can be so bold and take pictures like that, but be this embarrassed to show them to me?"

"Olivia has a way of making everything easy and comfortable." She looked up at him, scared of what she'd see on his face. His expression was unreadable. "I've never shown them to anyone."

"How can I make you more comfortable?"

"I don't know."

"I'll be right back." He climbed off her bed and went outside.

She slumped against her headboard and listened to the sounds of car doors opening and closing. Her stomach dropped to her knees. Was he leaving? Did the idea of her posing disgust him?

His steps sounded on the porch. Relief flooded through her veins. She straightened up as he walked back into her room with a crumpled shirt in his hand. He closed the door and sat back on the bed with her.

"I want to loan you my shirt to wear tomorrow, but I have two conditions."

She cocked her head to the side. "I'm listening."

"One, I get a kiss from you. Two, I get a picture of you in my shirt because, damn, there's something sexy about your girlfriend wearing your clothes." His eyes burned through her.

She swallowed hard. Had she known he'd like the idea of her wearing his shirt, she would've asked him a week ago. She frowned at the shirt in question. "Those are some steep conditions for a shirt that's been moldering in your car for god knows how long."

"That one's for me to drive home in." He leaned over her. "I'm planning on giving you the shirt off my back."

"That's a different matter entirely." Her heart sped up.

"Does that mean you agree to the terms?"

She nodded eagerly. She should play it cool, but wanted to see him shirtless. He made a show out of pulling off his shirt, muscles rippling. She knew he could easily pick her up, but she hadn't realized how cut he was. Well defined pecs led to abs she wanted to lick, especially when she followed the trail of hair that disappeared into the waistband of his jeans. His skin begged for her to run her hands over it.

He handed her the shirt and leaned in. His scent enveloped her, all male with a hint of spice. "I'm ready for my kiss."

She drank in the sight of his chest and arms bared to her. "You never specified when the kiss was to be given." She teased him to regain her equilibrium. "I'm thinking I'll do it next week or the week after that."

"That would be cruel." He hovered over her. "You wouldn't withhold kisses from me, would you?"

"Never." She leaned up and brushed her lips against his. "Besides, I wouldn't want you thinking I don't keep up my end of bargains." She wrapped her arms around his neck and kissed him again.

He leaned back and pulled her onto his lap. She let him take over the kiss so she could run her hands over the muscles on his back and shoulders. Her fingers tingled as she lightly skimmed his contours, taking her time to commit them to her memory.

His fingers tangled in her hair, holding her against him as he plundered her mouth. His other hand ran down her back and up her side. She surrendered herself to the delicious sensations running through her. His thumb brushed the underside of her breast and she moaned into his mouth.

"I think it's only fair that you take off your shirt too." He nibbled on her ear, sending chills racing through her.

"Now you're just being greedy."

"Can you blame me?" He ran his hands under the edge of her shirt and slowly worked it off of her. "I see you wore a sexy bra today."

She glanced down at the blue lace. "Guess it's a good thing I wore it."

She pressed her skin against his, reveling in the hot press of his body. Trailing her tongue down the column of his throat, she tasted his spicy flesh. She could spend the rest of the night learning every inch of him.

"Does everything match?" His voice rumbled in her ear as his hands glided down to her hips.

Before she could answer, a knock sounded on her door. Luke yelled, "Sammy, did Brad leave?"

She cursed under her breath. "No, he's in here with me."

"Good." The doorknob twisted.

"Open that door and I'll geld you." She scrambled for her shirt and opened the door a crack. "What do you want?"

"Andrew and I want to pick his brain about paint schemes."

"I'll be up in a minute." Brad lounged on her bed.

She closed the door in Luke's face. Brad opened his arms and gestured to her. She slid back onto his lap with a contented sigh. His warmth sank into her skin as she cuddled against him.

"You put your shirt back on." He grumbled.

"You didn't expect me to answer my door topless, did you?"

"Only if I'm on the other side of the door."

"I'll keep that in mind." She helped him make quick work of her shirt.

"Where were we?"

"You were asking if my panties matched my bra."

He kissed the soft spot on her neck and all of her thoughts scattered. "Are you going to tell me or do I have to discover it for myself?"

Olivia's panicked voice interrupted them. "Sam, I need your help. No one has anything that matches and everything looks like crap together. Tomorrow's going to be a disaster."

"I'll be up in a minute to help." She yelled through the door. She gave Brad an apologetic look. "If I didn't know any better, I'd say it's a conspiracy to keep you from getting any answers." She left his lap with a sigh.

He pulled her back against his chest. "Before we go upstairs, I have to know."

"Of course it all matches." She guided his hands to her hips.

"Can I see? I promise I won't do anything but look."

Had he asked before the interruptions, they'd both be way more undressed. She licked her lips at the thought of him naked in her bed. She swallowed hard at being the only one to strip. Taking a deep breath, she stepped out of the comfort of his arms.

SAM SHIMMIED OUT OF her jeans and turned to face him. Brad sucked in his breath. Blue lace cupped her breasts, lifting them high as though they were being offered to him. Her waist dipped in and he bet her hips would fit perfectly in his hands. Her matching panties barely hid her core from him.

He itched to trace every curve of her sweet body and find out if every part of her was soft and sweet. He opened and closed his fists to keep from breaking his promise. His body reacted and begged to toss her on the bed.

"You should get dressed or I'm going to break my promise. We won't make it upstairs if that happens." His voice came out rough. He raked a hungry gaze over her again. "You look way too sexy for your own good."

He waited until they were both redressed, took her hand, and joined her friends upstairs. Andrew and Luke pulled him into the tiny kitchen to discuss their minis, painting, and pricing. He kept his eye on Sam as she darted in and out of the apartment with different clothes, most of it lacy and sexy. Olivia debated combinations with her as they figured out details.

Sam's gestures drew his eyes over her curves. He wanted nothing more than to carry her back into her bedroom and taste every inch of her skin. He cursed the interruptions.

He turned his attention back to the guys at the table with him. The extra work was needed to grow his business. He took notes of what each of the guys wanted for their armies. Time flew by as he grew absorbed in the minutia of his business. He raised his head and looked around for his girl.

Andrew followed his look. "She went to bed hours ago. Olivia brow-beat her into getting some sleep."

"I should head out." Brad gathered up his things and waved good-bye.

He paused in front of her door. He should let her sleep, she had a photoshoot in the morning. He couldn't bring himself to leave without saying good-night and giving her a kiss or twelve. He tapped on her door and slipped in. She blinked up at him in the dim light.

"I was fairly certain you'd be asleep, but I figured I'd let you know I'm leaving."

"What time is it?" She rubbed her eyes and sat up.

He winced at the exhaustion in her voice. "Three in the morning."

"Are you sure you're okay to drive?"

"Probably." A yawn caught him out of nowhere.

"You don't sound like you're all that awake. Are you sure you don't want to crash here?"

He wanted to crawl under the covers with her and finish what they started earlier, but he didn't want to keep her up. The thought of sleeping on the couch while she was so close didn't appeal to him either. "I'm not a fan of sleeping on couches."

"I didn't say anything about the couch." She patted the bed next to her. "You look like you're about to pass out, it's snowing, and I don't want you driving."

He couldn't fault her logic. He crawled on top of her blankets. "Alright, you win."

"Are you seriously going to sleep in your jeans on top of the blankets?"

"Figured you'd be more comfortable that way." He'd be uncomfortable as hell, but it would be a small price to pay to spend the night with her.

"Not at the expense of your comfort. We're both grown-ups."

He stripped out of his jeans and joined her in the warm cocoon of blankets. He pulled her against him, her scent enveloping him. He traced her bare arm and down her side. It would be so easy to strip her out of the little tank top. He tamped down on his thoughts as his groin grew heavy.

"I can't promise to be a gentleman with you in my arms." He kissed her temple.

She snuggled against him and toyed with the edge of his sleeve. "I never asked you to be a gentleman."

"Now you're tempting me to keep you awake for the rest of the night."

She threw a mostly bare leg over his so she was half-draped over him. He couldn't help running a hand over her pert butt and down to the edge of her shorts. Her breath caught in her throat. He yawned again, exhaustion warring with needing her.

"Maybe temptation should wait until you've had some sleep." She let out a small laugh before kissing his cheek. "Good-night, Brad."

"Good-night, kitten." He settled in for a night of the sweetest torture because he was certain sleep wasn't going to come easy with her in his arms.

Chapter Eleven

Sam woke up oddly warm considering it was a cold winter day. She stretched slightly before remembering the man in her bed. She snuggled back in Brad's arms, warm and safe. She could get used to waking up like this, maybe with fewer clothes.

Olivia knocked on the door to remind her it was just about time to leave. Sam slipped out of the blankets with a groan and placed a kiss on Brad's forehead. He stirred a little with a grumbly noise before pulling her back onto the bed. She found herself pinned under his hard body.

She took a moment to savor the feeling of his weight pressing her into the mattress. The blanket tangled between them, hindering any real play time. They spent a few minutes kissing before he cursed at the blanket.

"I didn't think this through." He kicked at the blanket. "Not my finest moment."

"I'll blame it on the fact that you weren't awake yet." She extracted herself from the bed with a sigh. "I can't stay in bed anyway. Olivia will be back any minute to collect me."

"I should get going then." He untangled himself from the blanket. She filed away the image of him in her bed for later. It had been too dark last night to see him in his boxers properly, but now she could appreciate his muscular thighs and the V right above his hips. Not to mention the impressive erection tenting his boxers. "No point in staying in bed if you aren't with me."

She cursed at her need to leave. She really wanted to unwrap him like a present and explore his muscles instead of letting him slide his jeans back on. She tossed sweats over her pajamas and threw on shoes. She brushed a kiss on his cheek.

"I'll talk to you later."

He wrapped a warm arm around her waist. His breath huffed hot on her ear. "Just remember your promise. I get to see a picture of you in my shirt."

She nodded and swallowed hard. Her heart beat in her throat as she slid into Olivia's car. The cold wind chased away the last of his warmth. She huddled in her coat and hustled into the building.

Sam came to a halt when she saw the set. It never failed to impress her what her friend could do with the studio space. A large bed dominated the center of the room, heaped with white pillows and blankets. Other areas were set up to simulate windows and vanities. She looked over her wardrobe rack at Brad's shirt before sitting for hair and make-up.

Julie flopped into the chair next to her. "How'd you get roped into this?"

"You know Olivia, never ask for a favor if you don't want to pose for her in return." Sam squinted her eyes against the onslaught of hair spray.

"I think she owes us by now. Speak of the devil."

Olivia grouped them in pairs and bigger groups after doing a few test shots. She ran everything with ruthless efficiency. Once she had what she wanted, the girls hustled to change into the next outfit. Everyone else was cut when their racks were empty. Sam looked at her rack and realized there was only one outfit left.

Olivia pointed to the make-up chair. "Sit. I figured we could do this part in private."

"Why?" Sam frowned as she took her seat.

"You're the only one that had clothes from your actual boyfriend. I want to do a real boudoir shoot with you."

She groaned as the pins were pulled from her hair, the curls falling around her shoulders. After she wiped off the heavy make-up, she leaned back for her friend to apply a light amount of eye shadow and lip gloss.

"You, but a bit dolled up. I paired the shirt with your purple lingerie. Come onto set when you're dressed."

She took a deep breath before changing. Brad's scent wafted off the shirt, reminding her of their interrupted play. She turned around in the mirror to admire how it barely covered her butt.

She padded barefoot back to the set and earned a wolf-whistle from Olivia. She took her place at each station to pose. Her mind kept looping over the fact that Brad would see one of the shots. They tried a dozen or so poses before looking over them.

She wrinkled her nose. "Those look like crap."

"They're forced." Olivia pegged her with a look. "Stop thinking so hard about looking sexy and let it happen."

Sam climbed back onto the bed and knelt in the pillows. She held the shirt up to inhale his scent. She could almost feel his hands skimming her skin. Distantly, she heard Olivia clicking away.

"I think I got it." Her friend sounded triumphant.

Sam blinked a couple of times and laid back on the pillows. "One more."

BRAD'S COMPUTER DINGED. About time Sam logged on. He was almost out of minis to prime and base coat. He didn't trust himself to be able to focus on details while he waited for pictures of her. It was well into the evening and he was antsy.

Sam-Cat: Shoot's done.

Ubel: How'd it go?

S: Olivia seems happy. I'm dead tired.

U: I figured you'd be done earlier.

S: Hair, make-up, and costume changes for nine girls take a long time.

U: How'd the pictures turn out?

S: I'm copying them to my computer now. Check your email.

He scrambled to open the file. He stared at the button up shirt barely hiding her from his eyes, dumbstruck. She was all dolled up with her hair piled on top of her head. He drank in the sight like a man starving before remembering she was waiting for a reply.

U: You could've warned me they were super hot.

S: That one's tame considering some of the shots we tried out today.

U: You still owe me a picture in my shirt.

S: As promised.

The file loaded and his jaw dropped. Sam stared out of his computer, in his shirt with her hair fanned out around her. It looked like she had been writhing around on the bed, shirt rumpled around her waist to show off her purple panties. He pressed the heel of his hand to his aching erection, sure he would have an imprint of his zipper.

U: I think my heart stopped.

S: Does that mean you like it?

U: Hell yes. That one's my new favorite. I can't stop looking at it.

S: I'll see if Olivia will print a copy for you when she prints the stuff for her portfolio.

U: Are there more?

S: We took tons of pictures in a bunch of different outfits and groupings.

U: Show them to me.

S: Why?

U: I like looking at you. You're bold and pretty. Feminine.

Mine, his brain finished. He had never understood the lure of claiming a woman like Steve did until now. Did she feel the same way towards him?

S: It'll have to wait until later. I want to weed out the bad ones and anything without me. I desperately need a shower to get all the hair spray and make-up off.

U: I could come over and help you get clean.

S: I'd be asleep by the time you'd get here, but you're welcome to snuggle next to me. I have a morning shift tomorrow.

U: I'll let you get clean and sleep, as tempting as sleeping with you is.

S: Good-night.

U: Night.

He sat there long after she logged off, fighting the urge to see her anyway. The memory of her soft curves pressed against him that morning taunted him. He went back and studied the pictures she sent him. Need ripped through him, hot and wild.

He forced himself to close his email. Checking over his production schedule, he picked up one of Andrew's minis to finish. The sooner he got this unit finished, the sooner he'd have an excuse to see his girl.

"WAKEY WAKEY, SLEEPING beauty."

Sam groaned at Olivia's interruption. She was in the middle of an amazing dream where Brad followed up the scorching kiss from Thursday. She spent the week randomly sending him pictures from the shoot. He reciprocated by sneaking off with her at the store to kiss her senseless.

"It's too damned early on my day off." She had thought about inviting Brad over last night, but didn't want him to think he was just a booty call. "What do you want?"

"It's cookie making day. Time to get out of bed and help me bake all the cookies for Christmas." Olivia threw a peppermint striped apron on the bed.

Sam stretched as her friend bounced off. This was one of the few traditions they had started in college and she was determined to enjoy it while it lasted. Olivia whipped up the first of many batches of chocolate chips, knowing there would be cookie thieves. The boys took turns sneaking into the kitchen to distract and swipe cookies, but agreed to buy pizza in exchange.

A knock sounded at the door and Andrew greeted whomever it was. "Will you tell your girl to stop licking the knives?"

"What am I missing?" Brad leaned against the counter.

A wide smile broke over Sam's face at the unexpected boyfriend in her house. She skipped over to him and dropped a kiss on his lips. "We're making cookies."

"I can see that." He pulled her in for another kiss. "Nice apron." He gave her a heated look that said he wanted to strip it off of her and devour her. A shiver ran through her.

"They're licking the knives they're frosting the cookies with." Luke glared at her from his chair.

"What's a little spit among friends?" She winked at Brad.

Luke grabbed another cookie. "Your spit is disgusting."

"You know what's more disgusting than my spit?" She leaned down and licked Luke's cheek before blowing on it. "My cold spit."

Luke roared and leapt out of his chair. "Grab her!"

She put the table between them and darted back and forth out of his reach. Brad's warm arm snaked around her waist, holding her immobile. She squeaked in protest, unable to believe her boyfriend took Luke's side.

"Stop squirming and take your medicine." Brad pulled her more firmly against his chest, his breath hot on her neck. "I'll make it worth your while."

She stilled, glaring at Luke. This was not what she planned. He sauntered over, worked up a bunch of spit, and deposited it on her face. She tore out of Brad's hold, repulsed by the slime sliding down her cheek, and ran for the bathroom.

"That was super vile and way worse than what I did to you."

Brad followed her into the room and shut the door to block out the laughter. He took the washcloth from her and gently washed her face. "See? That wasn't so bad."

He invaded her space in the small room. His scent filled her head and her mouth watered. She couldn't stop herself from needling him.

"I hope you don't think washing my face gets you out of trouble for holding me while—"

His mouth covered hers, stealing her breath and words. He backed her up until she was pressed between the wall and his body. His tongue darted and thrust into her mouth, causing heat to surge through her body. Needing to get closer, she pulled herself up his broad shoulders.

He pulled back and grinned down at her. "I take it that I'm forgiven."

"I was never mad at you."

"Evil little—"

She stopped his words with a kiss. Looping her arms around his neck, she stared up into his deep brown eyes. "What are you doing here? Not that I mind seeing you, but you didn't say you were coming over."

"I finished a unit of Andrew's minis and came to collect my pay." He ran his hand down her cheek and neck, leaving a trail of warmth. "Added bonus is seeing you covered in frosting and wearing an apron."

"I'm not covered in frosting." Surely she would've seen if she was when she got into the bathroom.

"We could fix that." His eyes sparkled with promise. "Although, you're sweet enough without it." He nipped at her lips. "I could devour you whole."

"Devour?"

"I couldn't stop thinking about you this week."

"I'm guessing you liked the pictures I sent you."

"Liked is too tame of a word. You made it hard to get any work done." He ground against her so she could feel how aroused he was. "All I wanted to do was see you so I could peel the clothes from your body."

She arched against him. "I still have some of what I wore. What do you want to see?"

"You." He growled and nipped at her lips. She could get used to this possessive side of him. "But I've been dreaming of you in my shirt."

"I might have to switch it out for the one you're wearing before you leave." She ran her hands down his chest and under the edge of his shirt. "The one I have is losing the scent of you."

"Why's that?"

"I wear it to bed. It's almost like having you with me."

"Then I will make sure you get this one tonight." He kissed her nose before stepping back.

"Give me a few minutes to get changed." She kissed him one last time and rushed to her room. The cool air cleared her head a bit. Her hands shook with excitement as she pulled on the purple lingerie and Brad's shirt. She took a few deep breaths and arranged herself on her bed.

BRAD ADJUSTED HIMSELF after Sam left the bathroom. He wanted nothing more than to immediately follow her but hung around the kitchen for a couple of minutes to cool down. Olivia gave him a knowing look. He tried to ignore it and ate one of the frosted sugar cookies to cover his eagerness.

He let himself into Sam's room. She lay against the pillows, a vision in his shirt. He grew hard again at the sight of her lounging there, waiting for him with her toned legs peeking out from under his shirt. He ran one hand up the soft skin of her leg wanting to draw out the moment before climbing on the bed.

"I was right, you look absolutely sexy as hell in my shirt." He leaned over and placed a soft kiss on her lips.

She tugged at his clothes. "You know what would be even sexier? You, without a shirt."

"Your wish is my command." He helped her divest him of his shirt, smirking as she shoved it under her pillow. She hadn't been kidding about swapping shirts. The caveman part of his brain loved that she marked herself with his scent.

He leaned down, intent on taking his time kissing her. Her hands roamed over his shoulders and chest as though she couldn't get enough of the feel of him and he had to agree. She squirmed under him and pulled at him until he was flush against her. The heat of her arousal scorched him through his jeans.

He struggled not to rip their clothes off and bury himself in her slick heat, no matter how hot and wild she grew under him. His hands wandered a slow path up her silky legs starting at her calves and working his way up the outsides of her thighs. She wrapped her legs around his back and arched against him. His self-control unraveled even more.

He worked the shirt up her body, dipping his head down to lick and nip her skin as it was bared to his hungry gaze. She tasted like sugar and sweetness and all he wanted was to spend the day learning every inch of her. She squirmed in his arms and let out a little giggle. He grinned against her skin.

"Is my kitten ticklish?"

"Just a little bit." She wiggled away from his mouth.

"I think it's more than a little." He nuzzled her ribs and she gifted him with another giggle. He used the distraction to finish peeling the shirt off of her. Dark purple lace cupped her breasts, offsetting her pale skin.

She shifted under him and her hands went to the waistband of his jeans. He leaned back to give her room to work, grateful to no longer have the zipper grinding against his erection. She pushed his pants down as far as she could reach and made an adorable disgruntled noise when they stopped. He sat up so he could kick them off.

Missing her warmth, Brad pulled her up to straddle his lap. It took very little urging to get her to grind against him. Her soft moans were pure music to his ears, her slim hips fitting into his hands like they were made for him.

Heaven would be spending the whole day with her like this. Her nipples stood up through the lace of her bra, driving him to distraction with every brush of her body. He dipped his head to suckle one through the fabric. Sam sucked in a sharp breath and he snaked a hand behind her to undo the clasp. As soon as her bra was loose, she pressed her body against him and buried her head in his neck.

"Shy little kitten, do you want to stop?" He held her to him, savoring the skin-to-skin contact. He stroked a soothing hand up and down her back and struggled to rein himself in.

"Never." She caught him off-guard by pushing him onto his back. She pointed at the pillows, a clear demand for him to lay further up the bed.

His chuckle at her fierceness turned into a low moan as she trailed kisses and licks down his chest. Her nipples skimmed his skin, making him ache to taste them. He gripped the bed under him to steady himself against the onslaught. She slowly peeled his boxers off and took her time nibbling his hip bones. Her lips tortured him by being everywhere but his erection.

"Sam, you're killing me." His breath came out in short bursts.

"I doubt that."

Her mischievous grin was going to be his undoing. She kept her eyes on him as she finally put him out of his misery and took him into her warm mouth. He lost himself in the sensation of her around him. His hips bucked involuntarily and Sam choked.

Before he could utter an apology, she redoubled her efforts. His head spun and release coiled tight in his body. He tangled one hand in her hair and the other in the blankets to keep from thrusting and hurting her. He barely had a chance to warn her before he came with a hoarse shout. He struggled to catch his breath.

She crawled back up his body with a self-satisfied smirk. "That'll teach you to call me a shy kitten."

"If that's my punishment, I'll call you a shy little kitten whenever the mood strikes me." Brad flipped her over onto her back and she squeaked in surprise.

He urged her mouth open under his, needing to claim every inch of her. He trailed kisses to her neck laving the tender area behind her ear. She sighed and tilted her head to give him better access. His hands explored restlessly over her soft skin learning every curve.

His burning need momentarily sated, he could take his time tasting her skin. He sucked one of her rosy nipples deep into his mouth, her back arching off the bed. Her hands fluttered until they settled on his shoulders, cradling him to her. His urge to claim and protect her overwhelmed him.

SAM COULDN'T KEEP UP with the sensations running through her body. Brad's hands were everywhere as if he were memorizing her by touch. Every pull of his mouth on her breasts made her more needy. She followed his path of destruction through hooded eyes. He outlined her panties with his tongue making her bite back a plea to take her.

She swore if he didn't do something about her aching core soon, she was going to flip him back over and ride him. Mercifully, he raised her hips off the bed to strip her. He teased her bare slit with the tip of his finger, giving her the same evil grin she had given him earlier. She ground against him desperate for more stimulation.

Brad took his time kissing her hips and working his way down to her sex. His tongue flicked out and he growled before sucking her clit in his mouth. Her breath hitched as he slid a finger in her. She rode his hand, unable to stop herself.

He slid a second finger in her, ratcheting her higher. She just needed a little push to topple over the edge. She plucked at her nipples in time with his licks and thrusts. Her world splintered into a thousand pieces. He kept licking until she tugged him up for a long kiss.

His erection poked her hip and she bit back a grin. Long and thick, with veins running through it. She barely got her hand around it and she knew she'd be sore the next day.

She brought her leg around him and pressed her body against his erection. "Did you need something?"

"Just you." He ground against her. "I want to be inside you." A thrill ran through her at his desire roughened voice. She reached over and batted open the drawer to her nightstand for him to dig through. "There's nothing in here, sweetie."

"What?" She sat straight up and looked in the drawer. "I always keep condoms in there." She flopped back onto the bed in disappointment. "I must have given the last couple to Olivia. I don't suppose you have any on you."

"I wasn't planning on anything happening tonight." He laid down next to her, looking as dejected as she was.

"I could go upstairs and swipe some."

He pulled her against him. "I don't want to let you out of this bed, even if it means I don't get to be inside you."

She didn't know if she could stay in bed with him without begging him to be inside her. Her skin felt like an electric current ran through her. They couldn't stop touching and kissing each other. He pinned her under his hard body, her curves molding against him as though they were made for each other.

Brad slid a muscular thigh between hers and urged her to grind against him. She ached with him so close but so far away. Her hand stole between their bodies and grasped his erection. Her name fell from his lips as an agonized prayer. He slid in her hand, satin over steel.

She needed to feel him even if he couldn't possess her. She guided his shaft until he was pressed against her clit. She let out a cry as he thrust against her. So close, she was so close.

His hips jerked forward, faster and faster. Every move rubbed the veins of his cock against her sensitive flesh. His hand slid down her back to hold her against him. The slight shift in position was all it took to send her hurtling over the edge. A few thrusts later, he came in hot bursts over her stomach and chest.

"That was risky." She panted and stared up at him.

He swung a shaky leg off the bed and caressed her cheek. "I think it was worth the risk, don't you?"

He padded across her room to grab a towel, giving her an amazing view of his tight ass. There was not an inch of him that didn't call to her. She could take little bites out of him. He returned to her side and gently cleaned all of his seed from her skin.

She loved how his eyes softened when he looked at her. She curled against him after he rejoined her in bed, lazy and content. He trailed his hand along her back.

"Definitely worth the risk. If we stay in this bed much longer like this, I don't think we'll be satisfied with doing just that again." She placed her hand over his heart to feel the steady thump.

"Does my kitten want something?" He ran his hand down the side of her breast with feather light strokes.

The ache between her thighs rekindled slow and steady. She squirmed to alleviate it and kissed his shoulder. "I'm fairly content. But if you keep touching me like that, I might jump you, condom or not."

"You're feisty today." He let out an appreciative chuckle and pulled her on top of him until she was half-draped across him.

"I blame it on seeing you out of the blue."

"Maybe I should come over more often." His hand ran a possessive pattern over her back.

She couldn't help but shiver and snuggle closer. "You'd never get any work done."

"Work, shit!" He bolted upright, dumping her onto the bed with a thump. He scrambled for his clothes.

She pulled the blankets over her to block out the rush of cold air on her skin. "What did I miss?"

"I left Andrew's minis in the car with my laptop. I need to grab them before they freeze."

She sat for a second after he disappeared, disappointed at the abrupt change in mood. It was probably for the best. She didn't think she could resist begging him to fill her if they kept playing. She dressed quickly, putting a stop to her dangerous thoughts.

She popped into Olivia's room while Brad worked. Gone was her sweet lover and in his place was a confident businessman which was equally hot. Luke and Andrew pulled him into the small upstairs kitchen and out of her sight. Sam sighed and turned back to her friend.

"Of all the guys I know, he's the only one who doesn't keep one on him."

Olivia looked up from the picture she was editing. "I think it's sweet he doesn't assume you'll put out for him."

"Sweet but really inconvenient." She rummaged around in the nightstand. "I'm stealing a couple back, just in case."

"Be my guest. I'm fairly certain I owe you more than a couple."

Luke sauntered into the room and dropped a kiss on Olivia's head. "What are you girls conspiring about?"

"Just plotting your demise." Sam nodded her head at the heated tones coming from the kitchen. "What are you boys talking about?"

He shrugged. "Just commission stuff."

"It doesn't sound like commission stuff." She frowned at him, her stomach roiling with worry. "What aren't you telling me?"

"Nothing you need to worry about."

She trusted Luke as far as she could throw him. She stood and prepared to dart around him. Something was up. Before she could make a break for it, Brad appeared in the doorway and held out a hand to her.

"It's getting late, kitten. I should head home and get some work done." He stiffly hugged her.

She stood on her tiptoes to whisper in his ear. "Or we could go back to my room and finish what we started."

"Why don't we hang out here?" He avoided meeting her eyes. "We don't hang out with your friends all that often."

"If that's what you want."

"I do. I don't get to socialize with you guys except for work."

Brad pulled her onto the couch. She exchanged a confused look with Olivia. What the hell just happened? He kept his hands to himself as he engaged the guys in conversation. She dozed with her head on his shoulder, taking comfort that he didn't try to dislodge her.

He nudged her awake a few hours later to say good-night. After he left without a kiss, she trudged down to her room. Curling up on her bed, she tried to ignore how his scent clung to her blankets. She threw his shirt across the room, squeezing her eyes shut against the shards of glass clawing at her veins. A single tear escaped her eye before the choking sobs took over.

Chapter Twelve

Sam-Cat: You left in a hurry last night.

Brad stared at his laptop with a pang of guilt. He hadn't missed the confusion and hurt on her face when he left without kissing her. He should've taken her aside and explained everything, but he could feel Luke and Andrew judging his every move. Their threats didn't sit well, but he did love that she had people watching out for her.

Ubel: Sorry about that. I got an email from one of my clients while you slept. Rush job, they need them before a tournament in California. I get a bonus if they arrive in time.

S: That's amazing! Good luck with it.

He had a flash of inspiration to make up for his abrupt departure.

U: I want to take you out after it's finished.

S: Like a date?

U: Yes, kitten, exactly like a date. Think about what you want to do.

S: Anything you want to steer clear of?

U: No. I just want to treat my girl.

S: I'll leave you to work.

She logged off before he could stop her. He sat back in his chair with a groan. It wasn't a complete lie. One of his biggest clients had emailed him with a rush order. He contemplated turning it down, but the money was worth it and now he had proper motivation to try the impossible.

He dug out his smudged schedule and checked his other deadlines. If he pulled a few long days, he could get everything done without missing a thing. It would mean no more surprise visits to

Sam's house until it was done. Seeing as he couldn't stop touching her, it was a good thing to not go over until he could take her out.

He set up his painting area and laid out the minis he needed to spray. He spent the next few days priming and painting every minute he was awake, only stopping to eat and chat with Sam. She kept him motivated with cute and sweet pictures, his own personal cheerleader.

He went up to the store on Thursday just to see her and pick up a couple paints he ran out of. She worked by his side, hooking her foot around his. He savored the slight amount of contact between them. She pouted a bit when he barely kissed her and rushed home to continue working. He feared if he started kissing her, he wouldn't stop until he brought her home with him. He promised himself he'd indulge his need to be with her on their date and make up for his distraction to her.

Sam-cat: What are you doing?

He stretched and popped his back. If he wasn't careful, he'd get a permanent hunch. The paintbrush already fell into a divot on his finger. He wiped his hands off to answer her.

Ubel: Working.

S: I'll leave you to it then.

U: Don't. Just know that if I don't get back to you, it's because I'm covered in paint.

S: How'd you sleep? Any pleasant dreams?

U: I had a headache that shut down dream time.

S: I'm sorry. Anything I can do to help?

U: Change the weather so I can prime outside.

S: I gave up that power when I became mortal. Please don't kill yourself.

His headache abated slightly to a dull throbbing in his temples. He didn't have the heart to tell her how sick he made himself the previous night. Throwing up didn't help his head, so he cracked the window by his desk. He didn't enjoy the cold, but he preferred it to getting sick.

U: I have the perfect motivation to live. Have you figured out what we're doing for our date?

S: I've been trying to figure out something not super cliche like dinner and a movie. Veto if you want, but I was thinking either House on the Rock or the Domes.

He paused with his brush poised over a mini. Leave it to her to come up with random suggestions for their first date. He smiled at the unique suggestions, his imagination firing. She definitely put some thought into this.

U: Those are different. I assume you have reasons for both.

S: Of course. House on the Rock has all their Santas up. The Domes are tropical and warm. Both have nice secluded spots to steal a kiss or two.

U: I could use a kiss or two.

S: Do you need me to come over and keep you company?

U: As much as I'd love to take you up on that offer, I think you'd be too tempting of a distraction right now.

S: You sound like you need a distraction right now.

U: I should've taken advantage of the distraction on Thursday when I had the chance.

He glanced at the screen as he finished his current mini and picked up the next. Normally her answers came back lightning fast, but the minutes stretched by without a response. Was she mad at him for rebuffing her again? He couldn't blame her for it.

WHAT THE HELL WAS UP with Brad? He said he wanted kisses and distraction, but refused her offer. Sam wracked her brain for what could turn him hot-and-cold. Did he decide she was too easy?

She shook her head, he was just as eager as she had been. *Luke and Andrew.* They took Brad aside right before things got weird.

She marched upstairs and narrowed her eyes at Luke. "What did you do?"

"Context clues, please." He looked up from his textbook.

"What did you say to Brad when he was here?"

"Nothing important, just looking out for you."

"What. Did. You. Say?"

He held up his hands in surrender. "I might've, slightly, threatened to castrate him if he hurt or disrespected you. Andrew may have hammered the point home."

"Please tell me you didn't. Why?" Sam balled up her fist, debating on punching Luke.

"We just wanted to keep you from getting hurt."

"Stop butting into my life."

"Sam, I—"

"No, you made last week hell. We went from amazing to him barely talking to me, let alone touching or kissing me. Do you know how bad that hurt? Wondering what I did wrong? No, you don't because you didn't ask if I needed or wanted you to threaten my boyfriend."

She spun on her heel and stomped back down the stairs. She fumed all the way back to her computer. Save her from all the stupid men in her life.

Sam-cat: You should've told me the boys threatened you.

Ubel: That's nothing.

S: Bullshit. Explain the last week to me. And don't give me that crap about a rush job.

U: Fine, part of it was I think they're right. We rushed into bed without going on a proper date first, a week after you questioned if we're actually dating. Part of the last week really is that I have a rush job that will bring in much needed cash and prestige if I can get it done around the rest of my work.

Her anger slowly ebbed out of her. Brad had a point, not that it fully excused his behavior. He should've talked to her about his doubts instead of distancing himself from her. Her fingers stabbed at the keyboard.

S: Is that all of it?

U: No. Once I was out of your bed, I freaked out at how little self-control I had. All you had to do was ask and I would've thrown caution to the wind and been inside you. Protection be damned.

Sam swallowed hard and stared at his words. He echoed her thoughts so completely. How the hell did she respond to that?

U: And now I scared you.

S: Not in the slightest. I almost begged you to take me.

U: Kitten, you're throwing gasoline on the fire. Don't tell me that or I'll not stop next time. I don't want to be that guy.

S: Are you going to keep avoiding me until we go on a "proper date?"

U: It depends on how fast I can get this done.

S: How much is left?

U: Too damn much. And I miss my girl.

S: Let me come over to help. I know you say I'm a distraction, but this week has been hell.

U: I don't think having you here is a good idea based on what we just talked about.

S: Please, it's role playing night and they get loud. I need to get out of the house for a bit. I'll prime or base minis. I'll even run and get you snacks or food.

U: I really could use the help.

She seized the opportunity.

S: Do you want me to bring food or drinks with me?

U: I've been mainlining coffee. I'll make a fresh pot. I like Swiss Cake Rolls.

S: When was the last time you had a real meal?

U: I don't remember, I've been eating at my desk.

S: I'll be over in a bit. Don't bother making coffee, I'll do that when I get there.

She logged off and grabbed her painting supplies. Olivia caught her digging through the fridge. They packed enough leftovers to feed a small army or a very hungry boyfriend. She made it to the store to pick up snack cakes before she remembered she didn't have his address.

She stared at her phone and then at the house. The address matched, but there was no way he lived in the huge house. It was way bigger than her place and she split that five ways instead of three. Still, his car was parked in the driveway. She shrugged and hauled her stuff up the stairs. The door opened before she could ring the bell.

"You must be Sam. I'm Chuck." Inky black hair hung in his eyes. He reached out to shake her hand. "I'm so glad you're here. He's been a douchebag all week." He dragged her through the house, not allowing her to take in more than a blur of dark wood, and pointed down a set of stairs. "Painting room's down there. You're braver than I am, there might be something growing down there."

Sam felt like she'd been through a whirlwind. She crept down the stairs until she could peek around the corner. A bright section of the room drew her eye past the couch to a giant desk. Brad hunched over it, absorbed in his work. Classic rock played over the speakers, masking her setting things down. She waited until he was in between paint strokes before covering his eyes.

"Guess who."

"My girlfriend, who's the best distraction and helper in the world?"

117

"You got it on the first try." She placed a light kiss on the side of his neck. "You smell good."

"I just got out of the shower."

"You didn't have to clean up on my account."

He set aside the mini and pulled her onto his lap. "Yes, I did. I smelled about as good as this place looks."

"Does it always look like this?" The piles of plates, paints, and papers finally registered. She had no clue how he found anything in the mess.

"Not always, but I've been super busy lately and haven't gotten a chance to put anything away."

"Where do you want me?" It took her a second to realize how loaded the question was. "I mean, where do you want me to start helping with orders?"

"I adore how pink you turn when you're embarrassed. Is this the same woman who sent me heart-stopping pictures?" He nuzzled her neck. "I needed this."

She melted against him, his arms a warm anchor around her. The stress from the last week bled out of her. "I did too."

He gave her a scorching look before he devoured her mouth. She shifted on his lap to be able to match the ferocity of his kisses. He moaned in her mouth, the sound running straight through her.

"Sam, this was a bad idea." He slid a hand up the back of her shirt.

The line of heat licking up her spine didn't feel like a bad idea. "Or a great one."

"I'm not going to break my promise. I want to do things right, treat my girl with respect."

His girl. Her toes curled at the way he called her his. She pulled loose from his arms with a groan. "Fine. Work first, play later."

The sooner they finished this order, the quicker they could go on the date that was so important to him. His insistence on taking her out would be adorable if she wasn't crawling out of her skin with need. She wrinkled her nose at the cold coffee in the pot and the piles of dirty dishes. She took everything she could find upstairs. She popped the food she brought in the microwave and rummaged around the kitchen for supplies.

"Looking for something?" Steve lounged in the doorway.

She jumped with a squeak. "I'm putting a bell on you, you scared five years off of me." She gestured around the room. "Where do you keep your coffee, filters, and dish soap?"

He reached over her head for the coffee supplies. "Soap's under the sink."

"What?" She scrubbed out the coffee pot, Steve's eyes tracking her movements.

"Just happy you're here. I didn't realize you knew your place was in the kitchen." He chuckled and dodged the wet sponge she lobbed at him.

Sam carried everything back down the stairs, juggling to keep from dropping anything. "I swear that man had a death wish."

"Who?" Brad came to her rescue and took the coffee pot and set it to brew.

"Steve. He's cracking jokes about me knowing my place is in the kitchen."

"Need me to put him in his place?"

"Nah, I threw a wet sponge at him." She pressed the plate of food into his hands. "Eat." He devoured the food making yummy noises. A happy feeling bubbled up in her that he enjoyed her taking care of him. "You really haven't been taking care of yourself."

"I wish I could tell you I have, but I've basically been living down here."

"What's next?"

She spent the next hour cleaning up paints and items from completed jobs, trying to organize as she went. He apologized for the mess every time she unearthed plates or cups. She gathered up all of his mixing trays to scrape the dried paint off before washing them while he continued to paint. A sense of accomplishment filled her when they could finally see most of his desk.

She sorted through the scraps of paper he had scattered around. "You need a better system."

"Don't I know it." He set down the mini he'd been painting and pulled over a chair so she could base completed minis.

"When you're not slammed with a ridiculous amount of work, we need to sit down and work out a business plan for you."

"That sounds like a daunting task."

"Not really. It's just setting up a system for when orders come in, what you need to complete them, and when they're due. We could set it up as a form so you can easily see what colors you used the last time if it's for the same army."

He stared at her open-mouthed. "You'd really help me with that?"

She took advantage of his astonishment to kiss him. "Of course. Maybe we'll get crazy and set up a filing system and a way to organize your paints."

It was so different to see him at his own painting desk. Here, he was master of his dominion, never hesitating on where anything was. His concentration on the task was complete until she caught up with him.

His eyes tracked her as she took the dirty rinse cups to the bathroom to clean out and refill. She caught the hungry look in his eyes and shivered. Unable to resist his pull, she leaned over the back of his chair and kissed his neck. His scent made her mouth water. She was dying to continue what they started in her room.

"I'm not being a good harem girl." She nipped his ear.

He straightened like she electrocuted him. "How so, kitten?"

"I feel like I should be more at your beck and call, anticipate your needs, or at least be less dressed."

"Sam..." He groaned and set aside his paintbrush. He turned to pull her onto his lap, leaving smudges of paint on her wrists. "Why are you torturing me?"

She nuzzled his neck, drowning in his scent. "You're the one that wanted a harem of painting girls."

"Just you." He kissed her forehead and stared at the paint on her arms. "I can't even touch you right now without getting paint all over you."

"Some other night, that might be fun to play with." Images of outlining the contours of his muscles with paint filled her head.

"Wicked little minx. Stop being evil." He nipped at her lips.

"Let me at least feed you." She reached over to pull a snack cake out of the box, making a show out of pressing herself against him. He moaned against her neck.

She held up a roll to his lips. He took his time eating the treat, his eyes never leaving hers. Memories of his lips nibbling on her skin flashed through her. Desire pooled in her belly as he licked every last bit of chocolate from her fingers. She squirmed against him, every brush of his tongue sent a jolt of need through her. He brushed the back of his hand over her cheek.

Her phone alarm went off causing them both to jump. "Is it midnight already?"

"Looks like it."

"I have to get going." She didn't move from the comfort of his lap.

His voice rumbled in her ear. "You could spend the night."

"And make you break your promise? I couldn't do that." She loved teasing him.

"I am very much regretting making that promise right now. Especially when I have my personal painting goddess draped over me. Can I take it back?"

"Not tonight, I have to work in the morning." She forced herself off of his lap and gathered her things.

"Thank you for coming over and helping. I can get all of the smaller orders sent out and finish up the big order in the next couple of days. When's your next day off?"

"Wednesday." She zipped up her coat.

"I will come and get you for lunch and then we can go to the Domes to get warm." He grabbed her scarf and pulled her in for a passionate kiss.

She stepped away, dazed from the ferocity of his kiss. "Sounds wonderful. Good-night."

Chapter Thirteen

B rad smiled at his phone. Sam's face lit up the screen and he pressed the answer button. Her tear-filled voice filled his ear, incoherent words came from her.

"Kitten, slow down. What's wrong?" His phone creaked as he gripped it tight.

She took a deep breath. "I have to cancel our date."

"That's nothing to cry over. We'll just reschedule it for another time." He hated waiting, but he would for her.

"I don't know when I'll be back."

He leaned against the wall, sure he heard her wrong. "Where are you going?"

"Missouri. My dad..." She dissolved into tears.

Her tears tore out his heart. "It's okay, baby. Take your time."

She cried even harder. The need to get to her to comfort her sent him searching for his shoes and keys. Muffled noises on her side had him pausing.

"It's Luke. She got a phone call tonight. Her dad's in the hospital. He got hurt at work." The sounds of Sam crying grew quieter. "It sounds bad, man."

"Is he going to make it?" Brad couldn't imagine what she was going through considering how close she was with her father.

"They don't know. He was pulled under a forklift. He hit his head and hasn't woken up yet. He might lose his leg."

"What flight is she leaving on?"

"She's planning on driving."

He stopped dead and cursed. "What?"

123

"No available flights anytime soon and no one to pick her up." Luke sounded as frustrated with the idea as Brad was.

"Is anyone going with her?"

"No one can, it's finals week and we're all crushed at work."

"Keep her there until I get there. I'll drive her down. She shouldn't be behind the wheel in this state."

He ended the call. Tossing random clothes in a bag, he ran for the door. He drove to her house on autopilot, the urge to hold her making him break the speed limit. He took the front steps two at a time and let himself in.

"Thanks for doing this." Luke held out his hand. "Sorry for giving you hell about dating her."

Brad took the peace offering, barely caring as he kept moving to her room. "Don't think about it. I'd do the same if I was in your place." He tapped on the door and stepped in. Olivia held Sam in her arms. He knelt in front of the bed. "Sweetie?"

Sam launched herself into his arms with a sob. "You didn't have to come over."

"Yes I did. Shh, it'll be alright." He sent up a prayer that he was right. He looked up at Olivia. "Does she have everything packed?"

"I'll grab her things out of the bathroom." Olivia closed the door behind her.

He rubbed Sam's back and made soothing noises. Her tears tore out his heart. She stared up at him with tears streaming down her face.

"I'm sorry." She wiped her face with her hands. "I'm a mess. You shouldn't have to see me like this."

He swiped a tear from her cheek. "I love seeing you, no matter what you look like."

"What are you doing here?"

"Luke told me you were planning on driving to Missouri alone." He couldn't keep censure from his voice.

She backed up. "Are you here to stop me?"

"No, I wouldn't do that. I'm going to drive you there." He pulled her back into his arms. She opened her mouth, but he placed a finger over her lips. "It's either that or I worry all night about if you made it or not."

Olivia brought in the last things for Sam's bag. He picked it up and offered his hand to Sam. He loaded everything into her car while she hugged her friends. Tears streamed freely down her cheeks. He held the passenger door open for her.

"I can drive." She held out her hand for the keys.

"You are understandably worried about your dad. Let me focus on driving." He helped her into the car before getting in the driver seat and plugging in the address into his GPS.

"Driving would help distract me from thinking about what we're going to find at the hospital." Her voice was quiet and unsure.

"Curl up against me." He hated how helpless he felt. "We'll talk about whatever you want to distract you."

"Why are you doing this for me?" Her head lulled against his shoulder.

"I don't want you driving when you're worried about something like this." He turned on the wipers. "I'd rather you made it there in one piece."

"What about your work?"

Of course she'd worry about his business. "I can afford to take a break right now. I sent out the big order this morning. I'll notify the rest of my clients there will be a slight delay in my painting schedule when we get to the hospital." He leaned his head against hers. "Besides, this sweet girl helped me get ahead of my workload."

"You must have a great painting harem."

"The best."

He kept a running conversation about everything he could think of to keep her mind off of where they were going. Her answers came slower and slower until she fell asleep on his shoulder. The car ate up the miles until he finally pulled over to get gas. He shifted her gently so she wouldn't wake up. She looked so fragile.

"Are we there already?" She rubbed her eyes and looked around.

"No, I just needed to stop to get some gas and grab a coffee."

"I'LL GAS HER UP." SAM wiped the last bits of sleep out of her eyes. She couldn't believe she fell asleep. "You go inside." She took the keys from Brad with a kiss.

The cold wind woke her up while she put gas in her car. She hopped from foot-to-foot to stay warm. She got a good look at herself in the restroom mirror. Damn, she looked like hell, but there wasn't much she could do about it right now other than splash some water on her face.

She met Brad by the doors. He handed her a cup of coffee and held out his hand for the keys. She shook her head. "I'm good now. That nap helped. You should try and catch some sleep while I drive."

"Not a chance. Keys." He waited. "Now that I have coffee, I'm good for the rest of the drive. If you're awake, you can keep me company."

She relented and handed the keys to him. The way he took care of her was sweet. "If you get sick of driving, let me know. I know where we're going."

He held the door for her and she slipped into the seat. *Teleporting technology would be so handy right now.* She filled the car with nervous chatter, doing everything she could to keep her mind off of their destination. When she ran out of things to say, she rested her head on his shoulder.

"How'd they know to call you?"

Sam started awake. "Huh?"

"I didn't realize you fell asleep again. I was just wondering how the hospital knew to call you."

"I'm listed as his emergency contact for everything." She pointed to the exit. "Get off here."

He pulled into the parking lot and was at her door before she fully had it open. He took her hand and led her into the hospital. Her stomach twisted and she felt sick. He gave her a reassuring squeeze.

She walked up to the front desk. "Excuse me."

"Yes ma'am?" The nurse looked up from her screen.

"My father was brought in earlier today." She looked up at the clock and realized it was early morning. "I guess it would be yesterday now. His last name is Duke."

"Give me one minute." The nurse clicked a few keys. "And the first name?"

"Lewis. It would have been mid-afternoon when he was brought in."

"There he is. What's your name?"

"Samantha Duke, his daughter."

"You are his power of attorney?"

Her stomach twisted into a knot. "I am."

"I need you to fill out some paperwork."

She took the offered forms. The words swam on the page and she scrubbed the stupid out of her brain. *What if her father had allergies she didn't know about?* "I don't know the answers to most of this."

"Ma'am, is there any way Sam can see her father? We just drove seven hours to get here." Brad wrapped his arms around her, his strength helping to loosen the knot in her stomach.

The nurse gave them an apologetic look. "I need the paperwork filled out. He was brought in unconscious and we need to know some important information to treat him."

He leaned forward. "She lives two states away and wouldn't be able to focus until she sees him."

"It's okay." Sam signed her name at the bottom of the paperwork. "As far as I know, he's not allergic to anything and he's in fairly good health. I take full responsibility if I'm wrong until he can answer the questions himself." She vowed to have a talk with her dad about having information like this on file with her for the future.

"I'll get this inputted right away."

"I'd like to see my father and know what happened to him."

"I'll page a doctor to see you as soon as possible. Please have a seat over there."

She bit back her need to beg the nurse until she could see her dad. She collapsed in one of the hard chairs and leaned against Brad. "Thank you for coming with me."

He wrapped her in his warm arms and held her close. His scent calmed her pounding pulse. "Anytime you need me."

He shifted to get them into a more comfortable position. She smiled against his shoulder. She loved how he took care of her. She blinked a couple of times at the thought. It wasn't quite right. She loved him. The revelation hit her hard. She looked up at him to say something, but he had dozed off in the chair. She kissed his cheek. It could wait until they weren't in the hospital.

After a half hour or so, a doctor walked over to them. "Samantha Duke?"

"That's me." She bolted upright and blinked at the doctor. "Can I see my dad now?"

"In a minute." The doctor patted her hand. "I want to talk to you about what happened to him."

"He got hit by a forklift at work."

"It's a bit more complicated than that." He glanced at Brad. "Mr. Duke only has Samantha listed as his family. May I ask how you are related?"

"I'm Sam's boyfriend."

"Then I will have to ask you to excuse us. Patient confidentiality, you understand."

"Of course." Brad stood and walked across the waiting room. She wanted to call him back, but knew the doctor couldn't talk in front of him.

The doctor kept his back to Brad. "I have to say your father is extremely lucky someone noticed the accident and they were able to get the forklift off of him quickly."

Sam's eyes glazed over at the medical terminology being thrown out. "Plain English, please. It's way too late at night to follow medical jargon."

"The easiest way I can explain it is that we're not sure if we can save his leg. For now, we can't do surgery until some of the swelling goes down. Only then will we know how bad it is." The doctor offered her a smile. "He hasn't woken up yet, but his vital signs are strong. You can go in to see him in a minute. Your boyfriend will have to stay out here. Your father's wound is uncovered and we want to minimize the chance of infection."

"Of course."

"I'll send a nurse to show you to your father."

Brad was back at her side the second the doctor walked away. She raised an eyebrow at him. "Boyfriend, huh? How does that work if you avoid me for a week at a time?"

"I'm not living that down anytime soon, am I?"

"Not a chance."

"I still owe you a date to make up for that." He kissed her cheek. "Go see your father."

She slowly got up and followed the nurse. She looked back at him watching her like it killed him to not be with her. She wanted nothing more than to have him with her, but she couldn't risk her dad's health just to be more comfortable. Summoning courage borrowed from him, she took the mask and placed it on her face before entering her dad's room.

Her dad lay on the bed, pale and small looking and so at odds with the vibrant personality she was used to. IVs and cords snaked all over his body and bedside. The machines beeped with great regularity, incomprehensible to her. She avoided looking under the tented sheet covering his leg. She pulled up a chair and grabbed his hand.

"Oh, daddy." She bowed her head and cried. Tears quickly soaked the edge of her mask.

"Sam, what are you doing here?" Her dad's voice sounded rough and tired.

Her head snapped up and she watched her father slowly blinking at her. "I came to see you."

"Where are we?" He looked around the room, disoriented.

"We're at the hospital, daddy."

Panic flared in his eyes. "Are you okay?"

"Yes." She patted his hand to reassure him. "We're here for you. Do you remember what happened at work today?"

BRAD HATED LETTING Sam go down the hall by herself. She looked so tiny and fragile walking away. He pulled out his phone and sent off emails to his clients alerting them that their orders might be delayed due to an emergency.

Fast footsteps had him looking up. Sam rushed down the hall and launched herself into his arms. He carried her back to the chairs.

"What happened?"

She sniffled, pulled the mask off of her face, and grabbed a Kleenex. "My dad woke up and didn't remember getting hurt at work." She looked up at him with tears in her eyes. "That's not a good sign, is it?"

He soothed a hand up and down her back while he scrambled for something to say to make this better. "Not necessarily. They probably have him on a lot of medication to keep him out of pain. That's bound to mess up anyone's memories for a bit."

"I guess..."

He tilted her face up. "If he's anything like his daughter, he'll be fine."

"Thank you." She put her head against his chest.

His chest expanded. He held her while they waited for the doctor to come back with news. Her father had calmed down and he was no longer disoriented. They had given him something to help him sleep.

Brad walked her to her father's room and took up residence in a chair outside. *You'd think they'd make the chairs more comfortable so visitors weren't even more uncomfortable than they had to be.* He started awake and peeked through the window. She had curled up in a chair and dozed off holding her father's hand.

She looked so vulnerable and small. He wanted to hold her and shield her from the world. And there was not a damn thing he could do to make this better for her. He rested his head against the wall. Voices drifted from the room.

"Hey, kiddo."

"Hi, daddy."

"What are you doing here?"

"Do you know where we are?" Her voice sounded cautious. His heart ached for her and he looked in.

Brad studied father and daughter. Their attention was solely on each other. He could see where she got her coloring from, their dark heads bent to each other.

Her father patted her hand. "In the hospital. I remember what happened. I meant, what are you doing down here, young lady?"

"Sleeping in a really uncomfortable chair." She stretched. "You don't think I would stay up in Wisconsin, did you?"

"What about your job?"

"They gave me time off."

"Who's the guy?" Her father looked straight at the window. Brad gave an uncomfortable wave.

"Brad." She smiled back at him.

"Is Brad your boyfriend?"

"Not in the official we've gone on a date kind of way, but yes he is."

"How am I supposed to get grandkids if you aren't dating?"

He knew his face showed his shock. Grandkids? Did she want kids?

She turned bright pink and hid her face. "Cart before the horse much?"

"I just want to see you happy." Her father winked. "And I want grandkids to spoil."

"You can wait, old man." She chuckled.

A nurse nudged him aside and blocked his view of the room. He paced the hallway, confused on how to feel about eavesdropping on her conversation. He wandered down to the nearest vending machine and grabbed a cup of coffee while he mused on what he overheard.

Chapter Fourteen

A nurse bustled into the room and took her dad's vital signs. Sam took a deep breath and shook her head. Her father really had some screwed up priorities. Grandkids? Of course Brad overheard the whole exchange. How was she supposed to explain it to him?

A few minutes later, a doctor came into the room to check on the swelling. She got her first look at her dad's mangled leg and had to look away. Shock ran through her that they didn't take the leg off. The doctor remarked how much the swelling had gone down and would be back when they had a time for the surgery.

"You look green." Her dad patted her arm. "Is it that bad?"

"I'm honestly surprised they didn't take it off yesterday if it looks better today."

"You should go home and get some rest."

"I'm not going anywhere." She settled in her chair.

"I will have them call you when I know what time my surgery is, but your boyfriend looks completely exhausted."

She glanced up at Brad through the window. He had a cup of coffee clenched in his hand, looking for all the world like he wanted to come in. "You win this time, old man, but I will be putting in a notice at the nurse's station to be told when your surgery is. None of your tricks."

She kissed him on the cheek and reluctantly gathered up her things. She paused at the door to look back at him. A shudder ran through her at how her usually boisterous dad lay so quiet on the bed.

She tugged Brad out of his chair and stopped by the nurse's station. He passed out on the short drive to her dad's house. The car

133

ticked as it cooled down and she sat there watching him sleep. He had been so supportive through the entire ordeal.

"We're home, hun." She leaned over and kissed his cheek. "Let's get you into bed."

He made an incoherent noise as he stumbled into the house. She tucked him into her twin bed and he passed back out immediately. She stared down at him for a few minutes, debating crawling in next to him. She had woken up enough to need to get clean. She dug out a fresh outfit and jumped into the shower. She took her time scrubbing the smell of the hospital off of her.

Wide awake and feeling more human, she puttered around the familiar ranch style house. Her father's idea of redecorating was hanging up her most recent school picture in the hallway. They really needed to redo family pictures, it had been years. She wandered from room to room packing a bag for her dad. The old man would go crazy without something to read.

Brad came out of her room a few hours later, rumpled but better rested. "I woke up in a strange room and had no idea where you were." He pulled her into his arms.

She kissed his cheek. "My room is not strange."

"It's not what I pictured for you." He studied the hallway. "I do love the hallway shrine to you. I'll have to talk to your father for tips on decorating."

"I'll tell you his secret: it's just adding another picture every year and changing nothing else." She popped her head into her room and really looked at it for the first time in years. Neither she nor her father bothered to update the room since she was little. "At least I talked my dad out of keeping most of the stuffed animals."

He plucked a purple doll off the floor where she had been knocked down. "Who's this?"

"Shy Violet, and you be nice. I said most of the stuffed animals. We had to regrow the collection after the divorce."

"Why's that?" He pulled her onto his lap on the bed.

She cuddled the doll to her chest, old wounds she'd forgotten ripped open. "My mom wouldn't let me bring anything with me when I visited, which left us scrambling for clothes and toys. He didn't have much money because my mother sucked him dry, so it was a lot of trips to the thrift store. Shy was the first toy we found."

"She's adorable. I see why you like her." He toyed with the purple hair.

"WHY DIDN'T YOU MOVE down here to live with your dad?" Brad wanted to kick himself for bringing up the taboo subject, but Sam seemed like she needed to talk.

"The judge gave custody to my mother, even though I begged for dad to get it. By the time I found out I could appeal the judgment, I was so far into high school that it wasn't worth switching schools."

"At least she didn't take her temper out on you." He settled them against the pillows and snuggled her firmly in his arms. She gave him sleepy kisses.

"I'm guessing your father did." Her hand traced a warm trail over his chest. "And your mother did nothing to stop it."

He loved how Sam got him. "She's the type to believe her husband is the ultimate authority and can do no wrong. Even if he's beating her for no reason other than she made his toast slightly darker than he liked."

"My poor Brad." She pulled herself up to kiss him. "I want to go back in time and take you away from all that."

He savored the thought of her coming and stealing him during the times he hid under the bed to escape his father's wrath. "You would've been my angel." He kissed her temple. "You already are."

"This got heavy pretty fast." She blew out a breath.

He studied her. Dark circles shaded under her eyes and she didn't look like she had slept at all. "What did you do while I passed out?"

"Packed a bag for my dad and took a shower." She looked up at the clock. "We should get back to the hospital."

"Did you sleep?"

"Only what I got in my dad's room and the car ride down."

"Why didn't you nap with me?" He would've loved to have her in his arms while he slept.

She shrugged. "Too awake. I needed the shower to feel human."

"Why don't you lay down while I grab a shower and then we can go back?" She made a face at laying down. "I need a shower as well. I feel grungy." He was not above using anything in his power to get her to lay down for a few minutes. She had a hard night.

She gave him a slow nod and showed him where everything was. He tucked her into the bed before heading into the bathroom. The hot water relaxed his tense muscles. He rolled his shoulders and thought about the last twenty-four hours. If he could, he would rewind the last day and warn her father about the accident to save them the heartache.

He took his time cleaning up. Sam was right, he felt more like a human. Peeking into her room, she had curled up with the doll. Something about her vulnerability struck a powerful cord in him. He watched her sleep until the urge to crawl in with her overtook him. He eased himself into the warm cocoon of blankets and wrapped his arm around her. She immediately burrowed against him. It shouldn't make him this deliriously happy that she unconsciously sought him out. The sound of her breathing and warm presence of her body in his arms eased him back to sleep.

HE TRICKED ME. Sam struggled against the remnants of sleep. Brad held her so gently in his arms she almost gave into falling back asleep, safe and cared for. She reached for her phone and checked the time. Her nap hadn't been for more than two hours, but it felt longer.

She couldn't summon the energy to be mad at him, she probably would've done the same thing. Feeling impish, she tickled his nose with the ends of her hair. He grumbled and swiped at it, so she did it again. He growled and rolled on top of her.

"What do you think you're doing?" He nipped at her lips.

"Paying you back for tricking me into taking a nap."

"You looked like you were about to fall over. Sue me for wanting to take care of my girl."

His girl. She softened under him. "Fine. I'll sue you for five kisses."

"That I'll happily pay."

Her phone rang and flashed the hospital's number. Her heart dropped to her knees and she could barely hit the answer button. She shook the entire time she talked with the nurse. Brad kept his arms around her until she hung up.

"He's going into surgery in an hour."

He gave her a tight squeeze before helping her off the bed. "Then we should get going so you can be with your father." He held out his hand. "Give me the keys, I'll drive."

She briefly debated on arguing with him, but her stomach had tied itself into too many knots for her to concentrate on driving. Her heartbeat was too loud in her ears and it made her dizzy. She grabbed her dad's bag and slid into the car. Brad offered his hand on the way through the doors and to the nurse's station.

He was her rock until they got to her dad's room. He gave her a quick kiss on the cheek. "I'll be right here if you need me."

"Thank you." It was on the tip of her tongue to tell him she loved him, but she covered her face with her mask instead. She perched on the hard plastic chair. "Good morning, old man."

"I saw your not-a-boyfriend boyfriend giving you a kiss." Her dad's eyes twinkled. "Why didn't you kiss him back?"

"Because I didn't want you giving him hell when you meet him." She wagged her finger at him. "I know how you work. I kiss him and you threaten him with the shotgun. I don't and you give me grief for not showing enough affection." She heard Brad's chuckle through the door.

Her dad's surgeon walked in. All of her teasing died on her lips and she gripped her dad's hand. The explanation of what they were going to do buzzed in her ears, but nothing made sense.

"I love you, dad." She kissed her dad and took his glasses, choking back tears. She needed to stay strong for him. "I'll see you when you wake up."

"You'd better, I'm blind as a bat without those." His words slurred as the drugs took hold. "I love you too, Sam."

Brad wrapped his arms around her and watched them wheel her dad away with her. She held in her tears until the door swung closed. He whispered soothing words in her ear and held her tight until the choking sobs subsided. She couldn't get the thought out of her head of it being the last time she saw her father alive.

SAM'S SOBS TORE OUT Brad's heart. He felt powerless to help her. He gently brought her out to the waiting room and settled into yet another hard chair while she paced the floor, chewing on the side of her thumb. Every time she passed the clock, she glanced at it.

"You're going to wear a hole in the floor." He couldn't take the silence any longer.

She jumped. "How long did they say it was going to take?"

"About an hour, maybe longer. It all depends on how everything goes back together." He tracked her as she started another circuit.

"How long has it been?"

"Less than twenty minutes. You need to be distracted or you're going to gnaw off your finger." He pulled out his phone and patted his lap. "Come here, we'll watch stupid cat videos or something to pass the time."

"I'm fine." She resumed chewing her thumb and pacing.

He could easily overpower her and stop her damn pacing. He ground his teeth. Given her history, that wouldn't end well. He wanted to help her, not upset her further, but she was too damn stubborn.

"It's okay for you to allow yourself to be rescued every now and then." He patted his lap again, summoning all of his patience. "Let me be strong for you today. You can save me some other day."

She sank into his arms. "How do you know me so well?"

"You told me you didn't like being saved." He kissed her temple. "And I make a point to study what I like."

A happy glow filled her face. "So you like me?"

He tipped her head up so he could stare into her eyes. "Very much." She cuddled against his chest. He handed over his phone to stop himself from being overly sappy. Now was not the time. "Lady's choice on the first video."

She scrolled through his pictures, pausing at different ones of his work. She peeked up at him a couple of times to make sure he didn't mind, but there really wasn't anything he needed to hide from her. It was all tamer pictures of her, mostly stuff she sent him, and work. She finally switched over to browsing his video history. *Curious kitten.*

"You watched a tour of the Domes?"

"I was intrigued by your date ideas." He squirmed as she continued scrolling and found he had also watched one on House on the Rock. "And I wanted to impress you with my knowledge of plants."

"That's really sweet, but I didn't want to go because I had a burning desire to learn about plants."

He frowned at the top of her head. "Why did you want to go then?"

"It was someplace warm where we could talk and spend time together, just the two of us." She shrugged. "And I thought the color combinations might spark some really cool and unique paint schemes for your business."

He stared at her in shock. There was no way he heard her right. "You were thinking about my business?"

"Ever since the night I helped out, my brain's been ticking away. I have some ideas." She nuzzled her head into the crook of his neck. "I know discussing your business isn't the most romantic date ever so we can do something else."

Warmth spread in his chest. Never in a million years would he have guessed her motivation for their date. She was too good for him.

"Don't sell the idea short. I think it's amazing and romantic you put so much thought into our date. I'm humbled." He cleared his throat to dispel the tightness. "If you're done snooping on my phone, how about you pick something to watch?"

SAM SIGHED AND PICKED a painting tutorial. They took turns choosing something random from the suggestions bar and discussing the pros and cons of each technique. She glanced at the clock, shocked so much time had passed. Brad was good at keeping her brain from thinking too long on why they were there.

"It can't be good he's been in surgery for over two hours, can it?" Fear clawed at her throat.

Brad soothed a hand up and down her back. "It could just take awhile to piece the bones back together. He's a strong person, like his daughter."

She smiled at him, more grateful for his strength than she could ever express. "Thank you."

Her dad's surgeon walked into the waiting room hunched over. Her stomach back flipped at the prospect of bad news. She crossed the room on shaky legs.

"Miss Duke." He nodded. "Sorry for the delay."

"How is he?"

"Well, his leg was shattered. There's no other way to describe it. We weren't expecting that extent of damage when we went in."

"Is he...?" She couldn't put words to her fears.

"The surgery was a success. I was able to save the leg. There are a lot of pins and screws holding it together. He did lose some muscle to blood flow restriction, but, on the whole, he should regain some if not all mobility."

"He always wanted to be the bionic man." Relief made her loopy.

"We'll need to monitor him for a few days to make sure there's no signs of infection." The surgeon pegged her with a serious look. "That should give you time to find an assisted care facility for him to recuperate in."

"Why can't he come home?" Just like that, all of her worry came rushing back. "What aren't you telling me?" She wrapped her arms around her stomach.

"He won't be able to get around on his own for a while. There will be appointments he'll need to be taken to."

"I can take him." She straightened her shoulders.

"You live two states away."

"He's my father."

"Most children wouldn't put their lives on hold to care for their parents."

"I'm not most children."

"Are you willing to bathe him?"

The thought hadn't crossed her mind. She refused to think of her dad in a facility, no matter how brief the stay. "If that's what it takes for him to be comfortable in his own home."

"I don't think you understand how difficult this will be, Miss Duke."

"Look, I get it. I'll have to help him get in and out of bed and move around because he can't support himself. He'll need help using the bathroom and getting cleaned up." She met the doctor's eye and put steel in her voice. "What you don't understand is that he's my father and I will do everything in my power to make sure he gets the best care possible. If he chooses to do that in an assisted care facility or at home with me, that's his choice to make, not yours."

BRAD COULDN'T HELP but overhear Sam's conversation with the doctor. Her words punched him in the gut. She couldn't be serious about taking care of her father. He didn't want her to take off and leave him. Shame over his selfishness ate at him as he numbly followed her a few minutes later into her father's room.

She leaned over the bed and kissed the older man's cheek before handing him back his glasses. "How are you feeling?"

"Can't feel a thing, kiddo. These drugs are amazing." Her father's words were slightly slurred. He turned his attention to Brad. "Are you going to introduce me to your boy now or do I need to do it myself?"

She tugged him forward. "Dad, this is Brad. Brad, my dad, Lewis."

Brad straighted his back and held out his hand. He shouldn't feel this nervous about meeting her father, but he really wanted the older man to approve of him. Her father's handshake was firm despite the drugs still running through his system. Brad couldn't tell the night before because the room had been dim, but Sam got her piercing blue eyes from her father in addition to the brown hair.

"It's a pleasure to meet you, sir."

"Don't call me sir, Lewis is fine. I wish we were meeting under better circumstances. Thank you for making sure my baby girl made it here in one piece." Her father turned his attention to Sam. "I hear you've been arguing with the doctors."

"They want to put you in an assisted care facility. I didn't think you'd be comfortable in an old folk's home, although you'd fit in." She perched on the bed.

"I'm not a fan of the idea, but full time nurses are more expensive."

"I'll take care of you." She said it so matter-of-factly that Brad's knees gave out and he sank into the nearby chair. She really planned on leaving him.

"I don't want you to put your life on hold for me, young lady."

She shrugged. "It'll give me time to figure out what I want to do with my life."

Brad listened to them argue over whether it would be better for her to stay in Wisconsin or in Missouri. He bit down on his tongue to stop himself from siding with her father. Sam was strong, but she wanted to take on a monumental task. He could tell by the set of her shoulders she wasn't going to give in to logic.

"What if you hired a part-time nurse to help out with everything?" His voice was flat. He couldn't hide his dislike of her leaving. "It's a compromise between staying at home and going to a facility."

"You don't like my little girl staying down here." Her father was perceptive.

"I understand why she feels the need to do it, but I'm not in love with the idea." He avoided looking at her, not wanting to see how his words affected her. "I also know I have no say in whether she stays down here to help or not. My preference is selfish and has nothing to do with you."

"Honestly, I think I could learn to like you."

"If she got her streak of what's right from you, we both know you'll be recuperating at home with your daughter's help."

"Would you let her go without a fight?" Two sets of blue eyes focused on him.

"I'd find a way to make it work." Swallowing broken glass felt better than saying those words. "What kind of man would I be if I refused to let her help her family?" She beamed at him and squeezed his hand.

"I hear they'll be keeping me for a few more days. If you brought me reading material, there's no reason for you to hang around here."

She pulled out book after book from the bag with a flourish like it was a magic trick. "Do you doubt me, old man? Comics, whatever book was sitting in the bathroom, the one on your nightstand, and a couple from your to be read pile."

"That's my girl." Love tinged Lewis's voice. "Now, get out of here. Take your boy to Christmas Traditions or something.

"Dad, I'm—"

"Coming down to take care of me, I know." He plucked a book from the stack. "Which means you have packing to do. You should probably show your boy the better parts of Missouri. I'll hear no lip from you. It was nice to meet you, Brad. Enjoy your stay. Sam, I'll see you when you get back." He promptly ignored them to read his book.

She shook her head and kissed her father's cheek. Brad held the car door so she could get behind the wheel. He climbed into his side and turned to see her staring out the windshield. He covered her trembling hand with his.

"Kitten, what's wrong?"

SAM COULDN'T STOP SHAKING. "I think it just hit me. I've been on autopilot since I got the phone call." Tears threatened to spill. "I almost lost my dad."

"But you didn't." Brad brushed a hand against her cheek. "Your father is alive and you'll help him recover."

"Distract me. Please." Her mind spun with what might have happened.

"Where were you supposed to take me?" He kept his voice quiet and rubbed a thumb over her hand.

"Christmas Traditions. It's on Main Street in Old Town." She shifted the car into drive. She couldn't summon the excitement she usually could for the event.

"We don't have to go if you don't want to."

"It's not that I don't want to go. It's just..."

"You'd rather be with your dad." He understood her so completely. "Then you can tell me all about it and we can go back to the hospital."

"Thank you, but words don't do justice to the event." She navigated into a parking space.

"What is it?" His voice was full of curiosity.

She took his hand and led him up the small hill. Some of her excitement came back with the prospect of him experiencing it for the first time. "I'm not telling and ruining the surprise."

She watched as his confused frown slowly turned into wonder. The cobblestone street had been decorated with lights and garlands, lending the old buildings a festive air. A knot of kids raced between them and knocked their hands apart. She stopped to exchange pleasantries with one of the costumed characters.

"What did she give you?" Brad wrapped his arms around her waist and peered over her shoulder.

"Her card." She slipped one into his hand. "Every character has one. It tells you a bit of their history."

He pressed a warm kiss to her temple. "How many do you own?"

"I dunno. My dad and I used to do this every year. I'm sure he keeps them in one of the drawers in my room."

"Alright, Miss Tour Guide, who's the painter guy?" He pointed to an approaching character dressing in blue with snowflakes painted on his face.

"Pointing is rude." The actor stuck his nose in the air. "You have the pleasure of addressing Jack Frost."

Sam laughed. "The pleasure's all yours, Jack."

"Well, I never." Jack's eyes twinkled with mischief.

"Never had it dished back at you? I hear you've been mean to people up and down the street, nipping at their noses."

"Well played. Next time, perhaps it'll be your nose I nip at." He tapped her nose with two cards before bowing and handing them over.

"Do you know him?" Brad frowned at the retreating figure swallowed up by the crowd.

"Jack Frost? Not personally, but I've seen him enough to know he likes verbally sparring."

"It's good to see you smile." He hugged her tight.

She relaxed against his chest, content to be held by him. "It feels good to be here with you."

"How many characters are there?"

"It varies. If you want to collect all the cards, you check in with information to see who's not here." She gestured to the far end of the street. "It's usually around forty-five."

"That's a lot of walking."

"That's why there's a cookie and hot cocoa stand." She drew him across the street. "Two cups of cocoa, a snickerdoodle, and whatever cookie he's having, please."

"Chocolate chip."

BRAD TOOK HIS COOKIE and cup of cocoa from Sam. "I could've paid."

"My treat." She took a bite of her cookie and her eyes rolled back in bliss. "I forgot how good these were. Do you want a taste?"

Damn, he loved how she looked, all content and blissful. He'd never been more jealous of a cookie in his life. He ignored her outstretched hand and captured her lips. The cinnamon sugar layered over her natural sweetness. Hindered by his full hands, he couldn't stop her from pulling away. He groaned as the cold air replaced her warmth.

"Always with that trick," she chided, "when you can get a kiss whenever you want." Her smile told him how much she enjoyed it.

"Sometimes it's fun to catch you off-guard and remind you of our first kiss."

"Like I could forget." She finished her cookie and held out her hand. "Shall we?"

He threaded his fingers through hers and let the magic of the event wash over him. The afternoon slipped into evening as they poked in the shops and met more characters. He captured her under a tree for a lingering kiss, the lights twinkling around her. She swayed in his arms.

"Are you tired, kitten?" He shouldn't have kept her out this long, but he couldn't bring himself to break the spell.

She yawned, reminding him of how little she slept in the last day. "Getting there, but I don't want the day to end."

"Me neither, but we should head back. It's starting to get cold and you've barely slept." She pouted at him, making him regret saying they should leave. He ushered her over to the carriage rides. "But first, it's my turn to treat."

Her grin told him he had chosen wisely. He helped her into the waiting carriage, his hands lingering on her hips. Covering their laps with the blanket, he pulled her into his arms. His drowsy kitten curled up against him, all sweetness and contentment. When their ride ended, he debated paying for more until he was broke just to prolong the moment. He glanced down at her. Sam could barely keep her eyes open.

He stepped off the carriage and offered his hand to her. "Now we should get going."

"We never got around to ice skating." She slowed as they passed the rink, like a kid trying to get out of bedtime.

He kept a hand on her back to propel her to the car. "Good, it would've ruined a pretty perfect day." She gave him a confused look. "I don't know how to ice skate."

Chapter Fifteen

Sam woke up to a warm cocoon of blankets and Brad's body. *A girl could get used to waking up like this.* She inhaled his scent and closed her eyes. Five more minutes, she could hold the world at bay for five more minutes while she savored this.

He ran his hand down her back. "I like waking up to you snuggled against me." He stretched his legs until they hit the foot of the bed. "Although, I'd prefer a slightly larger bed."

"I have no problem fitting on it." She stretched her toes to barely brush the end.

"That's because you're little."

"Only compared to you." She poked him in the stomach. He captured her hand and kissed it. "I guess we should get up before my bed does permanent damage to you."

"Couldn't have that." He rolled onto his back and pulled her on top of him. He devoured her mouth like he couldn't get enough, leaving them both panting. "What's the plan for today?"

She knew their bliss wouldn't last long, but had hoped for more than a minute. "A quick run to the hospital before driving back to Wisconsin."

"Are you sure?" He stroked her cheek.

She leaned into his warm touch. "I want to bring the old man some more books to keep him from climbing the walls."

"I meant about going back so soon. We can stay longer if you want."

Her heart pinged. He really was too good to be true. "I think I've interrupted your work enough. Plus, it doesn't pay to stay here when there's so much to do up there."

"I don't want you to rush on my account. My work can wait a few more days if you need it."

"I'm sure." She forced herself out of the bed on into action. "We can't really do much more here." She shooed him into the shower while she scrounged up breakfast for them. Mentally, she added going grocery shopping once she came back. Her dad didn't keep much in the house that was remotely healthy.

They ate in silence, both too deep in their thoughts to make conversation. She left Brad to pack his bag while she hopped in the shower. She dumped the contents of her overnight bag on the bed, reasoning it didn't pay to haul it all up just to bring it back. The clothes hit the bed with a thump, more final than they should have. *My mind's playing tricks on me, this is just temporary.*

She kept the visit to the hospital short even though she could've stayed all day. She wanted to get back on the road so Brad could get back to work. She gripped the steering wheel, her mind racing with everything she had to do during the next few days. Her gaze skittered to the passenger seat. He stayed silent during most of the ride, only breaking the silence to offer to drive for a while. Only his clenched hands betrayed his thoughts.

The silence became too much to bear. "Thank you for coming with me. You didn't have to."

"I wanted to be there for you." He fell quiet for a moment. "When are you heading back?"

"In a week." The words tore her up. She fought back the tears threatening to spill. "Will you come over to say good-bye?"

He took her hand and gently brought it to his lips. "I hadn't planned on leaving your side for very long."

"Don't put your life on hold on my account." She would never forgive herself if his business failed because of this.

"You're part of my life too." He whispered against her skin, doing crazy things to her heart. "You won't be here for Christmas." He didn't ask.

It had never crossed her mind. She shook her head. "It doesn't feel right leaving my dad alone in the hospital on a holiday."

BUT YOU'RE FINE LEAVING me alone. Brad wanted to scream at how unfair this was. He swallowed back all of his harsh thoughts. "I have to run home and get your present after we get back."

"Do you want me to make a detour?" Sam glanced at him.

"Nah, I'll do it later. You've done enough driving today. I need to tell Chuck and Steve what's going on and grab clean clothes anyway." He stared out the window so she wouldn't see how torn up he was. He didn't want to make this more difficult for her.

They lapsed into silence for the rest of the drive. He could feel her pulling away from him and into herself and there was nothing he could do to stop it. He reached over and kept a hand on her thigh needing the contact to steady himself. She pulled up to her house and killed the engine. They sat there for a couple of minutes, listening to the engine tick.

She launched herself across the car and onto his lap. He almost missed catching her before her head hit the window. His heart broke in tiny pieces from how right this felt with her in his arms. *It's only a couple of months.* He could survive a couple of months without her warmth. She burrowed against his chest, all the world feeling like she was trying to crawl inside his heart.

"Sam, I..." He stopped and pressed his lips to her forehead. It wouldn't be fair to say it now. "I'm going to miss you."

"I'm going to miss you too."

He shifted slightly, cold slowly creeping up his legs. He could spend all day holding her, just not in the car. "Baby, as much as I love holding you, we should take this into the house. I'm losing feeling in my toes."

"I don't know if I can deal with their questions right now." She glanced fearfully at the house.

"Let me deal with your roommates."

She nodded and scrambled out of the car, letting in a fresh burst of snow and cold. He scooped her up in his arms and carried her across the driveway. She yelped in his ear and wrapped her arms around his neck. Luke must have been watching from the window because he met them at the front door. Brad nodded at him and carried Sam into her room.

He ran back out and grabbed her bag from the car. Not that it mattered because it was empty. He frowned at it. All of her roommates gathered in the living room and waited for him. He briefed them on how her father was doing and her plans of caring for him. He understood why she didn't feel up for this conversation, knives tore at him while he gave the explanation.

After their curiosity was sated, he slipped into her room. She had passed out in the middle of her bed, fully clothed except for her jacket and shoes. He pulled the blankets over her and dropped a kiss on her head. She didn't stir the entire time. *So much for spending time cuddling her before heading out.* She looked like she had been put through the ringer. He scribbled a note and left it on her nightstand to let him know when she woke up.

He made the drive home and sank onto the couch between Steve and Chuck. His friends were battling it out on some video game as usual. They paused as soon as he sat down.

"She's leaving to stay with her father while he recovers." His voice felt flat. Numbness had spread through him to dull the sharp breaking of his heart. Chuck offered him a beer but he shook his head. "I've got some work to do and I want to be able to go back over to her house to see her when she wakes up."

"You've got it bad for this girl. What are you going to do while she's gone?" Chuck took a pull from his bottle.

"I don't want to think about it." He pushed himself off the couch. "If you need me, I'll be in the basement."

He left his roommates talking about him and walked down the stairs. It took everything in him not to just turn around and head back to Sam's. He put in a few hours of work before turning in, but his heart wasn't in the job. He pulled an extra pillow against him and fell asleep with the image of Sam in his arms.

SAM WOKE UP AND LOOKED around her room confused. The last thing she remembered was driving back to Wisconsin and Brad carrying her into the house. She reached for him only to come up empty. A note on her nightstand told her to call him when she woke up. She snorted. *It's five in the morning, I'm not calling him this early.* Coffee was definitely in order.

She set the coffee to brewing and sat at the table with some paper. Her heart sank at the growing list: work needed to be contacted so she could use her family leave time, she needed to go to the bank and take out enough to cover her part of rent for the next two months. She scrubbed her eyes and poured herself a cup.

Eric stumbled out of his room and poured himself a cup. "Thought I smelled coffee." He turned her paper around to read it. "Whatcha doing?"

"Getting my head in order to make sure I get everything done."

"Did you call Brad yet?"

"It's too early." She sipped her coffee to calm her quivering stomach. She didn't want to think about what this was going to do to their fledgling relationship. "How'd you know I was supposed to call him?"

"He asked all of us to make sure you did, no matter what time you woke up." He tapped his mug against hers. "He had a feeling you would get up early and not call him. I wouldn't keep him waiting."

She waited until Eric went back into his room. She shook her head at the crazy hours he kept and refilled her mug. She carried it back to her room and looked over the note Brad left. "I figured you needed to get some rest. Ran home to do some work. Call me when you wake up."

He was too sweet. She picked up her phone and called him. She winced at how tired he sounded, but couldn't keep from smiling when he said he was showering and heading over.

Showering sounded like a wonderful idea. Feeling refreshed and awake, she printed out the paperwork she needed for work and finished writing her list. Brad let himself into her room and dropped an overnight bag by her bed. He hadn't been kidding about not leaving her side. He pulled her onto his lap and read over her list while she snuggled against him.

"Where do you want to start, kitten?" His voice rumbled under her ear.

"With work, that way I can get some boxes to pack my crap up." She sat and breathed in his scent, not wanting to move. "By the time we're done there, the bank should be open."

"Okay." He didn't move to dislodge her. Soft kisses pressed against her hair.

She shifted to capture his lips, pouring everything into the connection. They sat like that for a few minutes, both knowing they were procrastinating on starting. The longer this took, the more time she had with him. His arms tightened around her when she moved to get up. She smiled against his lips and stayed put until he loosened his grip.

She gathered up all of her paperwork and drug herself out the door. Cold wind whipped at them as they trudged into her work. He squeezed her hand while she went through all the paperwork to get family leave. He carried the load of boxes she salvaged from the warehouse to her car without a single complaint.

She ducked back into the store and grabbed a cart. She wandered blindly down the aisles, not really needing anything other than packing tape, but couldn't stop herself from stalling. Brad stayed by her side, a warm hand on her back as if he couldn't stop touching her.

Errands finally done, she dropped her bags on the floor next to the boxes. She flopped onto her bed worn out. "What's left on the list?"

"Packing." He settled next to her. "I think you're stalling on doing it because you didn't really need to walk the entire store looking for tape. Nor did you desperately need new books."

"I didn't hear you complaining about spending more time not packing." She rolled on her side to stare at him.

"I know how much you want to be with your dad." He pulled her on top of him and wrapped his strong arms around her.

BRAD HELD SAM'S SLIGHT weight against him. The whole day had been an exercise in self control to not beg her to not do this. Only her procrastination indicated her reluctance to leave him. He clung to the glimmer of hope that she would come back to him as fast as she could.

"I guess we should get started." She wrinkled her nose at the pile of boxes.

"We've delayed enough today that it can wait until morning." He couldn't loosen his arms to let her up, but she seemed content to let him hold her.

"What will we do to fill our evening if we're not packing my crap in the car?" She gave him a lazy smile.

"I want to give you your Christmas present." Worry settled on him with the thought she wouldn't like his gift.

Her eyes lit up. "That's a wonderful idea. I have yours under the tree."

She scampered off to grab it. He pulled the small box out of his bag and toyed with it. What if she didn't like it or thought it was cheesy? She reappeared with a box in her hands and shut the door before joining him on the bed.

"Here." He thrust the gift into her hands. The doubt killed him. *Might as well get it over with*. "I'm not sure if you'd like it, but it reminded me of you."

She tugged the bow off and gasped when she saw the necklace inside. She almost tackled him with her exuberant kiss. "It's wonderful. Thank you!"

His breath whooshed out of him. He had seen the golden tiger necklace in the store and knew he needed it for her. "Turn around. I'll put it on you."

She lifted her hair to reveal her soft neck. He slid his hands down the offered skin before bringing the chain around. He placed a kiss on the nape of her neck and clasped the chain over it, sealing in his kiss. He smoothed his hands along the chain.

"It suits you. Strong. Fierce. Feminine." *Mine*, his brain finished for him.

She toyed with the charm. "Thank you for it. It's beautiful." She turned in his arms to give him a lingering kiss sending his blood boiling. "It's your turn to open your present."

All he wanted was to unwrap her. She would be present enough for him. Brad looked back and forth between the present and her, curiosity over what she got him warring with his desire for her. Her nervous expression made up his mind for him and he tore into the present.

Inside the box was a photo album with a picture of her blowing a kiss on the cover. He thumbed through the book. Innocent pictures of their first tournament slowly gave way to increasingly sexier pictures of her. Most of the pictures were ones he had never seen. His girl was hot as sin in purple lace.

He looked up to find her studying him. "When did you have these taken?"

"A few days before my dad's accident. Olivia helped me put it together with other pictures she took of us."

"I can't believe you did this for me." He pulled her onto his lap and crushed her to his chest. He needed to hold her against him to keep his heart from leaping out of his chest.

She twisted in his arms so she could wrap her arms around him. She shifted against his growing erection and he groaned into her ear. "Guess that means you like it." She rolled her hips against him.

"Sweetie, don't tease." He thrust up against her, unable to stop himself. He claimed her lips.

She pulled away a few minutes later, panting. "You didn't check the bottom of the box."

"Show me." He didn't give a damn about what was in the bottom of the box. His girl was on his lap and he was going to give in to his burning desire for her. He ran his hands over her curves.

She reached into the box and pulled out the purple, barely there baby-doll dress she wore in the last couple of photos. "I wasn't sure with everything happening recently if I'd get to be there when you opened your present." She held up the scrap of see through fabric to her body. "But I do want to wear this for you at some point."

"At some point." Images of peeling the dress off her body filled his head. He took it out of her hands and set it aside. Right now, he was too damn impatient to let her put it on so he could take it off of her. "You put that on now and I swear it will get torn to shreds."

She wrapped her arms around his neck and pressed herself against him. "Then I won't put it on tonight."

He tangled his fingers in her hair and poured all of his desire into his kiss. She lit up in his arms and stoked the flames higher. Her fingers tugged at his shirt and he chuckled. His kitten could be persistent when she wanted something. He broke the kiss long enough to divest the two of them of their shirts. Her soft curves melted against him and he was in heaven.

SAM'S BRA LOOSENED and she worked to keep the smile off of her face. Brad liked his present and, by the way he was kissing and caressing her skin, he was forgetting his promise they wouldn't do anything before their date. Her body molded against his hard chest.

His lips trailed down her neck and marked a path to her breasts. She arched back in his arms, offering herself to him. A riot of sensations filled her. She clung to his strong arms and reveled in the ease with which he kept her from falling off the bed. She ground against him, cursing the clothing between them. She tore at his belt buckle and threw his belt across her room.

"Thank you, that was beginning to dig into me." Brad flipped her onto the bed and tore off the rest of her clothes. Heat spread throughout her body under his hungry stare. "My kitten."

She shuddered under the intensity of feelings those two words worked on her. It was on the tip of her tongue to tell him how much she loved him. She curved a hand against his cheek. "My Brad." Leaving the other words unsaid, she reached for the button on his jeans. "It's unfair you aren't as naked as me."

He pulled a couple condoms out of his back pocket and set them on the nightstand. Her smirk at his forethought lasted until he shed his jeans and rejoined her on the bed. She wanted him naked. She reached again for the waistband of his boxers, but he stopped her hands.

"I won't last long once I get naked. Let me make sure you are well taken care of before I join you." He plundered her mouth before starting his slow descent down her body.

His lips blazed a trail of heat down her body. Every nip and lick had liquid heat pooling between her legs. He took his time tasting every inch of her skin. She couldn't believe how lucky she had gotten to have such a thoughtful lover.

Her nerve endings zinged with anticipation as she watched him through hooded eyes. His eyes glittered with promise as he feasted on her, working her body to a fever pitch. She didn't know how much more sensation she could take and he hadn't even made it to her core yet. He paused to nip at her belly button. She giggled until his tongue dipped into the shallow indentation. A moan left her lips and her hips bucked in a plea for him to quench the fire running through her. Her hands twisted the sheets to keep from flipping him over and riding him.

Mercifully, he covered her sex with his mouth and his name fell from her lips. He smiled against her before sucking her clit into his mouth. Her world shrank to the powerful sensation of his lips on her, working her higher and higher until it shattered apart. Her breath was loud in her ears as she came aware of everything again.

"Please." She reached for him. She didn't care how needy she sounded on the heels of that orgasm.

"What do you need, sweetie?" He crawled up her body.

"You inside of me." She batted at the nightstand until she found the condoms he placed there.

He finally stripped out of his boxers while she tore open the foil packet. He rewarded her with a groan as she rolled the condom down his length. He settled between her legs and held her eyes while he shallowly thrust in. Never had she felt so connected to someone. She blinked back tears.

He stilled. "Kitten, did I hurt you?"

"No." She wiped away the moisture collecting in the corners of her eyes. She didn't know how to explain her tears. "Just a bit of emotional overload."

"Right there with you." He leaned down to sweetly kiss her.

He restarted his slow pace, his eyes never leaving hers. She tried to not read too much into his expression, there would be time to figure out everything when she came back. His hips jerked forward faster and faster, he hadn't been joking about not lasting long. She snaked a hand between their bodies to stimulate her clit so she could join him over the edge. Triumph flashed through his eyes when she came with a hoarse cry.

He buried himself deep inside her, her name tearing from his lips. He pulsed inside her, every one bringing a small aftershock through her. He kissed her reverently and rolled off the bed.

Sam rolled over to watch him walk across the room. Her eyes roamed hungrily over his broad shoulders and tapered waist. He turned to catch her staring at him. His smirk was pure male satisfaction.

"Enjoying the show?" He crawled back on the bed.

She snuggled into his shoulder. "Always." She threw a leg over him. "You have a nice butt."

"Thanks?" His chuckle reverberated under her ear. He curved a hand over hers. "I think yours is better."

"Agree to disagree."

BRAD LET THE SILENCE stretch between them, content and sated for the moment. He never had that kind of connection with anyone during sex, but he couldn't break eye contact with Sam once he was inside her. He felt raw and laid bare. If he spoke now, he wasn't sure what kind of sappiness would spew from his mouth.

She shifted to cover them with the blanket. She yawned against his chest. "I don't want to sleep."

"You sound like you need to." He brushed the hair off of her face so he could see her. "I'll be here when you wake up."

"Promise?" Her eyes found and held him.

He kissed her forehead, unable to deny her something so simple. "I promise."

"Can we do that again when I wake up?"

Yes please. "As often as you want."

She went quiet for a few moments. Her hand drew lazy lines around his muscles like she was memorizing them. He waited for her mind to sort itself out.

"I've never actually made love before."

"Honestly, kitten, neither have I."

"Really?" She propped herself up on an elbow to look at him. He shook his head and she settled back against his chest. "Well, you're really good at it."

"No, *we're* really good at it." He hugged her tight against him to stop his tongue from telling her everything he felt for her. If she didn't know by now, the words could wait until she came back to him.

They fought sleep as long as they could, whispering sweet nothings to each other. Something about the way she talked made him believe she was holding back saying her full feelings too. It gave him hope that they would be fine. He swept his hands over her skin, memorizing every inch of her. When they ran out of things to say, she crawled on top of him and they made love a second time. He drifted off with her safely tucked in his arms.

He woke to the feeling of lips pressing against his shoulder. He feigned sleep to see what Sam would do to wake him. Her lips worked their way up his neck and her slight weight straddled his body. Immediately, his cock woke up and twitched with excitement.

"Faker," she whispered in his ear. Foil tore and she unrolled a condom on him.

He smiled and still pretended to sleep. Her wet sex greedily sucked him in and Sam rode him fast. Wanting to watch her, he finally opened his eyes. Her head was thrown back and there was a franticness to her movements.

He curved his hands around her hips and thrust up against her. He could get used to waking up to this. Before too long, his balls drew up against his body. Needing to have her right there with him, he slid a hand down to rub her clit. Her body rippled around him and squeezed him like a fist. His brain went white and he held her against him until he could catch his breath.

Her lips stayed busy kissing whatever skin she could reach. He rolled them over and pulled out of her with a sigh. Cold air hit his skin and he wanted to bury himself deep in her and stay there until she forgot about leaving him. He turned to find her sitting up on the bed staring at the boxes across the room.

He sat against her pillows and pulled her into his arms. "I will take your wake up calls over an alarm any day."

"I was wondering if you were going to have me do all the hard work or if you planned on joining in." Tension ran through her body despite her teasing.

"I was curious how far you'd go to wake me up." He knew they couldn't put off packing any longer. He waved his hands around the room. "How much of this are you taking?"

"Clothes, painting stuff, a few books." She looked around the room. "And my computer and bathroom stuff."

Her painting stuff. All of the air whooshed out of him as the realization hit him she wouldn't be next to him on Thursday nights. He struggled to keep his voice neutral. "Where do you want me to start?"

"I figured you'd try to make this take longer, not jump in to get it done faster." Her arms squeezed around his.

As much as it killed him, he knew it was killing her too. "I'm not eager to let you leave." He swallowed a few times to get the glass out of his throat. "I'm trying to be supportive. If I had my way, you'd be tied to my bed and unable to leave me."

"I hate having to choose."

He tilted her face so he could look her in the eye. "I'm not going to make you choose. I know why you're going down there."

"Breakfast first. Then we can start packing." She sighed and pulled out of his arms to put on clothes.

He followed her lead and dug out clean clothes. A tray of cinnamon rolls sat outside her door with a thermos full of coffee. Silently, he thanked her friends for the gift and closed them back into the room. He sat cross legged on the floor and pulled her down next to him. He tore apart one of the rolls and held it up to her lips. She started in surprise, but opened her mouth.

As he withdrew his hand, she snagged his wrist and lapped the frosting from his fingers. He groaned, imagining her mouth wrapped around his cock. She gave him a knowing smile and reached over for the tray. They took turns silently feeding each other and sipping coffee until there was nothing left on the tray but frosting.

He pulled her shirt over her head before scooping her up and carrying her to the bed. The rest of her clothes ended up in a pile. He stroked a line down the center of her body before telling her to stay put. He returned a moment later with the plate of frosting. He scooped some up and deposited it on her nipples.

"Do you have a food fetish I should know about?" She tracked his movements.

"Nope, I just had an image of you covered in frosting stuck in my head since the day you made cookies."

He took his time cleaning the frosting off of her body. As much as he had a sweet tooth, he preferred her natural sweetness over the sticky frosting. They took their time playing around before he made love to her again. He could spend the rest of his life staring into her eyes as she came around him.

The next few days flew by with them only fully dressing to run to the bathroom or take a box to her car. They interrupted packing her room frequently with bouts of sex. Most of the time, all she wore was the necklace he gave her, even in the shower.

He loaded the last box in her car. "You're all set."

"Yeah, looks like." She buried herself in his arms.

He kissed the top of her head. "I'll be waiting for you when you come back."

"Don't make promises you don't know you can keep."

"Sam..."

She covered his lips with hers, stopping him from telling her he loved her. "I don't know when I'll be back. It could be six weeks from now. It could be six months. I don't want you to miss out on happiness if it comes your way."

He nodded although the idea of being happy with anyone but her burned like acid. "Call me when you get there so I know you're safe."

Chapter Sixteen

Brad looked at his phone for the millionth time. He didn't want to miss a single text from Sam, but his signal sucked in the basement. The computer dinged. His head whipped to see she had come online.

Ubel: How are things going with your dad?

Sam-cat: They're still not ready to release him to my care yet. They say it will be after Christmas before he can come home.

He could feel her frustration through the computer. She could've stayed another week with him instead of rushing to Missouri. He tamped down on the selfish thoughts.

U: What are you doing in the meantime?

S: Cleaning the house of a bachelor, making sure laundry is done because I don't want to know the last time he washed his sheets, spending as much time as possible at the hospital playing chess to keep my dad from climbing the walls. Tell me about your day.

He looked around the basement. Keeping busy seemed to be the theme of the day. His painting desk was already a huge mess. He needed Sam to come back and help him get everything organized again. *She'd be so pissed if she saw how fast he messed up all her hard work.*

U: Not much to tell. Chuck helped me set up a permanent computer in the basement.

S: What's wrong with your laptop and phone?

U: My phone doesn't always get signal down here and I got tired of lugging the laptop up and down the stairs, plus cleaning paint off of it was getting to be a pain. And there's this amazing girl I want to keep in contact with.

S: Aren't you worried about messing up Chuck's computer?

U: Nah, this is one of his old ones cobbled together to work.

S: What are you doing for Christmas?

He hadn't wanted to think about the holiday. He was used to spending the holiday alone, but this year felt different. A hollow pit opened in his chest.

U: Most likely painting and looking at this photo album this pretty girl gave me, why?

Basically the same thing I do everyday since she left. He had the order of the pictures pretty much memorized.

S: Olivia wanted me to invite you to the house for lunch.

He entertained the idea for a brief second and shook his head.

U: It would be weird without you.

S: Not so much. They're your friends too. I hate the idea of you not getting a home-cooked meal and working on a holiday.

It touched him how much she was already a huge part of his life down to her friends accepting him into the fold.

U: Maybe I'll make an appearance, just to make you feel better.

S: I already accepted the invitation for you. Olivia's expecting you for lunch at noon and will tell me if you back out.

U: Bossy much?

S: Just watching out for you. Gotta dash, the old man wants another book brought to him before visiting hours are over.

U: Bye, kitten. Drive safe.

S: Always. Miss you. Bye!

He leaned back in his chair. She ambushed him and he wasn't even sure he was mad about it. Her worry about him was sweet, especially with everything else she was dealing with. He shook his head and went back to the mini he had been painting before she logged on. He hoped she'd come back online before she went to bed.

"HEY, KIDDO, MERRY CHRISTMAS." Her dad set aside his book.

"Merry Christmas, Dad." Sam set down the boxes in her arms to give him a hug. "I snuck in some of the cookies Olivia and I made. I think they're on to me." She looked around the room like she expected the nurses to come in and confiscate the sweets.

"Yeah, beware of the nurses on the night shift, they're ninjas." He winked and reached for the cookies. "Are you fattening me up for the slaughter?"

"Not yet. I have to make sure it looks like an accident so I can get your insurance policy."

"Not likely, I'm cashing it in for hookers and blow. Wild party next weekend if you don't spring me before. I'm going a bit stir crazy."

"You're so weird." She tossed a pillow on the hard chair.

"Man only lives once. And remember, you got half of my genes. Open your present."

"I got the good half." She tore the paper off the gift. "These are amazing. I just ran out of minis to work on." She dug through the box to see which minis her dad got her. "How did you manage to score the variant of the leader for my army?"

"I asked Will at the Fantasy Store to pick one up for me at the last retailer convention he went to."

"You're the best dad a girl could hope for." She leaned over the bed in an awkward hug, her heart overfilled with love.

He studied her for a minute. "What'd your mother get you?"

The cursed subject every holiday. She sighed. "Money and a gift card as soon as I return the ugly ass dress she bought me. Three sizes too big this time and lime green."

"I'm sorry, sweetie."

"Don't be. It's not your fault she forgets about her first born until the last minute and doesn't take the time to find out anything about my likes. You are the far superior parent." She curled her legs under her and tried to get comfortable. "Have they told you when I can spring you from this joint?"

"Sometime this week, I hope. Otherwise, we'll go with the wild party idea to get me kicked out." He settled against his pillows. "You don't have to stay here if you'd rather go home and actually be comfortable."

"I'd rather stay with you." She shuddered at the idea of being alone in the empty house with nothing to do all day. "We haven't watched Rudolph or the Grinch together in years. I even brought a book for when you doze off on me." She dug through her purse and pulled out her phone.

"Are you going to call that boyfriend of yours?"

She sent off a text to Olivia followed by one to Brad. "We never went on our date at the Domes and we're pausing things while I'm here, so I don't know what to call him." Her heart ached and she pressed her hand to her chest. "Not that it's any of your business."

"It's very much my business if my little girl is happy. I saw the way he looked at you, he's definitely your boyfriend. And I remember you saying something about his family being crap. What's he doing for the holiday?"

"He's hanging out with Olivia and crew today." As if on cue, Olivia sent her a picture of Brad in front of her room at the house. Sam studied the picture. He looked thoughtful. "I'll call him when they kick me out today."

"You could call now."

"Hard pass, I don't need you eavesdropping on my phone calls."

"I don't drop eaves." Her dad pulled his best Samwise Gamgee impression.

"No, you just embarrass me by asking for grandchildren in front of him." She dug out the chess board. "Care for a game?"

"MERRY CHRISTMAS! I'M so glad you made it." Olivia barely had the door open before she pulled Brad into a hug.

"A little birdie told me I really didn't have a choice."

"You're right." Her phone chimed. "And right on cue, that's Sam checking in to see if you came."

His phone vibrated and he looked down at the smiley face Sam sent him. He shook his head and followed Olivia into the living room. He ran the tips of his fingers over the door to Sam's room, her absence kicking him in the teeth. *I shouldn't have come.* He looked up to see Olivia giving him a half smile.

"You can go in there if you want to."

"What good is the empty room?" He shrugged and forced himself away from the door. She wasn't on the other side. "Is there anything I can do to help?"

Olivia handed him a stack of plates. "You can help Andrew set the table."

He tried to numb the hole inside him with the simple domestic task and happy chatter filling the house. It had been years since he'd had a home cooked meal during the holidays. Most of the time, he snagged Chinese take out or left over pizza. Olivia put together an amazing meal. Gratitude filled him for being allowed to join.

He groaned when she passed around another bowl of food. Everyone seemed to be on the same page and skipped on the extra helping. He helped clear the table and fill the dishwasher until he was shooed out of the kitchen. Everyone collapsed in the living room.

He looked around for his jacket, unsure where it went off to. "Thank you for inviting me. I should head out before I crash."

"You haven't eaten dessert yet, you can't leave."

"Looks like there's no room for any other food coma victims." He looked around at the bodies littering the furniture.

"Sam's room's open. You can take a nap there." Olivia curled up on Luke's lap.

Brad ducked into Sam's room before anyone could see his hesitation. This was the last place he should be. He leaned heavily against the door and took a deep breath. *Big mistake.* Her scent assaulted his senses. If he closed his eyes, he could almost feel her just out of reach. His hand grabbed at the empty air in front of him.

She's not here. There's no magic in this empty room to bring her back to him. The thought cut through him. His knees buckled and he slumped onto the bed. *This is the stupidest thing I've ever done.*

He pulled one of her pillows against him to keep the ache in his chest. He would lie here long enough for her friends to fall asleep before making his break for it. He snorted. Sam had him wrapped around her finger so hard he wanted her friends to like him. He held the pillow to his nose and filled his head with her scent and images of her.

He jerked awake and looked around the dark room in confusion. It took him a minute to remember where he was. He pulled his phone out of his pocket. Missed call and a couple texts from Sam. He opened the texts and smiled at the selfie she sent of her and her dad.

Sam: Did you die? Olivia said you were napping in my room. Or are you creeping through my stuff?

He turned on her bedside lamps and plumped up her pillows to send a selfie of himself in her bed. His phone rang. "Your bed is really comfortable, even if it's a bit cold without you in it."

"Merry Christmas to you too." Her gentle chuckle filled his ear. "How was lunch?"

"Fattening." He exaggerated a groan to make her laugh. He could listen to that sound all day. "How was yours?"

"Dry hospital turkey, soggy green beans, but I give them props on their rolls and apple pie. Plus I snuck in cookies and pumpkin bars. Speaking of, have you had dessert yet?"

"There's more food?" His stomach rebelled at the thought of eating more. "I barely made it out of lunch intact. You'll have to roll me out of here if I eat anymore."

"Maybe that's my sinister plan, keep you too well fed so you can't run away."

Like she'd need to do that. He had no plans on going anywhere. He could hear her opening and shutting doors. "What are you doing?"

"Foraging for real food. I've been so busy cleaning and being at the hospital that I forgot to buy groceries. Frozen pizza it is."

"It doesn't sound like you're taking good care of my kitten."

SAM'S FACE HEATED UP. *His.* She would never get sick of the way Brad said that. "I had real food at the hospital, if that's what you call it. I'll go grocery shopping tomorrow after the store opens." She decided to bait him. "Or I could just eat cookies and pumpkin bars for dinner."

He rewarded her with a growl. "Please don't joke about that. I can't miss you and worry you're not taking care of yourself at the same time."

"All right there, caveman, you can calm down." She hopped up on the counter while she waited for the oven to preheat. "I'm making pizza to go along with dessert."

"That's not real food."

"Says the man who lived on coffee and pizza and junk food while on a crazy painting schedule."

"He also had an amazing harem girl who brought him real food and fed it to him." His voice deepened.

She shivered and suppressed the images of her actually playing the part of his harem girl. "Will it appease you if I promise to go grocery shopping and buy real food tomorrow? I'd do it now, but everything's closed."

"I guess it will have to, but I don't want to hear about you eating trash again."

"I swear the old man subsists on frozen pizzas and take out. I did have some fruit and frozen veggies I picked up, but I must've eaten it all already."

Brad kept her company while she waited for her pizza to cook. She took the chance to say hi to everyone at the house before letting him hang up. A smile ghosted across her lips. At least he wasn't as alone on Christmas as she was. She shook her head. It didn't help to dwell on it.

Her stomach rumbled. She hadn't lied about eating lunch, but they didn't give her enough to fill her up. She took a bite of her pizza and immediately regretted it. She chugged a glass of water to cool her burning tongue. *Smooth move, Samantha. Guess it's a good thing you don't have anyone to kiss right now.* She blew on her slice and took a cautious bite.

Cleaning up her dinner, she debated eating dessert right away. Most of the house had been cleaned within an inch of its life, with the exception of the kitchen. She had been dreading this room. She peeked inside the refrigerator, gagged, and slammed the door shut. *What a toxic wasteland.* Dessert would be her treat for cleaning. She'd hate to toss her cookies. Chuckling at her stupid pun, she grabbed a couple garbage bags and reopened the fridge.

Chapter Seventeen

"You're looking green around the gills, kiddo."

Sam swallowed down the bile creeping up her throat. "I'm fine."

She turned her attention back to what the doctor was saying about wound care, grateful her dad interrupted long enough to get her gag reflex back under control. She nodded in all the right places and asked just enough questions to make it seem like she knew what she was doing. Finally after an eternity, they finished the paperwork and she wheeled her dad out to the car. She left the motor running while she picked up his medication only to come back to him asleep in the passenger's seat.

Four stairs. She stared at the familiar sight of the front door. How had she forgotten there were four stairs leading up to the house? She shoveled them and made sure they were salted before leaving that morning. She nudged her dad awake.

He blinked at the house. "I forgot about the stairs."

"You weren't the only one." She helped him out of the car, his weight staggering her. "It's a good thing you didn't eat all those cookies."

"This is ridiculous, Samantha."

She shifted her arm around his waist for more leverage. "What's ridiculous?"

"You shouldn't have to carry me up the stairs."

"You used to carry me all the time." She grunted sweat pouring down her back despite the frigid air. They kept up a slow and steady pace up each stair. "Besides, it's not like I'm doing all of the work. Even though I'm glad you didn't get the split level we had looked at."

"Right now, so am I." He unlocked the door and used the knob for extra support up the last stair.

The squeeze in the front door made the step up interesting, but they did it in one try. "Okay, old man. Do you want to rest in your recliner or your bed?"

"Bed, if we can make it."

She nodded and grit her teeth. Of course he'd want the furthest option. They maneuvered down the hallway and into his room. After rearranging some pillows under his leg to elevate it, she went back out to the car to grab the rest of his stuff. Medication given, she set up his night stand with drinks, books, and his remote for the TV. The last thing she brought in was his walker, but she set that out of his reach so he wouldn't be tempted to get up without help.

Wandering back down the hall, she straightened out all the pictures they brushed against in their foray to his room. She took her time showering before peeking into her dad's room. Finding him asleep, she sat at her desk and turned on her computer. She barely logged in when Brad messaged her.

Ubel: How's your father doing?

She smiled at how sweet he was asking about her dad. She had spent the last week debating asking Brad to come down to stay with her, but stopped herself due to how much work it would be to relocate his business for such a short period of time.

Sam-cat: Resting. We had an interesting time navigating the few stairs to the house. He's worn out, plus his meds knock him out.

U: That sucks.

S: Not totally. His body needs rest. One minute.

She glanced at her phone before heading to her dad's room.

BRAD DRUMMED HIS FINGERS on his desk. He waited all day to talk to Sam and hated the interruption to his time. Guilt gnawed at him about how selfish he was when she had other demands on her time.

Sam-cat: That was awkward as hell.

Ubel: What?

S: Standing outside the bathroom while your father pees.

U: Why the hell would you do that?

S: He's not steady enough on his own to use the walker without supervision, so I have to help him out of bed and to the bathroom. And then back to bed afterward.

I am such a dick. All he could think about was how long he waited to talk to her and he forgot she was doing all of this hard work by herself. He wondered how she would feel if he came down to stay with her. It wasn't like he had to be in Wisconsin to work.

U: Awkward award of the day goes to you.

S: On the plus side, he can still mostly dress himself.

U: I don't think I want to know.

S: Best not to ask.

U: How are you holding up?

S: Fine, I learned about wound care today. Barf. Luckily the visiting nurse will get to do most of that gross job. Mostly missing you.

U: I miss you too, kitten.

He rubbed a hand over his heart. They chatted about whatever they could think of. He took a page out of her book and looked up questions to get to know a person better. She sent him a picture of her new painting set up in her room so he sent one back of how bad his desk had gotten in her absence.

S: I just got that disaster area cleaned up, damn it.

U: And you can clean it back up when you come home. ;)

S: I really do think you keep me around to be your harem girl.

U: Thought I kept you around because you're awesome, but I'm sure I can find a Slave Leia costume for you. You shall be the first of my harem.

S: I had better be the only one of your harem, mister. I hadn't realized you had a costume fetish.

U: I have a "get Sam into anything remotely sexy" fetish.

S: I'll keep that in mind.

U: I don't think I'll get anything else done today now that I have that image in my head.

S: That's not good for business. I'll paint with you to get your mind in the right mode to not kill your business.

He wished he could kiss her. She knew exactly what he needed to do and made it sound fun. They spent the next couple of hours sending pictures of their work back and forth.

He fell into the pattern easily. He woke up and logged into chat or text her good morning from his bed. She usually sent him a selfie from wherever she was at that moment. She bounced in and out of chat as her father's needs demanded. Knowing she could come online at any moment kept him glued to his desk, so he finished more work than ever. The week flew by without him noticing.

"You've been moping ever since Sam left." Steve threw a shirt at him. "Get dressed. We're going to game."

"Why do you care what I do?" Brad sniffed his current shirt and winced before pulling the clean one on.

"I don't. I just don't want Sam to find out how whipped she has you."

Honestly, he didn't care if she found out how much he missed her, but he didn't want her to think he was pathetic and couldn't live without her. He hadn't been back to the store to play since she left. He grabbed his stuff and allowed himself to be herded to the store. He set his stuff down at their table with a thump. It just didn't feel the same without her sunny presence. His eyes drifted from her empty chair around the room and settled on a new girl. He had to do a double take, her brown hair and bounce to her step reminded him very much of Sam.

"Who's the newbie?"

"She hangs out with one of Sam's friends. I didn't catch her name."

He stared at Steve like he had lost his mind. "That's unusual for you."

"She didn't seem interested in me." Steve shrugged and set up his army. "And she's very much not my type."

The girl in question stopped at their table. "Do you mind if I watch?"

"Not at all. I'm Brad." He offered his hand.

"Brad... Oh, yeah, Julie and Sam mentioned you. I'm Hannah."

Something about Hannah's name tickled the back of his brain, but he shrugged it off, Sam must have mentioned her. He gestured at the table. "Do you play?"

"Not yet. I'm just learning."

"What are you thinking about playing?"

"I like the leaders of Factionless."

"That's what Sam plays. She says they have style."

"I'd hate to duplicate her army." Hannah chewed her lip.

"There's plenty of choices that would keep you from even having any of the same minis."

"You seem to know a lot about them."

"I've spent hours debating army composition. I've learned a thing or two from her."

"With her gone, it would be nice to have someone walk me through the differences in leaders before I dive in." She stared up with pleading eyes.

While they didn't draw him in the way Sam's did, he couldn't help but notice flecks of green in her blue eyes. He shrugged. "If you have any questions, I'd be happy to help."

It would be nice to have the diversion of helping a new player. He walked her through the steps of the game while Steve trounced him. At the end of the night, Hannah left with the promise of coming back the next week so he could help her pick a leader. He went home and turned on his computer.

SAM DRUMMED HER FINGERS on her desk. Brad wasn't online like he usually was. She fiddled with her phone before setting it back down. If he was in the middle of something, she didn't want to interrupt him. She curled up on her bed with a book and tried to concentrate on the words until a ding brought her attention back to her computer.

Ubel: There's the girl with eyes like the sky.

Sam-cat: And there's the guy who's so full of shit his eyes are brown.

His cheesiness brought a much needed smile to her face. It had been a day from hell.

U: Ouch, is that anyway to talk to me?

S: Sorry. It's been a bad day. I didn't mean to take it out on you.

U: What happened?

S: We had a fun trip to the ER today. Dad's leg got infected. They cleaned it out and, from the yelling I heard, it hurt like a bitch. He's on a fun run of antibiotics to go with his other pills. Captain Crankypants is sleeping it off.

U: I'm sorry sweetie. Now I feel bad I had an okay day.

S: Don't be. I'm glad one of us had a good day. Tell me about it.

She tucked her legs under her and settled in. This was what she had been looking forward to. She held onto the normalcy of their daily talks and used it to stave off the loneliness of being by herself.

U: Steve pulled me to the Game Hut to play tonight. I met one of your friends.

S: Who?

U: Hannah. She seems nice.

Her heart stopped. Anyone but Hannah. The last thing she needed was that snake striking when she was four hundred miles away. Dots swam in her vision as she forced herself to breathe.

S: We're not friends.

U: Any reason why?

S: She's not nice. She stole both Andrew and Aaron from me and hates me for some unknown reason.

U: You did say your group is known for its hook ups and break ups.

S: She's not part of my group. She hangs on the fringes because she's Julie's roommate.

U: I'll concede the point.

S: Ask Andrew and Luke about her. They'll fill you in on her standard operating procedure.

U: Next time I see them, I will. I didn't mean to upset you.

S: It's fine. Did you play or paint tonight?

U: Played Steve. He stomped me into the ground.

She breathed a sigh of relief. Luke and Andrew would tell him all about Hannah's tricks. It didn't help the nagging feeling in the back of her mind. She should be there, staking her claim on Brad, but he was not a prize to be won.

Chapter Eighteen

"You are too fidgety for your own good, kiddo."

"Sorry, dad." Sam paused with the duster on the ceiling fan. Nervous cleaning made her feel better, not that the house needed it yet. She couldn't get the image of Hannah at the Game Hut out of her mind.

"We need to get out of the house, unless you want to tell me what's eating you."

"Why would you think something's bugging me?"

"You only clean that hardcore when you have something on your mind. Especially when the house is spotless already. Spill it." He crossed his arms across his chest.

She debated for a second about telling him her worries. "Where to, old man?"

He shook his head. "To the Fantasy Store to get me new reading material."

"Because there wasn't a box full of books that got delivered yesterday?"

"Those were novels, I need comics as well."

"Sounds like an adventure."

"You'll love it."

"I'm sure I will." She shifted his walker in front of his chair and helped him up. Everyday he got steadier on his foot. "Maybe afterward we can try something crazy and go grocery shopping."

"I don't think I should have my leg down that long."

"I'm not doing pizza again." She was sick of delivery and there wasn't much left from her last shopping trip.

"Chinese?" He looped his arm around her shoulders so they could navigate the front steps.

At least she could get vegetables with her meal. "Fine, but when the nurse is here tomorrow, I'm going grocery shopping. We're out of real food."

She folded his walker into the car. The drive to the game store was relatively quick and she found a close parking space. She followed her dad into the brightly lit store.

"Lewis, we had heard about your accident." A gentleman walked out from behind the counter, a huge smile on his bespectacled face. His short black hair was messy.

Her dad clasped his hand. "Yup, got taken out by a forklift. Will, this is my daughter, Samantha."

"Nice to meet you." Will reached out his hand for her to shake.

"Go look around, kiddo."

"I'll take care of your dad." Will grabbed a folding chair and set it down in front of the racks of comics.

She wandered around the store, marveling at how clean and organized it was. Comics and graphic novels dominated a third of the store, while another third was dedicated to games of all sorts, and the back housed tables and a board game library. She picked up a couple of new minis for her army and some paints. She added them to her dad's huge stack of comics.

"Are you buying out the store, old man?"

"Just making sure I have enough reading material to last a week or so."

She eyeballed the stack. "I think that'll do it, if you aren't going to subject me to any more westerns so you can read."

Will laughed. "She really is your kid, right down to the personality."

"Yeah, I lucked out in the kid department." Her dad grunted as she hefted him out of the chair.

"Not everyone would drop everything to take care of their father. World could use a few more people like that."

Sam ducked her head and grabbed their bags from the counter. Will held the door for them and waved as they settled in for the drive. She swung into the Chinese restaurant to grab dinner, Will's remark still rattling in her head. Was it so unusual for a kid to want to take care of their ailing parent? It didn't feel like a hardship, other than being so far from Brad and her friends.

Ubel: I was wondering if you were going to come on today.

Sam-cat: Just getting the kitchen cleaned up after dinner.

U: What did you do today?

S: Went to a comic and game store.

U: Are you cheating on the Game Hut?

She squirmed in her chair.

S: Sort of. My dad needed to pick up his monthly comics. I picked up a couple of minis and some paints.

U: Did you finish the ones you brought with you already?

S: Almost. I think some of them need a detail or two before I'm happy with them, but I have a lot of time on my hands these days.

U: How's your father doing?

S: Steady. He's getting better with his walker, although getting him standing still takes the both of us. Still bitching about doing his therapy. Nurse will be here tomorrow so I can get grocery shopping done. And then we get to go to his work the day after to do paperwork.

"HELLO AGAIN, BRAD."

Brad looked up from the mini he was painting. "Hi, Hannah."

She sat next to him and leaned over for a closer look. "You are an amazing painter. How do you get so much detail in something so small?"

"Years of practice and a good paintbrush." He tried to ignore the scent of her perfume, it smelled almost like the stuff Sam wore. His heart squeezed painfully.

"Do you teach?"

"Occasionally."

"Will you teach me?"

He edged away to give himself space to breathe. Now he understood why Sam was uncomfortable the first time he met her, if this was how overbearing he was. "I have a huge backlog of work I need to do."

"No, I get it. You do this professionally and I'd get in the way." Her head hung down and she stood to walk away.

He kicked himself for being so abrupt. Hannah at least deserved to know why. "It's not that, I can paint and talk at the same time. It's just, I'm trying to get as much done so I can visit Sam and I know you two don't get along."

"We used to be good friends."

"She said you were never friends. You're just Julie's roommate."

"Now, I'm just Julie's roommate. When we started college, the three of us hung out all the time. Four, if you count Olivia when she joined the group." She stared at her hands. "And then Andrew grew interested in me and dumped her. I feel really bad about how everything happened. I understand why she doesn't like me, and would hate to come between the two of you, so I'll leave you alone." She stood to leave.

He placed a hand on her arm. "I promised to help you pick out a leader for your army."

"You'd still help me even though I'm sure she warned you away from me?"

"I won't back down from my promises. Who were you looking at as potential leaders?"

"I like the looks of Shane, Fiona, and Ashley."

"Sam plays Ashley. She's a good leader."

"I'd rather not copy Sam's army. I want something that is mine."

He had to admire her conviction. He could see why the two girls had been friends. Their personalities matched. "Fiona's a solid choice, lots of spell power to play with, has a good variety of spells, and the mini is killer."

"Sounds perfect, thanks. I'll be back down in a minute." She patted his arm in passing.

He set to work on his latest commission and soon was absorbed in the work. He turned to say something to Sam only to realize a second too late Hannah sat next to him. *Maybe I can help them become friends again.* With that thought in mind, he helped Hannah put together her mini and discussed what other models might go good with her leader. It felt a bit like when Sam first joined the group. Heart aching and missing her more than ever, he cleaned up his mess and headed home to talk to his girl.

Sam-cat: How was your Thursday night?

Ubel: Slow without you.

S: Who'd you play against?

U: I didn't. I painted. Steve is making it a point for me to leave the house and socialize.

He stared at the screen, guilt at not telling Sam about hanging out with Hannah gnawing at him. *It would only upset her needlessly.* He'd get Hannah's side of the story and then slowly work at mending the rift. Sam was the one who had her heart broken and needed time.

S: Sounds like we had the same Thursday night then, minus the socialization. I finished one of my machines tonight.

U: Show me.

He hated not seeing her mini in person and could almost hear the pride in her words. His email dinged. He smiled at the picture of her mini posed with the purple doll. She even sent a couple from different angles without him asking.

U: That looks awesome. I like all the detail work on it, especially how it looks like it's slogging through the mud. I can't wait to see it in person. Even though the giant doll in the background looks like she wants to eat it.

S: Shy would never eat my minis. That's just mean.

U: Don't pout, sweetie. I think you should use her in all your mini pictures.

"WHY DON'T YOU COME up to the office?"

Sam eyeballed her father's boss. Something pricked the back of her brain. The guy was covering up something. She made a big show of looking up the staircase. "I think that's awfully far up for us to go."

"I think my daughter's right. My leg can't make that climb." Her dad pointed to a seating area by the vending machines.

His boss reluctantly led the way over to the tables. Sam fiddled with her phone while her dad discussed the use of his sick time and what was needed for workman's comp. Forklifts zoomed around the warehouse at speeds faster than she thought they should and people jumped out of the way. She flipped over to her camera and took a couple of pictures and video of the action.

The boss caught on to her interest in the forklift drivers and reached for her phone. "You aren't allowed to take pictures here."

"No signs posted against it." She held her phone out of reach. "But I guess you want to protect the drivers because it would be a shame if OSHA came in here and found none of your employees are driving safely, seeing as people are jumping out of the way and no one is using their horns." She gave him a sly look. "I'd bet my left leg one of them is the same guy who ran over my dad. Did he even retake his certification? How do you expect not to have a similar or worse accident happen?"

Her dad's head snapped up from his paperwork and took in the building around them while his boss stuttered over his words. "You know, she has a point. I love working here, so I was willing to overlook the unsafe conditions, but not anymore. I want to be around to give my little girl away at her wedding and play with my grandkids. You will be hearing from my lawyer."

She helped her dad back up and across the warehouse. She kept an eye out for any forklift drivers coming their way, but they made it out the doors safely. She helped her dad into the car and settled behind the steering wheel.

"I'm guessing the next stop is your lawyer's?"

He already had his phone out and paused his conversation to give her directions. They sat in the office and she handed over her phone so the lawyer could download the footage she shot. Her dad confirmed one of the drivers on camera was the one that hit him. The lawyer promised to be in contact as soon as he heard from OSHA.

The drive back to the house was quiet. Sam chewed over what she saw at her dad's work. If that was what he worked with on a daily basis, she really was lucky he was alive. They navigated back into the house and she tried to make him comfortable after having his leg down for most of the day.

BRAD'S COMPUTER DINGED and he quickly set aside the mini he was working on and cleaned off his hands. Sam had been gone most of the day and he had been impatiently waiting for her to come back to talk. *I'm so whipped.*

Ubel: How'd today go?

Sam-cat: I got a video of how unsafe my dad's work is. We went to his lawyer with the footage and he's getting in touch with OSHA. My dad's livid.

She certainly had been busy today. He shook his head at how tough and brave she had become. Pride welled up in his chest.

U: That's amazing for a day's work. How's your father doing?

S: Shaky, we pushed it too far today and his leg is really swollen. He had a dinner of pills and is sleeping it off in bed.

U: What's next in the great adventures of Samantha Duke?

S: Making real food for myself, doing a load of laundry, and missing you.

U: Sounds exciting. My bed's too big and cold without you in Wisconsin.

He mentally kicked himself for almost letting it slip that he didn't sleep much with her so far away. All he did was paint and message her. Hell, he left his laptop open when he went to bed. He missed her warmth and smile.

S: I've never been in your bed.

U: We need to rectify that.

S: As soon as we can. Even my tiny bed feels too big and cold without you hogging all the space.

U: Did you just call me a bed hog?

S: Only a little. I actually like you hogging the bed. Gives me an excuse to snuggle against you.

Her phantom weight leaned against him. He needed her curled up on him. He stared into space long after she logged off and thought about every moment he touched her, ever since he grabbed her hand at the tournament. Maybe he could get some sleep tonight.

Chapter Nineteen

B rad fumbled for his phone as it vibrated on the table next to him. "Hey Sam, is everything alright?"

"Sorry, I know it's Thursday. I just needed to hear your voice. It's been a day." Defeat stamped every word.

He gestured that he was stepping out. "I'm always here if you need to talk. What happened?"

"Dad decided he was sick of relying on me and tried to get out of bed by himself. The walker slipped out of his grip and he fell." She choked a small sob.

The need to hold her crushed him. *I could be there in seven hours.* "I'm sorry. Did he get hurt or angry?"

"Angry."

"Did he yell at you?"

"A bit." Her tone said it was more than a bit. "I found him like that. He had fallen too far away to reach his phone or walker, so he had been there for half an hour. If I hadn't thought to check on him..."

He hated the way she berated herself for things outside her control. "But you did."

"I guess."

"Kitten, don't beat yourself up over your father's fall. You had no way of knowing he would try to get up without you."

He sat on the stairway and listened to the worry and frustration leak out of her voice while she poured her heart out. This had been his worry, she took on this task and expected herself to be the perfect nurse with no training. His strong girl. When she asked about his day, he had a momentary twinge of guilt at not telling her he was teaching Hannah to paint. He shrugged it off and told himself she didn't need to worry about it on top of the rest of her burdens.

Hannah had told him her side of things. He found it unfair she took all the blame when it sounded like Andrew should be sharing it. Brad reminded himself he still needed to talk to Sam's ex about it, but hadn't found time to stop by the house. He had been swamped with last minute orders for an upcoming tournament.

"I'm sorry I interrupted your night with my rambling."

"Don't be. I miss talking to you. Hang on, it looks like the guys want me to put you on speakerphone." He nodded at the group crowded around him.

"Hey, Sammy-Sam, we miss your face around here," Steve shouted over the chorus of hellos.

"It's hard to miss yours. It's so ugly." Her sweet laugh came through the speaker.

"That just wounds me." Steve grinned.

SAM CURLED UP ON HER bed. Some of the tight knot in her chest unraveled by talking to everyone. She couldn't shake the feeling something was up with Brad, but someone would've said something to her if it was bad. *Maybe he's coming to visit and wants to surprise me.* The thought cheered her up a bit. He shooed everyone away and turned off the speakerphone.

"Are you feeling better, kitten?"

"Tons, thank you. I guess I hadn't noticed how alone I was until tonight." She shared a sigh with him. "Nothing to do for it though. Got to get the old man on his feet again."

"I hate not being there for you."

"But you are." She shook her head. He obviously underestimated how much it helped to have someone to talk to.

"I mean to pull you onto my lap and hold you when you need it." *I hate it too.* "Soon."

"How soon?" His frustration leaked over the line.

"Couple of weeks at the earliest, depends on what his mobility is after he's cleared to put weight on his leg." She struggled to keep hope in her voice.

"When's the latest?"

"Beginning of March if things aren't healing fast enough. We'll know more at his next appointment."

"I'm crossing my fingers for speedy healing. I miss my kitten."

"I miss you too." Her phone beeped. "I have to go, Dad needs something."

"Good night. I'll talk to you when I get home."

"Night."

BRAD RELUCTANTLY HUNG up the phone. He thumbed through the pictures of Sam on his phone as the reality of how much longer she was going to be gone crashed down on him. Another month or more of waiting around and feeling useless. He wandered back into the game room.

"That's not the face of someone who just talked to his girlfriend."

He didn't bother correcting Hannah about the status of his and Sam's relationship. "It's just taking her father longer to heal than planned."

"You miss her." She placed a comforting hand on his shoulder. "If you need someone to talk to, I'm here."

He absentmindedly patted her hand. "She'll be home soon enough. I think I'm going to pack it in and head home. I finished everything I had with me."

"Are you going to the tournament in a few weeks?"

"Of course. I have some work I need to turn in to my clients."

"It's my first tournament." She bounced around.

He chuckled. Her excitement was infectious. "Good luck to you."

She hugged him. "Thank you for all your help getting my army put together. I just wish there was more time to get it all painted."

"You're further along than most of the players. I'll see you next week."

SAM-CAT: YOU AROUND?

Sam flopped down in front of her computer. Dread gnawed at her at the coming conversation.

Ubel: For you, always.

S: Do you want the bad news or worse news first?

U: Neither, but if it's bad news...

Her phone rang next to her. She couldn't help but smile as she moved to the bed to be more comfortable. "Hi."

"I figured bad news deserves to be talked about over the phone." His voice rumbled in her ear.

"Bad news is I quit my job. The worst news is I'm stuck in Missouri until my dad's case goes to court." She choked and covered her face.

This was not how today was supposed to go. They were supposed to go to the doctor and be told her dad could put weight on his ankle. A few days of making sure he was good at getting around on his own and she'd be back on the road to Wisconsin and Brad. As much as she put on a brave face, she needed to be held by him something fierce.

"Start from the beginning." It sounded like he sat down hard.

"Work called and wanted me back ASAP and I can't go back because I'm still taking care of dad. So I quit. It's not like I really need the money right now."

"I get that. You're super smart and can get a job when you get back."

"That's what I was thinking." She gulped in lungfuls of air.

"I thought your father was getting better."

"Remember how he decided to get out of bed without any help? Yeah, he fucked up his ankle and it set back the healing process."

"Shit."

She wholeheartedly agreed with his curse. "And then the lawyer called. Dad's suing his company for negligence and I'm subpoenaed because I witnessed and took video of the forklift drivers along with the company's owner seeing them and doing nothing."

"When's the court date?"

"Not until May." Hopelessness pressed her into a small ball.

He cursed solidly. "What are you going to do until then?"

"Take my dad to physical therapy, paint, read, watch terrible westerns until my eyes bleed." Tears slid down her cheeks. "Basically the same shit I've been doing for the last month plus."

"No chance for you to visit while you wait for the court date?"

"Not unless dad gets better in a hurry. What about you visiting here?"

"Business took off and I'm backlogged with minis."

"That's amazing."

She was excited his business had taken off, even if it meant he couldn't come see her anytime soon. *I could be there if I had put Dad in a home like the doctor told me to.* She brutally squashed the thought. Even knowing how long she'd be gone, she wouldn't have done anything different except maybe ask Brad to join her in Missouri.

"It's great for business, not so great for having time with you."

"Still, it's better news than what I gave you. Sorry I don't get to go to the Valentine's Massacre with you."

"I hadn't thought about you not making the tournament. Fuck."

"Nothing for it. Have fun for the both of us. We'll go next year together."

SAM: GOOD LUCK TODAY.

Brad: It won't be the same without you here to be my good luck charm.

S: Win big and we'll celebrate when I get home. Slave Leia costume and all.

Brad stared at the kissy face she sent. He dropped his head against the steering wheel. *Not the same without her, that was the understatement of the year.* He briefly debated just going in and dealing with his business before bailing on the tournament. He snorted, Steve would put him through the ringer if he tried and then tell Sam.

He plunked down his bags and got to work, collecting payments and returning minis. Absorbed in his work, he barely got his entry in before the start of the tournament. He kept turning around, expecting to see Sam peeking over his shoulder. When he thought he saw her out of the corner of his eye, it was just Hannah. The hole in his chest gaped wide. Having her here made missing Sam worse, they were so similar. Despite his distraction, he did manage a respectable sixth place and best painted army.

Sam sent her congratulations when he sent her a picture of his award. He took his time getting back to the house, knowing the party would be in full swing. In no mood to socialize, he snagged a bottle of Long Island Iced Tea from the fridge and retreated to the basement. Getting blazingly drunk sounded like the best way to numb out the pain.

The bottle was halfway empty when light footsteps sounded on the stairs. Hannah poked her head around the corner. "I thought I saw you come down here." She nodded at the bottle in his hand. "Bad day?"

His head lulled against the back of the couch, too heavy to lift. "I've had a lot of those lately."

"Want to talk about it?" She pulled the bottle from his numbed fingers and took a swig.

"Not really, I'm not fit for the company right now." He took the bottle back and closed his eyes, hoping she got the message.

Her footsteps retreated to the stairs. After a few more pulls from the bottle, he set it down so he wouldn't drop it. *Perhaps getting shitfaced wasn't the best idea.* He lost track of time.

The couch dipped next to him and he leaned with it. Sam's perfume wafted over him. *When did she show up?* His brain scrambled to remember if she said she was coming to visit. He vaguely remembered her saying something about celebrating his win with him.

"Sam?"

She didn't say a word, just layered her lips over his. He couldn't open his eyes, they were lead weights. He let the gentle touch of her hands calm his racing mind. He tangled his fingers in her soft hair and deepened the kiss. He couldn't believe she finally came home to him.

Chapter Twenty

Sam stared at the email in disbelief. *No fucking way.* She warned Brad, but the picture Hannah sent curled against his bare chest proved he didn't listen. Numbly, she stared at the details of the picture, the tiny kernel of hope slowly dying as she recognized the couch in the basement of his house. That was definitely a naked Hannah laying on the couch with a partially naked Brad.

Her phone buzzed for the fourth time in the span of a few minutes. Brad's face lit up her screen and she sent it to voicemail. Her computer dinged, reminding her she hadn't logged out of the forums. He didn't seem to get the hint she didn't want to talk to him.

Ubel: Why aren't you answering your phone?

She closed her eyes. Angry tears leaked out the corners and she did nothing to stop them. *Anger was good.* It beat dealing with her heart breaking. Her fingers pounded the keyboard.

Sam-cat: Maybe because I'm busy with my dad. Maybe because I heard a nasty rumor and decided I had enough bad news to last a lifetime.

U: Was the rumor about me?

S: Wow, he got it on the first try. Is it true?

Her phone buzzed across her desk. She declined the call and tossed the damned thing onto her bed. There was no way she could hold onto her anger if she heard his voice.

U: Answer your phone. I want to hear your voice.

S: NO.

S: Is. It. True?

U: Kitten...

195

S: By avoiding the question, you are actually answering it. I think I deserve to hear it from you.

She dashed away the angry tears. The last thing she needed right now was to deal with that snake taking another guy from her. *Please say it isn't true.*

U: If the rumor is about me sleeping with Hannah, then it's true. I think.

Just like that, her world crashed down around her. Choking back her sobs, she grabbed onto the last remnants of her rage.

S: That's all you had to say.

U: I can explain.

S: You don't have to. And frankly, I don't want to hear about it right now. I need to go take care of my dad. Despite our best efforts, his physical therapy isn't going as fast as we want.

She logged off before he could respond to her. She didn't even feel bad about lying to him about her dad's progress. Her hands shook and she gave into a good cry-fest. Empty and hollow, she ducked into the bathroom to wash her face before heading into the living room.

She watched her dad flip through the western selection of his movies. "You won't find anything new in there."

"You've been crying." He turned his head.

She offered him the brightest smile she could muster. "Just the thought of another western movie marathon brings me to tears."

"You always were a terrible liar." He patted the seat next to him. "How about telling the old man what's going on?"

"It's nothing." She slumped onto the couch next to him.

"Boy trouble?"

"In a manner of speaking."

"What did Brad do?"

"He's dating someone else. Someone I warned him away from." She leaned her head on his shoulder, the wind out of her sails. "And it's my own fault for telling him he didn't have to wait for me."

"I'm so sorry, kiddo. If it wasn't for me getting hurt, you wouldn't be down here."

"There's nothing for you to be sorry about. Family comes first." She wrapped her pinky around his. "You and me forever, old man."

"So now would be a terrible time to tell you that you are starting to get underfoot?"

"The worst."

"You need to get out of the house." He held up a hand before she could protest. "Before you argue, I can take care of myself for the most part. I can get up on my own and around the house without your help anymore."

She hadn't failed to notice how he relied on her less and less. All she really did was drive him to appointments, grocery shop, and clean the house. "Are you kicking me out? Because that would be the epitome of bad timing."

"No, I like having you around. I've missed my chess partner." He paused and averted his eyes. "I was just thinking maybe you could get a job to keep you from going stir crazy. The Fantasy Store is hiring and Will would work your schedule around my appointments."

She gawked at her dad. *Tricky old man.* "How long have you been planning this?"

"Will mentioned it the last time we were in. I told him you probably weren't hanging around after I heal, but on the off chance you wanted to move down here, I thought getting you an application was a good idea."

"Thanks." Her phone buzzed with a call from Julie. "I should probably take this"

BRAD SET HIS ARMY BAG on the table next to Luke's. "How's it going?"

"Fine." Luke bit off the word.

"Just so you know, it looks like I should have a few more openings in my work schedule coming up, if you have anything you want to add to the docket."

"After you finish up my last order, I don't think I'll have anything else for you to paint." Luke picked up his bag and walked to the other side of the room. The bag full of unpainted metal told another story.

"What was that all about?" Steve took the vacated chair.

"Not really sure, but, whatever it is, it looks like I lost a client."

"Did you screw up any of his minis?"

"Not that I know of. He's always seemed happy with my work."

"Maybe he's having financial problems. I'm sure Sam would know."

His stomach twisted at the mention of Sam. "Except she's not talking to me right now." He drifted off. "You don't think this has anything to do with her, do you?"

"Could be. They did act like they were siblings."

Brad scrubbed his face with his hands. As if he didn't feel shitty enough about the situation, now it was affecting his business. He sent a message to Andrew telling him about having openings only to be rebuffed. By the end of the evening, he was pissed.

He packed everything up and stormed out of the store. If they didn't want his painting services anymore, he'd get their current minis finished as fast as he could. He dug out his notebook with his notes for orders.

He checked his computer out of reflex. Sam hadn't been online all day. He had to fix this. *I'll explain to Hannah this was a mistake and find a way to get Sam back. Grovel if I have to.* He dropped in his chair, his shoulders bowing under the weight of the task.

"Knock, knock." Hannah peeked around the corner. "I saw you weren't at the store, so I thought I'd stop by. Chuck let me in."

No better time than the present to get started. "Sit down." He gestured to the couch. "We need to talk."

"Sounds serious."

"It is. What happened on Saturday—"

"I knew it! You were only using me." She burst into tears. "Now you want to call it off because She's coming back."

He rushed over and pulled her into his arms. "That's not it at all." He swallowed past the sick feeling in his throat. "I'm not sure either of us were thinking straight at the time."

She shook her head against his chest. "I hadn't had a drop to drink." She sniffled and looked up at him. "Are you saying you only made out with me because you were drunk? Am I that repulsive?"

Sweat relief swept through him. They had never actually had sex. That explained why he still had his pants on the next morning. "Of course I'm not saying you're repulsive. I think you're beautiful."

A smile crossed her lips. "Then what did you want to talk to me about?"

"I was very drunk and not thinking straight." He threw up a prayer for Sam to understand. "That's not really the best way to start a relationship."

"So you're not breaking up with me?"

He tried to remember if they actually talked about dating during his drunken haze. The entire night was a blur. "I'm just saying maybe we should go on a date to see if we're actually compatible."

"HOW ARE YOU TODAY, Samantha?" Will held out his hand to her.

She reached over the table and shook it, not sure why her stomach tied itself in knots. "I'm fine. How are you?"

"I'm good. Is Lewis doing better?" She nodded. He flipped through some papers and frowned. "I guess I didn't notice before that you have a Wisconsin address."

"That's correct."

"Why are you applying here if you live up there?"

"I think a seven hour commute is fun," she deadpanned. They shared a chuckle and eased some of the tension in her shoulders. "Honestly, my dad's getting better since his accident and I've realized how little time I've spent with him over the years. I've heard great things about this store. I recently graduated college and feel like it's time to be a part of something where I know I can make a difference." *And to not have Hannah hounding my every relationship.*

"What special skills do you bring to the table?"

"I'm a wargamer with five years retail experience. I've lived with gamers of all types so I am at least passingly familiar with a lot of games."

They chatted for a few more minutes. It was the most relaxed interview she had ever had. They wrapped up with him letting her know he would call in a couple of days for a second interview or to be told she had not gotten one.

"Thank you for taking the time to interview me." She shook his hand on her way out of the office.

"It was my pleasure, Samantha."

"Please, call me Sam."

She wandered around the store and chatted with the staff about when a group for War Tactics met up. If her father wanted her out of the house, she would get back on the gaming horse, no matter how much it hurt her. She had just picked up her dad's comics when Will called out her name.

"Before you go, how do you feel about a second interview right now?"

"That's quick." Her head spun.

"Don and Sally, the owners, happened to come in to discuss how the first interviews went and want to meet you."

"Lead on." Unsure about the turn of events, she found herself seated in front of Don.

Sally, his wife, waved from a desk across the room. The couple resembled each other, both with salt and pepper hair and smile lines around their eyes. Sally's hair was swept into a neat bun. Sam immediately felt at ease with the older woman.

"If you don't mind my asking, what is your degree in?" Don bent his head over her resume.

"Theater management." She gave a humorless chuckle. "As far as business degrees go, it's mildly useless when trying to get a job."

"Why put your time into a degree you find useless?" His sharp eyes snapped up.

"I hadn't realized it was useless when I was getting it. I helped run the theater on campus where there was always something new to do or learn. As much as I joke about it being useless, the hands on business part of it was a great learning experience." She shrugged. "The fact it's a theater degree knocks you out of the running because everyone you're up against has a 'real' business degree."

"What was your favorite aspect of getting your degree?"

She thought for a moment. "I set up and ran one of the student shows every year, from promotion to scheduling the front of house staff. It makes me uniquely qualified to work in your store. Because I had to juggle my studies, work, and the theater, I know how to prioritize my time."

"How does that make you uniquely qualified for the store?" Will joined them at the table.

She had forgotten he was still in the room. She looked up in shock to see three pairs of eyes focused on her. "I'm guessing you run a lot of events here."

"Not as many as I would like."

"I spent my last two years of school finding events, hiring staff to run them, and promoting them. Not to sound cocky, but you need someone like me to take your events to the next level." She glanced around. "I checked your website and social media presence before coming here. The last thing you posted to the website is almost half a year old. When you post to your socials, you info dump and do multiple postings in a very short period of time."

"I do what I have time for." Will crossed his arms.

Well, that went downhill fast. "I don't mean to pick it apart. Even if you don't hire me, I can help you set up your social media in a way to make it effective."

THIS IS A REALLY BAD idea. Brad looked at himself in the mirror and ran his fingers through his hair. Why did he agree to go out with Hannah when he meant to break it off? He kicked the cabinet.

"Don't break my house just because you're a dumbass." Steve lounged against the door frame.

"Why not? At least I can fix the cabinet."

"Great, now you're feeling sorry for yourself. Do us all a favor: go out, make it really clear you aren't into her, and grovel to Sam." Steve walked down the hall. "I thought getting laid was supposed to put you in a good mood."

He followed to the closet and grabbed his jacket. "It does if you're with the right girl."

He still berated himself for not realizing it wasn't Sam kissing him. How the hell had he not realized sooner? Something had felt off, but he assumed it was because he was drunk.

"As much as I love Sam, she did give you permission to date while she was gone. Maybe you'll click with Hannah, maybe you won't. She's hot. Plus, if you're tied up, I have a chance with Sammy-girl."

The idea of Sam dating Steve burned like acid in his gut. "She's not your type." Brad snagged his keys. "I'm off to get this over with. Later, dude."

He pulled up to the restaurant Hannah picked and looked down at his clothes, grateful he chose a polo shirt over his normal t-shirt. This was too upscale for his tastes. With no sign of Hannah's car, he breathed a deep sigh and bellied up to the bar to wait. Two beers later, she finally showed up as he was ready to cash out and leave. *Fifteen minutes late, I shouldn't have waited.*

"I'm so sorry I'm late. I was on my way out the door and my mom called, freaking out about some committee she's on. I kept trying to hang up, but she wouldn't take the hint." Hannah dropped a kiss on his cheek. "Shall we get some food?"

He reluctantly nodded. It was too late for him to just leave and he was starving. His mind boggled at the price of food, but he sucked it up and ordered himself a steak. If he was going to go through with this farce of a date, he might as well enjoy the food.

Hannah kept up a steady stream of chatter to make up for his silence. He didn't want to be cooperative, but let himself get drawn into a discussion about his business. She seemed interested in how he set his own hours and pay. By the time dessert was over, he relaxed enough to be talked into dancing and drinking at one of the group's usual hang out. He ordered the first round of drinks, but quickly lost track of how many she bought him.

"You should walk me home." She wormed her way under his arm and stared up at him with big eyes.

"I really need to get some work done tonight. My workload is pretty hefty this week." He licked his lips. His mouth felt dry, but his last drink was already gone.

"I feel like I should insist. You've had a bit too much to drink and I would feel responsible if anything happened to you on the way home. I live just around the corner. Come over and at least have a bottle of water before heading home." She tugged his arm.

"I thought you were Julie's roommate." He weaved on his feet.

She looped her arm through his and led him out of the bar. "My parents decided to move me out of the dorms so I can concentrate on my studies."

He stumbled over his own two feet, too drunk to drive himself home. He allowed her to lead him back to her apartment. He sank into the couch and took a huge pull from the ice cold bottle she handed him. He waited for the room to stop spinning while he chugged the water. She took the empty bottle from lax hand.

She cuddled against his side. "You walked me to my door, but forgot to give me my goodnight kiss."

He struggled to remember why it was a bad idea. He mentally shrugged when the thought didn't come to him right away. *Must just be because it's our first date. I shouldn't have drank so much, I'm not making a good impression.* He didn't stop Hannah when she climbed onto his lap and initiated the kiss.

Chapter Twenty-One

Sam walked into the gaming space, her stomach in knots. The entire drive to Wisconsin had been an exercise in dealing with her nerves. She kept reminding herself her dad had everything he needed and could get around the house on his own. Plus he had friends checking in on him throughout the weekend. She just needed to get closure on this part of her life. Starting with her final night of gaming at the Game Hut.

She wasn't sure she really wanted to be here, but she couldn't bear to move without seeing most of the guys one last time. She frowned at some of the burned out lights and set her bag in her old spot out of habit. She scanned the room for a familiar face and felt a tap on her shoulder.

"Sam?"

She turned to find herself staring at Steve's amazed expression. "Surprise."

"What are you doing here?" He pulled her into a bear hug.

"Hoping to get in one last game for old time's sake." She returned the hug with feeling. "I'm moving to Missouri." The words tasted like ash in her mouth.

"Does Brad know?"

"Does it matter?" She snapped the words. "Sorry, that was uncalled for."

"Speak of the devil..."

She turned her head, heart beating against her tongue, and saw Hannah walk into the room. They locked glares before Hannah pulled Brad into a long passionate kiss before he could see inside the room. Hannah kept her eyes focused on Sam the entire time. Sam's stomach clenched and she turned back to Steve.

"Maybe coming here tonight wasn't the best idea." She wrapped an arm around her waist to hold herself together while she grabbed her bag. She just needed to get out of here without crying or being seen.

Steve covered her hand. "He's not the only person who would want to see you. Play against me for old time's sake." He raised his voice. "Either get a room or knock it off. You're making me ill."

"Thank you," she whispered. She kept her back to the door while she set up her army and struggled to get her emotions under control. "Is that normal?"

"Nope, I think that was for your benefit."

"Awesome." She shared a look with him.

A few minutes later, Brad came over to their table. "What the hell was that about?"

"We have a special guest today." Steve gestured at her. All she wanted to do was sink into the floor.

Brad turned and did a double-take. "What are you doing here?"

"Playing a game." She shrugged with a nonchalance she didn't feel. She kept her hands busy with her army so she wouldn't give in to the urge to hug him. Her eyes drank in him greedily until she spotted the red mark on the side of his neck. She turned away before her expression could betray her. "In a couple of days, moving most of my crap to Missouri."

"You're moving down there for good?" His voice cracked.

"I'm not a fan of a seven hour commute for work."

"When did you get a job?"

"Last week. Dad hinted not so subtly I was getting underfoot now that he can move around the house on his own. All he really needs me for is driving to appointments."

"You didn't tell me." His voice held a hint of disappointment.

She raised her chin. "You aren't around to talk to anymore and you have a girlfriend. What I do isn't any of your business." She turned back to the table. "Steve, are we playing or what?"

BRAD FELL INTO THE nearest chair. Sam came to the store and saw him kissing Hannah. *I'm so fucked.* He should've known something was up with Hannah pulling him into a passionate kiss good-bye. There went any chance of setting things right with Sam.

He spent part of the evening trying to get her attention so he could explain himself to her, but she kept her focus on the game in front of her with the exception of talking to the other guys she knew. Every hug made his insides burn. Steve caught his eye and shook his head. She didn't want to talk to him tonight, not that he blamed her.

He packed his bag and headed to the door. He obviously wasn't getting any work done at the store tonight and he couldn't take her ignoring him anymore. He glanced back and caught her broken expression before she turned her head back to her game. Steve's hand covered hers. Brad turned to go to her but his friend waved him off.

He leaned his head on his steering wheel. All he wanted was an easy relationship with Sam, what went wrong? *Easy, you're a colossal dumbass.* He let himself get tricked into sleeping with Hannah that night in the basement. Not that he could remember any of it. He shook his head.

A couple of days. That's all the time he had to finish Andrew's last couple of minis for an excuse to see her. And in that time, he needed to figure out how to break it off with Hannah. And figure out how to beg Sam to stay in Wisconsin with him.

He headed to his painting desk, feeling a bit better with his vague plan. He pulled up short when he saw Hannah sitting like a statue on the couch. "What are you doing here?"

"I guessed you'd be home pretty quick. And wanting to talk." She bowed her head.

"And you're okay with that?"

"I think breaking up with me because Sam came back is a shitty thing to do, but I understand you only wanted me as a distraction and bed warmer." She picked some fuzz off of her pants, keeping her eyes down.

He knelt next to her, stomach acid churning. "It was never like that."

"But you are breaking up with me." She sniffled. "You were exactly like I feared you'd be. I was so stupid to think you'd be a good guy."

"You're not stupid. And I never wanted you as a distraction from missing her." He moved to the couch and pulled her onto his lap. "Sam's not coming back. She's only here to pack her stuff before moving to Missouri."

"But you're still breaking up with me."

I'm so sorry Sam. He kissed away his last chance to make things right. "I'm not breaking up with you. We'll take some time and see how everything works with us. I hate how we started."

She squealed and wrapped her arms around his neck. "You mean it?"

"Yeah, I mean it." His heart bled in his chest as he shifted her onto the couch with a kiss. "I do have work to get done tonight."

"I understand. I won't get in your way." She kissed him and skipped off.

He sank into his work chair, emotionally exhausted. *What the fuck just happened?* He spun a paintbrush around his fingers before settling in to work. Begging Sam to stay was off the table, but he still needed to see her one last time and beg for her forgiveness.

SAM RAN A PIECE OF tape down the box she finished filling. Most of her stuff was packed and in her car for the morning. Just the large pieces remained for her step-father to pick up and put into storage until she found a place for herself. "Can we sit out on the roof?"

"It's the middle of March, in Wisconsin, and you want to sit out on the roof?" Olivia looked at her like she'd lost her mind.

Maybe I have. She rubbed the ache in the center of her chest. "It might be my last chance to do it. We'll light a fire in the holder. It'll be fun."

"You're crazy." Olivia dug out the metal candle holder they occasionally made small fires in from the upstairs' closet.

Sam pulled on her coat and opened the upstairs' window. She swept the lingering snow off of the porch roof and stuck her hand in to get the blanket they used. She set the plate and metal holder in the middle and coaxed a small fire to life. Olivia climbed out next to her and closed the window most of the way.

"What are you going to do now?"

Sam stared at the fire and poked it with a chopstick. "I've got the job at the game store. That'll keep me busy while I figure out what to do with my life."

"I can't believe he drove you to move away."

"Brad has nothing to do with this decision." She caught her friend's look. "Okay, he had a little to do with this. But this whole thing with my dad really made me think about how alone he is down there. I want to spend more time with him."

A familiar car pulled up in front of the house. "Speaking of the devil. Look who just appeared."

"What is he doing here?" Her heart beat in her ears, painful and full of hope.

"I don't know." Olivia stuck her head in the window and had a brief conversation with Luke. "Sounds like he's bringing Andrew's models back."

"Oh." All of her hope crashed around her and she tossed more papers into the fire, trying to ignore the ache in chest. She leaned back near the window to listen to the conversation behind her. "What was that about the guys not giving him any more work?"

"Luke and Andrew are pretty pissed about him getting with Hannah and are choosing to show their solidarity by not giving him work."

She snorted, her heart full at her friends' support. "Tell those two I appreciate the concern, but not to take it out on him. I gave him the go ahead to live his life before I left. I think dating Hannah is punishment enough."

Olivia climbed through the window and left her to her thoughts. Sam curled her arms around her knees and watched the moonlight shine down. *I'm going to miss this.* Her heart gave a painful lurch. Someone scrambled through the window onto the porch roof.

Brad sat next to her. "Isn't it a bit cold to be sitting out here?"

She shrugged through the glass in her veins. The breeze brought his scent to her. "It's like everything else, you get used to it after a while."

"Kitten..." He scooted closer and put his arm around her.

"Please stop." She pushed his arm off of her. As much as she wanted his touch, she couldn't do this with him. "I'll tell the guys to stop giving you shit about dating Hannah. What's going on with us should not affect your business. But you can't act like you don't have a girlfriend around me. Things like this," she gestured between them. "They make reality that much harder."

"AND WHAT IS REALITY?" Brad wasn't ready to say good-bye to her. *Just a few more minutes, hours, days.*

"That thing where you have a girlfriend who hates me and I have a new life waiting for me in Missouri." Sam's voice was dull. She held herself like she was trying to not fall apart.

"Why are you moving?" He stared at her, wishing he had the balls to take out his phone and take her picture. "And no lies."

"For a few reasons. One, this accident with my dad made me want to spend more time with him. We have such a great relationship, but we never get to see each other. Two, I can't watch you and Hannah together. Given my past with her and other boyfriends, I think you'll understand."

"I never got the story of what happened with your other boyfriends."

She made an angry noise and glared at him like she wanted to push him off the roof. "I asked you to do one thing when she popped up in your life: ask the guys about her." She looked away. "The last reason I'm leaving is I'm excited about my new job."

"Where are you working?" As much as it broke his heart, he needed to keep her talking. Maybe they could mend their friendship if he couldn't fix their relationship.

"The Fantasy Store. You know, the comic and game store my dad shops at."

"You're cheating on the Game Hut by taking that job." Venom laced his words. He shouldn't be surprised, she'd been talking about that damned store since she went down there.

"I was never in a relationship with the Game Hut." Her words pierced him. He read between the lines at the real accusation and she was right. "I have the opportunity to have a fresh start at a good life with none of this baggage. The least you could do is be happy for me."

He ached to pull her into his arms. "I'm going to miss you."

"I'm sure you'll be kept plenty busy now that I'm out of the way." She kept her face away from him.

"That's hardly fair."

"Sorry. That's the other reason I'm moving. If I stay, I'll turn bitter and angry. At least down there, I will have other things to think about and won't have to watch history repeat itself for a third time."

"Is there anything I can say that will make you change your mind?" He pleaded to her back, watching her shoulders shake with silent tears.

"Not really. I start on Monday."

"I'm sorry."

"I am too. But that doesn't change anything."

He choked back the lump in his throat and dropped a kiss on the back of her head. "Good-night, Sam. I'd ask you'd let me know you made it there in one piece."

He climbed back into the window. Olivia ducked out onto the roof the second he was clear. He could hear her comforting Sam and it tore his heart out of his chest. He ignored the looks Andrew and Luke gave him. Nothing they could do or say would make him hate himself worse than he already did. He looked up at the girls huddled on the roof and knew the sight would haunt him for the rest of his life.

He pulled into his driveway and heaved a sigh. *Great, like he didn't already feel like shit.* Hannah's car was parked across the street. He drug himself into the house and put on a happy face for his new girlfriend.

She popped up from the couch and stalked across the room to him. "Where were you?"

"Delivering the last batch of minis to Andrew." He dropped a kiss on her cheek on his way to the basement.

"And seeing Her?"

His hand clenched at the tone she used to refer to Sam. "Saying good-bye to a friend, yes. She goes back tomorrow."

"Ding dong, the bitch is gone." Hannah did a little dance.

"What did you say?" He couldn't have heard her right.

"I said the bitch is gone and I couldn't be happier."

He studied her face. She was way too happy about this. "She's not a bitch. I thought you two were friends."

"I just meant that you weren't giving this relationship a fair shake with the idea of her coming back." She smoothed her hand across his forehead. "You're all frowny. It's like you want to believe the worst in me."

"Sometimes it's hard to believe the best when you say things like that."

Chapter Twenty-Two

"You didn't bring back much, kiddo."

Sam looked up from the box she was unpacking. She hadn't heard her dad walk up. "I only have one car." She carefully placed more books on the bookcase. "And I brought most of my stuff when I came down in December. Whatever I didn't bring this time James is putting in storage."

"How is your mom and her family?" He sat on the edge of her bed.

She hated doing this dance. "I don't know. Good, I guess. She's not talking to me because I chose you over her. James came because that's what he does, but I haven't seen her or Victoria in forever."

"I'm sorry."

She shrugged and played off like it didn't hurt her. "Not a great loss. I hear Victoria acts like her. At least the father figures in my life are decent."

"I'll leave you to unpack. When do you start your job?" He grunted as he pulled himself up with his walker.

"Tomorrow."

"You didn't leave much time to get settled in."

"I need to be busy."

She broke down the boxes she brought in and headed back to her car to grab the last load. A wave of sadness crashed into her and staggered her. She shook her head. There was nothing she could do except move on with her life. It didn't take her long to get everything set up in her room. A quick shower and dinner had her feeling more settled than she had been in awhile. She dropped a kiss on her dad's head and climbed into bed, nervous about her new job.

"Good morning, Sam." Will met her at the door when she showed up for work the next morning.

"Morning." She stowed her purse and set down her cup of coffee. "Where do we start?"

"First thing every morning is to get the money out of the safe, count up the drawer, and run to the bank."

He walked her through the day, shadowing her when she talked to customers. She endured the curious stares of the clientele while she learned the ropes. As the week went by, he gave her more freedom to do her duties without supervision. She meshed well with the other clerks and they complimented each other's skills. By the end of her second week, she had collected a long list of comics everyone thought she should read.

"I knew working there would make a comic junkie out of you." Her dad nodded at the stack of books she worked her way through.

"Or I want to be able to sound like I know what I'm talking about. Although, 'what's your favorite comic' usually takes the pressure off of me. And the customers are learning I'm a mini gamer more than anything else."

"A mini gamer that doesn't touch her stuff."

She twisted in her seat to alleviate the pang of guilt. "I just wanted to get settled into my job before scoping out the local game scene."

"I'VE MISSED YOU THIS last week." Hannah wrapped her arms around Brad's neck and leaned against his back.

He set aside his work. "I missed you too." He lied to keep the peace, but hadn't really been bothered by her silence. "I've been so busy with work and you with school."

"My schedule is super hectic this semester." She pouted. "I miss my snuggle-bear."

He flinched at the pet name. "We should make plans for this weekend."

"I can't. I have a mountain of homework and sorority stuff." She tapped her finger to her chin like she was thinking. "You should move in with me!"

"I don't know…"

"No, it's perfect. I'll get to see you around all of my activities and not have to visit this smelly basement."

"I don't know if it'll work. I need space to prime and paint."

"We'll make a corner of the living room into your workspace." She peeked at him and her face crumpled. "You don't want to live with me because this is a temporary relationship." Tears leaked out of the corners of her eyes.

"Don't cry, sweetie." He kicked himself because his hesitation caused her to cry. "I didn't mean for it to sound like I didn't want to live with you. I just worry my painting will take up too much space and I'll smell up the apartment when I prime."

"We'll work something out. Maybe get some extra shelves so you can organize better."

"If it's that important to you, I'll do it."

"You're the best!" She squealed and kissed him. "I have to go, I'm going to be late."

He was sure he had been hit by a hurricane. He followed her upstairs to grab something to eat. She left with a trail of excited chatter.

Steve glared at him. "Dude, you got played. I thought you were going to break up with her."

"I said I was thinking about breaking up with her, not that I was actually breaking up with her. Maybe this is a chance to see if there's anything between us."

"She's not Sam."

"You think I don't know that?" The knife twisted in his heart and he slammed his cup on the counter.

"I just don't want you to keep punishing yourself because you got drunk and made a mistake."

"I'm not punishing myself. I'm trying to move on. She has, so why can't I?"

"She's still ignoring your messages, isn't she?"

He slumped against the counter. "She looks right at home in her new store."

"I saw the pictures she posted of her with the rest of the clerks. The store looks amazing, not like the shit hole we game at. Maybe I'll take a road trip down there when they host a tournament. You're more than welcome to tag along."

"I don't want to bring Wisconsin baggage down to her. She's got her fresh start and is making the most of it." He rubbed his chest to loosen the ache. "I'm glad she's happy with her new job."

"HOLD IT RIGHT THERE."

Sam turned to face the guy with a hoodie pulled low over his face. "Can I help you?"

"Give me all your money."

Fear slithered down her back and she inched closer to the door to work. "I'm pretty broke right now. I can't help you."

"Give me the blue bag." He pulled out a gun.

She froze. Images of her dad having to identify her body flashed through her head. She threw the bank bag at his feet. *I don't want to die,* her brain wouldn't stop repeating. Time slowed and his hoodie slipped back for her to see his face.

The gun went off as he reached for the bag. She hit the ground as he grabbed the bag and ran. When she was sure he wasn't coming back to kill her for how little was in the bag, she sat down hard on the steps and called 911. After explaining the situation to the dispatcher, she called Will to let him know what happened. She let herself dissolve into tears at her narrow escape.

Will showed up while she was giving her statement to the police. "Are you alright?"

"I think so." Her voice shook. "It was Troy Kelly. He pulled a gun on me. It went off after I threw the bank bag at him."

"You're one hundred percent certain?" She nodded, having sold his comics to him the day before. "How do you know?"

"His hoodie fell away from his face when he went for the bag." It hit her that she had thrown store property at the guy. "I'm so sorry, I didn't know what else to do so I threw the money at him."

"You did everything right, I promise." Will clapped her on shoulder. "I'm going to call Don and Sally to let them know what happened. Out of curiosity, how much was in the bag?"

"A roll of quarters and two rolls of pennies." She let out a shaky laugh. "He caught me on my way back from the bank."

"Why don't you take the rest of the day off with pay?"

The thought of going home and having time to dwell on her close encounter had her shuddering. "If it's alright with you, I'd like to work. If I go home, all I'll do is think about it."

She went in and tried to lose herself in the daily hustle and bustle of the store. The other clerks gave her hugs when they heard what happened. All she wanted was to forget how afraid she had been. Late in the afternoon, the phone rang and Will called her over.

"They caught him. Troy still had the bag in his possession when he tried to knock over a gas station. The cops want you to go to the station and confirm his identity." She nodded, unsure if her voice would work. "Do you want me to go with you?"

She took a shaky breath. "Please, I'm not sure how I will react to seeing him again."

He grabbed his keys and let the other clerks know where they were going. "It'll make it easier for me to tell him he is banned from all of our stores as well."

"I'M SO GLAD YOU MOVED in with me."

Brad kept his head buried in the box he was unpacking so Hannah wouldn't see his expression. *A fresh start, that's what this would be.* "I'm glad too, hun."

Hannah kept him busy getting everything set up just so. He couldn't take a breath without her dictating it. He snuck Sam's photo album under a stack of his clothes in the back of the closet. It wasn't fair to Hannah, but he couldn't make himself get rid of it. It was the only thing he had to show for their short relationship. He patted the pile to make sure none of the box showed and broke down another box.

"I think that's the last of my stuff in the bedroom."

Hannah poked her head out of the bathroom. "I got your stuff all set in here."

He tossed his box on the pile growing in the living room. "Looks like all I have left is my painting stuff and dvds."

"We'll have to get rid of all the extra boxes to make space for your new painting table. Why don't you take them down to the dumpster while I get started on putting away your movies?"

He hefted a huge stack into his arms and headed to the dumpster. He kept repeating to himself it was a fresh start, even if it meant a new desk because his old one wouldn't fit in the apartment. When he returned to the apartment, it looked like she was about to start a fight, so he grabbed the rest of the boxes quickly and took his sweet time tossing them out. She was in an extra happy mood when he got back. He mentally shrugged and chalked it up to the stress of moving into a tiny apartment together.

She helped him open the box for his new desk and handed him parts as he needed them. The cheap furniture went together quickly and he bolted the shelves to the wall. He dumped the contents of his boxes onto the shelves and desktop, promising himself he'd organize it later. He was too worn out to care at the moment.

"It looks good." Brad pulled her into his arms and laid his head on top of hers.

"Do you want to go to dinner to celebrate our first night living together?"

"Sure, but I will have to get some work done tonight."

Hannah sighed and shifted to kiss him. "Always under a deadline."

"Got to pay the bills somehow."

"Do you want to shower first?"

His hands itched to get back to painting. "How about you clean up and I'll shower while you're getting ready?"

"Look at us, being domestic." She gave him a huge smile before sashaying to the bathroom.

SAM WOKE IN A PUDDLE of cold sweat and ran her hands over her body for any signs of wounds. Her ears strained for any sound of her father, but figured she hadn't screamed out loud when no sound came from his room. She leaned over and switched her light on to banish the lingering nightmare away. *The bullet missed me.* She needed to find something to take her mind off of it.

She paced around the room, debating on taking a shower, before settling in front of her computer. She rubbed her arms to warm up while she waited for it to boot. Strains of classical music soothed her nerves while she mindlessly surfed. Somehow, she ended up on the gaming forums.

Ubel: Long time, no talk.

She jumped with a squeak when the message popped up. Damn, she was too high strung for her own good. She stared at the screen torn on whether to talk to him or not. She clung on to the lifeline he offered.

Sam-cat: I can't sleep.

U: Why not?

S: I keep replaying today in my head with the worst result.

U: Did something happen to your father?

S: No, he's good, sneaky with the walker. They're going to upgrade him to a cane soon.

U: Then what happened today?

She chewed on the side of her thumb before typing the words. The nightmare felt too real still. She needed someone to comfort her more than she needed her pride.

S: I was held at gunpoint this morning.

Her phone rang on the nightstand. She rushed across the room to answer it before it woke her dad and saw Brad's picture on the screen. "You didn't need to call."

"You sounded like you needed to talk. What happened?" Concern tinged his words.

Immediately, her hands stopped shaking and she curled up against her pillows. "One of my customers caught me as I came back from the bank run. He pulled a gun and demanded the money. I threw the bag at him and the gun went off."

"Are you hurt?" She could hear the panic in his voice.

"No, I hit the ground pretty quick. The bullet hit the building. The cops say he missed me by a few inches." *Too close for comfort.*

"You must have been so scared. I'm sorry this happened."

"My boss got there almost as fast as the cops. They caught the guy this afternoon."

SAM'S VOICE SOUNDED so small. All Brad wanted to do was pull her into his arms and shelter her from the world. He slipped into the hallway to keep from waking up Hannah. The last thing he needed was to be caught talking to Sam.

He kept her on the phone for hours, talking about her new job and how her father was progressing. Classical music provided the background for their conversation. She reciprocated by asking about the group and his business. They danced around the subject of his significant other. Now he had her talking to him, he loathed hanging up and losing the connection to her.

"I really didn't mean to keep you from your work."

"You aren't." The lie came automatically from his lips. He knew where her statement was leading.

"Liar, it's three in the morning. Either you were working or you were getting ready for bed."

He smiled at how she knew his schedule. "I mean, I should be working, but you shouldn't be sorry about talking to me. I hope it helped."

"It did. Thank you." She yawned. "I should let you get to bed or back to work. I need to be up in a couple of hours for work."

He frowned. "They didn't give you time off?"

"They tried. I knew if I took any time off because of this, I wouldn't ever have the nerve to go back. It's better to just work through it."

"Always so brave." Just when he thought he had her figured out, she did something that surprised him.

"Thank you for taking the time to talk to me."

"Anytime..." He caught himself before he called her kitten. "Let me know if you can't sleep. I'll stay up with you."

"Good night." She hung up.

He leaned his head against the wall and closed his eyes. He'd give anything to be in Missouri, holding her and making sure she was really okay. He beat his head against the wall a couple of times. No, he was a man of his word and would give this thing with Hannah a fair shot.

Chapter Twenty-Three

"Hey, Sam, what's with the extra body?"

Sam looked up from the shelves to her customer, Robert. He had become her first friend since the move. "We have to have two openers from now on."

"Since when?"

This story was getting old. It seemed like every other customer wanted to know. "Since I was held up for the bank bag a couple of weeks ago."

"Oh shit. Are you alright?"

"Other than a couple of sleepless nights, I'm good." She wasn't about to tell him how many nights she laid awake and refused the lifeline of Brad's voice. If she was going to make this a clean break, she couldn't keep calling him. "A little upset about not knowing what to do in a situation like that."

"If you want to learn some self defense, we train martial arts in the gym every Tuesday and Thursday night." Robert handed her a card.

She looked it over and pocketed it. "We'll see. I'm not sure if it'll be for me."

"Just a thought. It's a good group of guys." He headed for the game room.

She chewed over the idea for the rest of her shift and snagged a pizza on her way home, not really in the mood to cook. Her dad joined her at the table and munched in silence for a few minutes.

"You're quiet tonight." He tapped the table in front of her. "The other week is still bugging you?"

"A bit." They rarely talked about it after the first few days. "One of my customers offered to let me take a martial arts class with him." She slid the card across the table. "Not sure how I feel about it."

"It could help with the nightmares." He raised an eyebrow at her. "Maybe make them come less."

"They're going away on their own." She ignored the pointed look he gave her. She had woken up the night before in a cold sweat. "I'm already gone more than I feel comfortable with."

"I'm on the mend and can get around the house without you." He reached across the table and took her hand. "You've taken good care of me, now it's time to think about yourself."

"I'm beginning to think you want me out of the house more."

"You do put a cramp on my love life."

"Yeah right." She rolled her eyes at the thought.

"I worry, kiddo. I don't like seeing you get hurt because of not knowing how to handle yourself."

"I'll look into it."

"YOU SHOULD TAKE ME out on a date right now."

"I need to get this order finished. I'm working." Behind Brad, Hannah landed on the couch with a sigh. *Oh, fuck, here we go again.*

"You're always working. You never have any time for me anymore."

Ten, nine, eight... He took a deep breath and turned around. "You knew when you started dating me that I have to work a lot to build my business."

"Yeah, but you just sit there and ignore me everyday. It's like you don't want to be with me." She stuck out her bottom lip.

"Of course I want to be with you, why else would I have moved in?" This discussion had become too familiar. He figured he'd cut it short tonight. "Give me ten minutes to get this cleaned up and we'll go out. What do you want to do?"

"Really? Can we go out dancing?"

He groaned inwardly. "If that's what you really want to do, of course."

She squealed and skipped away. He looked over his table and sighed. He had just put paint on his palette. Now he was going to wash all that money down the drain. His mind calculated how much paint he had wasted and multiplied it by the dozens of times this scene had played out. *It's time to invest in a covered palette.* He shook his head and changed into clean clothes.

Twenty minutes later, he sat on the couch, waiting for her to finish getting ready. The painting table beckoned, but he knew the second he sat down to work, she'd be out bitching at him. He sat, growing more and more annoyed as the minutes ticked by. She finally walked out of the bathroom and he groaned. It was going to be one of those nights.

She twirled, short skirt flaring just enough for him to see her thong. "How do I look?"

"Like a vision." He bit back his criticism and pulled her into his arms. He almost gagged on her overpowering perfume. "Are you ready to have some fun?"

"Always." She flashed him a smile. "I hope you don't mind, but I told the girls where we were going. They might join us later."

They might join us later, my ass. He followed Hannah into the packed club, her friends already there and a couple of drinks in. He pulled out a chair for her and was promptly ignored for a round of shots. He sank into a chair and watched her shake her ass on the dance floor. When it looked like other guys were showing too much interest, he went over and pulled her tight against him.

"What are you doing out here?" She shouted over the thumping music.

"Dancing with my girlfriend. I thought that's what we were doing tonight."

"You left all of our purses alone? Go back to the table. I'll dance with you when someone sits down." She shoved him back towards the table.

He slumped in the chair and glared at her back. He should've known they weren't actually going out dancing together. All she wanted was someone to watch her and her friends' stuff while they danced. Any time there was a chance to join her on the floor, she begged exhaustion. He settled for texting Steve and plotting out the next week's worth of work while ignoring the fact his girlfriend was bumping and grinding with other men. When the girls had enough, he half carried her home and tucked her into bed. *What a waste of a night.*

"AND JUST WHERE DO YOU think you're sneaking off to, old man?" Sam peeked her head into the living room.

Her dad maneuvered his way to the front door. The sight of him with a cane instead of a walker warmed her, although it made tracking his movements harder. "It's Thursday, bowling night."

She snorted. "Like you could bowl with your bum leg."

"I sit and keep score."

"The lanes keep score automatically. I think what you meant was: you sit, bullshit, and drink." Not that she was going to complain when he got out of the house and enjoyed himself.

"Right, that's what I meant."

"Do you need a lift?"

"Nope, one of my buddies from work is picking me up. Speaking of leaving the house, aren't you running late for your martial arts class?"

"Heading out the door now." She hefted her gym bag onto her shoulder and edged around him. "Don't forget I have a miniature tournament this weekend. You're on your own for dinner on Saturday."

"Be safe."

"Always. You too."

"Don't wait up."

She saluted and hustled to her car. She dashed into the gym, pausing only to bow and take off her shoes. Robert nodded at her and pointed to the clock. She slid into her place with a minute to spare.

She wiped the sweat off her face. Warm ups and rolling killed her every week. She was sure they wanted to see how far they could push her before her body gave out entirely. Her legs shook as she made the minor adjustments the instructor gave her. She groaned with relief when they finally bowed out.

Robert sat next to where she collapsed. "You're getting better."

"Doesn't feel that way. Every week I think I've regressed." She blindly pulled her water bottle out of her bag and downed half of it.

"That's just you realizing how much you don't know." He wiped his face off with a towel.

"That's not as comforting as you think it is."

"Trust me, it gets easier. You're getting better at not freezing up when someone attacks you." She nodded her thanks for the compliment. "Are you ready for your tournament?"

"No, but it's time to get back in the saddle."

"What's kept you from playing?"

"Memories." Flashes of Brad played in her mind. She put a stop to it before the gaping hole in her chest could reopen. "Both good and bad."

"Let me guess, your ex plays."

"Got it in one guess. What gave it away?" She slung her bag over her shoulder and held the door for him.

"You had that look. The one that says it's still pretty raw."

"Yeah, we really hadn't started dating before my dad had his accident. Snake of a woman swooped in while I was here and snagged him despite my warnings." She kept her eyes focused over Robert's head.

"Well, his loss." He cleared his throat. "Good luck on Saturday."

"Thanks." She waved and headed home where a long shower and bed called her name.

"BYE, SWEETIE! DON'T forget I have a sorority meeting tonight."

Brad set down the mini he was working on right before Hannah crashed against him and gave him a kiss. "Have a good day."

She wiggled her fingers at him and shut the door. He waited for her second appearance at a forgotten item and heaved a sigh of relief when she was truly gone for the day. He studied his paint desk and pulled out more minis. He hid those last night after he finished them just for this purpose.

Pushing back thoughts of how fucked up this was, he grabbed his wallet and keys. He could do the drive by heart, even with construction. His heart beat faster as he swiped his membership card before entering the Domes. Breathing in the humid air, the knot in his chest loosened.

He waved to the workers he had come to know in his weekly trips since the last time he talked to Sam. Here, he pretended he hadn't screwed everything up by not waiting. In his mind's eye, he imagined she was just around the curve, waiting for him to catch up. This had been a great idea for a first date and he had picked up more than a few unique paint schemes for his business. He snapped a picture of a different plant to test out if he could reproduce the color palette, feeling Sam leaning over his shoulder. His heart broke a little when he had to leave and she wasn't with him.

He swung by the Game Hut on his way home to pick up his order of paint. Trudging up the stairs to the apartment, his phone went off in his pocket. *Great, Hannah texting to see where I am.* He opened the door, rearranging his grimace.

"Where have you been?"

"I was running low on peacock green." He held up the bag like a shield. "And this army uses a lot of it."

"But you didn't tell me you'd be gone."

"I'm sorry, sweetie. It was going to be a quick run and I didn't think you'd come home while I was out."

"My class let out a little early and I came home to see if you wanted to take me out to dinner before my meeting, but now I have to dash." She placed a quick kiss on his cheek and skipped out the door.

He dropped into his chair. *That was too close for comfort.* That would be the last time he'd go to the Domes for a while. The last thing he needed was Hannah to figure out he was slipping to a place Sam wanted to take him.

He turned his focus to the table in front of him. He pulled up the game forums while he checked his email for orders. As always, Sam logged off as he logged in. *I'm good enough to talk to when she can't sleep, but not good enough otherwise.* He leaned his head in his hands. He needed to stop pining for the girl he lost and focus his energies on the one he had.

Chapter Twenty-Four

"Hey, kiddo, do you have a minute to talk?"

Sam looked up from the stack of comics she was putting away. Her dad driving himself places took some getting used to. "Only if you don't mind me filling some back issues while we talk. Or I can take my break early if it's important." She scanned her dad's suit. "You look spiffy today."

"I met with the lawyer." He paused. She hated this trick. He wouldn't tell her the rest until she asked, even though he was vibrating with excitement.

She let the silence lengthen between them and went back to filing comics. He gave her a smug smile and pulled up a chair. "Old man, what did the lawyer say?"

"Work offered a settlement." He folded his hands behind his head.

"And?" She was tempted to take his cane and beat the answers out of him. The wait was unbearable. This was the first they'd heard since they started the case.

"It's quadruple what we were suing for."

"That's amazing! That means our case is legitimate and they're scared."

"The lawyer's pushing me to take it. They also threw in a hundred shares of stock in the company."

"Dummy talk this to me, dad. Are you actually thinking about taking the offer?"

"I am. We're already working on the paperwork."

She frowned. "But I thought this was to make sure no one else gets hurt, not for the money."

"Sweetie, a hundred shares of stock gives me voting rights in the company. OSHA is putting them under some very strict oversight. Big changes are being made to ensure no one else has to go through this." He grabbed her hand. "I just want this to be done."

It's over. The things keeping her in Missouri were finally done. Her dad was on the mend. She could pick up her life like she had never left.

Her heart ripped open and reality crashed in. She couldn't just pick up her life. Brad was lost to her and under Hannah's spell. Even her old room was gone. Eric would probably give it back if she asked, but there wasn't much point. She didn't have a job up there anymore.

Her father watched her like a hawk, no doubt reading her every thought. She gave him a smile. "It's amazing news, old man." She squeezed his hand. "I'm glad we can put this nightmare behind us."

"YOUR SUIT IS FRESHLY pressed and ready to go." Hannah called from the bathroom.

"Thanks, but why is it freshly pressed?" Brad barely glanced up from his table. *What did he get roped into this time?*

"Because we're heading to my parents' house for dinner, remember? It's a formal Easter dinner. You have to wear your suit and tie."

He had forgotten about their dinner plans. "I hadn't realized it was a formal affair."

"Well, it is, and you need to get cleaned up and ready to go." She pushed him into the bathroom.

He tugged at his tie. He hated these damned things. It slowly strangled him. Dread settled in his stomach as he stared at the huge house in front of him. She came up next to him and tsked at the state of his tie.

She straightened him out and pulled the knot painfully tight against his throat. "Perfect. Are you ready?"

"I guess so." He debated bolting down the street, but allowed her to pull him into the house.

All around him were signs he was out of his league. Chandeliers glittered with freshly cleaned crystals and every picture had a gilt edged frame. He knew her folks were loaded, but they gave Steve's parents a run for their money. Her parents sneered at him during introductions, having judged him and found him wanting. She got her coloring from her father and her features from her mother, right down to the pursed lips.

He held out Hannah's chair for her before taking his assigned seat next to her. He fumbled his way through the appetizers, despite trying to follow her lead. *Fuck formal dinners. Give me a Christmas around Olivia's table any day.*

Hannah's father stared holes through him. "What do you do for a living, young man?"

"I own my own business."

"What type?"

"He paints miniatures for a living, daddy." Hannah patted Brad's arm and giggled. "People pay him to paint little people."

"That sounds... nice." Her mother chimed in.

"It doesn't sound like it pays very much."

"He pays his share of the bills." Hannah trivialized all of his hard work with one sentence.

He straightened in his chair, seething. "Actually, while the pay isn't steady, it's a very rewarding line of work. I get to set my own hours, I do all of my own bookkeeping so I can track my hours on a project versus payment, and I am constantly marketing my skills while learning new ones."

"It sounds like a lot of work for very little return." Her father sat back in his chair. "You should find more financially stable work to keep my little princess in the lifestyle she's accustomed to."

"If money becomes an issue for us, I'm sure she'd be more than happy to pitch in to keep our household afloat." Shock vibrated around the table. *Well, I stuck my foot in it.*

She tittered and patted his shoulder. "He's only joking, daddy. Brad's a fine provider and when he finds a good job, he'll switch to make me happy."

He blinked at her. *Did she really just say he'd get a soul sucking job?* She gripped his hand under the table and squeezed. He took the hint to shut his mouth, but it cost him. He spent the rest of the evening answering questions as blandly as possible.

She stayed silent throughout the drive back to the apartment, radiating the same anger brewing in him. He relished the thought of this fight. He held the door for her so they could do it in private.

"How dare you embarrass me in front of my parents?" She threw her shoes into the closet with a loud thump.

"What the fuck did I do that was so wrong?"

"Telling them I would be more than happy to get a job to keep us afloat? Like that would ever happen." Her dress followed the path of her shoes. "Now I have to do damage control with them to keep them from freaking out."

His mind reeled. "What, do you really expect me to be the sole breadwinner here?"

"Of course." She didn't seem to get that he hadn't planned on being the only income. "When I graduate, my parents stop paying for all of this." She waved her arms around the room.

"How the hell do you think my painting business can pay to keep you in your extravagant lifestyle?"

"I figured your little painting business would be a passing hobby."

He sputtered for a second. *Little?* "You knew when we started dating I owned a painting business and it was what I wanted to spend the rest of my life doing. I never led you to believe otherwise."

"I just thought when you got a taste of the good life, you'd do everything in your power to keep it."

He raked his hands through his hair. "Tonight you belittled my dream in front of your parents and made them believe I wasn't upholding my end of this relationship. I've never skimped on paying my share of anything or pitching in to do anything you've asked."

He threw the stupid tie in a puddle and stalked to the shower. He needed to wash the stink of entitlement off of him. He took his time cooling down before dressing in comfortable clothes.

She huddled on the bed, tears streaming down her face. "I'm sorry about tonight. It's my parents' expectations that I can't seem to shake. They have this image in their heads of how a relationship is supposed to work. Every time I go over there, I get sucked in."

"Parents can do that to you." He tossed his towel in the hamper. "I'm going to get some work done."

"DON WANTS TO SEE YOU in the office."

Sam looked at Will, her heart in her throat. He didn't give her any indication what was going on. She checked her conscience as she walked to the back. Nothing came to mind for her being in trouble, her last monthly review was stellar and she was always on time for her shifts. She knocked on the office door and let herself in.

"You wanted to see me?"

"Come in. Shut the door and have a seat." Don pointed to a chair across the table from him. She slid into the seat and sat on her hands to keep from fidgeting. "We haven't talked much since you started. How are you doing? Is the job meeting your expectations?"

"I'm fine. Other than the one incident with being held up, it's been wonderful."

"I'm sorry I didn't really get a chance to talk to you after all of that. Are you doing okay?"

She relaxed a tiny bit. *Maybe he met with everyone during their first few months.* "I started taking martial arts so I can feel like I can defend myself. Everyone's been amazing about helping me."

"Will's been going on about how you've helped set up events around the store and got the social media running smoothly. The other managers are jealous."

She flushed at the praise. "It's nothing. I'm glad I could put some of my skills to work."

"I'm sure you're wondering why I asked you back here." He steepled his fingers and she nodded, a lump forming in her stomach. "The company is doing better than expected. We attribute much of that success to the clerks in the stores. With as much business as we are doing, it has brought up two things I wanted to talk to you about. The first is to find out if you'd be willing to drive to the other stores and help them do their social media like you do at the St Charles store."

She rocked back into her chair. He wanted her to help out in all the other stores? "Of course, if Will can spare me, I can work with them on getting things set up."

"Good, we're planning on hiring another part time person for the store to cover the hours." He made a note on his pad. "The second thing is more speculative in nature. We're looking to expand to another location. There's nothing solid yet, but we're looking to train the next manager so that when we find the perfect location, they will be ready. After much deliberation, we decided to offer you the job. There will be a slight pay raise while you are training and another when you take over the store."

She sat in stunned silence for a few minutes. "Why? Not that I don't appreciate the offer, but there are plenty of people who've been here longer than me. I've barely worked for you."

"We talked to all the managers at the last meeting to come up with a list of people. Your name topped the list. I know it might not be ideal to run a store with your responsibilities with your father."

"He's actually on the mend and doesn't need me anymore. His old job settled out of court, so I don't even have that on my plate anymore. Any idea of where this new store might be?"

"We're keeping our eyes open. We'd rather keep it nearby, but you never know what will come up."

Chapter Twenty-Five

B rad stepped into the game room. He could cut the tension with a knife. The guys stood in little quiet knots, talking in hushed tones. He set down his bag and joined one of the groups.

"What's going on?"

"Alex said he had something he wanted to tell everyone. It sounds serious, like bad serious."

They didn't have a chance to speculate any further because Alex walked into the room. "I'm glad to see all of you here. It does my heart good to see my regular guys gathered for this." He sat on one of the tables. "I need to close the Game Hut."

The guys all chimed in their dismay. Brad studied the owner. "Why?"

"It's been a long time coming. Every year, we've made less and less money. The internet's killing my business. With that said, I feel it's time for me to sell off the business and move on before it completely drains my bank account."

"How much are you selling it for?" The idea of losing this place killed Brad. Even with how rundown it had gotten, it held a special place in his heart. He choked at the dollar figure Alex threw out. "When are you closing if you can't find a new owner?"

"I haven't decided yet, I'm looking at the end of July, maybe sooner if business doesn't stay solid."

The owner exchanged nods with the group and left. The room stayed silent for a few minutes before they broke into small groups and muttered amongst themselves. Those who wanted to buy the business scrambled to figure out how to scrape together the funds.

He headed out the door and to Steve's house. He let himself in and dropped onto the couch next to Steve. His friend paused his video game and stared at Brad in disbelief when he told him what happened.

"I can't believe he's closing the store." Steve hung his arms over his knees.

"He's willing to sell it." Brad couldn't keep the hope out of his voice.

"That's a losing investment if he's telling the truth on what's going on."

"Tell me you wouldn't want to own a game store."

"Don't get me wrong, the location's prime and all that, but I wouldn't want to contemplate the amount of money it would take to get that place up to par."

He slumped back, deflated. "You were the only one that remotely had the kind of money Alex wants."

"When are you going to tell Sam?"

He covered his eyes. This would break her heart, he had no doubt about it. He always thought of the Game Hut as their place. "I hadn't thought about it. Probably when we know for sure if the store's closing. I don't want to tell her over messenger or the phone if I can help it."

"Don't wait too long. She'll want to come up to see it before it closes down. We'll hold a party."

"I wish I had your conviction that she'll come up."

SAM STEPPED OFF THE train and looked around. As expected, her mother was nowhere to be found. *Fucking peachy.* She should've known better than to get her hopes up that the woman would be on time. She sat on a bench and pulled out her current book.

"Sam!" Her step-father, James, ran up to her a few minutes later, his shaggy brown hair completely frazzled around his head. She smiled, her mother definitely had a type: tall, brunet, and muscular. "I'm so sorry I'm late. Your mom said she was coming but had something come up last minute. I got here as fast as I could."

She gave him a hug, noting he was still in his suit from work. "It's okay. Thank you for getting here so fast."

"Did you have a good trip?" He grabbed her suitcase before she could.

Shaking her head, she picked up her purse and backpack. "It was fine. I read most of the way when I wasn't napping."

He looked over at the book in her hand. "'The Way of the Sword,' I didn't take you for a martial arts connoisseur."

"Just started taking a class a month ago. I needed to feel like I could defend myself."

"Any reason in particular?" He hefted her suitcase into the trunk.

"I, um, had a shitty year. I got assaulted in a bathroom." She glanced at him when he gasped. "I didn't get raped. I had some amazing friends who saved me."

"Are you okay? I hadn't heard about that."

"I'm fine now. It was a rough time." She waved away the fear threatening to creep back into her throat. "But I did get held up at gunpoint at work."

James pulled her into a tight hug. "Sweetie, I'm so sorry. Why didn't your mom tell me?"

"I guess I forgot to tell her. By the time she calls, it's far enough in the past that I forget she doesn't know."

She climbed into the car and caught James up on everything going on in her life on the way home. He told her about her half-sister's play and academic achievements. By the time they pulled into the driveway, she had almost forgotten her frustration. Almost, until her mother met them at the door.

"My sweet daughter." Her mother pulled her into a tight hug, choking her on a cloud of perfume. "Sorry I missed your train. Victoria needed some last minute clothes for her program tonight and I broke a nail and needed to get it fixed."

"I guess it was a good thing you had James to pick me up." Sam looked over her mother's overly dyed red hair and long glittery talons. "I'd hate to be left at the train station because you had a nail emergency."

"It was your choice not to drive."

Yup, being punished for making her pay for me to come. She followed the trail of perfume into the kitchen. James set her suitcase in the living room. "Where am I sleeping?"

"The couch."

"What's wrong with the spare bed in Victoria's room?" She remembered why she stopped visiting after she went to college.

"We got rid of it when we got her a new bed." Her mother turned and frowned at her clothes. "You could never dress yourself properly. It's a good thing I bought you a dress for tonight."

Dread coiled in her belly as a box was thrust into her hands. She lifted the lid. Inside rested a hideous floral printed dress, three sizes too big. She stared at the gift in shock.

"You don't look pleased with your gift." Her mother stared daggers into her.

Sam set the box on the counter. "It's not really my style and way too big to fit me."

"I can never remember what size you wear." Her mother dismissed her with a wave of her hand.

"We could go shopping and pick out something together." She didn't know why she still wanted her mother to connect with her. "We have time before the play."

"I can't. I have plans to go out with your sister."

"Half." The correction came out of her mouth automatically.

"What was that?"

"Victoria's my half-sister."

"I haven't forgotten." Her mother glared at her from across the room.

"But you've forgotten everything else about me."

"Now you're being dramatic."

"How much thought did you put into my dress?"

"I wracked my brain."

Victoria sauntered into the room, all willowy and perfect. Sam always envied her dark blonde hair and grace. "She spent less than five minutes in the store, grabbed the first dress she found, and said 'this'll do.'" Her half-sister snagged two cookies from the jar and handed one to Sam. "And at that, Dad was the one to remind her you didn't know to bring a dress."

"Thanks for the honesty." She staggered back at Victoria's niceness.

"No problem. We have time before I have to leave for the play. Want to go shopping for something not hideous?"

"Please."

James tossed Sam the keys to his car with a wink. *Looks like he countered mom's terrible influence on Victoria.*

"DEAR GOD, YOU ARE SO fucking mopey lately."

Brad cast a look over his shoulder at Hannah. "I'm working, not moping."

"You've been on the phone and upset for over a week now. The store's closing, get over it." She waved a dismissive hand.

"How can you be so blase about it? That's where we met." *And I met Sam.*

"Sure, we met there, but we fell in love over at Steve's house. Are you going to pitch a bitch if he sells it?"

He didn't correct her about falling in love. "No, because if I wanted to, I'm sure he'd sell it to me."

"Well, it would be better than this dump." She flopped onto the couch like the weight of the world was on her shoulders. "I've seen you scribbling numbers. What's all that about?"

"Just running numbers on everyone that wants to pitch in on buying the store." He spent the last week trying to talk more people into investing in the store with little to no success.

"You can't be serious." She popped back up. "That place is a money pit. I forbid you from spending our future happiness on it."

He snorted. "Don't worry about it. There's only five of us seriously thinking about it, and we don't have even half of the asking price."

She sighed. "Good. I'd hate for you to have another business where you'd rather spend your time than with me."

He tried to tune out her negativity. He wanted to get this piece done before he headed out to the store tonight. It constituted the last of a rather large commission and enough money to keep him from worrying about rent and utilities for a couple of months, more if he was careful.

"If I could wave a magic wand to get all this painted, I would so I could have more free time."

"Hire an apprentice." Hannah repeated this solution every time they had this discussion.

"That requires more money than I have to spare right now. If you want to spend more time with me, you could help out with basing or something."

"That's menial labor. Hard pass."

"Then you are stuck with me working like a dog to get things finished." He shrugged away the thought of how different she was from Sam. He carefully finished the last stripe of green on the plaid pattern.

He barely had the mini set down when Hannah wrapped her arms around him. "You do good work. I just want more time with you."

"Then come with me to the store tonight, I promised one of my clients I'd bring their order to them and Steve wants to game. You used to like painting and spending time with me there."

"I can't. Sorority meeting." She kissed him. "I'll send you a text when it's winding down."

Chapter Twenty-Six

Sam stared at the door her mother just slammed. After thwarting the hideous dress, the woman didn't speak to her all night. Victoria, on the other hand, turned out to be a better ally than she had ever been in the past, talking late into the night. James and her sister were the bright spot in the visit.

Her mother started in on Sam early this morning, banging pots and pans around the kitchen to ensure Sam couldn't sleep. Sam tried to ignore the racket, but gave up and poured herself a cup of coffee which earned her a lecture about assuming she could eat or drink anything she wanted. She didn't relish the idea of an argument, so she dumped her cup back into the pot and walked up to the corner gas station to get her caffeine fix. She came back to a fuming mother and things escalated until she snapped and told her mother off. The older woman left in a huff.

Yup, this trip is going as expected. Sam didn't know why she hoped it would be different this time. "James, can you drive me to the Game Hut? I really don't want to be here when She gets back."

He handed her his keys. "Take it. I have my company car if I need to go anywhere."

"You really are the best." Impulsively, she kissed his cheek.

He looked taken back. "I'm sorry this trip has turned out bad for you."

"It's not your fault. You've been nothing but nice to me, even when I wasn't so nice to you."

"You were an angry kid who had no say in where you lived. You thought I was trying to take your dad's place."

"I don't think I've ever said thank you for everything you've done for me, including trying to keep me as part of this family."

"It's not even out of my way. I worry about all my kids. Even angry little girls."

She choked up and gave him a tight hug until she could talk again. "Is there any way we can stay a family without having Her in my life?"

"If you choose to cut your mom out, I will do everything in my power to make sure Victoria and I are still in your life."

"Thank you." She could never express how much he meant to her. Regret at the way she treated him when she was a child ate at her.

She waved good-bye and hopped in the car. James had all the fun toys and the little red sports car was one of her favorites. She pulled into the farthest parking spot at the Game Hut so no one would hit the car. Patting it, she snuck up behind Steve as he got to the entrance of the building and covered his eyes.

"Guess who."

He pulled her hands off his eyes and did a double take. "What are you doing here?"

"Avoiding the egg donor until I leave the state." She returned his hug with feeling.

He held the door for her. "Egg donor?"

"My mother. We had our come to Jesus talk about her not treating me like one of her kids. I don't think she listened, but I know my step-father did." She sat on one of the tables. The game room was dingier than she remembered. And a third of the lights were burned out. "I figure this'll be good for a couple of holidays without dealing with her."

"You're awfully blase about that."

"It's been building to this for way too many years." She waved at a couple of guys walking in. "Ever since my parents' divorce, I was the one thing she could use against my dad. It became more apparent when Victoria was born. And now I'm free." She flopped back with a contented sigh.

"Who's the dead body?" Brad's familiar voice had her head snapping back up. He dropped his bag in shock and scooped her off the table. "How have you been? How's your father? What are you doing here?"

Her heart strained in her chest and her hands itched to run themselves over his face and neck. "Good, fine, Mother's Day or avoiding my mother depending on if you mean in Wisconsin or here specifically." She ticked off her answers on her fingers to keep herself busy and ignore how good it felt to be in his arms. "Longer answers?"

"Please." He gently set her back on the table and pulled up a chair.

She took a moment to memorize his face. There were a few more frown lines than the last time she saw him and the ghosts of shadows under his eyes. *When was the last time he got a full night's sleep?* She forced down the worry bubbling up about him.

"I'm doing good. After that one incident, I'm taking martial arts to learn how to defend myself. I'm next in line for a promotion at work when a store opens up. Dad's doing much better than we hoped. He's driving himself around and actually owns shares in the company he used to work for."

"Why'd he buy shares in a company he's suing?"

"Right, you don't know. They settled out of court. He now owns enough shares to make an improvement to the way things are run."

"THAT'S AMAZING." BRAD envied the way Sam's eyes lit up when she talked about her life. *Leaving here really was the best thing for her.* The thought settled like a rock in his stomach. "What are you doing here?"

"A girl can't miss this dingy place?" She looked around the room with distaste. "My mother threw an epic level fit for me to come up for Mother's Day. We got into it almost as soon as I walked into the house. It all came to a head today and now I'm avoiding her until I can leave tomorrow."

His heart dropped at how soon she was leaving. "If you hate it up here so much, why didn't you leave today? Not that we don't love seeing you." *And having you rip open old wounds.*

"Train doesn't leave until the morning." She shrugged.

"And your car wouldn't have been a better option?"

"I wanted to make sure she paid for the trip. If I drove, she'd find a way to weasel out of return trip gas." She gave the room another once over. "It's awfully somber here. What gives?"

He caught the look Steve gave him. He hadn't come up with a good way to break the bad news to her. "Alex is closing the Game Hut."

"What? No!" She slumped forward on her perch. "Why?"

"He's been losing money for awhile and wants to sell it and move on."

"That's terrible. What's going to happen to it?"

"He's offered to sell it to our group, but no one has even a tenth of what he wants for it. Steve's the exception, but who would invest in a failing business?" It tore out his heart to tell her.

"I wish I could help. I love this place." Her eyes drank in their surroundings. "I have good memories here." She briefly glanced down at him before looking away.

"You wouldn't happen to know anyone with the money to buy it?"

"My boss, Don..." She looked thoughtful before shaking her head. "He wouldn't buy it if it's just a money sink. I could talk to him."

"I'd hate to lose our place, even if it means having it run by someone who's a blood sucking leech."

"Who's a blood sucking leech?"

"Your boss. Alex has been telling us—"

"All about the businesses Don has forced to close." She finished his sentence with a hard look at him. "I know the stories. The truth is most game store owners aren't businessmen. Don is. He goes in and tries to help or buy their stock when they close."

Her defense of her boss stunned Brad. "Never expected you to be so passionate about your boss."

"He's a good guy. He has a reputation for being the eight hundred pound gorilla in the room, but he's not like that. I wouldn't work for him if he was."

"I get it, don't judge a book by its cover." He held up his hands in surrender.

"Do you think he'd buy this place?" Steve butted in and took the words out of Brad's mouth.

Sam tapped her finger to her lips and thought for a moment. "I don't know. He's looking to expand, but I don't think he's planning on leaving Missouri with the next store. I'll bring it up to him when I see him."

Brad tried to not get his hopes up. He gave himself a mental shake. Here he had Sam all to himself and they were being fatalistic about the store. "We should do something. It's not everyday we get a Sam to spend time with."

"My house is always open to pretty girls." Steve winked at her.

"If it's one of your infamous parties, I should grab my suitcase and return James's car. That is, if there's room for me to crash and someone to take me to the station in the morning."

"I have an open room just for you and I happen to have the day off to be your personal chauffeur." Steve held out his hand.

Brad bit back a growl. "I'll drive you over to the house."

"I'll drive you." Steve countered and leaned in so she wouldn't overhear. "I don't think she needs to be in the car when you tell your girlfriend you're partying with Sam."

Just like that, the illusion shattered and reality set back in. *Hannah.* He'd have to bring her with to the party and there went any chance of spending time with Sam. He numbly nodded.

"Whichever of you is going to drive me. Follow me back to my mother's house." Sam rolled her eyes and walked out the door.

SAM DRIFTED INTO THE house after Steve. She waved at Chuck who was setting up the bar. *I shouldn't have come here.* So long as she didn't go into the basement, maybe she could keep the memories from crushing her.

Steve set her suitcase into a room. "You can bunk in here tonight."

"I'm afraid to ask who's room I'm stealing."

He avoided her eyes. "It's no one's."

"Meaning it's Brad's old one." Her heart lurched and a sick feeling settled in her stomach.

"That's exactly what I meant. If it bothers you, you can sleep in mine and I'll take this one."

"I'm not kicking you out of your room. I'm a big girl, I can handle sleeping in my ex's room for the night." She swallowed against the lie. "If I'm sufficiently drunk enough."

"Your wish is my command." He gave a gallant bow.

She smiled. "Thank you for taking me in."

"I wish I could do more for you."

She sat on the edge of the bed and ignored the waft of Brad's scent coming from the blankets. "It's not just the store, is it?"

"Shit's gone bad, Sam. He's stuck with Her and can't seem to get himself out of it."

"He's a big boy that makes his own choices. I tried to warn him."

"I know, but she plays his good guy instincts against him all the time." Steve paced the room. "Just when I think he's going to get free, she pulls him back in with honeyed lies."

"There's nothing I can do for him." She wiped her hands along her jeans to rid herself of the nervous energy crawling through her.

"I know. I just wanted to warn you before they show up tonight. Let's get you a drink." He took her hand and guided her to the bar. "If I remember right, you enjoy girly drinks."

She took the offered drink and nursed it while the house filled up with guys from the store. She nodded and chatted with most of them. A whoop caught her attention and she turned her head to see Brad and Hannah walk in the door. Immediately, Hannah turned her attention on some of the guys and did shots with them. Sam watched, mesmerized by the sight until Brad snagged a bottle from behind the bar and retreated downstairs.

She waited a few minutes and followed after him. He sat on the couch taking long pulls from the bottle in his fist. The room looked wrong without his mess of paints and papers on the desk. She knocked on the wall.

"Do you mind if I join you?"

"It's a free country."

She perched on the arm of the couch and studied him for a long moment. He looked like he had been put through the wringer. "Is everything alright?"

He snorted. "Depends on who you ask." He tipped the bottle back. "If you ask her, everything's fine except I need a better paying job to keep her happy."

"I didn't ask her, I asked you. But I can see you just want to be alone with your bottle." Her hand itched to rip it out of his hand. "I'll see you later. I have no interest in watching you kill yourself."

"SAM, WAIT." BRAD COULDN'T let her walk away from him. He snagged her warm wrist. "Stay. I'll stop drinking if it means you'll sit and talk to me."

"Fine." She snatched the bottle from his grasp and took a swig. Her face contorted into a grimace. "How do you drink this?"

"The drunker you are, the less you taste it." He took the bottle back and set it carefully on the floor. He struggled to sit up straight.

"I'll take your word on it." She looked everywhere but at him.

"How did you become friends with Hannah?" The question popped out of his mouth without a thought.

She frowned at him like he was crazy. "As you recall, I told you she was never my friend."

"Fine, tell me how she came into your life."

"Julie and Eric grew up together. She's a year younger, so I was already friends with him and dating Andrew by the time she came to college with us. Hannah was assigned as her roommate and seemed shy, so we went out of our way to include her." Sam slid off the arm and onto the couch.

"And in thanks she stole your boyfriend." He grimaced as the pieces slowly fell into place.

"Honestly, Andrew and I were at the point where we were more friends with benefits. We were comfortable with continuing with the way it was until something better came along. It didn't cross my mind that she was jealous or whatever at the time."

"What changed your mind?" He mirrored her pose to face her on the couch. He tapped her foot with his when she took too long to answer.

"Aaron." She squirmed a bit mentioning her ex's name. "He has... needs in the bedroom that I wasn't comfortable meeting."

He leaned forward a bit, intrigued by her reluctance. "Like threesomes or something else?"

"Like tying up his partner and taking a crop to them." Her face turned pink and she looked away. "Hannah overheard me talking to Julie and Olivia about it and pursued him armed with the knowledge. She pretended to be a submissive version of me." She cocked her head to the side. "I can't believe you didn't ask Andrew or Luke about this when I told you to."

It was his turn to squirm. "I got slammed with work and was in over my head before I knew it."

"What happened? How'd she get to you?" Sam curled her arms around her legs.

"She showed up on Thursday nights wanting to learn how to play and paint. I needed a distraction and thought I could find out more about how you two fell out. And..." *God, I had been so stupid and blind.*

"You thought you could get us to be friends again."

He nodded. "I got beyond drunk after the tournament and..." He couldn't bring himself to tell her the nitty gritty details. "I wanted to own up to my mistake right away, but then she freaked out on me and accused me of using her."

"She knew exactly which buttons to push."

"Yeah, we've been fighting on and off since. She and her father belittled my business. When I confronted her about it afterward, she told me she thought I'd outgrow it."

"That fucking bitch. I wish there was something I could do to help."

His chest warmed at the venom in her voice. A kernel of hope bloomed in him. "Stop being mad at me?"

Her eyes softened a bit as she looked across the couch at him. "I was never mad. Disappointed, yes, especially after I tried to warn you. Heartbroken, definitely."

"You moved away."

"Did you really expect me to stay up here? I couldn't watch history repeat itself a third time, not with you, so I got a job near my dad."

"You're harshly honest tonight."

"It's been that kind of trip." She sighed. "I'm going to head up to the party."

He watched her go up the stairs without a glance backwards. *Not with you.* The words bounced around in his head. Did it mean she still had feelings for him?

Chapter Twenty-Seven

Sam rolled over and buried her face in the pillow. Brad's scent filled her head and she reached for him. *They hadn't woken up together in forever,* she thought joyfully. Coming up empty, she cracked her eye open with a groan. Memories of the night before came flashing back with a sharp headache hot on their heels.

I'm never drinking that much again. She dressed and followed the scent of coffee in the hopes there were some pain killers in the house. Steve stood in the middle of the kitchen making food. She dropped into the nearest chair and laid her head on her folded arms. A cup of coffee and a couple of aspirin appeared in front of her. She nodded her thanks.

"Morning, sweetie. You looked like you had a blast last night." Sarcasm laced his words. "I was beginning to think you were going to finish that bottle of rum by yourself."

"I'll buy you a new one." The coffee woke her up enough for the pounding in her head to increase. "It was a bad night."

"I'd say, you gave Hannah a run for her money on getting stupid drunk." He squeezed her hand before sliding a plate in front of her. "I overheard part of your conversation with Brad."

"Awesome." Just what she needed, an audience for her honest talk.

"Sorry, I went looking for you when I noticed you missing." He dug into his plate and made a gesture to hers. "It'll help your hangover before you get on the train."

She dug into the eggs and toast, mulling over the trip. Steve left her to her thoughts without much prying. She wondered how much he overheard, but couldn't summon up the energy to ask. Feeling more human, she grabbed her suitcase and carried it out of the room. He took it from her and loaded it in the car.

"Thank you for everything. I appreciate it." She hugged him.

"I wish I could've done more." He kissed her cheek. "I've missed you."

"Missed you too. You should come down and see my work sometime."

"I've been meaning to. Let me know when you have a War Tactics tournament."

"I will." She waved and boarded her train, feeling a bit better about her trip.

I should've driven, at least it would be a distraction. Her thoughts chased themselves around her head while she stared out the window until her exhaustion overtook her. Her train finally spat her out at her stop near midnight and she snuck into the dark house an hour later.

Her alarm woke her a few short hours later. Contemplating calling in, she forced herself up and into the kitchen. She watched the coffee pot drip while she waited for it to finish brewing.

"You look like someone kicked your puppy, kiddo." Her dad limped into the living room and settled into his chair with a sigh.

She poured a cup and brought it to him. "Never had a puppy, mom wouldn't allow it."

"I would have if you lived with me. Do you want to get a puppy?"

"Not making this any better." She scalded her tongue in her rush to inhale the caffeine.

"Rough trip?"

"The roughest."

"Want to talk about it?" He held out his arms.

She curled up in his arms like she was a little kid, avoiding his bad leg. "Fought with mom."

"About what?" He rocked her and the knot in her chest loosened.

Tears threatened to fall, but she choked them back. "That she doesn't treat me like her kid. Don't think I got through to her, but James got it. He promised to keep her in line. Victoria and I bonded."

"That's good. Anything else happen?"

"Found out the Game Hut's shutting down. Saw Brad." His arms tightened around her. She took all the comfort she could to keep talking. "Watched him drink himself stupid. Had an honest talk with him. Drank too much and slept in his old bed."

"How do you feel now?"

"Hollow. I don't know how I should feel. Maybe all this closure hasn't hit me yet."

"I'm proud of you, sweetie."

"When it sinks in, I'm sure I'll be proud of myself too." She glanced at the clock and kissed his cheek. "I need to get to work. Thanks for listening. I love you."

"YOU'VE BEEN MOPING since the party." Hannah stepped between Brad and the coffee maker.

"I'm worried what the loss of the game store will do to my business." He reached around her to grab the pot. He needed caffeine if he was going to deal with her attitude this early.

"You weren't this upset when you first heard the news. I think this has to do with seeing Her again." She sniffled. "You're thinking about leaving me."

He counted backwards from ten before answering. "This has nothing to do with Sam's visit." The partial lie tasted sour on his tongue. He sipped his coffee to wash it away. "Maybe some of my mood has to do with the way you acted at the party. I can't say I loved seeing my girlfriend flirting with my friends."

"Oh please, I was just having fun." She rolled her eyes.

"How about trying to have fun with the person you're dating?" Rage simmered in his veins.

"You could've joined me."

"The last time I tried that, you bit my head off and sent me back to watch your purse." He stomped to his desk.

"I need to get to class. Maybe when I get back, you'll have pulled the stick out of your ass." She slammed the door behind her.

He sat at his desk for a few minutes after she left, stewing over their conversation. She always made him out to be the bad guy. After staring at his work without touching any of it, he got up and went into the bedroom. He tossed a bunch of clothes into a duffle bag and dug around the upper shelf for Sam's photo album.

The box felt too light. He let out a blistering curse. The box was empty. *That bitch hid Sam's present.* He finished packing his bag and sat to wait for Hannah to come back.

She came sauntering a few hours later and stopped short when she saw the box. "What's this?"

"Why don't you tell me? When I moved in, this held a photo album, but it's no longer there." He applauded himself for how calm he sounded when all he wanted to do was ring her neck.

"Pictures of another woman. Naked photos. Why would you keep those?" Her voice rose with every word.

"They were a gift from a friend. A gift I put away and didn't look at because I was with you."

"Then why did you pull it out today?" Her eyes landed on his bag. "You're leaving?"

"I'm going to spend the night with friends. I need time to 'pull the stick out of my ass.'" He stood and picked up the duffle. "Now, where is the photo album?"

"I burned it. I thought about leaving the ashes in the box for you." She crossed her arms and raised her chin.

Red filled his vision. Sam's gift, burned to ashes. The gaping hole in his chest reopened. It was the one thing he had to prove she had been his, even for a short period of time.

"I'll be back tomorrow. We will discuss this relationship after I've cooled down." He brushed past Hannah before he did something he regretted and headed to Steve's.

"DON, MAY I HAVE A MINUTE of your time?" Sam hovered in the doorway to the office, praying she wasn't interrupting anything. Even after all this time, her boss still intimidated her.

"Of course." He smiled and gestured to the chair across from him. She slid into it and toyed with a pen. "I hear you've been picking the brains of the other managers while you're in their stores."

"It helps me figure out what they need from me and allows me a chance to see how other perspectives on managing affect the outcomes of their sales."

"I'd love to hear your theories and insights."

Her shoulders relaxed a fraction. "Anytime you have a spare minute."

"How was your trip?"

"As expected, full of drama." She shifted in her seat and took a deep breath. "I wanted to talk to you about something that happened while I was up there."

"You're not thinking about moving back, are you?"

"No." She waved away his concern. "While I was at my mother's, I visited my old game store, the Game Hut. The owner, Alex, is selling the business."

"Do you know why?"

"The guys say he's losing money. No one there has the capital and willingness to buy it." She sighed knowing the chance of Don saving the business was slim. It tore her up to lose the space, even if she didn't play there. "I figured if nothing else, we could buy some of his stock."

"Tell me about the store." He flipped to a new page on his notepad.

"It's like St Charles minus the comics. And dirtier. I couldn't tell you the last time the store had been cleaned." She wrinkled her nose. He indicated she should elaborate. "It's really more the community that shops there that makes the place so great. They band together and cheer each other on."

He grilled her about the stock mix and community for over an hour. Will came in to check on her partway into the conversation. Finally satisfied, Don set his pen down.

"I will check into the store and talk to Alex. It sounds like they have some product we could use if we can get it cheap enough."

Defeated and empty, she nodded. "I figured it would be a good opportunity for the company."

"Thank you for bringing it to my attention. I'll see you at the meeting on Monday."

"I CAN'T BELIEVE YOU took her back." Chuck flopped onto the chair. "You had the perfect out."

"She had a perfectly reasonable excuse for why she burned it." Brad's words lacked conviction. He still didn't understand Hannah's animosity toward Sam.

"She always has a reasonable excuse." Steve cracked open a soda. "That's the problem, you always allow her to talk her way back into the relationship."

"Dude, you could've convinced Sam into coming back if you weren't balls deep in crazy."

"Don't call my girlfriend names." Brad leaned back and stared at the ceiling. "Besides, Sam's happy in Missouri. And she's gotten over me."

Steve snorted. "Keep telling yourself that."

"What's that supposed to mean?"

"You didn't see her after your little chat the other night." Steve gestured to Chuck. "Chuck had to peel the bottle of rum out of her hand. Liquid courage to be able to spend the night in a room that smells like you." Chuck nodded. "I don't think she's over you and you're not over her."

"Fuck." Brad couldn't catch a break. His heart leapt to attention. *Sam needed courage to sleep in my old bed.* "Hannah said something like that as her reason for burning the photos. Why would I keep sexy pictures of another woman when I'm with her?"

"You should've left them here, dumbass. I would've taken real good care of them." Steve smirked at him.

Brad chucked a pillow at his friend. "She's not your type."

"You never know until you have them in bed with you."

Brad shook his head to clear it of the image of Sam laid out on his bed, so strung out on bliss that she couldn't ever leave again. "It doesn't matter, she's happy with her new job."

Chapter Twenty-Eight

"One last piece of business for today." Don looked around the table. Sam pasted on an interested look, but the day had drug on for the past ten hours. "I've spoken to Alex, the owner of the Game Hut in Wisconsin. He is asking a lot for his business and isn't willing to just sell off his stock. I told him before I commit, I want to go over his records and store. He has six months left on his lease, so if we were to buy him out and keep the store, I would need a manager for it. Any takers?"

She slumped in her chair. There was no way she was volunteering for the job. No way she would have to see Brad every time he needed paints or played a game. Everyone stared at her.

"Why is everyone looking at me?"

"I think they are waiting for you to volunteer."

"I couldn't. I've barely worked here." She shook her head vehemently.

"Sam, in the time you've been here, sales have gone up eleven percent company-wide. You brought up the idea of buying the Game Hut. You already know the clientele. What seems to be the problem?"

I moved to Missouri to get away from one of the customers. The words hung in her mouth unsaid. She squirmed under the scrutiny of the room. "It seems like a huge responsibility to give a new manager."

"We're not going to make a decision today, but Sally and I are going up on Friday to start looking into the opportunity. Why don't you come with us and see how it feels to you?"

She was cornered and she knew it. She couldn't get out of this without explaining why she didn't want to go back. "Sounds like a plan." She forced a smile on her face. "I just need to get my shifts covered."

"I got you covered." Will nodded in her direction.

"Thanks."

She drug herself in the house after the meeting, not understanding why they lasted all day. It didn't seem like everything got done on the agenda, even after ten hours. She dropped her bag next to the couch. Her body crashed into the cushions.

"Long day, kiddo?"

"The longest. I hate meeting days especially because I'm not a manager yet." She looked over at him. "I hope you ate, I'm not up for cooking and we got pizza."

"Do you need a sounding board?" He set aside his book.

"How do you know?"

"I'm a parent, I know things. You have your deep thought face on."

"I'm supposed to go up to Wisconsin with Don and Sally on Friday to look over the Game Hut to see if we're going to buy it." She stared dully into space. "If we do, they want me to run the store."

"That's amazing, Sam." He paused for a couple of seconds. "That's the store He shops at, isn't it?"

"The old man gets it in one try." She flopped back like she was on a therapist's couch. "What do I do?" Her brain and her heart were conflicted and she wasn't sure which one to follow anymore.

"Honestly? Go to Wisconsin. Look at the store. Give your honest feedback. Don't worry about whether or not you'll be asked to run it. You'll know the answer when it comes up. All you have to do is follow your heart, but you knew that without me telling you." He leaned over and patted her head. "Besides, you can't hide in Missouri the rest of your life."

Sometimes she hated how well he knew her. "I could, but then I'd be stuck doing your laundry for the rest of my mortal life."

The week flew by faster than she wanted it to. She woke up ridiculously early and got in her car for the long drive. She pulled into the parking lot of the Game Hut and stared at the store, working up the nerve to walk in. Her feet found the stairs before she registered where she was heading.

"Sam? What are you doing here? Why didn't you let me know you were coming?" Brad scooped her up in a tight hug. "I've missed you."

She reveled in the feel of his strong arms around her. She returned his hug with feeling before forcing herself to step away. "Missed you too. This was a last minute decision. Bosses say 'drive to Wisconsin,' you do it."

BRAD TOOK BACK EVERY bad thing he'd ever said about Sam's bosses. Hope filled his chest and he could barely breathe. "Bosses?"

"Slow down, buddy. This trip means nothing except they are looking into a possible lead."

"And you?"

"I'm only here to assist Don and Sally because I know my way around the store." She didn't meet his eyes.

"Sam? A moment of your time, please." A woman gestured from the doorway.

Sam gave his arm a squeeze before following the woman out the door. He rubbed the spot. She was lying about something to him. He waited for her to reappear with a piece of paper in her hand and a thoughtful expression.

His curiosity got the better of him. He snatched the paperwork out of her hand. "What do we have here?"

"Work I have to do for my job." She grabbed for it, but he kept it out of her reach. "And it's private, so give it back."

He darted around the tables. "Let's see here. 'Changes you would make to the store. Which clerks fit with your vision of the store? Product lines you'd like to add.' Sammy-cat, if I didn't know any better, I'd say these questions were for the person who would be running the store."

"Stop fucking around. I have work to do." She glared at him.

He touched a nerve. "I'll give it back if you answer one question. Would you be the one running the store if they bought it?"

She gave him an exasperated look. "Sally and Don want me to, but I'm not convinced it's a good idea."

"Why?"

"It's too much responsibility. I'd be left without the support system of the other stores being close together." She held out her hand. "That's two questions. Now give me the paperwork."

It wasn't like her to doubt her ability to run a store. He stalked around the table and she retreated a step. He set the paper on the table, but kept his hand on it so she couldn't take it.

"There sounds like there's more to the answer."

"Is there an answer that will get you to leave me alone to work?"

He pushed her too far, but wouldn't back down. "Just the truth. That's all I want."

"The truth is I have a week to help my bosses decide if they are going to buy this place. I didn't want to come with them, but no one else wanted to come and I got tossed under the bus." She pointed at the paper and he stepped back. She gathered all of her things and walked to the door. She glanced back at him. "I've missed this place, but there are too many memories associated with it that I don't want to think about."

He stared after her, open-mouthed. He hoped her bosses liked the store and forced her hand to make her stay to run it. He could find a way to make it up to her and fix everything. Hope welled dangerously in his chest. He needed her to come back so he could fix this. He settled into his chair and worked on base coating a mini while he waited for his client to show.

SAM LEFT THE BASEMENT before her mouth got her into any more trouble. She almost told Brad that he was the reason she didn't want to come back. The lie soured in her mind. No, the situation with him and Hannah made her not want to come back and continue to hide in Missouri.

She poked around the different parts of the store she couldn't as a customer to satisfy her curiosity and to push the conversation with Brad out of her head. Layers of dust coated boxes in the warehouse and front room, some of them looked like they had barely been opened. She frowned at the stacks and moved on, intent on asking about them later.

Don found her hours later, leaning on the counter and asking the clerks questions. "Where's the nearest place to get real food?"

"There's an Italian place around the corner that most of us used to go to. Food's really good." The words were out of her mouth before she remembered the night of the tournament. The breath whooshed out of her, but it was too late to take back the suggestion.

"Do you want your friend to come along?" Sally joined them.

"Friend?" Sam thought for a minute until she realized who Sally meant. "Oh, you mean Brad. It depends on if you want to talk about the business in front of customers or not I guess."

"Can he be trusted?" Don grew serious.

She almost snorted. *With business secrets, yes, but not with your heart.* "He knows how to keep his mouth shut when he needs to. He's kind of the leader in the miniatures community around here."

"He was the one who brought up Alex selling?" She nodded to Don. "See if he wants to give us his insights."

She gave a nod and headed down the stairs. She could just wait at the bottom for a minute and then go back and tell her bosses he didn't want to come. He didn't have a high opinion of her bosses anyway. She wavered near the door. *Coward.*

She strode into the game room and tapped Brad on the shoulder. "My bosses were wondering if you wanted to come to dinner and offer up your insights about the place."

"Give me a minute to pack up and I'll come along." He studied her. "Unless you'd rather I didn't."

"No, come with." She forced herself to not take him up on the offer. "They want to hear from the customers to get a better idea of what's going on. You're the person I can depend on to give them straight answers and keep mum about the behind the scenes talk."

"Of course."

BRAD DROPPED HIS BAG off at his car. Sam didn't want him to come to dinner, that much he knew. Why she bothered to ask him to come along was beyond him. He followed in silence on the way to the restaurant. He stopped short. *Did Sam realize this was the restaurant they went to the first time he met her and after her first tournament win?* She pulled a breadstick out of the container and broke it in half and placed half in front of him. His heart pounded in his ears. *Of course she remembers.* She avoided his eyes while introducing him to her bosses.

He fidgeted in his seat, overly conscious of his every move and how it affected her job. He'd hate for her bosses to see her in a bad light because he stuck his foot in his mouth. The talk quickly turned to business and he had to respect them for knowing exactly what they were looking for. Sam shone as she showed exactly how smart she was. He made a note to see if she would be willing to straighten up his business.

"The numbers just don't add up. The amount Alex is spending on AW doesn't equal his sales, but his shelves are empty." Don stabbed the papers with his finger.

"Not to mention the shelves are covered in a layer of dust." Sam pointed out, obviously disgusted at how dirty the store had gotten. "May I?" She shifted her barely touched plate out of the way and took the paperwork. Brad itched to slide the food back in front of her. "This is almost all core material. And it's repeated almost exactly every month. Look."

Don picked up a couple of pages. "That's what I don't understand. These items have empty space on the shelf. Do you think someone's stealing?"

"I think it's more simple than that. I was looking into the warehouse and that extra room near the front. They are filled to the ceiling with boxes from just about every distributor."

"You think it's sitting in the warehouse."

"If you were a super lazy clerk, you would make sure special orders were pulled and then you'd dump the rest of the box in the warehouse. Forget it needs to be worked. The next time your rep calls to make sure you have core items, you're out so they ship more. Continue the pattern until it's too overwhelming to even think about fixing."

"I want to test your theory tomorrow." Don turned his attention to Brad. "What has been your experience with shopping at the Game Hut?"

He had dreaded this question. Here was where he talked them out of buying the business. He shifted under the scrutiny. "Honestly, sir..."

"Call me Don."

Brad looked at Sam. She nodded encouragement. He pushed her plate back in front of her and grabbed a breadstick. He broke it and gave her half with a gesture to eat. She arched an eyebrow at him, but dug into her pasta.

"Honestly, Don, I continue shopping and gaming there because it's the closest store to my apartment. Over the past few months, it's gone downhill. Sam can tell you how much better it was at the end of last year when the shelves were stocked and the customers were appreciated. We used to have amazing tournaments that brought in people from all over the area."

"What do you attribute the change to?"

"Alex checked out. He leaves his clerks in charge of just about everything but doesn't pay them enough to run the store. You rarely see him, shelves are consistently empty of product, clerks have attitude. I couldn't tell you the last time the bathroom's been cleaned." He swallowed back the thought that he was the last person to clean the bathroom and why. "Terrain needs to be fixed or replaced. We used to get together a couple times a year to repair it, but we stopped getting any kind of recognition for it and there is a new group of guys that go out of their way to be rough on it so it doesn't stay fixed for very long."

"There's a lack of oversight and caring from the store itself?" Don made a few notes.

Brad nodded, his stomach cramping at the thought of swaying them away from the store. "Yes, sir. Most of my group has been playing at other stores for the most part, especially because they stopped holding tournaments. They only come to play here if they need something specific from the store or me."

Sam gasped and looked up from her half full plate. "No more Thursday night painting?"

"It's hard to paint when half the lights need new bulbs." He didn't tell her he shifted around the burned out bulbs so their spot was always lit.

"Thank you for your honesty." Sally smiled at him.

He couldn't shake the sinking feeling as he sat back and let Sam take the spotlight for the rest of dinner. Her bosses left the two of them at the door to the store. "Do you think they'll buy it?"

"I wouldn't get my hopes up. I saw some of the numbers for the store. It looks really bad." She tried to give him a brave face, but he could read the writing on the wall. "Still, we've come all this way. He won't make a decision until we're gone through everything. I'll let you know first thing either way."

"Thanks, Sammy." Impulsively he squeezed her hand. "I never really realized before that you're kind of a wiz at this whole business thing."

"I've been learning a lot from working with Don and Sally. They've sharpened my skills."

"How much would you charge to whip my business into shape?"

"A million dollars." He gaped at her. She covered her mouth with her hand to cover her giggle. "You were serious. You really want my help?"

"I feel like I've stalled out with my own knowledge. I could really use your help."

"Let me get through this store thing and then we'll talk."

Chapter Twenty-Nine

Sam walked out of the warehouse, coated in dust and bone tired. She spent the better part of the week sorting out the pile of boxes in the back room. She shuddered at the idea of what was in the front room. *What a waste of retail space.* She wiped her hands off on her jeans as she walked to the office.

"Out of ten boxes, all ten have similar contents, slight variation if they have more in them."

Don looked up from the paperwork strewn on the table. "How much would you say is in the boxes?"

"Our cost or retail?"

"Our cost."

She flopped into a nearby chair and hoped Sally came back from the coffee run soon. "About two or three hundred dollars, depending on the box."

"How many are there?"

"Nineteen, just for AW."

"Hmph." He made more notes.

She could never figure out what he was thinking when he made that sound. She sat on pins and needles while he scribbled. "There are thirty-two other boxes in the warehouse I haven't even cracked into from other distributors."

"If we went low and said the other boxes had a hundred dollars worth of product, that's seven thousand dollars sitting collecting dust."

"What a waste of money." She needed to fill the silence and riffled through her notes. "How can you justify pissing away seven thousand dollars? And that's not counting the extra room full of stuff that could be retail space."

He made a few more notes before looking up at her. "If you aren't business minded, it's just the cost of doing business. It trickles out a little bit at a time without much notice."

"Is that why all of your stores have tight budgets?"

"It keeps the stores from overstocking and spending more than they can afford. It also makes the managers more conscious of what really sells in their stores." He passed her a paper full of numbers. "Will you check my math?"

She took her time going over the lines. "Looks right to me. What's it all mean?"

"That's how much the store costs to buy." She choked at the figure. He continued tapping the columns as he went. "How much product in the store is worth roughly, and how much the store costs to run each month with minimum product coming in."

She pulled up the last couple months worth of sales. "That's way less than it's making now."

"I noticed that too. My calculations included your pay raise, which makes me wonder how much Alex is pocketing and how much he's just overspending."

Sally walked in with a tray of coffee and glanced over Don's shoulder. "Do you have it all figured out?" He nodded. "I'm guessing we can have our discussion now."

Sam took the offered cup and looked back and forth between her bosses. "I'm confused. I swore you said something about my pay raise being part of your calculations."

"I was wondering if you caught that." Don cleared his throat. "We know you're reluctant to consider taking this job."

"And it's not just the workload." Sally smiled across the table. "Every challenge we've given you, you've exceeded at. You moved to Missouri to help out your dad, but something else made you stay. It isn't any of our business, but we need you to consider taking over this store."

Sam slumped in her chair. "What happens if I say no?"

Don shrugged. "We put in an offer for the product we want and go back to Missouri."

"Why can't you have someone else run this place?"

"No one else in the company wants it." He gave her a pointed look. "You know the clientele which would make the transition easier. If we took over the lease without a manager in place, we would be up here trying to find a suitable replacement. That's more work than we are willing to put into an acquisition so far from our base of operations."

"If I refuse, this place shuts down." Her heart sank to her knees. Could she do that to her friends just because she didn't want to see Brad and Hannah together?

"Alex might keep it going after getting rid of the excess product, but more than likely, yes. It's a lot of hard work, but I know you can rise to the challenge. If you accept the position, we will give you a twenty-five percent raise, an additional week of vacation every year, and moving expenses. Sally and I are going to stay for the next couple of months to get you comfortable and get this place on the right track."

"How long do I have to think about it?"

"We'd like to put in the offer before the week is out."

BRAD KICKED HIMSELF for how much time he spent in the Game Hut during the last week. His business suffered because he couldn't do much detail work in the gloomy basement, but he couldn't stop himself from wanting to catch glimpses of Sam. As if his thoughts summoned her, she wandered into the game room lost in thought. She was absolutely adorable, covered in dust from digging through the store. He tried to catch her eye, but she kept looking around the room like it would give her all the answers to the universe. She nodded to herself and flew back out of the room.

"I wonder what that was all about." Steve stared after her.

Brad rooted himself to the spot so he didn't follow after her. "No idea, but I guess she'll tell us when she's ready."

A few minutes later, she skipped back into the room, her face glowing with excitement. She waved him over. "They're going to start negotiations to buy the store."

He let out a whoop and spun her around. "That's amazing."

"It is." She grinned and hugged him tight before squirming out of his arms. "I need to go apartment hunting. See ya!" She waved.

"Wait, what?"

"Oh, the other part is I'm taking over this location." She skipped out of the basement before her words sank in.

"Sam, hold up." He raced after her. "Stop and say that again." He grabbed her arm to keep her from going up the stairs. He was afraid his mind was playing tricks on him.

"Don and Sally putting in the bid to buy this place was contingent on me taking over as manager. I just told them yes, so I have to go apartment hunting."

He pulled her into his arms, trying hard to not crush her in his excitement. "That's the best news I've heard all day."

"I need to breathe." She pushed against him until he let go, but she grinned up at him. "Where do I start looking?"

"Do you want my help?"

"Please."

Anything for her, even if it meant being late and dealing with an angry girlfriend. He pulled up nearby apartments and set up a couple appointments for the afternoon. She traipsed through one bedroom apartments and studios with him in tow. He kept trying to steer her toward something with a bit more room in the hopes he'd find a way back into her life, but she pushed for the smallest available space she could find near the store.

"I think this one's perfect." She stared out the window.

He snapped a quick picture of her. "It's awfully small, Sammy-cat." He ran a finger along the counter. "Dirty too."

"I don't need much space, it's just me and maybe some plants I'll kill." She climbed into the lofted space and sat with her feet on the stairs. "I'll sleep up here, put my painting area over there near my TV, and have enough space for a small table in the kitchen area." She stood. "Besides, rent is cheap because it's been empty for a while, it's close to the store, and I can move in right away."

He squinted at the space and tried to see her vision. He could see her making the apartment comfortable no matter the size. "I love that you're moving back. It will be like you never left."

She descended the stairs. "Except this isn't the House that Gaming Built. I'll be on my own for the first time ever." She hopped down the last stair. "You're helping me move in."

He stood toe-to-toe with her, fighting the urge to pick her up and kiss her. There was no question in his mind he'd help her move in, but her presumption rankled. "How do you figure? Your bosses are hiring a moving company."

"Movers don't unpack your stuff or put it away." She stepped up a step so she could stare at his eyes. "I'm offering a trade. Help me move and I will help you with your business." She stuck out her hand.

"Just like that? It seems like a lopsided trade. You have no idea what kind of mess my business is in."

"I've seen your business, Brad." She raised an eyebrow. "You have to be here for the entirety of the move in. Every minute you're late, I charge extra to straighten out your mess."

"Deal." He clasped her hand in his and damn near crowed with excitement. Sam was back and life was looking up.

Chapter Thirty

Sam pulled into the driveway and slumped against her steering wheel. She looked at the little red car parked behind her dad's. *One of his work friends must be visiting. At least he wasn't alone the entire time she had been gone.* The thought lifted some of her worries about moving away. She grabbed her suitcase and let herself into the house.

"I'm home." She dropped her suitcase and followed noises into the kitchen. Her dad was locked in a passionate embrace with a woman. Neither him or the red head looked up when she entered the room. She gagged and backed up. "Oh, yuck. There is not enough eye bleach in the world to get that out of my brain."

Her dad broke off the lip lock and stared at her with wide eyes. "Sam, you're home early."

"Apparently I wasn't expected." She backed up slowly. "I'm just going to go to my room. And scrub my brain." She bolted down the hall.

The slow thump of her dad's cane followed her. "Did you have a good trip?"

"It was fine." She frowned at her dad's messed up hair. "Are we going to talk about how I came home to find you making out with a woman where I eat?" She shuddered. "Please tell me you will scrub down the counters and table before I need to make food."

"Samantha, I'm old enough..."

"To have a girlfriend, I know. I just don't need to see you making out in the kitchen." She made a face. "I'm happy you'll have someone to keep an eye on you after I leave."

"You accepted the job." He didn't seem surprised.

"Accepted it and got an apartment. Boxes are in the car so I can pack. Movers will be here in a couple of days. And then I get to take over my new store." She couldn't keep the grin from splitting her face. "My own store. With my own clerks." She burst into cheesy dance moves.

"Congrats, kiddo." He pulled her into a tight hug. "You deserve it."

She perched on the edge of her desk. "So, who's the woman you were sucking face with?"

"Her name is Mary."

"And how did we meet her?"

"She works in the office."

"Aw, office romance. How cute."

"Smart ass."

"Better than being a dumbass." A movement in the hall drew her attention. Mary peeked around the corner. "Does she know you're a big dork?"

Mary leaned against the doorway, her copper red hair hastily smoothed down. "Not only does she know, but she thinks it's adorable."

"She sticks up for you." Sam high-fived her dad. "Way to pick 'em."

"Your dad has good taste. He talks about you all the time."

She had to give the woman points for sucking up to her. "He's a good learner. He only made the mistake of a shitty woman once."

"Samantha Marie, that is no way to talk about your mother." His scolding held no heat.

Sam held her hands up. "I never mentioned her. You're the one that assumed." She schooled her expression. "I'm going to grab my boxes and leave you two to whatever it was you were doing when I came home. Please close the door and maybe put a sock on it so I don't walk in on you."

"I'VE BEEN THINKING."

Brad bit back a groan. No good ever came from Hannah uttering those words. He glanced at the clock and mentally cursed. He needed to leave to get to Sam's to help her unpack. He hoped to get there early, but it looked like his girlfriend had other plans.

"What have you been thinking about?"

"I've been absolutely horrible to you since you moved in." She draped herself across the back of his chair. "I hadn't realized how much work it takes to have a live-in relationship."

"It's definitely hard work." *Especially when your girlfriend was making you late.*

"It's really hard to keep the spark alive." She nipped at his ear, oblivious to his need to leave the conversation. "I got you a gift."

She grabbed his hand and led him to the couch. With a push, he flopped onto the cushions. She handed him a box with a flourish. He looked at the box with a sick feeling in his stomach. Dutifully, he opened it up to find a photo album with a picture of her blowing a kiss.

Flipping through the pages, his worst fears were confirmed. Hannah replaced Sam's gift with one of her own, meaning she found out Sam was moving back and wanted to keep him from leaving. Each consecutive picture was more explicit than the last. He wanted to light the damn thing on fire and never see it again, but plastered on what he hoped was a grateful look on his face.

"Do you like it?"

"Thank you." He leaned in and kissed her. "It's unexpected."

"I figured you'd want something to look at when our lives get crazy busy." She pulled the book out of his hand and crawled onto his lap. "Now, show me how grateful you are for my gift."

He closed his eyes with a sigh. He wasn't going to make it to Sam's on time. Turning his attention to Hannah, he picked her up and carried her to the bedroom.

"YOU GUYS CAME!" SAM hugged Steve and Chuck as they entered her apartment. "Thanks for helping out."

"Anything for you, sweetness." Steve looked over her helpers. "Looks like you have plenty of help."

She glanced back at the apartment full of her friends. Just about everyone was there to pitch in. Her heart welled up. "Yeah, Olivia put out the call and everyone showed up."

"I thought Brad was coming." Chuck caught a swift elbow from Steve.

Just like that, her warm fuzzies were killed. "He said he'd be here. We're exchanging his muscles for my business knowledge." She shrugged as if his absence didn't hurt. "If he doesn't show, he has to pay me to overhaul his business."

"Well, put us to work." Steve flexed. "We have muscles aplenty for you."

"There's a box of cleaning supplies in my car, if you'd bring them up." She tossed her keys at him.

Olivia organized a full scrub down of the apartment the second the supplies made it in the door before a single box was brought in. Sam climbed on the counter to clean out the cabinets. She spent most of her day directing where all the boxes should be stacked, not that she needed to because everything had been labeled. The morning flew by in a blur of cleaning and unloading.

She called in for pizza for lunch before the real unpacking started. She looked around at her friends, eating on her floor, content for the first time in awhile. "Thanks, you guys, for all of this."

"Anytime, sweetheart." Luke reached over and squeezed her hand. "It's good to have you back."

"Here's to having our Sam back." Steve raised his plastic cup in a toast. "And to her starting a new, more exciting chapter of her life."

She teared up. "Here's to having the best group of friends a girl could possibly ask for."

"Alright, enough mushy shit." Andrew stood up and collected the empty plates and cups. "Let's get her fully moved in."

"Let me at the bookcases." Julie dove at the boxes labeled books and Eric followed her.

BRAD HOVERED IN SAM'S doorway, unsure how he would be received. He should've been here hours ago. The knowledge ate at him. He turned to leave.

"You're late." Steve dropped some empty boxes off by the door.

"Got held up."

"You're just in time to put together the furniture." Sam passed a box to Steve. "How are you at reading directions?"

"I'm pretty good. Put me to work." He needed to find a way to make it up to her. He'd spend all day making furniture if she'd smile at him.

"Olivia's fiending to put away my clothes. Please help her build my closet shelves and drawers." She patted his shoulder and turned to set up her desk.

He opened his mouth to apologize to her, but Sam moved on too quickly. He went over to the loft stairs "Sam said you need some help."

"You're late." Olivia sized him up. "Screw these drawer slides into those holes." She pointed at the spots. "What held you up?"

"Girlfriend," he grunted, focusing on the task at hand and hoping Olivia didn't pry.

"She found out where you'd be today." It wasn't a question.

"I think she hoped I'd get here too late to help." They worked mostly in silence for a few minutes. "I just don't get it."

"Hannah knows she's not your first pick. How would you feel if you were her?"

He started. "Shouldn't you be advocating in Sam's favor or something?"

"I could, if you want, but I think you need to figure out all of this yourself." She handed him the drawers. "But you should also think about how seeing you with Hannah makes Sam feel."

She kicked him in the gut with her words. "Are all the girls in your group this harshly honest?"

"We look out for each other." She handed him the last drawer and stepped back to admire their work. "That's finished." She shooed him away from helping unpack Sam's clothes.

Everywhere around him, people were laughing and setting up Sam's life. He looked around, an outsider to all the happiness. He wandered toward the back of the apartment in search of Sam.

She stood on the edge of her tub, struggling with the shower curtain. "A little help?" He grinned at the adorable picture she painted before taking the rod out of her hand and hanging it. "Thank you."

"It looks like you're almost all unpacked."

"Everything but the bathroom and my painting stuff."

He nodded at the box for her bathroom shelves. "Do you want a hand getting that set up?"

"If you don't mind. I know everyone's getting ready to head out."

"I was late, it's the least I can do."

"Why were you late?" She lowered her voice. "I thought we were exchanging moving me in for business help." She kept her eyes on the box in front of her.

He sorted out the pieces. "I think you know why I was late."

"Your girlfriend wasn't thrilled by you coming over." She choked on the word girlfriend. She handed him the pieces he needed almost before he asked for them.

He brushed her hand every chance he could get. "To say the least." The shelves were built and installed before he knew it. "All done. Anything else you need built?"

"I didn't really need this. I don't have that much stuff." She cracked the tape on the boxes. "How much trouble will you be in when you get home?"

He filled her shelves with fluffy purple and gray towels. "Too much for what I actually did today." He studied her as she settled a wicker basket full of girly stuff on the top shelf. "Seeing as I was late, how much will I owe you for the business advice?"

"It all depends on how much work your business needs." She waved good-bye to her friends and motioned to the box for her desk shelves. "We can discuss it later."

He took the offered screwdriver. "I think you mean, it's going to be expensive as hell."

"Exactly." She grinned down at him. "But worth every penny."

Chapter Thirty-One

"Sam, wait up!" Steve raced to catch up with her outside the store, bringing Chuck in tow. "We have a favor to ask of you." He took a few of the files threatening to fall out of her hands.

She nodded her thanks, dreading the amount of work ahead of her. She wanted to have the weekend for nothing but fun, but her store needed more work than anticipated. Meaning she had to do paperwork at home.

"What is it?"

"We need your help to break up Brad and Hannah."

She stopped walking and stared at Steve like he grew another head. "What? No, I won't have any part in it. Brad's a big boy, he can handle his own relationships."

"But he's not."

"What do you mean?" She knew she was getting reeled in, but couldn't stop herself.

"After you left, she started gloating about how she got rid of you. Not always around him, but we've all heard it at some point. Things got better for a bit. I'd bet good money she's screwing around on the side, but I can't prove anything. He's stuck there, missing everything. He's miserable and can't shake her."

"I did promise to save him after all he did for me." She sighed. "What do you want me to do?"

"We want you to make him stand up and notice you. Remember things can be better than they are. It's karaoke night. With your voice, it shouldn't be that hard."

"How do you know I have a good singing voice?"

"You sing along to the radio when you work."

"How am I supposed to get him to notice me? He's relegated me to the friend zone."

"You actually believe that? You two are so stupid sometimes. He's just as in love with you now as he ever was."

She ignored Steve's jab and how her heart skipped a beat. "And after he notices me?"

"I'm hoping he finally breaks up with her."

"That's not much of a plan." *Lord save her from the stupid guys in her life.* Like she didn't have enough to juggle without these two adding to it.

"That's all we can think of. I think he's forgotten how un-crazy other girls are." Chuck put his arm around her. "Please, Sam. We know you adore him."

She ran the plan over in her head. "The plan is: tart Sam up, parade her in front of Brad, and hope he falls for her and breaks it off with Hannah?"

"Everything except the tarting up part." Chuck gave her a once over. "As much as we'd like to see you wearing very little, Hannah likes to whore herself up before going out."

"Got it. Find something sexy but not slutty. That's not a challenge." She dumped all of her paperwork in her car. "I'll see you there." *What the hell did I just get myself into?* Out of her depth, she pulled out her phone and made a couple of calls.

Half an hour later, Olivia burst into Sam's apartment with Julie in tow. "We haven't gotten ready for a night out in a long time. I've missed my girls."

Julie flung herself onto the couch. "Far be it for me to question girl time, but we haven't done this since—"

Sam held up a hand. "I have an ulterior motive for tonight. I need your help finding something eye-catching but not slutty."

Olivia clapped her hands. "I love a challenge."

"Has someone caught your eye?"

"Sort of. I've been wrangled into helping break up Hannah and Brad." Sam spilled her conversation with Steve and Chuck.

"Are you sure you're up for this?" Julie raised her eyebrow.

"I never got over him. Moving didn't help. Whatever I do now can't be worse than not doing anything at all." *Except maybe him rejecting me again*, she thought bitterly.

"We're here to help, no matter what." Olivia hugged her. "Now, let's go through your wardrobe."

Sam leaned over the back of the couch and watched her friends look at and reject most of her clothes. She couldn't help but laugh with them as they got crazier with suggestions. Olivia held up a deep v-neck blue shirt and lacy tank top. A push-up bra followed the clothes.

"It brings out your eyes. And gives a great eyeful of cleavage without being trashy." Olivia winked.

Julie threw a pair of tights and a jean skirt. "Short, cute, and you."

"WHAT ARE WE DOING TONIGHT?" Hannah pounced on Brad the second he opened the door.

He took his time setting his work bag on his desk. She had asked this question every night since Sam came back. "It's karaoke night. There's a group going."

"We haven't gone out to karaoke in forever."

Because you grind on other guys. He debated on starting the fight, but decided it wasn't worth it. "Then it's about time we go."

"Do you want dibs on the bathroom?"

"I'll grab a quick shower when you're done. I've got some work I want to finish up."

He settled at his desk and prepped some of his work for the week. He shoved some papers out of his way to make room for paint bottles and mulled over his problem with Hannah. Could he finally break up with her tonight? Every time he tried, she pulled the wounded bird act on him. He didn't want to make her cry, but it was pretty inevitable.

He glanced at the clock and blinked in surprise at how much time had passed. He pounded on the bathroom door. "Save me some hot water."

"I'm deep conditioning." The water shut off. "I thought you liked it when I looked good."

He could hear her pout through the door. "You usually look good. I just don't want a cold shower."

"Just usually? You mean there are times when you don't like the way I look? Why are you so horrible?"

"That's not what I meant and you know it." He wanted to beat his head against the wall. He hated how she twisted his words. "Just do your thing." He flopped back into his chair and raked his fingers through his hair. Not able to bring himself to do more work, he settled for cleaning up his paints and brushes.

"That's the cleanest I've seen your desk since we moved in."

"Figured it was due. I really should be more organized with my business." He looked up at her still in a towel. "Do you mind if I grab a quick shower while you do your make-up?"

"And let the humidity ruin my hair? No." She spun on her heel and closed the bathroom door.

He sighed and went back to cleaning up his desk. He took his time checking over his paint brushes and rubbing cleaner into them. He really had let his tool care fall to the wayside and hoped most of them were salvageable because replacing them would be a pain. Or not, because Sam would order him new ones at the store.

A cloud of perfume descended on him. "Bathroom's all yours for a shower. I'll need it again for final touch ups."

He brushed past her and stepped into the shower. He was rewarded with a cold spray of water. *Guess that's what I get for being a gentleman.* He kept his shower quick and found something clean to throw on. He tried to ignore how little Hannah was wearing. He looked again to confirm she wasn't wearing a bra.

He pulled on his shoes and stood waiting for her to finish getting ready. Hearing the perfume spray again, he ushered her out of the apartment.

SAM SLID INTO A CHAIR next to Chuck. "I'm guessing I haven't missed anything yet."

"Not yet, they're usually late." He gave her the once over, lingering on her cleavage. "I like the look."

She snapped her fingers in front of his face. "My eyes are up here."

"You can hardly blame me. Your shirt shows off some wonderful cleavage."

She brought a book in front of her, ignoring the urge to pull her shirt up and undo all of Olivia and Julie's work. "I guess we should prepare our plan of attack."

Steve joined the huddle and selected songs for maximum impact. The table slowly filled up as their friends showed up. Everyone was brought up to speed on the plan. They filled out the last slip when a hush fell over the table. Brad and Hannah had arrived.

Stomach quivering, Sam gathered up all of the requests and walked up to the DJ. She flashed him a bright smile. "If you could, please keep these in order."

"I'll see what I can do." He flipped through the stack.

"If you can't get them all in, these are the most important ones." She pointed to a handful of slips with stars. "The rest are just icing on the cake."

Steve intercepted her on her way back to the table. "You look like you need a drink."

"Or several." She glanced at Hannah's sparkly scrap of an outfit. "You guys weren't kidding when you said she whores herself up."

"I'm hoping she wore underwear this time. I see she's not wearing a bra, so odds aren't very good."

"Seriously? How do you..."

"She flashed some guys one night while Brad was in the bathroom. I got an eyeful."

"Ick, sorry." She took a swig of her drink to get rid of the bad taste the visual gave her.

"Now you know why I drink so much. Are you ready to do this?"

She took a deep breath. "I think you strengthened my resolve."

"He's looking over here. Quick, laugh like I'm funny." She threw her head back and laughed, touching Steve's arm. "You're really good at this. He doesn't look happy about the attention you're showing me."

"Guess our plan's off to a good start." She tapped her glass against his. "Carry my drink for me?"

She looped her arm around his and made their way back to the table, whispering in each other's ears. She soaked up the venomous looks from both Hannah and Brad. Chuck stood and pulled out her chair. She made sure to give him a big smile.

Steve set her drink in front of her and leaned into her ear. "If we weren't trying to save the world, I'd be tempted to snag you for myself."

"You'd fail." She arched an eyebrow at him.

"But the chase would be so much fun."

"Don't you two look cozy." Hannah raked a nasty glare across the table. "I see we are dressing for comfort."

Sam looked down at her high tops. "I could dance and sing all night in this." She gave Hannah a quick glance. "At least I don't need to be practically naked to get attention."

"You bitch. You're just jealous because I got the man." Hannah poured herself onto Brad's lap, causing him to spill most of his drink on her and the table. She screeched and ran for the bathroom, cursing his clumsiness the whole way.

"COULD YOU BE NICER to my girlfriend?" Brad slammed the last of his drink down and gave the empty glass a glare. He needed all the alcohol he could get to make it through this night.

Sam leaned across the table to hand him some napkins, giving him a great view of her cleavage. "I will be as nice to her as she is to me." He cursed and she grinned at him. "I'll try not to antagonize her while you have a drink in your hand."

"That's the least you can do." He mopped up the drink off the table.

"No, the least I can do is buy you a replacement drink. Long Island, right?"

He nodded, his mouth watering for a taste of her. The way her hips swayed to the music as she made her way to the bar made him want to follow her. She returned with his new drink and gave him one of the sweet smiles he missed. She rushed to the stage to sing, some ballad of love lost. He leaned back and enjoyed watching her. Was it his imagination or did she keep seeking him out in the crowd?

As the night wore on, he tried to join in with the group's dancing, but Hannah crawled onto his lap again. He choked on her perfume. "Are you planning on singing tonight?"

"And leave you alone with the vultures? Not a chance." She firmly planted her ass in his lap.

Brad rolled his eyes when she wasn't looking. He debated calling it an early evening seeing as he couldn't enjoy himself. Sam's flirting with his friends slowly ate away at him. He tasted bile watching her grind against Chuck during a sexy duet. He tracked her every move back to the table and ground his teeth at the huge hug Steve gave her.

"I'm bored, let's go home." Hannah whined over the music.

"If you want to go home, I'm not stopping you. But I'm staying here to celebrate with my friends." He brushed her off his lap and leaned back. He wanted just one breath of air not clogged with her perfume.

"Why are you being cruel?"

"I'm not. I said we were going out for karaoke. It's you who decided not to sing and join in on the fun, and it's you that keeps pulling me back into my chair when I try to have fun with my friends. If you're bored, go home, but don't sit here and bitch when the rest of us are trying to have a good time."

"Why do I put up with you?"

"That's a great question." One he'd been wondering about for a while.

Hannah stormed off right before Sam's name was called for another song. He settled back to enjoy the view, but Sam seemed to have another idea. She stepped off the stage and wove her way through the crowd, dancing with people along her trail to the table. Chuck pulled her against him to grind with him. Unable to resist her, Brad stood and turned her to dance with him.

They battled to keep each other close. Every nerve in his body fired at their pressed bodies. He leaned forward to kiss her, but she stepped back to finish the song. The bar broke out into thunderous applause. She took her bow and whispered something to Steve before hustling out of the room.

Chapter Thirty-Two

Sam ran to the bathroom and stood in front of the mirror, breathing heavily. Her reflection stared back at her, a little too wide-eyed and conflicted for her taste. Being that close to Brad and not kissing him killed her a bit, but he noticed her which had been the goal. It had been written all over his face how much he wanted her, but she held on by the tiniest of threads to her promise to not kiss him. Her stomach twisted in knots at playing with his emotions, but she was at a loss on how else to get him to cut ties with Hannah. Sam's breath evened out and she headed back toward the bar.

She almost crashed into Brad. "We need to put a bell on you."

"Where are you going?"

"Back to our friends." She stepped to go around him.

He grabbed her arm and pulled her back to the wall. His grip burned through her skin and set her heart racing. "What was that stunt you just pulled?"

"You of all people should know not to grab me like that." She kept her voice even, much to her own surprise. He dropped his hold like she electrocuted him. "And I have no idea what you're talking about."

"Dancing with me, making me think you were going to kiss me." He leaned in close, leaving her no room to escape. "You're causing trouble."

Says the man in my personal space. His scent invaded her head and left her mouth watering. "Me? Who was it that came up and ground against me? Oh, I think it was you."

He placed his hand on her cheek and ran his thumb over her lips. She froze under the gentle touch. She wanted to kiss him, but clung on to her promise not to unless he was solely hers. They stood there, breathing in each other's air, daring the other to make the first move.

She opened her mouth to say something about playing with fire, when a blur moved in her peripheral vision. A fist clipped her cheek and eye and sent her head back into the wall. Her vision hadn't cleared before another fist hit her mouth. She slid down the wall, her knees buckling under her. She blinked up to see Hannah glaring down at her.

"You slut!" Hannah grabbed a handful of Sam's hair and pulled her to her feet. "How dare you try and steal my man?"

The burn in her scalp helped clear Sam's head. She smiled and tasted blood. "You act like he's a prize to be won or an object to be stolen. If that's the case, game on."

"Whore." Hannah's fingers pulled hard and tipped Sam's head back painfully. "Cunt."

She covered Hannah's hands and spit a mouthful of blood at the girl's face. "Name calling only shows how low I'd have to sink to be on your level."

Sam mashed their hands against her head, grateful for the little bit of training she had. In the back of her mind, she waited for Brad to help get his psycho girlfriend off of her, but refused to take any more punishment. She twisted and threw Hannah to the ground and pinned the thrashing girl the best she could. Strands of her hair floated to the ground around them. She blinked through the pain up at his shocked face.

A pair of bouncers came up and separated her and Hannah. The large man in front of her gently helped her to her feet and looked her over. "Miss, if you would come with me? I'll get you some ice for your cheek. The police are on the way and will have some questions for you."

BRAD STARED AFTER THE bouncer and Sam as she was ushered away. What was that move she did? Pride welled in his chest at how well she handled herself, too quick for his intervention. He nodded to another bouncer and agreed to stick around the bar until the cops showed up.

He rejoined the group around their table. "I think the night's pretty much over. Hannah and Sam got into a fight in the hallway."

"Is she alright?" Steve bolted out of his chair.

What Brad wouldn't have given to have Steve's instincts. He had no doubt his friend would have jumped in the fray to save Sam some of the pain the short fight caused her. He sighed. *One more thing to add to the growing list of stupid shit I've done.*

"I don't know. Hannah hit her pretty hard. The bouncers took her to the back."

"What did you do?" Steve pegged him with a hard look.

"Nothing, it was over pretty quick."

"You're such a dumbass. Why didn't you pull your crazy girlfriend off of Sam?"

"It was over before I could. You'd be proud of her. She handled herself like a pro." Brad snatched up her jacket. "I have to go and answer some questions."

He fled the inquisition like the coward he was. He found the bouncer who had helped Sam and pressed her jacket into his hands to give her before heading to the police station. Every chance he got while filling out his statement, he made sure to point out Sam was only defending herself from Hannah's attack. He signed his name to the paperwork and looked at the officer.

"Can you tell me if Samantha Duke is still here?"

"She's filling out some paperwork. It'll be awhile."

He thanked the woman and headed out. Not wanting to go home, he wandered the streets and eventually made it to Sam's apartment. He slumped in front of her door and contemplated the shit show his life had become. He dozed off waiting for her.

"What the hell are you doing here?" Sam stood in front of him, fatigue etched in her voice.

"I wanted to see if you're okay." He squinted up at her. She had the beginning of a black eye and her eyeliner had been smudged at some point. He wanted to run his hands over her to check her for injuries, but stayed where he was.

She stepped around him and unlocked her door. "I'm fine."

"You don't sound fine."

She whirled around at him. "I'm tired and thirsty. I smell like sweat and stale liquor. I got the shit kicked out of me by your girlfriend while you watched. And then I got to spend a couple of hours talking to the police. I have a shit ton of paperwork to do tomorrow before I head into work on Monday to explain to my bosses why I've been fighting with a customer."

"Why are you yelling at me?" He pushed himself to his feet to see her expression without a light behind her.

She looked at him like he was stupid. "Shall we start with the part where you stood by and watched her beat me?"

"What did you want me to do? Hit her?"

"Pull her off of me or defend me. Anything at all." She hugged her arms around herself.

Defend her. Sam hated being saved, but here she was asking why he didn't do it. The same question that had been plaguing him all night. "You managed to defend yourself before I could step in and help." He shrugged in an attempt to dispel the tightening in his shoulders. "Besides, it would've made things more complicated if I had stepped in."

"And there's the heart of it. Complications." Sarcasm laced her voice. "It's nice to know friends rate below complications with your psycho girlfriend."

"Why are you pissed at me? It's not like I hit you."

"No, I got hit because of you. You were right. There was trouble. Too bad it was caused by you cornering and touching me. Good night, Brad." She shut the door in his face.

The deadbolt sliding home reverberated through his chest. He couldn't be sure, but he thought he heard her slide down the door and let out a quiet sob. His heart tore into pieces at the sound. He laid his hand on the door and imagined he could feel her warmth through it.

"I'm so sorry, Sam," he whispered.

When she didn't open the door or respond, he made the trek back to his apartment. Hannah's perfume lingered in the air, reminding him of every bad choice he made. Still clothed, he threw himself on the bed and passed out.

His phone woke him a few short hours later. Without looking at the screen, he answered. "Hello?"

"You have a collect call from Hannah Stratton, do you accept the charges?"

He sat up as the memories of the night before flooded back. "I do."

"I need you to come and bail me out." Hannah's voice brooked no argument.

"How much is bail?" He scrubbed his face and tried to get his brain to function.

"A thousand dollars."

"That's a lot of money. I don't have that kind of cash to spare." He didn't want to tell her he had been setting aside money to move out.

"Put it on a credit card or something. I'm panicking about being here." She whimpered. "Please, Brad, I need you. My dad will pay you back. Why are you being difficult about this?"

He hadn't gotten enough sleep to deal with this. "Because you assaulted one of my friends. I should let you sit in there until your dad decides to bail you out."

"I'm sorry. I saw you standing so close to her and I freaked. I swear it will never happen again. Just please come and bring me home."

He sighed. "Fine. I'll scrounge up the money and be there as soon as I can."

He took his time transferring the funds to his checking account, hoping he'd get the call that her father let Hannah out. He called Sam a couple of times on his way to the station, needing to hear her voice. On the third time, it went straight to voicemail, crushing his hope that she'd forgive him after a night's sleep.

Chapter Thirty-Three

S am trudged through the parking lot, oversized sunglasses hiding her face, hoping she could make it into the office without being stopped. Her eye had mercifully not swelled shut, but turned a lovely shade of purple. She ran her tongue over the split lip and groaned at the sight in front of her. Brad waited for her outside the store.

"You didn't answer my calls or texts yesterday."

After the second call, she turned off her phone. "I had work I had to get done."

He stepped between her and the door. "Are you still mad at me?"

"Just disappointed in you." Jesus, she sounded like a broken record. She sighed, her paperwork growing heavy in her arms.

"What can I do to make this up to you?"

"Right now, pray my bosses don't ship my ass back to Missouri and shut this place down."

"They wouldn't do that." His voice lacked conviction.

"They might. This place is on borrowed time as it is. They could take all the product to their other stores and not really have lost much in the bargain. I have six months to turn this place around and prove their investment was worth it or they'll pull the plug." She pushed the sunglasses onto the top of her head. He rewarded her by wincing at her black eye. "What will they do when they find out I've been fighting with customers? If I were them, I'd call it a failed experiment and close it down. Maybe even fire me. Let's find out."

She brushed past him and into the office before he could respond. Worry clawed at her over what her bosses were going to say when they saw her. She spread out her paperwork on the table in an effort to keep her brain occupied. She was deep into orders when the door opened behind her, bringing the smell of fresh coffee.

"Sorry we're late. There was a huge line to get coffee." Sally set a cup in front of her. "And then they got Don's wrong... What happened to your eye?"

Sam took a deep breath. "A group of guys from here went out to karaoke. One of their girlfriends didn't like them talking to me. Her fist met my face. I got to talk to the lovely police officers."

"Are you okay?"

"I'll live. It looks worse than it is. Paramedics said I was lucky she didn't hit any higher and shatter bone." She shrugged at her injuries.

Don slid into the chair across from her. "Why would she hit you?"

She hadn't expected concern from her bosses over her wellbeing. "We have history. Lots of it. Couldn't give you a good reason why she targets me all the time."

"I hate to ask, but will this affect the store at all? Because you run it, he'll stop shopping here?"

She winced. Here came the backlash she was expecting. "She doesn't come in here very often. He feels bad. There shouldn't be much blow back."

One of her clerks knocked on the door and popped his head in. "Sam, Hannah's here to see you. She looks pissed."

"Looks like I spoke too soon. Excuse me." She made her way to the front of the store. "How can I help you?"

"Where's my boyfriend?" Hannah looked like she hadn't slept in a couple of days.

"He was outside an hour or more ago. I've been in the office all morning and haven't seen him since I came in."

"You're lying to me. I know he's been with you. He isn't answering my calls and barely spent any time with me after he bailed me out. Get him or I'll start messing up your store."

Of course he bailed his girlfriend out of jail instead of leaving her to rot. "Mess with my store and I'll call the cops. Get out, you are no longer welcome here." Sam turned on her heel and walked back toward the office. Her head yanked back. She was really getting sick of having her hair pulled. "This is a game you will lose."

Hannah let out a yell as Sam peeled her fingers off her head. Hannah took a big swing, but went wild and knocked boxes off the shelf, all while screaming about how a poor person like Sam shouldn't have things she didn't. Sam sidestepped and blocked attacks coming her way, hoping to wear Hannah out. In the background, she heard Don calling the cops. Seeing an opening, she kicked out Hannah's leg and got her in a hold to ensure no further damage would be inflicted on her store.

Sam looked up at Don, panting. "How will this affect the store? I'd say she's going to cause trouble, don't you?"

Don didn't say anything until the cops showed up. He pointed at Hannah. "She came in here and assaulted my store manager. I have the whole thing on security footage."

Sam found herself at the police station for the second time in a week. After filing her statement, she met Sally in the waiting room. "Not the best start to taking over a store." Her stomach sank to her knees. "I guess this means you'll be firing me or shipping me back to St Charles."

"We discussed it on the way here. Obviously we don't condone fighting in the store. There was a lot of product knocked all over the floor. But we aren't blaming you for it. I would like to know why she came after you."

After Don joined them, Sam gave the abbreviated version of her history with Hannah. She finished up over her cold coffee while surveying the destruction in her store. She rolled her neck to dispel the tension growing in it. There was so much work to be done without the extra crap from the fight.

"If we ban her from the store, how will that affect the group's shopping?" Don looked over the wreckage.

"None of the other guys like her. They will be thrilled to have a Hannah free area." She waved a dismissive hand she didn't feel. "Brad might stop coming, but that's neither here nor there."

"Alright, get this cleaned up and we'll get back to the work in the office."

Her clerks shooed her away from the mess and back into the office. After a few hours of paperwork, her body stiffened up from the fight. She wandered through the store to loosen up her muscles and found herself in the basement facing most of the guys fixing terrain.

"What are you guys doing down here?"

"Steve felt bad for getting you beat up, so we decided to go through the terrain bin and get it fixed for you." Chuck brushed his knuckles against her bruise. The light touch had her wincing back. "I think he should buy you something special for the amount of damage that bitch did to you."

BRAD FLED HIS APARTMENT and rushed to the store after he got the call from Hannah to bail her out again. He berated himself for ever believing she'd leave Sam alone. She screeched at him to let her out, but he wanted nothing to do with her lies anymore.

He practically flew down the stairs to the basement. He hovered in the doorway and watched his friends baby Sam. His fists clenched to keep himself from tearing through them to pull her into his arms. He hated feeling like an outsider with his friends, but he'd damaged all of the relationships around him.

She smiled at Chuck. "I'll live. It's not Steve's fault she went ballistic. It was bound to happen sooner or later." She shrugged. "She came after me in the store again today, screaming about how 'a poor person like me shouldn't be allowed to have things she doesn't.'"

Steve pulled her into a tight hug. "Sammy, I'm so sorry for all of this."

"Don't be. You had no way of knowing what would happen." She yawned and stretched. "I'm going to head out. It's been a long couple of days and I feel the need for a long soak in an epsom salt bath." She turned toward the door and finally caught sight of Brad.

He positioned himself so there was no way she could get around him. "Hey, Sammy-cat."

"Please get out of my way." Defeat stamped itself over her features.

She looked so small and tired. All he wanted was to pick her up, carry her back to her bed, and spend the day taking care of her.

"I wanted to talk to you."

"Did you pay her bail?" She fixed a hard stare at him.

"Yes."

"Let me pass. I don't want to talk to you. You're on my personal shit list."

"Why are you mad at me?"

"You bailed my attacker out of jail!" Anger flared in her blue eyes.

"I don't understand why this pisses you off. I'd bail you out."

"She attacked me. Twice! One of those after you let her out of jail." She ducked around him. "It shows where I rate in your life."

He watched her walk away, dumbfounded by her accusation. He turned into the room and took an empty seat. Everyone's stares bored into him. "What?"

"You bailed Hannah out after she beat Sam?" Steve looked at him like he'd lost his mind.

"Why does everyone think I did something wrong? She claimed to be having a panic attack in the jail."

"Because you did, dumbass. Sam is the sweetest girl we know. Hannah is a psycho bitch. We've kept quiet all this time because we thought you'd wise up and dump her ass." Steve grabbed his arm as Brad stood to leave. "I'm not done with you. Where are you going?"

"I need to go to my apartment. Hannah's parents' lawyers managed to get her out again. She and I have to have a serious talk."

"I hope it's to break up with her." Steve's voice echoed after him.

Brad walked into his apartment and settled in to wait for his girlfriend to appear. Half an hour later, she walked in with her parents in tow. They didn't say anything to him, but walked into the bedroom, leaving him alone with Hannah.

She threw herself into his arms. "I'm so glad to see you."

"We need to talk." He peeled her arms off of him.

"I take it my dad called you." He shook his head in confusion. "They're taking me home to give me time away from the toxicity of your friends. They want us to break up." She choked back a sob.

"The toxicity of my friends? The friends you treated like shit for years for 'having something you didn't?'" He didn't care enough to lower his voice.

"You're angry."

"Damn right I'm angry. You said it wouldn't happen again. And then you went straight for Sam the second you were out."

"She was hiding you from me. Why else wouldn't you answer my calls?"

He pinched the bridge of his nose and counted back from ten. "Maybe because I was upset that you went after one of my good friends and didn't want to talk to you? You know what? I can't sit here and listen to you make up excuses as to why you do crazy shit anymore."

"What are you saying?"

"I agree with your parents. We should break up." He paused to let it sink into both of them. Elation bubbled up his body. "No, we are breaking up. I'm done with this shit."

"You bastard! You were only using me as a stand in for Sam this entire time." She slapped him.

He let the hit reverberate through his body. It was no more than he deserved. "No, I tried to make this work. It's you that brought Sam into this relationship. Goodbye, Hannah."

Her parents came back out into the living room with a couple of suitcases and ushered her out the door. Once he was sure they were gone, he let out a sigh of relief. Now the only question was how did he go about fixing all the relationships he ruined while with Hannah?

Chapter Thirty-Four

"You want me to revamp the store and document the entire thing?" Sam stared at Don like he'd lost his mind. Did he realize how much extra work the project would add to her load?

Don nodded. "I think it would have a bigger impact on the community and draw people to the store if we show them we are making progress on updating and cleaning the store."

"I agree it would be an amazing opportunity to use our social media to better our image. Do I have a budget to hire a photographer?"

"Why can't you or your clerks do it?"

She raised an eyebrow at the question. "When? We're retraining the entire staff, scrubbing down and repainting the store, digging out two full rooms of overstock, and making a new section for the store. When do we have time to take pictures of all that?" She pegged him with a hard look. "And don't say after hours because I'm barely keeping up with learning paperwork."

"When you put it that way, go ahead and get some bids for photographers." He held up his hands in surrender.

She pulled out her phone and punched in a number. "Olivia, I have a question for you. We're taking bids from photographers to document the remodel of the store. Are you interested? I know this isn't your usual shoot."

"Of course I'm interested. I could always use more work. What's the scope of the project?"

"A couple of months. You don't have to be here everyday, just enough to get some action shots and before, during, and after shots of the changes."

"Five thousand dollars."

Sam choked. "Say that again."

"Five thousand dollars. For the scope and man hours, it's pretty low for professionals." Olivia chuckled. "I'll make a deal because it's you. Five hundred dollars and you owe me two photo shoots."

Sam should've known this would end in owing Olivia more than money. "What type?"

"Sexy gamer girl and one of my clients wants you as a model. I've been meaning to call you to set something up after your eye heals."

"What client?" Who would want to use her and what pictures had Olivia shown people?

"I'm sworn to confidentiality. Trust me, this is tamer than the stuff we did in college."

Sam scribbled down the amount and showed it to Don. He gave her the thumbs up. "You're hired. Swing by the shop today or tomorrow when you have free time." She hung up. "That was a fast yes."

"It was way less than I expected." Don smiled. "It's a good thing you have a photographer friend. Sounds like she wanted something else."

"Just a favor for one of her shoots. Apparently one of her clients saw some pictures of me and wanted to hire me."

"HOW'S BACHELORHOOD treating you?" Steve flopped onto the couch.

"Better than dating Hannah." Brad looked around the quiet apartment. It looked like a hurricane had hit it. "You've been here a lot lately, what's up?"

"Chuck's got a new girlfriend. They've been sucking face all over the house. I just need a break from the schmoopy faces."

"That bad? Don't you have a girl of your own?"

"Nah, I broke it off with Zora."

"How long ago was that?"

"Couple of months."

Brad set aside the mini he was painting. "Shit, I'm sorry. I've been so out of it."

"Not a problem. You've had your hands full of crazy." Steve flipped a few channels. "When are you going to ask Sammy to overhaul your business? I'm surprised you can find anything."

"I really can't, I missed a deadline this week." Brad was drowning in disorganization, but shook his head. "She's busy with her store remodel. Plus, I fucked up helping her move in. I'm afraid to see how much she'd charge me."

"You'll never know unless you ask."

"I'm still trying to figure out a way to make it up to her for fucking everything else up."

"You two are meant for each other. Just take your time and show her how much she means to you." Steve stood to leave. "And get her over here to fix your business. Or at least organize your desk."

Brad stared after Steve and then at his desk. It had overflowed onto the floor and coffee table. Invoices mixed with empty paint bottles and coffee cups. He needed help badly.

He ran his fingers through his hair and belatedly realized he had green elixir all over his hands. Cursing his luck, he ran into the bathroom to inspect the damage. Yup, green elixir smeared all over his hair and forehead. Muttering an oath, he hopped into the shower.

He spent the next couple of hours gathering up papers and cleaning up empty dishes. He knew he was procrastinating, but fear kept him from calling Sam. He rationalized it with her being busy with her store. Once most of the mess was corralled, he couldn't delay any longer.

"Hello?" She answered on the third ring.

"It's Brad. Am I interrupting work?"

She let out a laugh. "These days? Always. What's up?"

"Remember how you offered to go over my business with me? I know I fucked up hard lately, and I will totally pay you, but I could really use your help." He rushed out the words before she could respond. "I'm drowning."

"Slow down and breathe." He could hear her smile in her voice. "You already paid your debt. You helped me move."

"I was hours late."

"That's very true. Then let's call it a swap of favors. You'll owe me a future favor."

"Why do I feel like you'll enjoy having me in your pocket?" Not that he minded if it kept her talking to him.

"I learned from Olivia. When were you thinking about scheduling your consultation with me?"

"Whenever you have time, I know you're busy with your store. I wouldn't have called if it wasn't an emergency."

"I have some free time Friday night. Does that work for you?"

"You are a goddess."

"Just a sucker for a sob story."

He hung up with a smile. Friday. He groaned and took in the state of the apartment. He needed to clean the place up so she didn't know how bad it really had gotten.

"SMILE."

"I'm doing paperwork." Sam blinked up at Olivia's camera. "What are you doing?"

"I figured you'd want staff pics for the website."

"Maybe wait until my black eye's gone."

"It's almost healed." Olivia clicked off a couple of pictures of the office. "Woah, paperwork mountain."

"Yeah, Don and Sally are trying to make sense out of it all."

"What are you doing?"

"Back here, I'm learning the day to day operations: invoicing, bills, etc. After the bosses go back to Missouri, it's all on me. The real challenge is out in the store. The entire staff is being retrained on how to give good customer service." She stretched and popped her back. "Plus, I'm overstaffed."

"Are you going to fire people?"

"Soon. Everyone's been warned they're on probation. At the end of the month, one will be promoted to assistant manager and a couple will be let go."

"You look exhausted."

"It's just stress." She waved a hand around the room.

"Tell me what's going on." Olivia pulled up a chair.

"Staff retraining's not going so great. I'm asking them to actually give a damn and work."

"You sound pissed."

"They were less than six months away from being jobless. You'd think they'd be happy to still be working." She blew out her breath. "While I'm doing that, we're tackling all the overstock Alex left behind, trying to deal with all this paperwork, and cleaning an entire store."

"You have your hands full. What can I do to help?"

"Take pictures of everything? Come back at least once a week to capture progress?"

"What are you going to do when everything's set up?"

"Sleep. We're talking about turning the current warehouse into another game room."

"You need a day off."

"I have a day off, remember? We're doing the Ren Faire on Saturday."

"I'll have your costume for you on Friday night."

"Can you drop it off earlier in the day? I promised Brad I'd look over his business and get him back on track."

"You're helping him out? Are you getting back together?"

Sam squashed the kernel of hope in her chest. "No, I said I'd go over his business in exchange for a favor later."

BRAD FIDGETED IN HIS chair. Sam had been silent for way too long, her pizza forgotten as she looked over his pile of papers. She made a note in her notebook and flipped to a new page. He winced at the paint splatters over everything on his desk. The worst of the mess had been taken care of, but there was no way he could hide how disorganized he was.

"When was the last time you changed your prices?" She glanced up from the papers.

"Uh, never?"

She made a tsk-ing noise and wrote something down. They had been at this for more than an hour. He had a sinking feeling she was disappointed by his every answer. The silence lengthened until he couldn't take it anymore.

"Feeling like this is an inquisition."

She looked up from her notebook in surprise. "Think of it more as an intervention. You have next to no organization, no real pricing structure, no future plans for your company. I'm shocked."

"I've been doing this by the seat of my pants for years, it seems to be working." He crossed his arms over his chest, hating being so defensive with her when she was helping him, but not able to stop himself.

She set her notebook aside and gave him a hard look. "Working like a dog with barely anything to show for it?" She touched his arm lightly. "You're better than that, Brad."

Her touch burned through him. "I don't want to lose customers over raising my prices."

"I think you'll find even if you lose customers, you'll gain more by valuing your services for what they are actually worth. Pricing yourself too high, and you get nothing. Price yourself too low, and people think your quality is low." She pulled a sheet out of her notebook. "Look this over and tell me what you think."

He glanced at her figures, shocked at how much thought she put into this restructure. He risked a look at her and she pointed at the paper. He looked at the sheet again. "You raised my single figure prices."

"It's all based on how much time you spend on each piece." She scooted her chair closer and he caught a hint of her perfume. It had been too long since she had been close enough for him to smell it. It reminded him of better times. "Your base cost per model is pretty much the same whether you're painting one or a hundred. The only difference is you're spending more time on single figs than you are on rank and file. Your prices should reflect that."

"You're amazing. What's all this stuff at the bottom?"

"Olivia's rates for production pictures. I took the liberty of asking for you. You need to invest in your business, either by paying someone to take better pictures of your work or you need to figure out how to do it yourself. The pictures you post don't do justice to your work."

"Anything else I'm screwing up?" He hadn't expected her to find fault with every single facet of his business.

"Don't take that tone with me. I'm just trying to help." She grabbed her bag and headed to the door. "Look over what I came up with. You're worth more than you think."

He pushed down the thought she meant that as more than a painter. "Sam, wait. I'm sorry." He raked his fingers through his hair. "I'm an ass. I didn't think I was doing that bad at running my business. This paper proves how much I'm fucking up." He looked at the sheet again. "What's this 'Sam's organizational help' about?"

"That's what it would cost for me to help you straighten out your invoices and set up your invoicing software as well as organizing your desk again. I did a rough estimate of hours."

"You'd seriously input all of my mess of paperwork?" She always managed to floor him.

"I don't come cheap, but you may want to outsource some of your office work to lighten your load and give you more painting time." She gave him a brief hug. "Think about it. I need to go and get some sleep."

"Night, Sam."

Chapter Thirty-Five

"It's Ren Faire day!" Olivia sang over the phone. "You'd better be up and in costume. We're on our way to you."

"About the costume..." Sam tugged on the flaps comprising the gladiator skirt.

"It was specially made for you by Aaron. He said something about you talking about wanting to be a warrior for faire, so you're a warrior."

"Aaron made this?" She ran her hands over the tight brown leather bodice and glanced down at the generous cleavage it showed, even without her lacing it tightly. "I should've seen his handiwork when I put it on."

"We're at your front door. I'll do your hair and make up when we get there."

She tossed her phone and wallet in the pouch on the costume and ran for the door, leather slapping her thighs. Now she was moving, she could definitely see her ex's stamp all over the warrior costume. Wondering what Olivia had to do to get Aaron to part with such an exquisite piece, she slid into the car.

Self conscious, Olivia had to pull her forcefully out of the car. Luke chuckled as Olivia turned her around and pulled the laces tight. Sam gasped for breath and covered her cleavage with a hand. She closed her eyes to avoid the looks she got from the passing people as she sat on the trunk to have her hair and make up done.

"REMIND ME WHY WE'RE going to the Ren Faire." Brad grumbled from the passenger seat, his mind still turning over his conversation with Sam the night before. She all but gave him the green light to spend more time with her.

"To see pretty ladies scantily dressed while day drinking." Steve smirked from the driver's seat. "Besides, Olivia said Sam will be there." Brad sat up straight. "And she has a super sexy costume for the day."

"How super sexy?" Brad didn't want anyone else staring at her if her body was on display.

"Olivia didn't say." Steve parked in the overflowing lot. He pulled out his phone and texted someone. "They're near the front entrance."

Brad followed Steve through the crush of people and cars, keeping an eye out for Sam. Lightning streaked through him at the sight of her. She sat on the trunk of a car, eyes closed and looking like a goddess while Olivia finished up her makeup. Sexy was an understatement for how she looked. He licked his lips, imagining peeling the bodice off of her, not to mention how much of her legs the short gladiator skirt showed off.

"I'm in my own personal hell." Sam looked like a warrior goddess that he wasn't allowed to touch.

Steve clapped him on the back. "Cheer up, buddy. Maybe day drinking will make her forget she's still upset with you."

SAM OPENED HER EYES and stared at her reflection in the small mirror Olivia handed her. That girl could do wonders with a bit of leather wound through her hair and a bit of makeup. She jumped off the trunk and did a whirl, the leather of her skirt flaring out. *If you can't beat them, join them.* Other patrons passed them and gave her a few compliments.

Sudden heat had her looking over and seeing Brad eating her up with his eyes. Now she understood why Olivia insisted on the costume and she silently thanked her friend. He wore a pair of shorts and a tee shirt, doing nothing to hide the muscles she loved so much. She tried to still her fast beating heart by looking away, but a familiar head of light brown hair appeared from between the cars.

"Aaron!" Sam ran and got caught up in his strong arms. "Thank you for the costume. It fits like a dream."

"It should. I made it specifically with you in mind." He brushed a lock of hair off her cheek. "Did Olivia talk to you yet?"

"About what?" She frowned.

"When would be a good time for you to model for me. She said you agreed."

"You're the mystery client she's been talking about? I'm going to kill her. She didn't tell me who it was."

"Sweetie, I have a whole line of new corsets that will hug every curve on your luscious body. I can't wait to see you in them."

Her eyebrows shot up at Aaron's loud proclamation. "What are you doing?"

"Olivia let me in on what's been going on." He winked and made a couple small adjustments to her costume. "Relax and play along." Before she could reply, he grabbed her hand and spun her around. Her skirt flared out. He gave her an appraising look and ran his hand along her neck. "Absolute perfection. The only thing missing is a necklace." He offered her his arm. "Shall we find one to match?"

"She already has one. Not that she bothers to wear it." Brad muttered as he brushed past, his hand briefly touching hers.

Her stomach twisted. She moved toward him, reaching for his hand, but Aaron pulled her back. She turned to her ex. "What is Olivia playing at?"

"Nothing, sweetie."

"Bullshit, Aaron. What the hell is going on?"

"Olivia is baiting Brad into realizing how miserable he is without you. She wants him to have a taste of what he put you through." His hazel eyes flashed with mischief.

"That's terrible." She glanced at the group. "Or it's brilliant. I'm not sure which."

"Go along with it until you make up your mind."

"And the crack about the necklace?" Her heart broke at the dejected look on Brad's face.

"I know all about him giving you one you don't wear. I'm betting you keep it someplace close though, based on your expression." Aaron kissed her cheek. "Don't worry. I'm not planning on buying you jewelry or making a play for you. I like having you as a walking advertisement for my leather work."

BRAD WAS IN THE WORST kind of torture. He followed behind the group like a tool, snapping pictures of Sam in her hot as hell costume, but unable to do anything about the burning desire coursing through him. She would be stopped every so often by another patron and would point to the asshole who was never far from her side. He jammed his fists into his pockets before he punched the guy.

Steve picked up on his mood. "You want to grab a drink?"

"Hell yes." Brad raked a hot look over Sam. "I don't know how much more I can take."

They ducked into a nearby tavern and grabbed a couple beers. The rest of the group followed shortly behind them. The asshole glued to Sam's side pulled her onto the small dance floor. Her smile lit up the building.

Steve pulled the cup out of Brad's hand. "Dude, careful. You almost crushed the thing, booze and all."

"Thanks for the save." He wiped his hand off on his jeans.

"Anytime. Do you want to get out of here?"

"Yes and no." He couldn't peel his eyes off of her. He didn't want to miss a moment of the sexy way her hips swayed.

"Are you going to do something about that or just torture yourself?"

"What am I supposed to do? She's mad at me and it looks like she's moved on." He snatched back his cup and downed it in one gulp.

Steve scratched his neck. "Maybe you should do something to make up for bailing Hannah out."

"I would've done the same for her! I don't know why she's still angry about it."

"Other than her black eye and the fact that bitch gave her more bruises after you let her out, I can't imagine why she'd be mad."

"Don't be a dick."

"Just pointing out that you had her against the wall and were rubbing your hands on her right before Hannah took the swing. I think that might have something to do with it." Steve handed him another cup of beer. "While you think about it, I'm going to dance with a pretty lady or two."

Brad looked at the dance floor where Steve stole Sam from the asshole. He quickly stole her back, her breathless laughter filling the area. Steve detoured on his way back to offer a pretty little blonde a dance. Brad shook his head at how smooth his friend was.

Olivia took the vacant seat next to him. "Having fun today?" Her voice held an edge to it.

"I take it you had something to do with this." He nodded at the dancing couples.

"I invited Aaron and Rebecca to join us. Figured Sam needed to be reminded of how nice Wisconsin can be."

"She does deserve something nice in her life." *God knows I've fucked it up enough.* He gestured for another beer.

"Are you planning on spending the entire faire drunk?"

"Seems like the thing to do." He nodded at other groups hitting all the taverns in the place. "Did you want something?"

"Sam to be happy."

"She looks happy right now." The sight twisted his guts in knots.

"Aaron won't keep her happy. They're great as friends and she adores his sister, Becca, but they'll never date again. Too much history."

"Then why invite them?"

"You really are thick." She hopped off the stool. "Enjoy the rest of the day."

Steve rejoined him. "What was that all about?"

"I have no earthly idea." Brad stared into his beer like he could divine the future. "Did you know Sam and Aaron dated?"

"Yeah, Rebecca just told me. She's hoping her brother doesn't screw it up this time. Why?"

"Olivia invited him, knowing they wouldn't get back together, but wanting Sam to be happy. Then called me thick. What the fuck did I miss?"

"The look on your face when he touched her." Steve snorted. "This was a set up to make you as miserable as you made Sam. And to show you how much you want her back."

"Are you fucking kidding me?"

"They told me about it after I almost went after Aaron for the crack about her necklace."

"Is Sam in on it?"

"She wasn't this morning, but she's probably figured it out by now."

"When were you going to tell me?"

"When it became apparent you had no clue and weren't going to do something about it. Go cut into their dance or buy the girl a flower or something. I'm sick of you moping."

SAM WIGGLED OUT OF Aaron's arms. "I don't think I can keep this up anymore. It doesn't feel right."

"Come on, Sammy. We're having a good time."

"It's not fair to Brad or Becca."

"What does this have to do with Becca?"

"Does she know about today?"

"No, she showed up late."

"You missed how her eyes lit up like it's Christmas when she saw us. She's always wanted us to get back together."

"No way."

"She's told me she wants me as her sister and she gets in the way of any other woman in your life."

"That little shit."

"You need to come clean with her about this... Whatever the fuck this is." *And I need to come clean to Brad.*

"Why me?"

"Because you're her brother and were in on this from the beginning." She kissed his cheek and pushed him toward Rebecca. "I'm going to do the same with Brad."

Sam looked around the tavern and came up Brad-less. He had been hanging out at the bar looking absolutely miserable and drowning his sorrows. She tapped Olivia on the shoulder.

"Have you seen Brad?"

Olivia looked around and shrugged. "No, the last I saw him, he was at the bar. Wait, here he comes."

Sam's eyes zeroed in on him. He carried a purple snapdragon in his hand. As he neared, he dug in his pocket and answered his phone. His expression turned from nervous to thunderous in no time flat.

"He doesn't look happy."

Chapter Thirty-Six

"Son of a bitch!" Brad shoved his phone in his pocket, the purple snapdragon he bought for Sam forgotten in his other hand.

Steve abandoned dancing with the blonde girl and ran to his side. "What's up?"

"Hannah's parents have come to move her out of our apartment and are refusing to cover her half of the rent." Brad ran his hand through his hair and calculated the number of hours he would need to put in to cover the rent until he found a new place. "I can't cover it all on my own."

"When does your lease run out?"

"We're month-to-month. Rent's due next week." His savings had just gotten to the point where he could relax about money, once Hannah's dad paid him back for bail. "I can cover it for now, but I'm going to eat through everything I have saved quickly. That place is expensive."

"I still have your old room open at my place."

Gratitude flowed through him. "You are a lifesaver. Anyone have a truck to move my furniture?"

Everyone shook their heads. He turned on his phone to look up truck rentals when Sam touched his arm. "Let me call my bosses and see if I can use the company van."

"You're the best." Brad itched to hug her, but settled for handing over the slightly mangled flower. She squeezed his hand briefly before bringing the flower to her nose. He treasured the slight smile on her face. Maybe he had a chance to fix them.

Before he could get his hopes up, he needed to finish dealing with his ex. He found himself climbing into a red van outside the game store. Much to his dismay, Sam had changed out of her costume and into jeans and a t-shirt. She had left her hair wrapped with the leather strap, lending her an air of fierceness.

"Decided against being a gladiator?"

"As comfortable as it was, it seemed impractical for moving you."

"You don't have to come if you don't want to."

"Actually, I do." She made a gesture to the van. "I'm the only one allowed to drive the getaway car."

"I mean, you don't have to come up. I know you don't want to see Hannah."

"I'm not afraid of her. I offered my help and I won't let her scare me off."

"Fierce little tiger." He breathed the words, knowing she hated him calling her any nicknames, but awed by her determination.

SAM'S HEART WARMED at Brad's words. The only thing missing was him calling her his. Shaking her head at the thought, she pulled into the parking lot of his apartment. He led the group up a flight of stairs and opened the door to a wall of yelling. She squared her shoulders and followed everyone in.

"What the hell is she doing here?" Hannah screeched. "I want her out."

"Well, princess, you don't get to dictate everything." Sam patted herself on the back for how firm her voice was. "I'm helping a friend move after he broke up with his girlfriend." She grabbed the tape and made boxes with her back to a wall so she could keep an eye on Hannah and her fists.

The guys worked fast, filling boxes as fast as she could make them. Everything was packed into the van and assorted cars with brutal efficiency. It seemed like no one wanted to be here any longer than necessary. Brad spoke in low tones with Hannah's parents and accepted something from them. She leaned against the wall and waited for him.

"You must be Samantha." Hannah's father extended his hand.

She eyed him warily, but took his hand. "I am."

"I just wanted to say how sorry I am for everything that happened. If there's anything I can do, let me know."

"Make sure to pay for the damage your daughter did to my store."

"Consider it done, so long as you drop the charges against my daughter." He smiled the wide grin of someone used to getting his way.

"Not a chance in hell. She attacked me, twice, causing me bodily harm. Both incidents were caught on camera showing her to be the aggressor and me merely defending myself." She returned his toothy grin. "All dropping the charges would accomplish is allowing you to sweep this under the rug. Considering all of the documentation done in this case, I'd be a fool to drop the charges."

"You'll regret this, little girl. I will bury you."

"Now we know where your daughter gets her charming personality." She opened the door. "Enjoy meeting with my lawyer. And fuck you." She slammed the door behind her, nervous energy bubbling in her system.

Brad slid into the passenger seat a few minutes later. "Did you really tell Hannah's father to fuck off?"

"Basically. He wanted me to drop the charges against her. I told him where to stick it."

"That's pretty ballsy. He's really rich and will come at you with the best lawyers."

She shrugged. "I'd be more worried, but everything's on camera and I have the company's lawyers and Aaron's dad's firm backing me." She patted his knee. "Let's get you home."

"I'm sorry I interrupted your day off. It looked like you were enjoying yourself." He looked at her out of the corner of his eye like he wanted to say more.

She stopped at a red light and turned so she could give him her full attention. "Why'd you buy me the flower?"

"I wanted to apologize for everything that happened. I was hoping it would start a conversation on how I can fix our friendship."

"Oh." They drove in silence until they got to Steve's. Her mind churned over how to tell him it wasn't their friendship she wanted to fix.

"Now I owe you two favors. One for consulting on my business and the other for helping move me."

"I'll clear them both if you come with me to my game distributor on Monday. Don and Sally are letting me fill my store with new products. They said I could bring a trusted customer to help me. It was broadly hinted that you should be that customer."

"Done." He answered almost before she finished.

She bit her lips to stop her smile. "You do realize you have to be at the store by eight in the morning. Think about this before you commit, Mr. Night Owl."

"I said done."

SAM TAPPED HER FOOT. Damn Brad for waiting until the last second to show. She already wasn't looking forward to the drive and now she had to play catch up with her bosses. She checked her watch again and took a swig of her coffee. His car slipped into the space next to hers.

He rushed over. "Sorry, I had to fight to get into the bathroom. Chuck's girlfriend stayed over."

"The bosses left a few minutes ago in the van." She handed over his cup. "We'll still probably beat them there. Hop in."

She was hyper aware of the heat pouring off of him as she pulled onto the highway. Glancing over, she saw him staring at her. "What?"

"Why me? Of all the customers in the store, why was I asked to come along?"

"You're one of the few they know. We're friends and you're not afraid to speak honestly in front of them."

"How do you know all that?"

"I asked." She shrugged and grabbed for her coffee cup. Her hand brushed his and she pulled back like it burned.

"Can we talk about the pink elephant in the car?"

"There are no elephants, pink or otherwise." Her denial came too fast, but she wasn't sure she was ready to have this conversation.

"It's going to be a long drive if we aren't going to talk." He eased his seat back and closed his eyes.

She took a long swig of her coffee, knowing full well he wasn't actually sleeping. She settled in to wait him out, but she couldn't handle the silence. "What do you want to talk about?"

"I knew you couldn't take the quiet." A sly smile crossed his face.

"I could just turn up the music and let you fall asleep if you're going to be that way."

"Sorry, Sam. Can I ask you a question?"

"Why not?" She sighed.

"You didn't look happy at the Ren Faire when I came back with the flower. Why?"

"Because I couldn't take it anymore. Our friends set up whole day to be a big fuck you. They decided you needed to see me happy with someone else so you'd know what you put me through."

"You weren't happy to see me twist?"

"I didn't know about it until after Aaron made the crack about my necklace. I made him tell me what was going on. I went along with it because I wasn't sure if it was a brilliant idea or a terrible one."

"What changed?"

"I saw how upset it made you. You were day drinking. I was going to tell you, but then we had to leave to move you out of your apartment." She peeked over at him. "Sorry."

"I got to see you stand up for yourself against Hannah's father. I've never been so proud of you." He reached over and squeezed her hand before retreating to his side.

She let out a slow breath to calm herself. *He was proud of her.* "Thanks. I'm glad we got the pink elephant out of the car. It was ruining my gas mileage."

"Not by a long shot."

"I'll bite. What's the issue?"

"Our unresolved feelings for each other."

"I don't have any." She caught his sideways look at her fast words. "I think this will take more than the rest of the drive."

"I'm willing to wait."

She snorted. "That'd be a first."

"That was a low fucking blow, even for you." Hurt laced his words. "I recall someone giving me permission to date because she wasn't sure when she was coming back to Wisconsin. And then you went and got a fucking job down there. What did you expect?"

"Slow down there, buddy. I got the fucking job so I wouldn't have your new relationship thrown in my face." She covered her mouth as though she could take back the words.

"You stayed there because I was dating her?"

In for a penny. "Why else would I stay after my dad got better? My life was up here." She shrugged off the hurt. "Knowing I was going to be gone for a minimum of four months, you didn't even wait two before finding someone to warm your bed."

"Is that really what you think of me?"

"What else am I supposed to think, Brad? I was putting my life on hold to take care of my dad and you were here, fucking her, even after I warned you about her." She dashed the traitor tears off her cheeks. "You know what? This isn't the time or place for this. We're here."

SAM PULLED INTO A SPACE and killed the engine. Brad never saw anyone bail out of a car so fast. He climbed out at a slower pace, while she paced away to pull herself together. He hadn't given it much thought when she said she couldn't watch him date Hannah, but now he realized he drove Sam away. She gave up so much, his strong girl, when she left. He numbly shadowed her and her bosses into the enormous warehouse.

She looked around like a kid in a candy store. "Is it in any kind of order?"

"Most of the board games will be at the end, but no, not really." Sally grimaced. "The best way to approach it is to go row by row. Take your time, we have all day. Don and I will organize everything and let you know when you're getting close to your limit."

"Any hints on how much that is?"

"It's more than St Charles spends on comics in a month. Have fun." Sally waved them off.

He waited until they were out of earshot. "How much money is that?"

"Over twenty thousand dollars." Her eyes danced as she held up the gaming books she picked. "Let me know if you find more of this brand."

"Is that what I'm here for? Your extra set of eyes?" He was still raw from their argument.

She whirled on him. "What do you want from me? Just spit it out instead of being passive aggressive. You're here as my customer advocate. Which means you're advising me on what you think the store needs."

"Truce." He held up his hands.

Every time she filled a cart, he brought her a new one, chewing over how to make things right between them. He dropped a few paintbrushes into the cart and pretended like they magically appeared. She raised her eyebrow and tossed in a couple more with a wink. The tightness in his chest loosened a bit and they took a break for a drink.

"Where are we sitting for our spending?"

"You haven't spent a quarter of what we set aside for you." Sally handed Sam a bottle of water. "I think you're being too conservative with your choices."

Sam took a long pull off the bottle before handing it to him. She acted like they were dating without realizing it, but he wasn't going to point it out. "I don't want to buy a bunch of stuff for the sake of spending money. Besides, the board games are going to eat through it fast."

"What do you think, Brad?"

He almost spit out a mouthful of water and handed the bottle back to Sam. "All of the stuff she's picked out seems to go with the general feel of the store. I'm sure she'll grab extras of things like paintbrushes."

"You sound as cautious as her."

"I run my own small painting business. Cautious is in my blood." He accepted back the almost empty bottle and drained it.

"This is me telling you two you are being too cautious. The returns we brought in are more than enough to cover what we plan on spending here today."

"I hear and understand." Sam saluted. "We're hitting an area with more miniatures and painting supplies. I promise to spend a ton of your money before the day is out."

"Good, but let's take a break for lunch."

They didn't talk on the way to or from lunch. He kept opening his mouth, but the right words wouldn't come out. He trailed behind her, keeping all of the chat to business. By the time they reached the end of the warehouse, they were both worn out.

He helped load the product into the van and flopped into her car. She didn't seem to want to start up the conversation again, so he let the ride be quiet. He just didn't have any energy to argue with her again.

"Thank you for coming with me today." She pulled in next to his car.

"Not a problem, sweetie. It was enlightening."

Chapter Thirty-Seven

"Night guys." Sam waved to the last group of customers as they left the store.

Brad lounged against the counter. "Are you heading out soon?"

"Nah, I've got some more work to do before I call it a night." Her stomach twisted when she realized they were alone. Their unfinished conversation still hung between them.

"How late are you planning on staying? You got here before we did today."

"I want to finish setting up the game room." She yawned before she could stop herself.

"You look worn out." He patted her hand. "Why don't you leave it for tomorrow?"

She wasn't going to deny how tempting it was to put off the project again. She had been putting it off all week since they came back from the distributor. "It's my day off and Chuck's birthday party. Which means I'll be spending tomorrow and Sunday doing paperwork for Monday's meeting."

"You're going to work yourself to death."

She smiled at his warning. "I'll be fine. Most of the extra work is done. I'm taking some time off in the next week or so." She shooed him to the door. "Scoot so I can get this project finished."

"Yes, ma'am." He saluted before she locked him out.

Leaning against the door she sighed and looked over her store. While she relished the challenge of running her own store, she had to admit she may have bitten off more than she could chew. Closing the store and counting down the register took no time at all.

Before she knew it, she stood before the open door to her new board game room. Boxes and shelves littered the area. This project kept getting put off while she put out little fires throughout the store. Tonight she was determined to finish it if it killed her. All of the other product they picked up had been put out on the shelves, all that remained was the new board game area.

A tap on the window pulled her from her thoughts to see Brad holding up a cup of coffee and a sandwich. She unlocked the door. "How did you know I needed those?"

"I saw how tired you are and you haven't eaten much all day." He twisted the lock behind him. "And I know you won't ask for help."

She took a bite of the sandwich and swooned. Her stomach roared to life and she inhaled the rest of the food. "I can't ask you for this."

"You helped me move and consulted on my business, consider this me returning the favor." He pointed at the room. "Don't you need Olivia to document this?"

"She already got the before pictures. She'll be back in the morning for the after."

"What about during? Shouldn't there be pictures of you working?" He pulled out his phone and snapped some pictures while she chased after him to take the phone away.

"Delete those." She couldn't keep the smile off of her face. "We already have some of me painting."

"A couple of these are pretty good." He slid his phone into his pocket. "Put me to work."

She handed him a box cutter and they lingered over their hands touching. "You unbox and I'll price."

She took an extra step back from him. The close proximity, her exhaustion, and the magnetic pull between them combined to make her forget her promises to herself. She took a pull from the cup. Damn, the man even got her coffee order right.

The flow of work washed away all thoughts of curling against him. For a while, they barely talked while they worked. After all the games were priced, they debated back and forth about the best arrangement of the shelves and games. They cleaned up all the trash and she stepped back to admire their work.

He stepped behind her, heat beating between them. "We make a good team."

"Thank you for this." She turned and hugged him tight. "I couldn't have gotten this done without you."

His lips pressed against her forehead. "You're welcome. Let's get out of here."

She grabbed her paperwork and let them out. They talked about more ideas for the store on the way to their cars. He hovered near her and she was sure he was going to kiss her. She leaned slightly towards him, but he squeezed her hand and headed to his car. She frowned after him, disappointed and confused.

WHEN DID I BECOME SUCH a wimp? Brad beat himself up as he sat behind the wheel. He could feel Sam wanted him to kiss her. But what did he do? He walked away, not wanting to misread her and ruin their newly mended friendship.

Steve looked up from the video game he played. "How'd it go?"

"I'm such a tool." Brad flopped onto the couch.

"She gave you the whole 'let's be friends' speech?"

"No, I chickened out. Hell, we stood at her car and talked after we were done. I'm pretty sure she wanted me to kiss her, but I walked away."

"What the fuck, man? I thought the whole point of staying to help was to get her back."

"It was, but I kept thinking about if I was wrong. What if she's still pissed at me?"

"Sam wouldn't have helped you move if she was pissed at you." Steve glanced over. "You two are morons."

"You aren't wrong."

"My advice? Tell her you want to talk tomorrow during the party. Lay it all out for her and find out if you have a chance. If she rejects you, at least you aren't stuck in limbo wondering."

"I'll think about it. Night." Brad headed to his room and laid on his bed looking at the ceiling. If he didn't send her a message soon, he'd chicken out again. He pulled out his phone.

Brad: Are you up?

Sam: Just got home, what's up?

B: I was just wondering if you were coming to Chuck's party tomorrow.

S: I wouldn't miss it for the world. I took the weekend off special for it.

B: Do you think I could have some of your time during the party? There's something I'd like to talk to you about.

S: Is everything alright?

B: It's nothing bad. I just need to talk to you about some stuff.

His phone rang. "What kind of stuff?" Her voice trembled over the phone.

"Sam, it's nothing bad, I promise. You didn't have to call or worry. I just want to talk."

"Okay... Why don't we talk now? Or while we were working earlier?"

"We were busy earlier and I'd rather not do this over the phone. Please, don't worry about it."

"Well, now I'm worried. Can I have a hint as to what you want to discuss?"

He covered his face with his hands. This was not going how he'd hoped. "Just stuff. I want to talk about our friendship... stuff."

"Friendship stuff. Color me confused."

"Look, I'll explain it all tomorrow night. Please don't worry about it."

"Fine. I'll see you at the party."

"Good night, Sam."

"Night."

His heart sped up as he hung up. He was really doing this. Tomorrow night he would either get back with Sam or lose her forever.

He barely slept and was up before either of his roommates. He kept himself busy getting the house cleaned and set up for the party so he wouldn't think about his looming talk with her. After a quick shower, he wandered down to the basement with a bottle of liquor to wait.

SAM WALKED INTO THE house, heart in her throat, shortly after the party started. She sat in the driveway for way too long, but she hadn't wanted Brad to know she was nervous about their impending talk by showing up too early. She wiped her sweaty palms on her jeans and looked around the room.

"Happy birthday, Chuck!"

The birthday boy swooped her up in a hug. "My favorite store manager is here. Grab a drink. Cupcakes are in the kitchen."

She grabbed a glass of rum and coke and meandered around the party trying to be casual about looking for Brad. When she couldn't find him, she stopped Steve and he pointed towards the basement. She tiptoed down the stairs, dread growing in her belly. Brad sat on the couch, staring into space. She tapped on the wall to get his attention.

"I was wondering if you were going to show up." His head lulled towards her.

"Are you drunk?"

"Not yet." He pointed at the nearly full bottle at his feet. "If you had shown up in an hour, I might have been."

She picked up the bottle. "Premixed Long Island Iced Tea."

"A great version of liquid courage."

"I'm not sure I want to talk to you when you've been drinking." She set the bottle down and turned to go.

"Sam, please." He touched her arm, but made no move to grab her. "I haven't had much."

She perched on the arm of the couch. "What did you want to talk about?"

"What happened after you went down to Missouri?"

"I don't think—"

"You deserve to know." He stared into her eyes and took a deep breath. "You were right. While you were putting everything on hold to take care of your father, I was with another woman. I didn't mean for it to happen, but she showed up on Thursday nights to paint and learn how to play. She reminded me of you."

"I'm not sure I like being compared to her." Sam's stomach soured.

"She acted like you. She played Factionless and had the same group of friends. Sold me a sob story about how you used to be friends. I thought I could help you get back together."

"She played you."

"After the tournament, the group came here to celebrate and I came down here to wallow. I got very drunk and stupid." He looked away. She wanted him to stop talking, he slowly twisted a knife in her heart with every word. "For a while, I thought she was you. My eyes were closed and she wore your perfume. When I woke up, I realized what happened and went to call you. She woke up, started crying, and said I just used her for sex. Turns out that was a lie and we hadn't had sex that night.."

"And you decided to prove you weren't using her." She took a big swig from her cup and let the burn cut through the lump in her throat. "I gave you permission to go after happiness while I was gone, so there was nothing standing in your way." She didn't apologize for the bitterness in her voice.

"In a way. Things went well for us for a while."

"What happened?"

"Things unraveled. You took the job in Missouri and she started changing. Saying things like 'thank god the bitch is gone.'"

"Showed her true colors. I hear that's her M.O."

"I tried to break it off a few times. She'd freak out and things would go back to being good before unraveling again." He snorted. "And then you moved back."

"And she beat the hell out of me for it."

"If I'd known she was going to go after you again, I wouldn't have bailed her out. She swore she wouldn't do it again and I believed her. I didn't want you to get hurt."

She reached over and squeezed his hand. "I know. You do know that entire night was a setup like the faire."

"Chuck admitted to it after the fight. He felt so bad for you getting hurt."

"It didn't tickle. She throws a mean sucker punch."

He reached over and ran his thumb over her cheek. "Is it healing okay?"

"No permanent damage." She covered his hand and leaned her cheek into it, needing the comfort of his touch more than her next breath. "Where does that leave us?"

Chapter Thirty-Eight

B rad wanted time to stop while Sam leaned her head against his hand. He wasn't sure he could handle Sam rejecting him. "It all depends on you. I completely understand if you don't want to be with me anymore."

"Would you be okay with that?"

Fuck, cards on the table. "Not really, but I would try my damndest to not let it interfere with our friendship."

"I missed being friends with you." She brushed her soft lips against his knuckles.

"I missed it too, Sammy-cat." He tugged her hand to his lips. He hoarded as much contact as she'd give him. "I don't know how to fix this," he whispered against her skin.

She pulled her hand back to her lap. "I don't know either."

"Hannah found the photos you gave me. She torched them all."

"That bitch! I can't really blame her, I wouldn't want you to have pictures of your ex like that, but damn it, I never got to wear the lingerie except for the shoot."

"She never found it, it never left my car."

"I'm surprised you kept it." She leaned over and kissed his cheek. It felt like her final good-bye. "I'm going to rejoin the party."

"Just let me know. If you think of anything I can do to fix this." He stared blankly at the wall so she wouldn't see how she tore his heart out.

"Of course." Her steps halted at the bottom of the stairs. "One last question: when she first tricked you into making out with her, where were you?"

He didn't want to put the final nail in the coffin, but he promised he'd be truthful with her. "Here. I ended up with a crick in my neck from sleeping on the couch."

"Oh." He strained to hear her words. "I want that night."

He hung his head. "If I could go back in time, I'd change it."

"No, Brad, I want that night tonight. We start again here, where things went wrong."

"You're crazy." He couldn't keep hope from his voice.

"Or a genius. We start over tonight or we need to stop talking about it."

He launched himself off the couch and pushed her against the wall. He knew he should be more gentle with her, but couldn't stop himself. "Are you sure?"

"Never been more sure of anything in my life." She captured his lips and worked her hands under his shirt.

He chuckled as she pulled his shirt off. "A little eager?" He tugged her shirt off and molded his hand against her breast. "Do you still match your underwear?"

"Yes." She arched into his touch.

"Show me."

She wiggled against him while she shimmied out of her jeans. Every movement brushed against his growing erection. She clutched at his belt. "Take yours off too."

He stilled her hands. "Slow down, sweetie." He laced his fingers with hers and pinned them above her head. "I plan on taking my time tasting and teasing you."

Steps sounded on the stairs. He cursed under his breath and handed her his shirt. She dropped it back on the floor before pulling him against her.

"Interruptions don't mean getting dressed."

He growled in her ear, "seriously?"

Steve glanced at them and the clothes scattered around them. "Upstairs bathroom is occupied and I thought you two were just talking."

"Obviously, we're not." Brad kept Sam covered with his body.

"I'll warn everyone against coming down here." Steve closed the bathroom door.

Brad looked down at her. "Exhibitionist much?"

"I knew you'd keep me covered and the whole putting on clothes to take them off slows down the whole evening." She ground her body against him.

"You don't like it slow?"

"I do, but this dance has gone on long enough."

God, he loved this woman. He kissed her, his tongue teasing her lips until her mouth opened under his. His fingers worked into her silky hair, tugging her head where he wanted it. Her tongue dueled against his, ratcheting up his need for her. Her hands grabbed for any purchase on his arms and back. He nudged her thighs apart with his. Her heat scorched his thigh every time she ground against him.

He leaned his entire body against her soft curves while Steve passed them again. When he was sure the coast was clear, he couldn't wait any longer and undid her bra. He kissed his way down her neck and across her collarbones. Taking one rosy nipple in his mouth, he took his time relearning exactly what she liked.

His hands skimmed her sides and peeled off her lacy panties. His mouth traced a path down her body until he found her clit, his tongue darting and sweeping over it. He had forgotten how good she tasted, all sugary sweetness. Her knees buckled under his assault and he gripped her harder against his hungry mouth. He slipped two fingers into her, working her into a frenzy.

SAM'S WORLD SHATTERED into a thousand fragments. She leaned against the wall, catching her breath. Brad smiled up at her as he easily held her up. He eased her away from the wall and turned her towards the couch so he could scatter kisses up the backs of her knees and thighs.

She shifted from foot-to-foot, restless for him. He kissed her lower back. "Is there something you want, kitten?"

"You naked, inside me." She peered over her shoulder. "Please."

He moved away from her and she shivered at the sudden kiss of cold air. His clothes thumped against the floor before his warm arms wrapped around her. He rubbed against her. "Is this what you wanted?"

"Almost." She rocked back, desperate for more friction. "I need you in me. Please."

He adjusted his angle and slid slowly into her. Her head fell forward at the delicious intrusion. She missed the way they fit together. He held himself still against her, breathing hard. She moved against him, urging him to thrust. She moaned as he clutched her ass and thrust into her hard.

The first thrust caught her off-guard and she grabbed blindly at the back of the couch to keep from falling over. Each thrust was harder, rougher, as though he needed to brand himself on her. She pushed back, wanting him deeper until all memory of being apart was obliterated. His hips slapped against her as they raced towards orgasm. Her fingers curled into the back of the couch and she flew apart. His hoarse cry filled her ears as he joined her over the edge. They tumbled onto the rug in a naked heap.

"Fuck, this floor is cold."

She rolled on top of him and snuggled into his shoulder. "But you're warm."

"Kitten, I'm all for cuddling, but I'm going to make a wild suggestion to relocate to my bed." His chuckle rumbled under her ear.

"Just for cuddling?" She couldn't keep the smile from her face.

He ran his hand down her side, making her hungry for him again. "And anything else you want to do."

"Let's go!" She bounced up and ran for the stairs.

"I know you have a disdain for clothes getting in the way, but I'm going to suggest you put on some clothes so the guys don't get an eyeful."

"Right, there's a party going on up there." She grinned and snagged his shirt off the floor. "You just like me in your shirt."

He pulled her back against him. "Damn right I do. I have to stake my claim somehow."

Tempted as she was to continue their fun on the couch, she wanted to take her time getting to know him again. She slipped on his shirt and dug around for her panties. "Hurry up and put on some clothes. I want to get upstairs and naked again."

He pulled on his jeans and grabbed the rest of their clothes. They raced upstairs and through the party. Her cheeks flaming, she curtsied at all the wolf whistles they got from their state of undress. There was no way she was living this down anytime soon. She snagged some cupcakes and bottles of water on their way through the kitchen.

She winked at Chuck. "Figured we'd need some fuel to keep us going."

"If we don't see you in a few days, we'll send a search party."

"Happy birthday." She kissed his cheek and bounced into Brad's bedroom.

Brad slammed the door behind them and took the sweets out of her hand. "You're a genius."

"I know. I'm starving." On cue, her stomach growled.

"I was thinking about covering you in frosting and licking it off, but I guess we could actually eat them. Did you eat dinner?"

"No, I spent the day doing paperwork and had to rush to get here. I was also worried about our talk so I forgot to eat."

He set the cupcakes on the nightstand and gently brushed a lock of hair off her face. "I told you it wasn't anything terrible." He scooped her up and tossed her on the bed. She bounced a couple of times, stunned by his action. "Stay right there. I'll get you real food."

BRAD STALKED OUT OF his room. For the first time, he understood Steve's need to care for his woman. Sam needed to take better care of herself, the hours and stress she put herself under had taken their toll on her body. He paused to consider if he was some of the stress.

Steve clapped him on the back. "Finished already, minuteman?"

"Eat shit, numb nuts. Sam didn't eat dinner and I'm guessing lunch. I need her to have plenty of energy to go all night."

"Say no more, man. Feed your woman. She's looking like she's lost a bit of weight."

"More than a bit."

He filled a plate full of food and grabbed a pint of ice cream from the freezer. He juggled everything to get his door open. He shut it with his foot and drank in the sight of Sam sprawled on his bed where he left her.

She crawled off the bed and took some of the food from him. "Nachos and ice cream, that's a weird combination."

"Chuck wanted a nacho bar for his birthday. The ice cream goes with the frosting I'm planning on covering you in."

She fed him the first chip. "Guess it's good finger food."

"Get back on my bed, woman, so I can feed you," he growled at her.

She took her time stripping off her clothes and settling against his pillows. He didn't know if he could concentrate on getting food in her when she looked so damn sexy. He sat next to her and fed her a chip, cheese dripping onto her chest.

"I thought you wanted to lick frosting off of me, not cheese."

"That was an accident. Let me clean it up for you." He licked a trail all over her stomach and chest until he finally got to the cheese. They were both breathing hard when he looked up.

"Food or sex..."

"Trying to figure out which one's more important right now?" She nodded as he placed another chip in her mouth. "Food first, then sex. I don't want you passing out on me before I'm finished with you."

They fed each other until she couldn't eat another bite before he shucked his jeans and climbed over her. Every inch of her skin needed to be worshiped and he planned on taking his time. She seemed to have a similar idea, exploring and playing with his body. When he couldn't take anymore, he made love to her, unable to look away the entire time. She curled up in his arms afterward, making content noises. He covered them and dozed off.

A thought woke him. "Sammy, are you on birth control?"

"No, why?" She raised herself onto her elbows and blinked sleepily at him.

"I wasn't planning on doing anything so I didn't have any protection on me. I was so intent on being with you, I didn't even think we're forgetting it." Realization dawned on her face. He was such an idiot, he couldn't stop screwing things up with her. "I'm so sorry."

"Is this the part where you tell me you have an STD?"

"No, I'm clean. This is the first time I've forgotten." His stomach turned, waiting for her to freak out.

She snuggled back into his arms. "Then don't worry about it. I'll grab some Plan B in the morning."

He frowned, not the reaction he expected. "You're awfully calm about this."

"I'm not going to let it ruin the best night of my life."

"The best night?" She nodded. He ran his hands over her back, still not sure this wasn't a dream. "You don't wear your tiger necklace anymore."

She touched the spot where the charm should have rested. "I took it off when I was trying to forget you. All it did was remind me of what I left behind."

He pulled her closer, anger at himself welling in his chest. "I hate you stopped wearing it, even if it was my own fault." He pressed a kiss to her forehead, silently vowing she would never have reason to doubt his love for her. "Will you start wearing it again?"

"Of course, I never kept it far from me." She wiggled out of his arms and dug through her pockets. "Will you put it back on me?"

He took the necklace from her. He let it rest in his palm to warm the metal up. He pressed a line of kisses along the back of her neck before clasping it on her. He nuzzled her ear, content she was his again.

"My kitten." Fierce joy surged through him. He let his hands roam her body. "I love how it looks on you."

She turned around. "I've missed wearing it."

He laid back and pulled her on top of him. "Never take it off."

"Never."

"I don't think I can get enough of you." He tugged her up for a long kiss. "I need to be in you again."

She guided him into her wet heat and slowly rode him. She looked so gorgeous taking her pleasure while wearing the jewelry he gave her. He wanted this night to last forever.

Chapter Thirty-Nine

S am woke up to hands stroking her back. A warm body cradled hers and it took her a minute to remember the night before. Brad's scent filled her head. She smiled up at him and reached up to trace the thought lines on his face.

"What are you thinking about?"

He looked at her and blinked. "It's nothing important. Just a passing fantasy."

"Tell me." He looked away. Her stomach twisted at his action. "Please?"

"It's nothing, sweetie."

"If it's nothing, you can tell me." He remained silent. "You're starting to scare me."

"I don't want to freak you out or sway your thoughts." He took a deep breath. "I was just thinking maybe it wouldn't be a terrible thing if you didn't take it."

"Take what?"

"Plan B."

She bolted upright, sure she heard him wrong. "Say that again."

"Shit, I freaked you out."

"I'm not freaked out. I just want you to say it again so I'm sure I heard you right."

He stared over her head. "I was thinking it wouldn't be such a bad idea if you didn't take Plan B."

"Why's that?" She watched the color climb his cheeks.

"Never mind, it was a stupid idea."

"Are you blushing?" She cupped his face in her hands. He kept avoiding looking at her and the weight of the conversation hit her.

"You're wanting me to not to take the pill in the hopes of knocking me up."

"I didn't say that."

"It's implied by the whole reason for taking it."

"Would it be so bad?"

She studied him, wondering what brought this up. "Why do you want it?"

"Just forget I said anything."

"No, I want to know your thoughts on this. It's not just my decision to make."

"Sam... Fuck." He scrubbed his hands through his hair. "I want kids. I like the thought of you carrying my child. It would be tangible proof of how I feel about you."

Her heart beat against her tongue. "And how is that?"

"I love you, Sam." He said it with such conviction her heart felt like it would burst from her chest. He finally met her eyes and she could see the love in them.

She kissed him with all the crazy feelings bouncing through her. "I love you too."

She curled back up in his arms, content to be held by him. Her brain churned over the conversation. *Kids.* They had never talked about starting a family, but then again, they hadn't had much time together before things went sideways. She drew lazy circles on his chest and stomach as she sorted through her thoughts.

His hand covered hers. "Penny for your thoughts."

"Just thinking about what you brought up."

"Do you care to enlighten me?" He folded his hands behind his head, caution lacing his voice.

She resumed drawing on him. "I was thinking maybe we shouldn't put the cart before the horse. We just got back together. I'd rather not complicate the relationship so soon."

"Fair enough."

"You're disappointed." She couldn't look up at him to see the effect of her words.

"Yes and no. You have a very valid point. We are back at the beginning of our relationship and shouldn't complicate it until we've gotten to know each other again."

"There's a but in there."

"But I had this image in my head of you with our child."

For a moment, she couldn't speak. Images flashed in her head of herself pregnant, him caring for their child, quiet nights of the three of them cuddled together. She had to admit it was tempting to chance it.

"How about a compromise? We try living together for a few months and then talk about it again."

DISAPPOINTMENT SLAMMED into him, but Brad wasn't going to sway Sam into doing something she didn't want to do. He had a lot of work to convince her to stay with him.

"Deal. When are we moving your stuff in?"

"Or you could move in with me." She restarted doodling on him with her finger.

He did not want to pack his crap up again and move. "Your place is too girly."

"The hell you say."

"I'm just saying we need to man the place up a bit before I'd feel comfortable."

"What about my apartment is so unmanly you aren't comfortable in it?" She sat up and gave him a piercing stare.

He scrambled for ideas to have her move instead of him. "All of the clothes under the loft stairs."

"There are no closets in the place. Your clothes would be there too."

"The purple blankets on the bed."

"We'll buy green pillowcases and sheets to match."

"Will you stop being the voice of reason?" He squeezed her hand. "I'm trying to find reasons not to move my stuff again."

"If you don't want to move in with me, you just have to say so. You're the one who brought up starting a family. I'm suggesting we take the first step towards it."

He pulled her on top of him and wrapped his arms around her. "I want to live with you, but I don't understand why I have to move instead of you."

"Two reasons. One, I have a lease on the apartment and don't want to pay to break it. Two, as much as I love Chuck and Steve, I want a place where it's just the two of us. No wolf whistles every time I go to the bathroom."

"I can't promise not to whistle at you, especially if you wear as little as you did last night." He kissed her hair.

She smiled up at him. "I would wear less and sexier if we weren't around two other guys."

"Seriously?" She nodded and images of her in sexy lingerie filled his head. "You know how much I love having you naked." He ran his hand over her curves, marveling at how she fit against him.

Her hand wove a slow path down his chest and stomach. "Just think, naked painting harem girl." He groaned as her hand paused on his stomach. "Won't happen in the cold ass basement."

"That's playing dirty."

"No, playing dirty is promising it and never going through with it." She crawled on top of him and ground against his growing erection. "You know I'll actually do it."

He threw his head back and lost himself in her. "Is this you will paint with me naked or you'll be naked and I get to paint on you?"

"Both."

"Done. I'll start bringing my stuff over right now."

"Sex first. Then coffee and moving." She writhed on him.

He pulled her down for a long kiss. He couldn't get enough of this woman. "Your wish is my command."

MOVING BRAD INTO HER apartment took no time at all. Steve and Chuck were way too happy to move him out. His desk fit into her space perfectly. Sam shook her head. Their space. It was no longer just hers.

"What's left to do?" She came up behind him and wrapped her arms around his waist.

"Just getting my paints set up. You put my clothes away quick." He turned to give her a kiss. "And you need to take your pill." He nodded at the package on the counter.

"Right, almost forgot." She took longer than necessary to read the instructions and warnings, waiting for him to stop her. Taking a deep breath, she ripped the package and tossed the pill in her mouth before she could give in to her second thoughts. "All done."

"Just like that?"

"I guess." She buried her head in his box of paints.

"How about I unpack and you organize?"

She stared at him like he grew a second head. "You trust me to set up your painting area?"

"Of course, you're the one keeping everything from going to absolute shit. If I set it up, it'll make no sense whatsoever."

She grinned. "You just want me to run the business end of your business so you can do nothing but paint."

"Would I do that?" He gave her a wide eyed look.

"Yes." She leaned down to kiss him. "I love that you trust me to do it, but I'm not always going to have the time. I'll set up some simple systems so you can input data as you go and make it easy to keep track of your shit."

"I love you."

Those three words filled her with unimaginable joy. "I love you too."

"You're the best." He handed up a load of paints for her to put away.

The day passed in a happy haze. Her stomach cramped a few times and she ran to the bathroom thinking she was going to throw up. She cursed her stupid decision of taking the pill.

"I think it's time for dinner." Her stomach growled.

"Is it that late already?"

"We did spend most of the morning having sex."

"We should end the day the same way." He wrapped his arms around her waist and gave her a serious look. "Unless you're still feeling bad."

"I'm better. I think the worst is over. Let's grab food."

They had just exited the building when she was pushed out of the way by a blur throwing itself at Brad. She blinked to clear her vision and found Hannah with her arms around him. "I'm so glad I found you."

"What the hell are you doing?" He disentangled himself from Hannah.

"Is that anyway to greet the mother of your child?"

He exchanged a confused look with Sam. "Say what?"

"I'm pregnant with your baby, Brad." Hannah's eyes filled with tears as she touched his shoulder. "I want to try again for the sake of our child."

Sam stood outside the exchange, forgotten. She fought the urge to rip Hannah's hand off of Brad. Looking at him, she choked back a sob. Hannah just offered him what she refused. And the look in his eyes showed all types of hope.

"This is a bit sudden, Hannah. Let me take it all in." He took a couple steps away. "I'll call you."

Sam watched in growing horror as he walked off without a backwards look at either of them. Hannah gave her a smug look and rubbed her belly. Sam clenched her fist and swallowed back the urge to wipe the smirk off Hannah's face. She turned on her heel and continued walking as though her entire world wasn't crashing down around her.

Sitting down at her favorite cafe, she thought about the look on his face, the hope of a kid. Food turned to ash in her mouth the longer she sat there. She kicked herself for taking the damn pill when she had second thoughts about it. When it became obvious he wasn't coming, she trudged back to the apartment and let herself in.

"WHERE WERE YOU?" BRAD lifted his head out of his hands to watch Sam come in. After he wandered around the neighborhood lost in thought, he came home to find her still gone.

She changed into her pajamas. "I could ask you the same thing. You left me on the sidewalk."

"Sorry about that." He couldn't meet her accusing stare right now. His head was too full of the possible changes in his life.

"Heavy thinking?"

"You could say that."

"I want to make a suggestion." Caution laced her words.

He didn't want rational thinking at the moment, but hoped it would soothe the churning thoughts in his head. "Go ahead."

"I think you should insist on a paternity test."

His head snapped up. "You don't believe her?"

"I believe she's pregnant, but it's damn convenient timing if you ask me. With as much as she flirted with you around, I can only imagine what she did when you weren't there." Sam settled at the table with her paperwork.

"Is that all you're going to say about the situation?" He frowned at her.

"What am I supposed to say? I know you want kids and I just took a fucking pill to ensure what we did last night won't result in them." She hunched over the paper in front of her.

"True."

She flinched at his response, but didn't say anything else. Did she regret taking the pill this morning? He stared at her bent head for a few minutes. When it became obvious she wasn't going to be done anytime soon, he got up and sat at his desk. This was not how he envisioned their first night living together, but she had said something about a meeting the next day.

He let the flow of painting blank out the squirrel running through his brain. He barely registered the scratching of her pen in the background. Hours passed without either talking. He finished the mini in his hand and turned to show it to her, but she was nowhere to be found.

Her paperwork was neatly stacked on the edge of the table next to her purse. He frowned and looked up to the loft. A lump under the blankets indicated she went to bed without saying good night. He shut off the lights and crawled in after her. She didn't move from her curled up position, so he rolled onto his side to face away from her. Just when he needed her comfort, she pulled away. Story of his life.

Chapter Forty

Brad laid in bed until he was certain Sam had left for the day like he'd done for the past week. He couldn't face the look in her eyes when she talked about the fact she ensured they weren't having a kid anytime soon. He shouldn't have put the thought into her head so she didn't beat herself up for her choice. Today he would get the first of the answers he needed: if Hannah was actually pregnant.

He showered and dressed to meet the possible mother of his child. Bile climbed his throat, Sam should be by his side during this difficult time. Hell, Sam should be the one getting the tests and having his baby, not Hannah. He listened with half an ear to the doctor, Hannah was far enough along the child could be his.

"When can we do a paternity test?" He finally found his voice.

The doctor raised an eyebrow. "You don't think it's yours?"

"I want to be sure I'm not saddled with raising another man's baby. I have questions about her faithfulness while we were together."

Hannah broke down into tears. "How can you question me?"

"Do you really want to get into this in front of the doctor?" Brad dispassionately watched her try to get sympathy from the doctor. "There were plenty of times you made out with other guys. My friends saw you."

"Lies."

"If the kid is mine, I'll apologize for my hasty words. If it's not, then you and I both know you were never faithful to me. I do find the timing of you telling me to be convenient and I wouldn't put it past you to pass off another man's child as mine." He turned back to the doctor. "Sorry to air our dirty laundry, but I need to be sure I'm not screwing up my future."

"Considering your concerns, I'm surprised you're here. We can take a sample of your blood today and do a follow up appointment next week."

"I will not have you hurting my baby for his paranoia." Hannah hugged her belly.

"There's no need to do anything with the baby. The father's DNA is in your bloodstream. We will just be matching up his with yours to see if Mr. Werner's is in there."

Brad held out his arm for the vial of blood to be drawn. "Thank you very much."

"I look forward to seeing you again, young man. Not many men would come with an ex when they have doubts about the parentage of the child."

"Until proven otherwise, it's my kid. She was my girlfriend when she got pregnant." He shook the doctor's hand and left without waiting for Hannah.

She caught up with him in the parking lot. "That bitch has poisoned you against me. Against our family."

"She has a name. I won't have you talking bad about my girlfriend. Sam has done nothing to you, but you delight in hurting her. The person who's poisoned me against you is you."

"What about our baby?"

"If it's mine? I'll help raise it and care for it, but we're not getting back together." He turned on his heel and got into his car. He drove for hours to clear his head until he couldn't avoid going home any longer.

SAM SHIVERED. DAMN Brad, where was he? She'd been waiting for hours in ridiculously thin lingerie for him to come home from Hannah's appointment. She strained her ears, still no sound of him.

Screw it. She got up and put on real pajamas. She stuffed the dark purple lingerie in the drawer with more force than necessary. This was the last time she tried that bright idea.

She crawled up to the bed and avoided the clock. Some time later, the apartment door opened. She followed the pattern of his steps as he walked to his desk. A pause, pages flipped, and the book slammed shut. He crawled up and she tried to keep her breathing even like she was asleep.

The bed dipped under his weight. And then, nothing. She peeked over her shoulder and saw he had his back to her again. She swallowed back the tears threatening to fall. Every night had them drawing further and further apart.

The next morning, she rolled out of bed more tired than when she laid down. She trudged down the stairs. Brad dogged her every step until he brushed past her. She stumbled to a stop at the bottom of the stairs.

"What the fuck is this?" He stabbed a finger at the photo album she left on his desk.

She clung to the railing, confused at his anger. "It's a gift. For you."

"A gift of you being submissive to another guy? Why the fuck do you think I'd want this shit?" He threw the book across the table. She cringed away from his anger. "You could just be honest and tell me you want to go back to him."

"Is that what you really think?"

"Why else would you pose for him?"

"I owed Olivia a favor for all the work she put in at the store. Aaron asked for me because I can take direction well."

"His own personal plaything." He spat the words.

"Photographic direction, Brad. He needed a model to show off his leather work."

"So the whole world is going to see these? At least I got to see them first." He paced away.

"No one but you is going to see the ones in the book." She backed up a couple of stairs. "I only agreed to take those for you. I thought—"

"You thought what, Samantha? I'd like to know that someone else wants you? That you'd play dress up for him? Go back to him if that's what you want."

"I don't. I wanted you. I made sure all I had to do was show off the items. My face is in none of the pictures used on the website. The only time I looked at the camera was when Olivia suggested I replace the book Hannah burned." She straightened her spine, refusing to be made into the bad guy. "I guess I was wrong to assume my boyfriend would want pictures of me, not when he could be playing house with his ex. I waited for you to come home last night for hours, freezing my ass off in stupidly skimpy lingerie in the hopes you'd remember I existed."

Tears burned the back of her eyes, but she refused to let him see how bad he hurt her. She dug through her dresser and dressed in a rush. As she passed him, she threw the tiny outfit at his face and slammed the bathroom door. The brush ripped through her hair as she tried to get her emotions in check. *I have to get out of here.*

Brad reached for her as she walked past. "Don't touch me!"

He backed up like she burned him. "Sam, wait."

"No, you wanted me gone so I'm going." She kept her back to him and grabbed her purse. "Congratulations, you got your wish. You have no right to treat me like that, I'm not Her. But you'll never see it."

IT WOULD'VE BEEN BETTER if Sam had slammed the door on her way out, but the soft click was ten times worse. Brad saw fear in her eyes, fear he put in there by rushing to conclusions. He sat down hard on one of the kitchen chairs. When was he going to learn she was nothing like Hannah? He chalked up today's screw up to the shock of seeing pictures of her tied up and staring over her shoulder.

He drained his coffee cup before pulling out his phone and punching in Steve's number. "I fucked up and Sam just walked out on me."

"Good morning to you too." Steve yawned. "Did she leave you for good or just to cool off?"

"I don't know." Panic gripped Brad's throat. "I'm guessing to cool off because she only took her purse."

"What did you do?"

He described the events of the day before and the morning, sparing his friend no small detail including the way she yelled at him not to touch her. The more he talked, the stupider he felt. He finished his story and waited.

"Well, you're an idiot."

"I already knew that. I was calling for help."

"Grovel."

"I was thinking I should move out and give her some space."

"After telling her to leave you? It sends the message that you want to be with someone else and are looking for an excuse to leave."

"I didn't think of that."

"You're in deep shit. Call one of her friends for ideas. Don't do anything stupid like accusing her of wanting to be with anyone else. She fought for you, dumbass. Remember, she's not that other bitch."

He hung up and dialed Olivia. "I owe Sam the biggest apology for being an asshole. Can you give me ideas?"

"She just called me crying. I'm tempted to let you twist for the way you treated her and the gift she gave you. The only time I ever see her nervous during photo shoots is when she knows you're going to see the end product." He stayed silent while she chewed him out. After she finished ripping into him, she gave him some ideas on how to win back his girlfriend.

He spent the afternoon with his stomach in knots as he put his plan into action. He chewed on his thumb while he waited for her to come back. What if she spent the night at one of her friends' houses? The door finally opened and she tossed her purse on the table on her way to the bathroom. A gasp told him she found his note.

She walked out of the bathroom with a white carnation in her hand. "'My beautiful kitten, in my stupidity this morning, I forgot to tell you how gorgeous you looked. Thank you for coming home so I had a chance to.' What the fuck is this?"

"I realized too late I'm an idiot and put my foot in my mouth."

"And this is your idea of an apology?" She held up the note.

He swallowed past the knot in his throat. "No, that was to get your attention. Where did you go?"

"Work. I figured I could put my anger to good use and get the office set up."

"How'd it go?"

"Didn't get much done."

He held out his hand to her. Disappointment punched him as she stayed across the room and out of touch. "I'm sorry. I wasn't even thinking about you replacing my old photo album with a new one. All I saw in my mind was the other guy touching you. I wasn't thinking straight when I got home last night and thought you were telling me something. I get it if you don't want to forgive me and throw me out."

SAM HESITATED. SHE spent the day torn between kicking Brad out and shaking him until he understood she loved him. "I don't get why you'd assume something like that."

"I'm unlearning the bad habits I got while with her." She made a face. "All of the bullshit lately is screwing with my head."

"It's screwing with mine too." She dropped into a chair and fiddled with the flower.

He sat across the table from her. "I want to fix this. I need to."

"You've been absent a lot lately."

"Sorry if I'm a little freaked out by the fact I might be a father."

"It's not that. You disappear a lot. It makes me wonder if you're with her, playing house." Bile crawled up her throat.

"How could you even think that?"

"You want a family, Brad. On the same day I denied you what you wanted, another woman gave you the chance." She held up her hand, needing to finish without him interrupting. "Even when you're here, you're not. I sleep next to you, a foot away from you, your back to me. You won't talk to me and ignore every advance I make to you. Where else can you be?" She hated the tears in her voice.

"I've been down by the lake thinking a lot." He sighed and stared at the table. "I went with her to her last appointment. She's truly pregnant."

His words cut her open. "How far along?"

"Not quite three months."

"Far enough along for it to possibly be yours."

"We're seeing the doctor next week." Of course they were. She walked across the room so she wouldn't have to look at him while he broke her heart. "I want you to come with me. I need you to be there."

"Why?" She fiddled with the papers on her desk.

"It's the day we get the result of the paternity test."

"Won't she object to me being there?"

"I don't care what she wants. You're the one I care about." He stood behind her, careful to not touch or crowd her. "Look, it's early and you look like you haven't eaten yet today. Let me take you out for food."

"Fine, but if you run off on me before we eat, I'm changing the locks."

He held the door for her. "I have no plans on leaving you if you still want me around."

They walked in silence to the cafe. She didn't know how to bridge the gap. He brought their food to the table, never once losing the wary expression on his face. As much as it pained her, she wasn't ready to forgive him for the last week. After they finished eating, she expected they'd go back to the apartment, but he turned in the other direction.

"I want to take you someplace, please." She nodded and followed him into another shop. "I'm Brad Werner. I have an appointment for this evening."

The receptionist typed for a minute. "If you'll wait in the next room, we'll come get you when they're ready."

He led Sam into a dimly lit room with candles and serene music. She studied the waterfall in the corner with a frown. "What is this place?"

"A massage therapy studio. You've been working so hard lately I thought you needed a chance to relax. Well, we needed to relax. I booked us a couple's massage. So this might be a bit selfish."

"When did you set this up?"

"About an hour after you left. After I let Olivia chew me out."

"Olivia called you?" She stared at him with her mouth open.

"No, I called her, after I called Steve." He leaned forward in his chair. "I fucked up and was out of my depth. He suggested I call your friends for ideas on how to apologize."

"Smart man."

"Olivia said you've been way too tense lately and I should give you a massage. I figured you wouldn't want me touching you, so this was the next best thing."

"Why wouldn't I..." Their conversation from the morning came back to her. "Because I yelled at you not to touch me."

"I made you afraid of me this morning. I never want to see fear in your eyes when you look at me."

"Thank you."

Chapter Forty-One

S am settled on the chair next to him, but Brad made no move to cuddle her against him, as much as he wanted to. He watched as she slowly relaxed while she stared at the waterfall. If he had to, he'd put in extra hours every month to treat her to this just so he could make sure she de-stressed.

A woman entered the room. "Mr. Werner, Miss Duke, I'm Tracey. I'll be one of your therapists today at Serenity." She looked at her paperwork. "I see we're getting a couple's massage. Have either of you ever had one?"

He looked at Sam. She shook her head. "Not professionally."

"Okay, in a few minutes, you'll be taken into another room where you'll strip down to whatever's most comfortable for you and slide under the sheet. We'll knock before entering to make sure you're ready. Each of you will have a therapist to work on you. We want this to be a relaxing and enjoyable experience for you. Do you have anything we need to focus on?"

"Sam's been under a lot of stress at work lately and moving heavy boxes." He waited for the therapist to make a few notes. "I hunch over my desk all day."

"I'll be back with Naomi and we'll show you to your room."

Sam waited until Tracey left the room. "I could answer for myself."

"Sorry. I just wanted to make sure you got everything worked on." He silently beat himself up for speaking for her.

She studied him. "What other surprises do you have up your sleeve?"

"It wouldn't be a surprise if I told you."

Once they were in their room, he turned his back so Sam could undress without him staring. He glanced over as he slid onto his table and caught her staring at him, still partially dressed. She blushed and turned to finish undressing.

"What?"

"It's just been a minute since I saw you naked." She slid under her sheet.

A knock kept him from answering her. Their therapists came in and for a while, he forgot she was in the room. Tension melted off of him as the knots in his back unraveled. A soft groan from across the room brought his attention back to his girlfriend. She needed this after the last few months. Contentment spread through him. At least he did one thing right today.

Once they were alone again, he dressed quickly and turned to her. Sam still laid on her table. He brushed a hand on her shoulder. "It's time to get off the table, kitten."

She grumbled at him, but took his hand so she could sit up. He grabbed her clothes and knelt at her feet to help her dress. "You don't have to do that."

"You look so relaxed I'm afraid you'll fall over." He took more time than necessary to tie her shoes.

Her hand played with his hair. "Thank you for this. I think we both needed it."

"Can I take you home?"

"Please." She smiled and wrapped her arms around his bicep.

He wanted to freeze time and just soak up the moment. He paid and let them back into the apartment. Unable to resist any longer, he stole a soft kiss from her before helping her into her pajamas. She frowned at him.

"You have me relaxed and content and you're putting me in pajamas? I thought you'd try for something else."

"I'd love to, but I don't want to push my luck. Tonight's all about your comfort."

Her arms wrapped around his neck. "You are my comfort. Come to bed with me."

"Sam, I..."

She covered his lips with a finger. "You've apologized enough for one day. Come to bed, I've missed you."

He couldn't deny her anything. He climbed the loft stairs behind her and took his time undressing her. Touching every inch of her soft skin was like coming home. Her hands traced their own path over him, telling him without words how much she loved him. He took his time filling her, wanting to enjoy every moment of the evening.

SAM PACED THE WAITING room. As expected, Hannah threw an epic fit at her presence and refused to let her into the room while the results were given. The last week had been wonderful, minus the constant texts from Hannah wanting Brad at her beck and call. She chewed her nails and made another lap. He finally came into the room.

"Well?" She looked over his head, bracing herself for the worst.

He scooped her into his arms. "It's not mine."

Relief stole her breath. "Thank goodness." She kissed him. "But the timeline?"

"She was cheating on me." He kissed her again. "Let's get out of here."

He held the car door for her. Hannah tore out of the office, crying and screaming into her phone. They sat for a moment watching the dramatics before he turned to her with a serious expression.

"What would you have done if it was mine?"

"That all depends on what you did after finding out."

"How so?"

"If you wanted to play house with her and have this 'perfect' version of a family, I'd let you leave and realize what a mistake it was, but I wouldn't take you back." She stared out the window.

"Harsh."

She turned to look at him. "I've been through this scenario with you once already and I refuse to be put through it again. I obviously had plenty of time to think about this when neither of us was sleeping."

"Was there an option B?" He eyed her with a wary expression.

"I'd help you raise the kid when you'd have it so long as Hannah wasn't in our lives. We'd share custody, but not our lives with her."

"You'd raise a kid that wasn't yours?"

"Of course, because it's yours."

He pulled her across the seats and kissed her fiercely. "I love you."

"I love you too." She smiled against his lips before settling back in her seat.

He put the car into drive. "Let's go buy a ring. I want to marry you."

"You need to ask my dad first. He's old fashioned that way. Not old fashioned enough about having a grandkid out of wedlock, but he'd kill you if you proposed without his permission. Which might take some doing based on the on again off again status of our relationship."

"Much groveling."

"I'll put in a good word with your parole officer." She winked at him. "And you might want to make up for the week you neglected me before getting on your knees to ask me to marry you. The massage was great, but that was penance for accusing me of cheating."

"I'll do anything you ask me to, kitten."

"Take me home and ravage me?"

"Your wish is my command."

GAME ON

Acknowledgements

I need to start by thanking my hubby, Greg. From listening to me complain about my characters not doing what I want them to to putting up with my crazy writing schedule, this book wouldn't have happened without him.

To Mei mut for keeping me company while I wrote and for forcing me to take a break, even if it was just to feed her or let her outside.

A huge thank you to my family (both birth and the one I married into) for believing in my dream and cheering me on. Especially my mom for alpha reading my book and having long conversations on slang.

To my beta readers: Claire, Jen, and Sarah, thank you for your sacrifice in finding all of the issues and giving me some solutions. You ladies have made me a better writer by pointing out my blindspots and being excited for what I'm working on.

Finally, to everyone who's been following the journey and inspiring me, especially the Heart Breathings community, thank you from the bottom of my heart.

They say it takes a village. And I have a great village.

Don't miss out!

Visit the website below and you can sign up to receive emails whenever Dawn Dalton publishes a new book. There's no charge and no obligation.

https://books2read.com/r/B-A-YOQDB-LEAXC

Connecting independent readers to independent writers.

About the Author

Dawn Dalton writes romances that speak to her nerdy heart. She's been writing ever since she figured out that it meant she didn't have to keep her stories in her head and hasn't stopped since.

She loves fantasy romances, role playing games, coffee, and sushi. Not always in that order.

When she's not writing, you can find her in the dojo, hiking, or hanging out with her elderly puppy, Mei.

She lives in the Midwest with her husband and dog.

Read more at www.dawndalton.com.

Milton Keynes UK
Ingram Content Group UK Ltd.
UKHW030250190324
439698UK00015B/1074